Disney
Moana

ALSO FROM JOE BOOKS

Disney Frozen Cinestory Comic
Disney Cinderella Cinestory Comic
Disney 101 Dalmatians Cinestory Comic
Disney Princess Comics Treasury
Disney • Pixar Comics Treasury
Disney Darkwing Duck: The Definitively Dangerous Edition
Disney Frozen: The Story of the Movie in Comics
Disney Big Hero 6 Cinestory Comic
Disney • Pixar Inside Out Cinestory Comic
Disney • Pixar Inside Out Fun Book
Disney Gravity Falls Cinestory Comic Volume One
Disney Gravity Falls Cinestory Comic Volume Two
Disney Gravity Falls Cinestory Comic Volume Three
Disney • Pixar The Good Dinosaur Cinestory Comic
Disney • Pixar The Good Dinosaur Fun Book
Disney Zootopia Cinestory Comic
Marvel Thor: Dueling with Giants
Marvel Captain America: Sub Rosa
Marvel Sif: Even Dragons Have Their Endings
Marvel Guardians of the Galaxy: Castaways
Disney Winnie the Pooh Cinestory Comic
Disney Descendants Wicked World Cinestory Comic Volume One
Disney Descendants Wicked World Cinestory Comic Volume Two
Disney Alice in Wonderland Cinestory Comic
Disney • Pixar Finding Nemo Cinestory Comic
Disney • Pixar Finding Dory Cinestory Comic
Disney Star vs the Forces of Evil Cinestory Comic
Disney • Pixar Finding Dory Graphic Novel
Disney Zootopia Graphic Novel
Disney Princess Comic Strips Collection Volume One
Disney Darkwing Duck Comics Collection Volume One

Don't miss our monthly comics…
Disney Frozen
Disney Darkwing Duck
Disney • Pixar Finding Dory
Disney Pirates of the Caribbean
Disney Princess
Disney Star vs the Forces of Evil

Disney

MOANA

Comics Collection

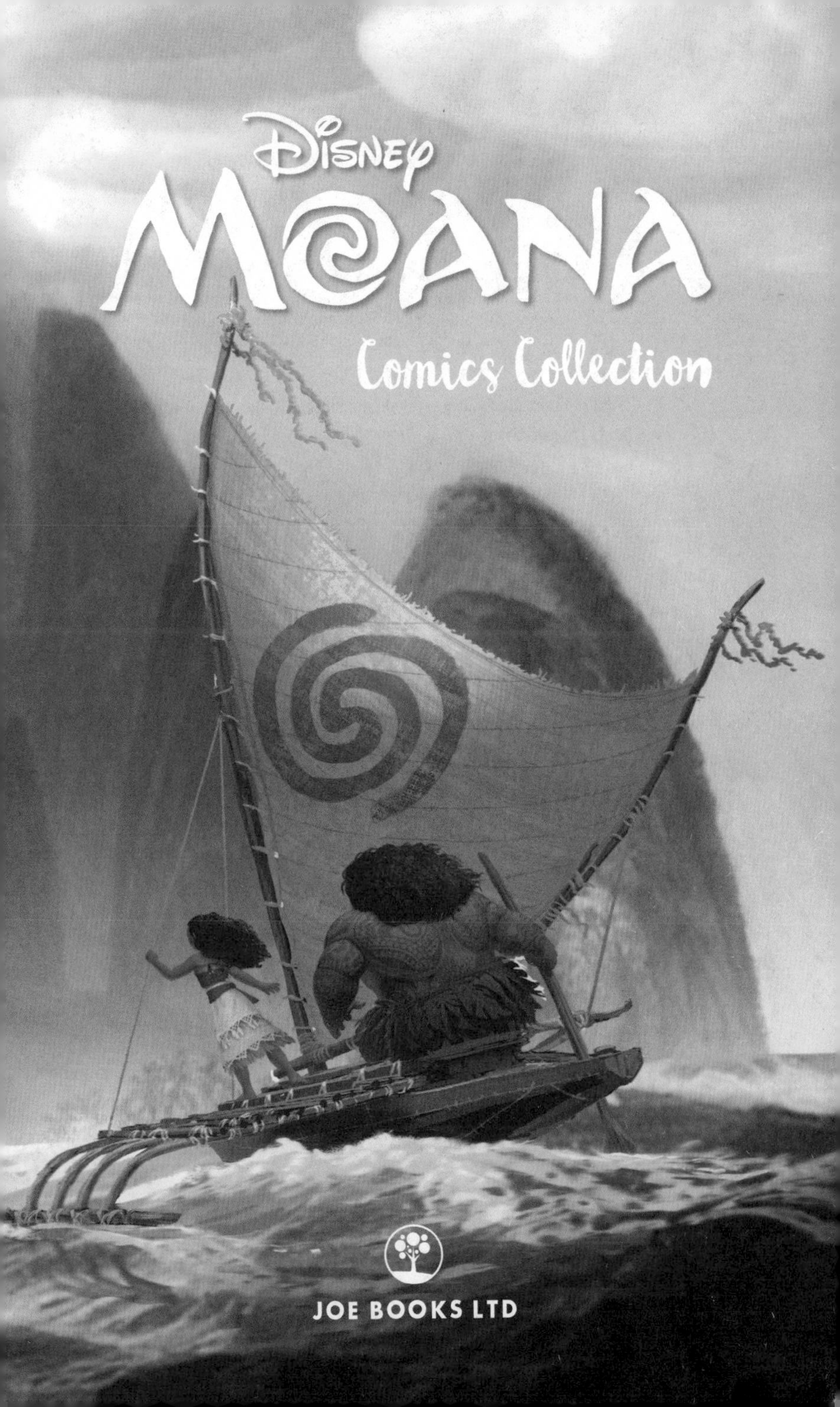

JOE BOOKS LTD

Published simultaneously in the United States and Canada by
Joe Books Ltd, 489 College Street, Suite 203, Toronto, Ontario, M6G 1A5.

www.joebooks.com

First Joe Books Edition: December 2016

Print ISBN: 978-1-77275-461-2
e-ISBN: 978-1-77275-480-3

Library and Archives Canada Cataloguing in Publication
information is available upon request.

Printed and bound in Canada
3 5 7 9 10 8 6 4 2

Contents

TO ITS INHABITANTS, MOTUNUI IS MORE THAN JUST AN ISLAND—IT'S THEIR WHOLE WORLD, A PARADISE THAT GIVES THEM EVERYTHING THEY NEED. MEET THE ONES WHO CALL MOTUNUI HOME...

Moana

Moana has always been drawn to the ocean and its hidden wonders. But her father keeps her away from the ocean for she is the future leader of Motunui, and her place is on the island. Torn between what Tui wants for her and what she wants, Moana is still looking for her true self. The answer lies beyond the reef...

Tala

Tala is Moana's wise and unconventional grandmother who shares her special connection to the ocean. Tala knows well the heritage of her people, while most of the islanders have chosen to forget it. Her stories feed Moana's imagination and will help her make the right decision when the time comes.

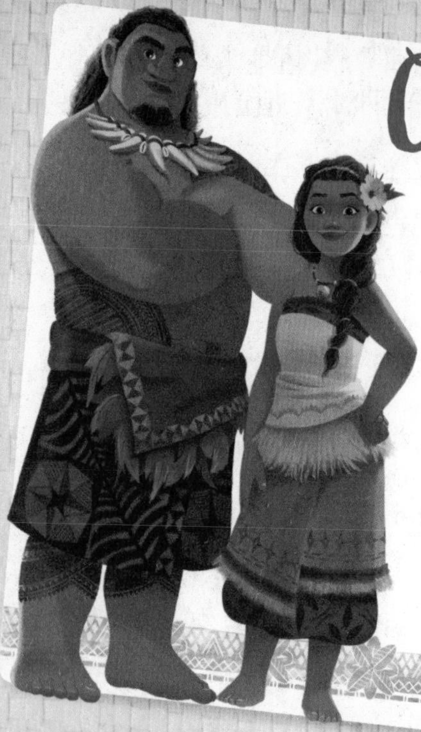

Chief Tui and Sina

As the leader of the people of Motunui Island, Tui is only interested in the common good, which does not include exploring the sea beyond the reef. Unlike his wife Sina, Tui does not understand why Moana cannot just follow his teachings and learn how to become the next great chief of their people.

Heihei

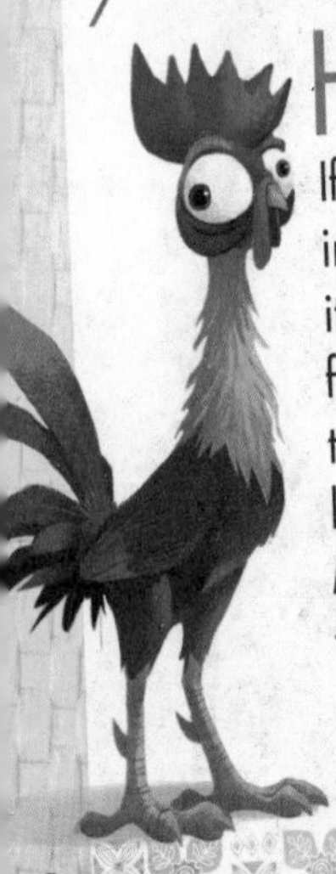

Heihei is not like any other chicken. He's dumber. If there's one way to get into danger, Heihei will find it. If there are two, he will find both of them. And still, there's no logical reason behind his actions. Yet, Moana believes there's more to him than meets the eye and that he does not deserve to be cooked and eaten!

Pua

This small, adorable pig is Moana's loyal pet & friend. Not afraid of water or boats, Pua is always ready to jump on a canoe to help Moana achieve her heart's desire: to reach the open ocean!

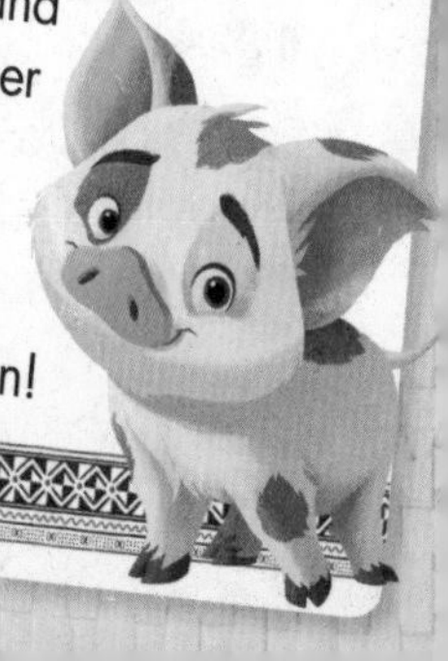

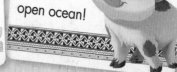

THE WORLD BEYOND THE REEF IS DANGEROUS AND UNFORGIVING, HOME TO HORRIBLE MONSTERS AND THOSE FAR MORE POWERFUL THAN HUMANS...

Maui

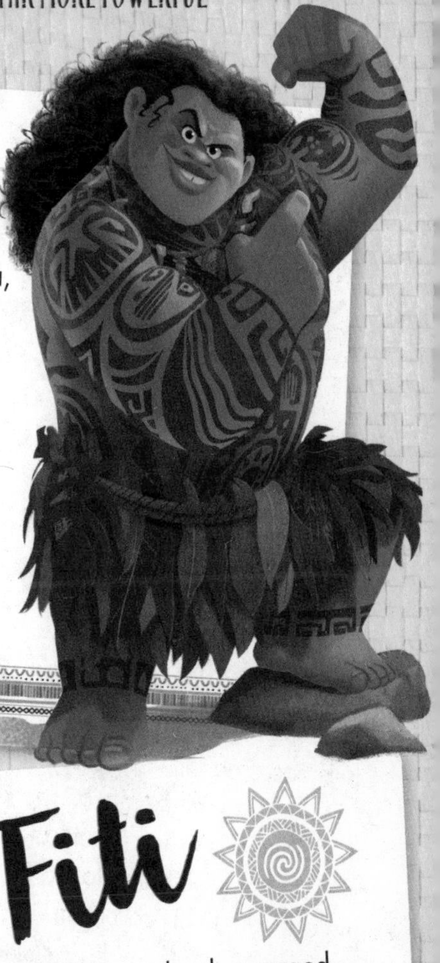

Once the greatest hero in Oceania, Maui is now just a legend, a forgotten demigod. After stealing the heart of Te Fiti, Maui has been confined to a small island, his only friend being one of his tattoos, a mini version of himself. Maui just wants to forget about his past and recover his magical fishhook, which allows him to shape-shift into all kinds of animals.

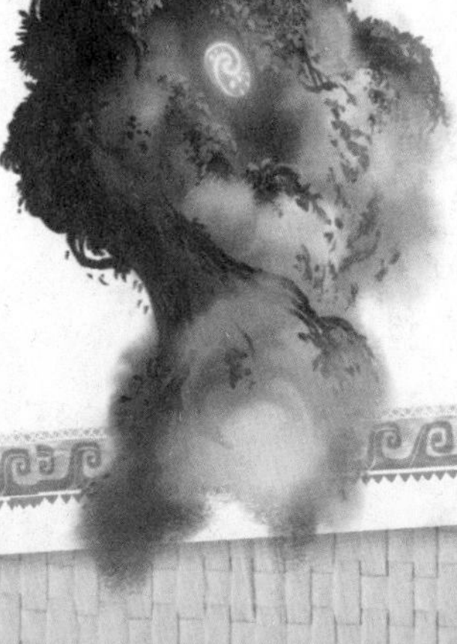

Te Fiti

Te Fiti, the mother island, emerged from the ocean at the beginning of time and created life. She made plants, humans and animals flourish. But when Maui stole her heart, darkness began to spread among the islands...

Kakamora

They may look cute, when you look at them from a distance, but these little warriors are just murdering pirates! They paint angry faces on their coconut-shell armor and attack any vessel crossing their waters to the dreadful beat of their big drums.

Tamatoa

Tamatoa is a scavenger, a collector of treasures, who lives in Lalotai, the land of monsters. He is obsessed with any shiny object that can make him as sparkly as a diamond. When Maui lost his precious hook, Tamatoa found it and added it to his collection.

Te Kā

Te Kā is a gigantic lava monster, a demon of earth and fire. Surrounded by ash clouds and volcanic lightning, Te Kā walks on land and cannot touch water. A very long time ago, Te Kā defeated Maui, separating him from his hook.

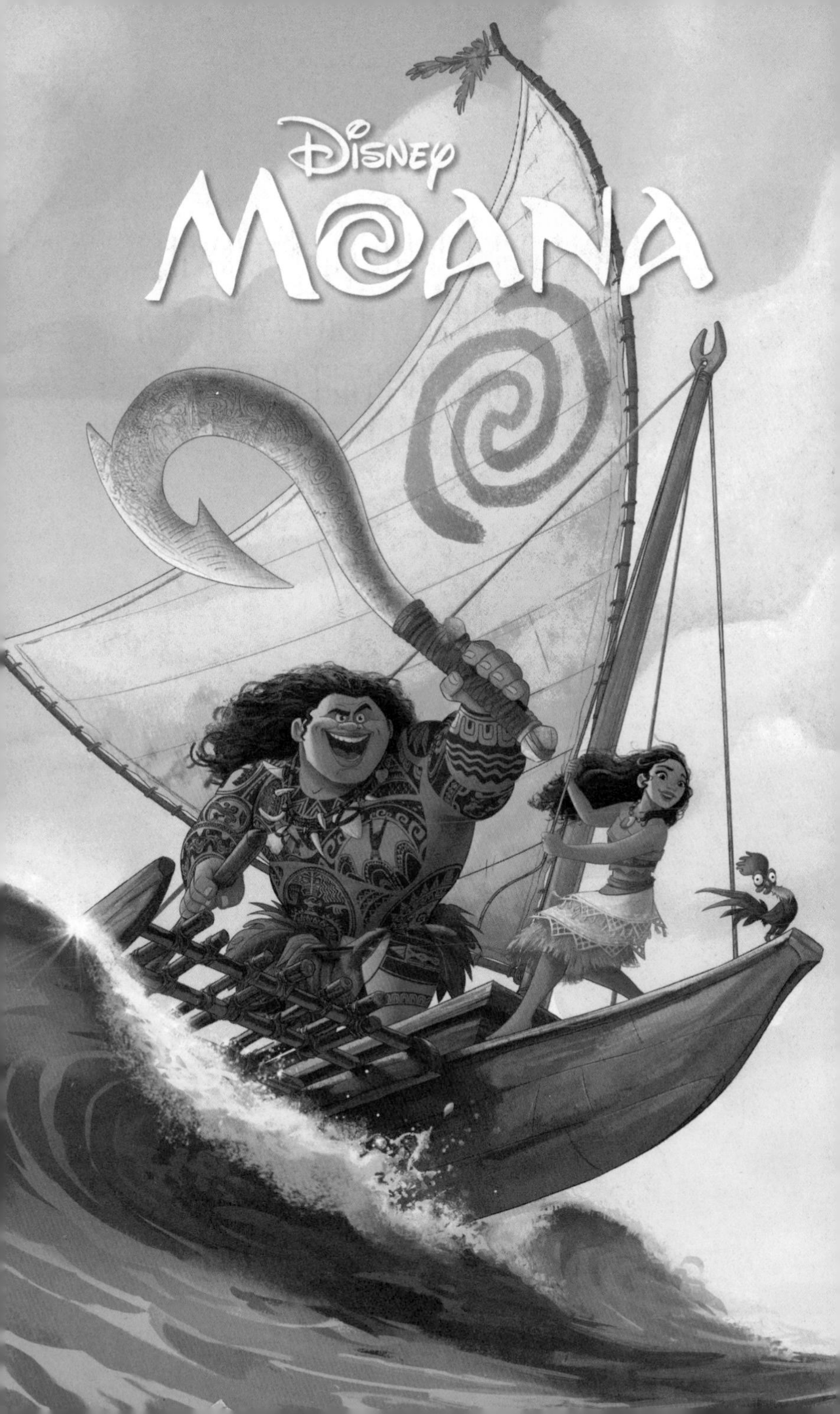
Disney
MOANA

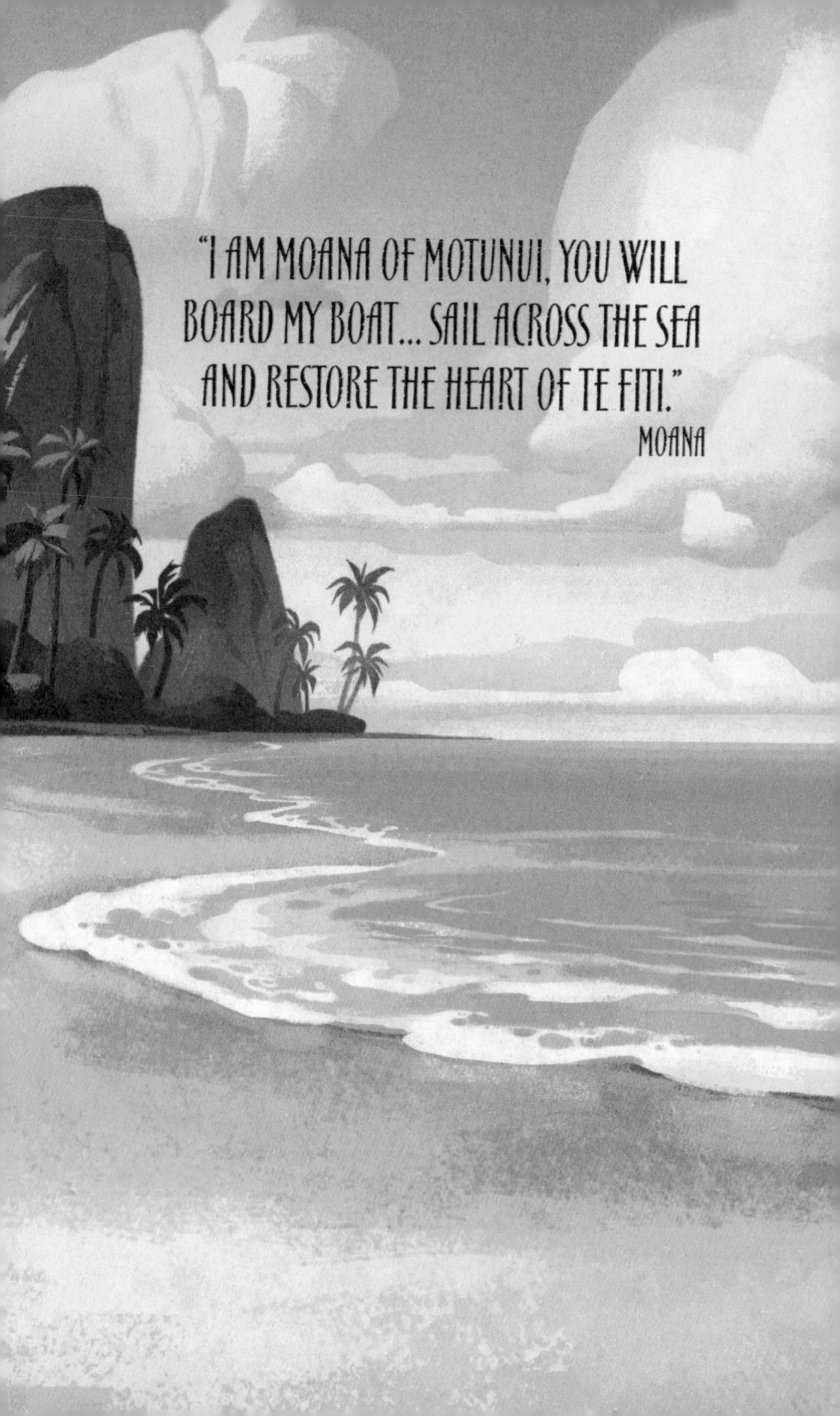

"I AM MOANA OF MOTUNUI, YOU WILL BOARD MY BOAT... SAIL ACROSS THE SEA AND RESTORE THE HEART OF TE FITI."

MOANA

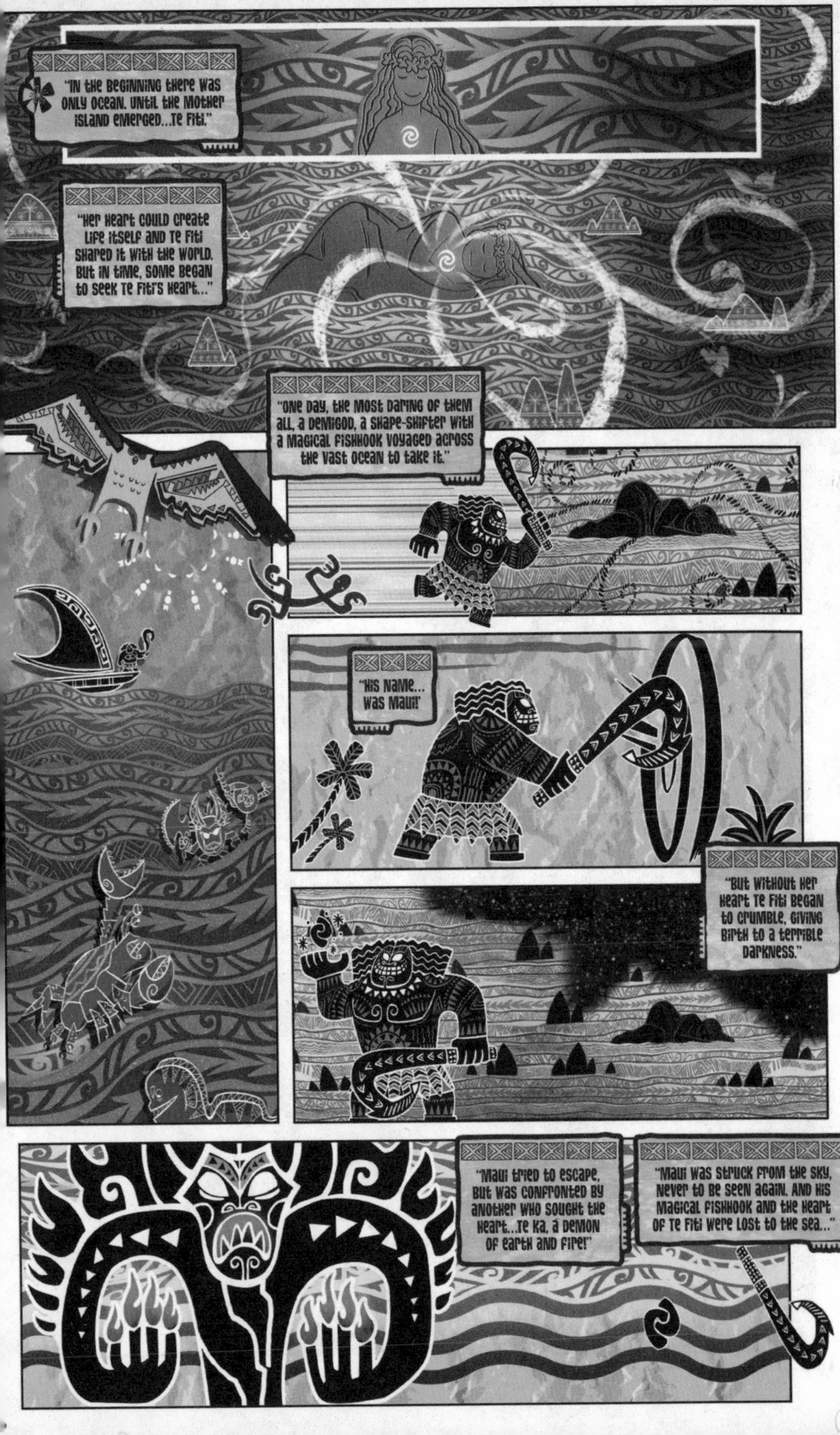
"In the beginning there was only ocean. Until the Mother Island emerged...Te Fiti."
"Her heart could create life itself and Te Fiti shared it with the world. But in time, some began to seek Te Fiti's heart..."
"One day, the most daring of them all, a demigod, a shape-shifter with a magical fishhook voyaged across the vast ocean to take it."
"His name... was Maui!"
"But without her heart Te Fiti began to crumble, giving birth to a terrible darkness."
"Maui tried to escape, but was confronted by another who sought the heart...Te Ka, a demon of earth and fire!"
"Maui was struck from the sky, never to be seen again. And his magical fishhook and the heart of Te Fiti were lost to the sea..."

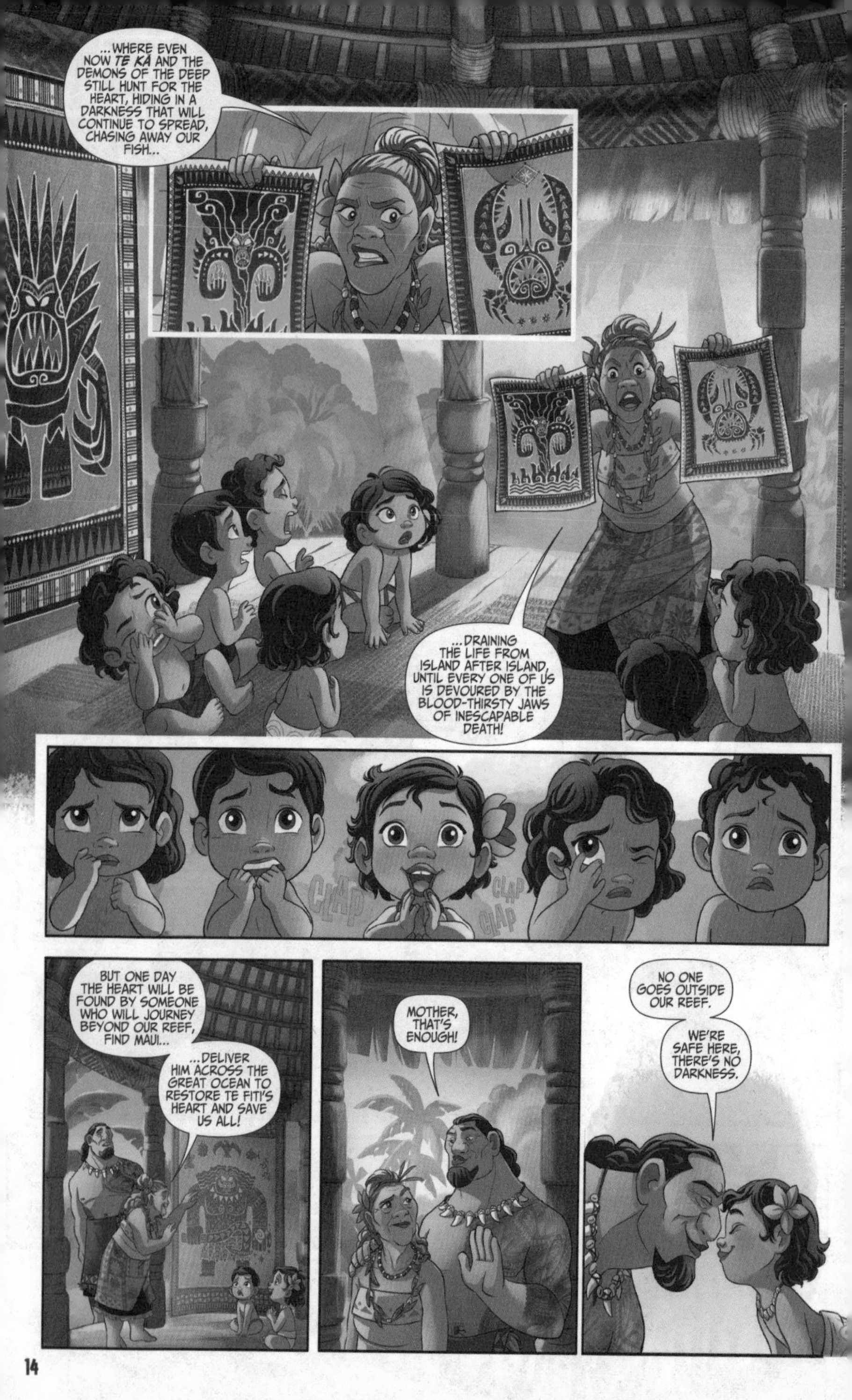
...WHERE EVEN NOW TE KĀ AND THE DEMONS OF THE DEEP STILL HUNT FOR THE HEART, HIDING IN A DARKNESS THAT WILL CONTINUE TO SPREAD, CHASING AWAY OUR FISH...
...DRAINING THE LIFE FROM ISLAND AFTER ISLAND, UNTIL EVERY ONE OF US IS DEVOURED BY THE BLOOD-THIRSTY JAWS OF INESCAPABLE DEATH!
CLAP
CLAP
CLAP
BUT ONE DAY THE HEART WILL BE FOUND BY SOMEONE WHO WILL JOURNEY BEYOND OUR REEF, FIND MAUI...
...DELIVER HIM ACROSS THE GREAT OCEAN TO RESTORE TE FITI'S HEART AND SAVE US ALL!
MOTHER, THAT'S ENOUGH!
NO ONE GOES OUTSIDE OUR REEF.
WE'RE SAFE HERE, THERE'S NO DARKNESS.

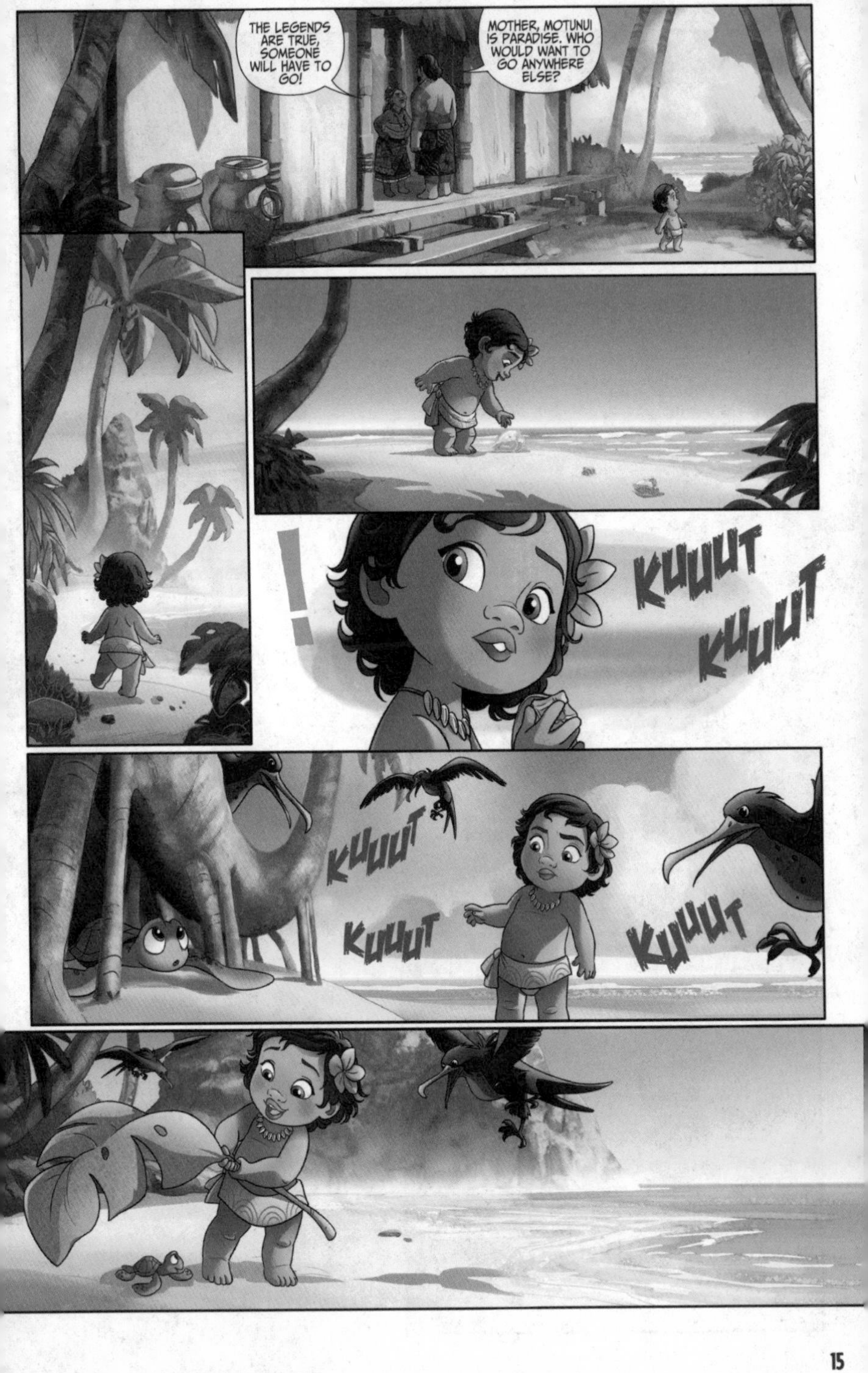
THE LEGENDS ARE TRUE, SOMEONE WILL HAVE TO GO!
MOTHER, MOTUNUI IS PARADISE. WHO WOULD WANT TO GO ANYWHERE ELSE?
!
KUUUT
KUUUT
KUUUT
KUUUT
KUUUT

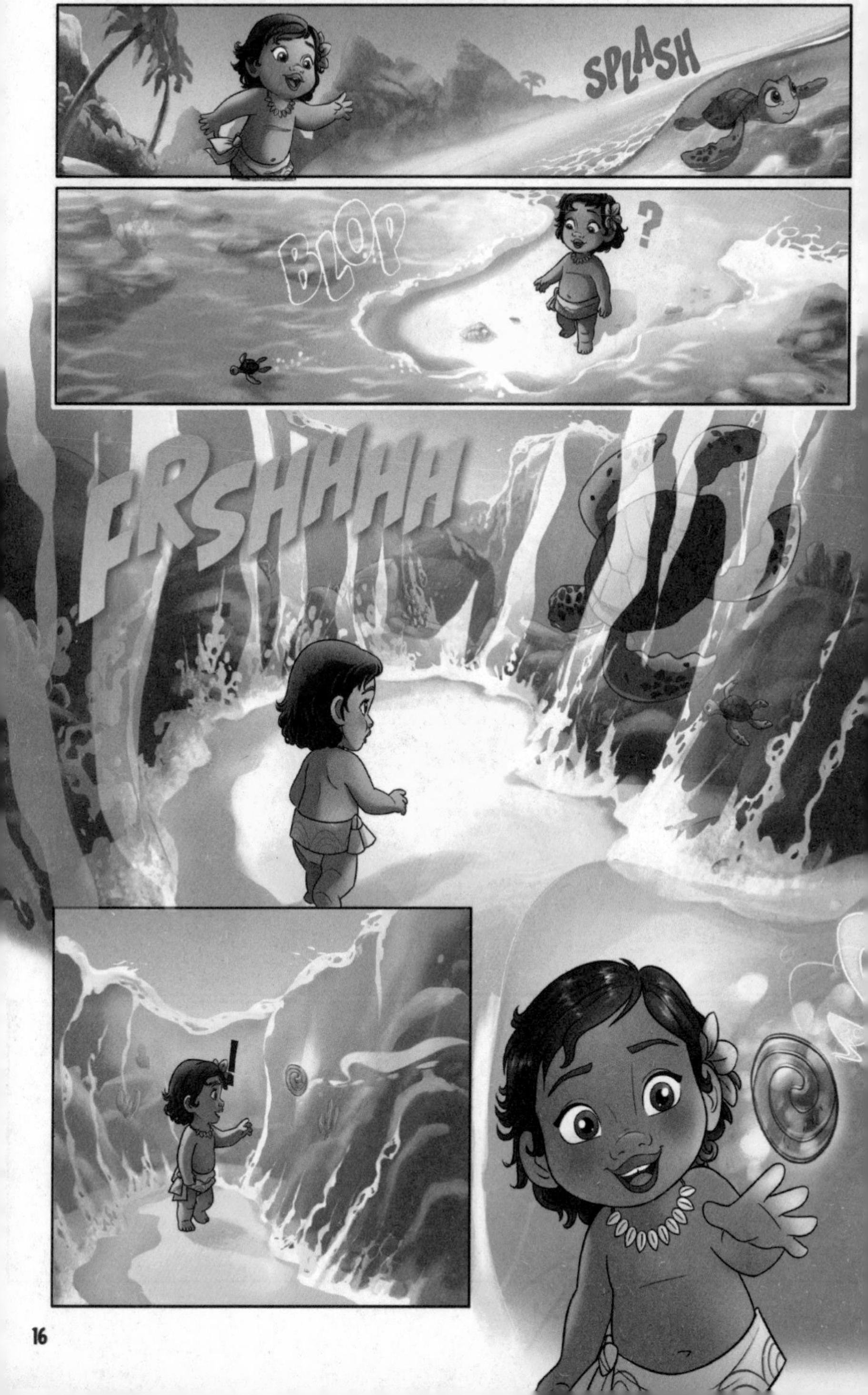
SPLASH
BLOP
?
FRSHHHH
!

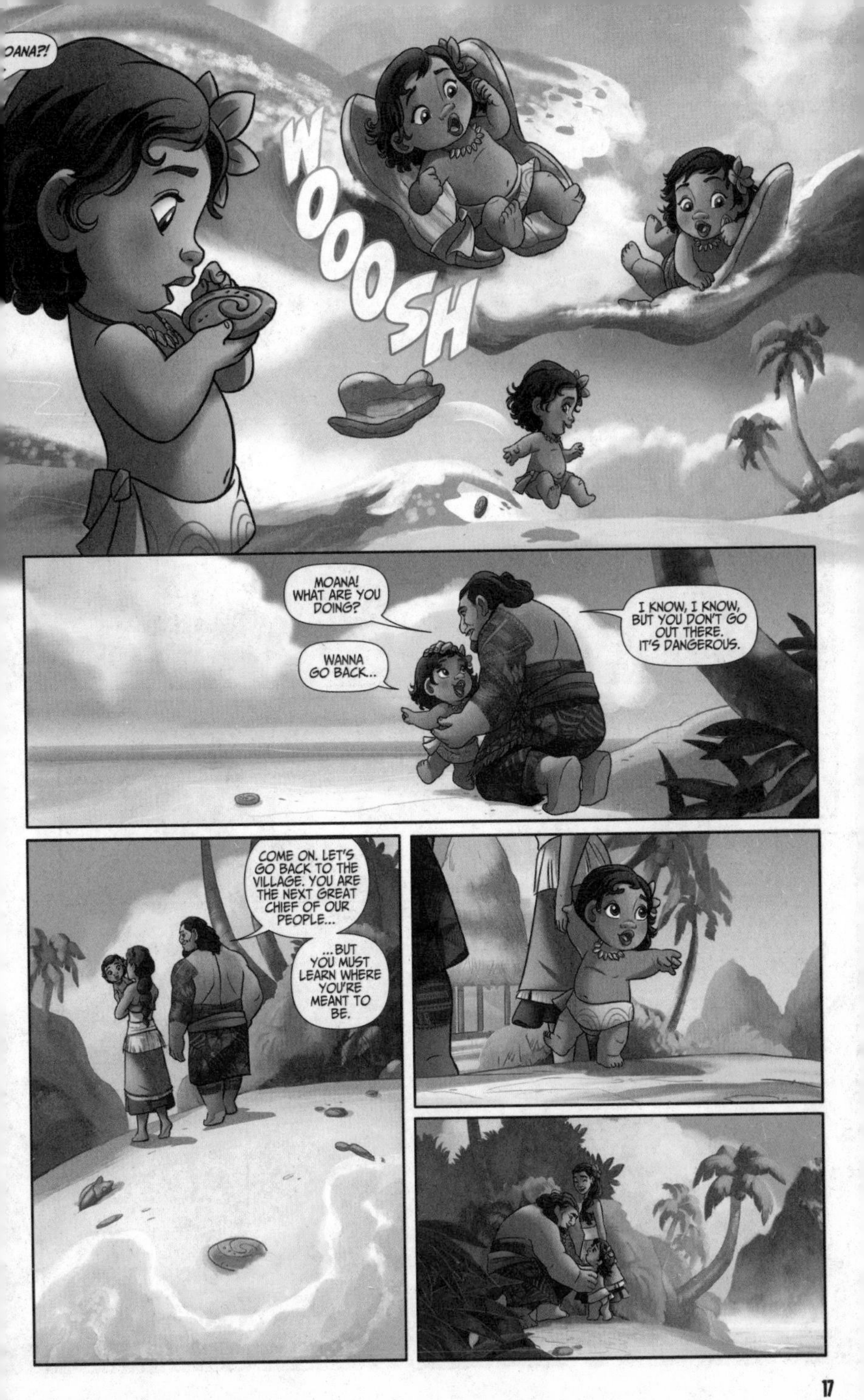

OANA?!
WOOOOSH
MOANA! WHAT ARE YOU DOING?
WANNA GO BACK...
I KNOW, I KNOW, BUT YOU DON'T GO OUT THERE. IT'S DANGEROUS.
COME ON. LET'S GO BACK TO THE VILLAGE. YOU ARE THE NEXT GREAT CHIEF OF OUR PEOPLE...
...BUT YOU MUST LEARN WHERE YOU'RE MEANT TO BE.

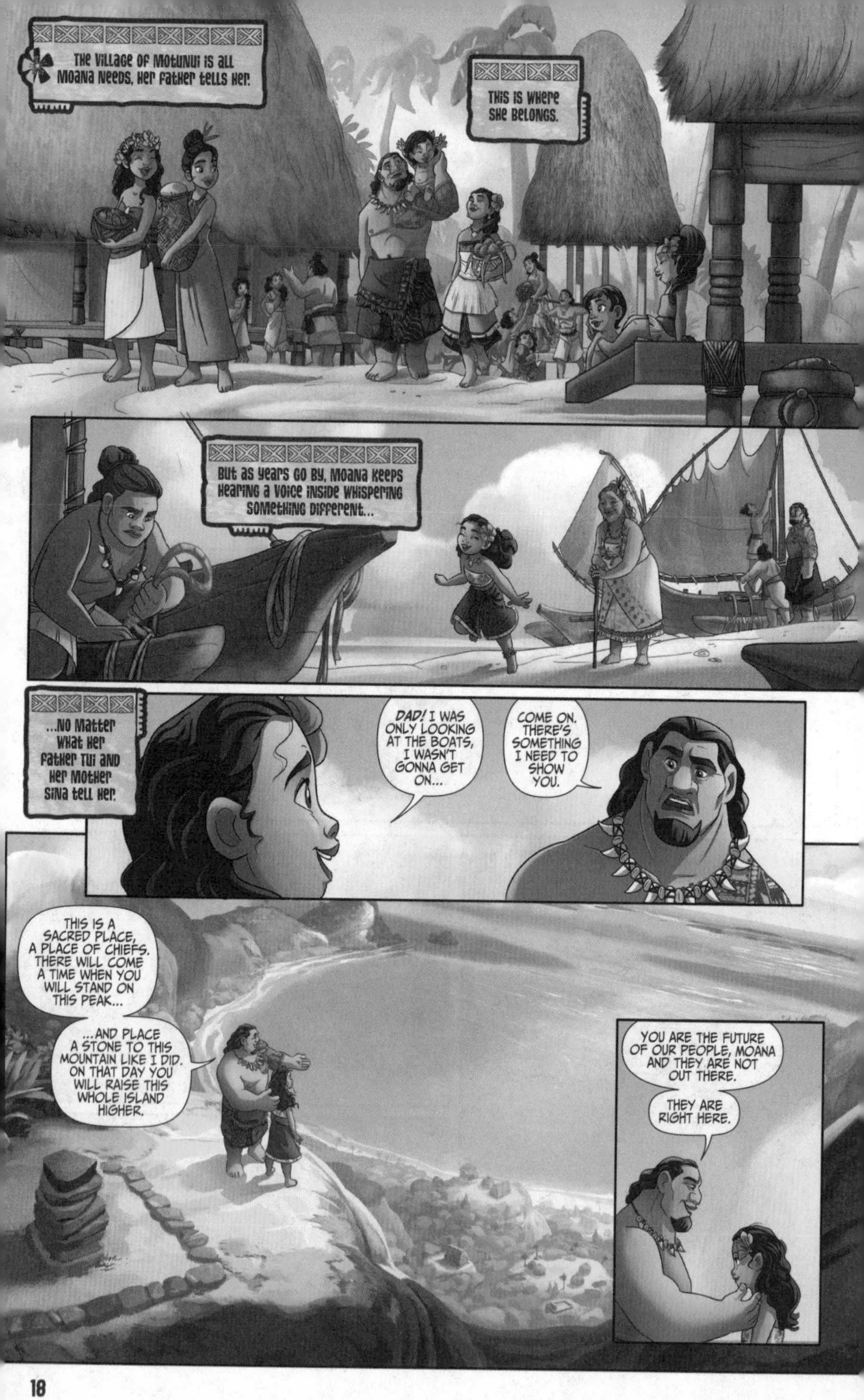
The Village of Motunui is all Moana needs, her father tells her.
This is where she belongs.
But as years go by, Moana keeps hearing a voice inside whispering something different...
...no matter what her father Tui and her mother Sina tell her.
DAD! I WAS ONLY LOOKING AT THE BOATS, I WASN'T GONNA GET ON...
COME ON. THERE'S SOMETHING I NEED TO SHOW YOU.
THIS IS A SACRED PLACE, A PLACE OF CHIEFS. THERE WILL COME A TIME WHEN YOU WILL STAND ON THIS PEAK...
...AND PLACE A STONE TO THIS MOUNTAIN LIKE I DID. ON THAT DAY YOU WILL RAISE THIS WHOLE ISLAND HIGHER.
YOU ARE THE FUTURE OF OUR PEOPLE, MOANA AND THEY ARE NOT OUT THERE.
THEY ARE RIGHT HERE.

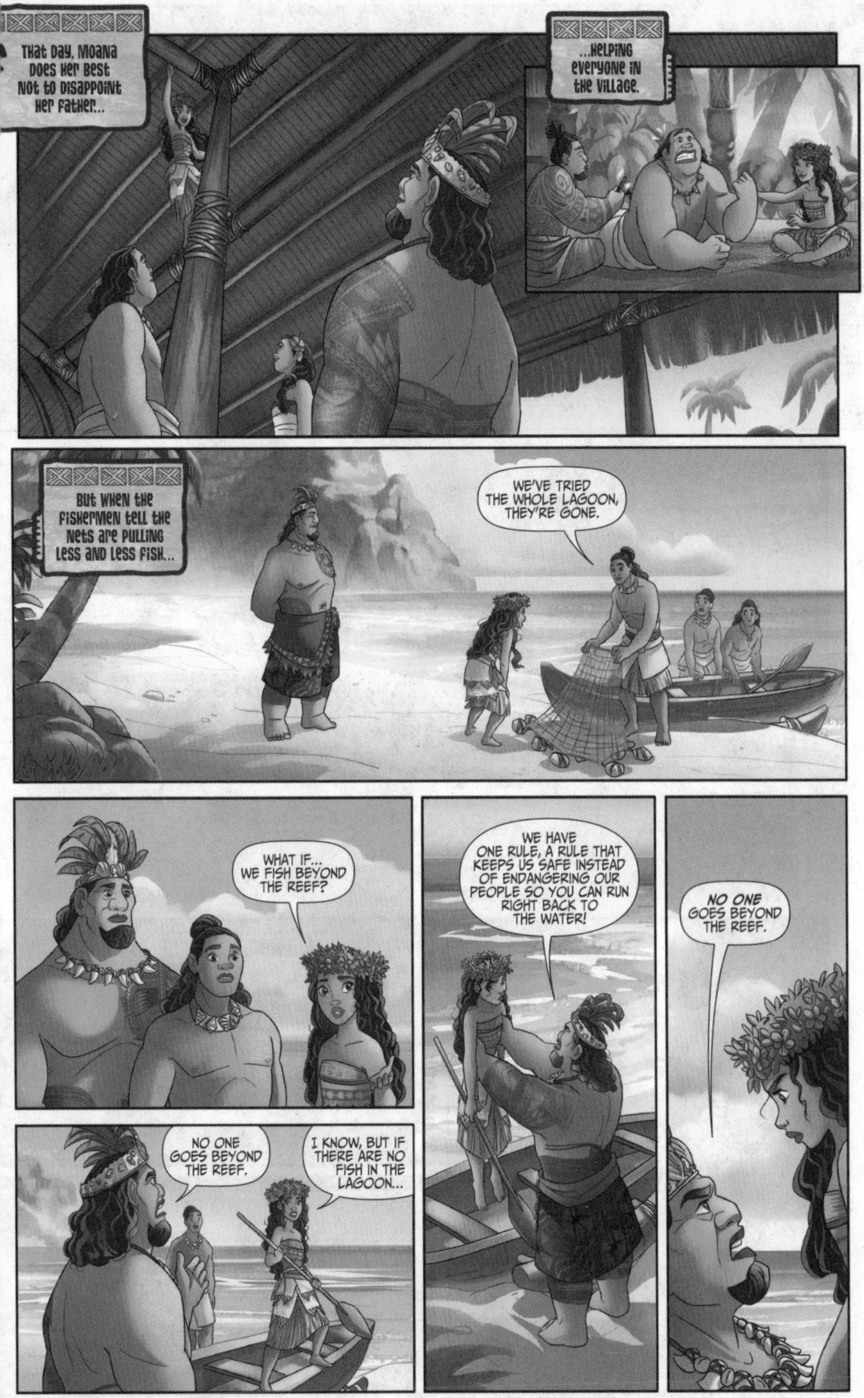

That day, Moana does her best not to disappoint her father...
...helping everyone in the village.
But when the fishermen tell the nets are pulling less and less fish...
WE'VE TRIED THE WHOLE LAGOON, THEY'RE GONE.
WHAT IF... WE FISH BEYOND THE REEF?
NO ONE GOES BEYOND THE REEF.
I KNOW, BUT IF THERE ARE NO FISH IN THE LAGOON...
WE HAVE ONE RULE, A RULE THAT KEEPS US SAFE INSTEAD OF ENDANGERING OUR PEOPLE SO YOU CAN RUN RIGHT BACK TO THE WATER!
NO ONE GOES BEYOND THE REEF.

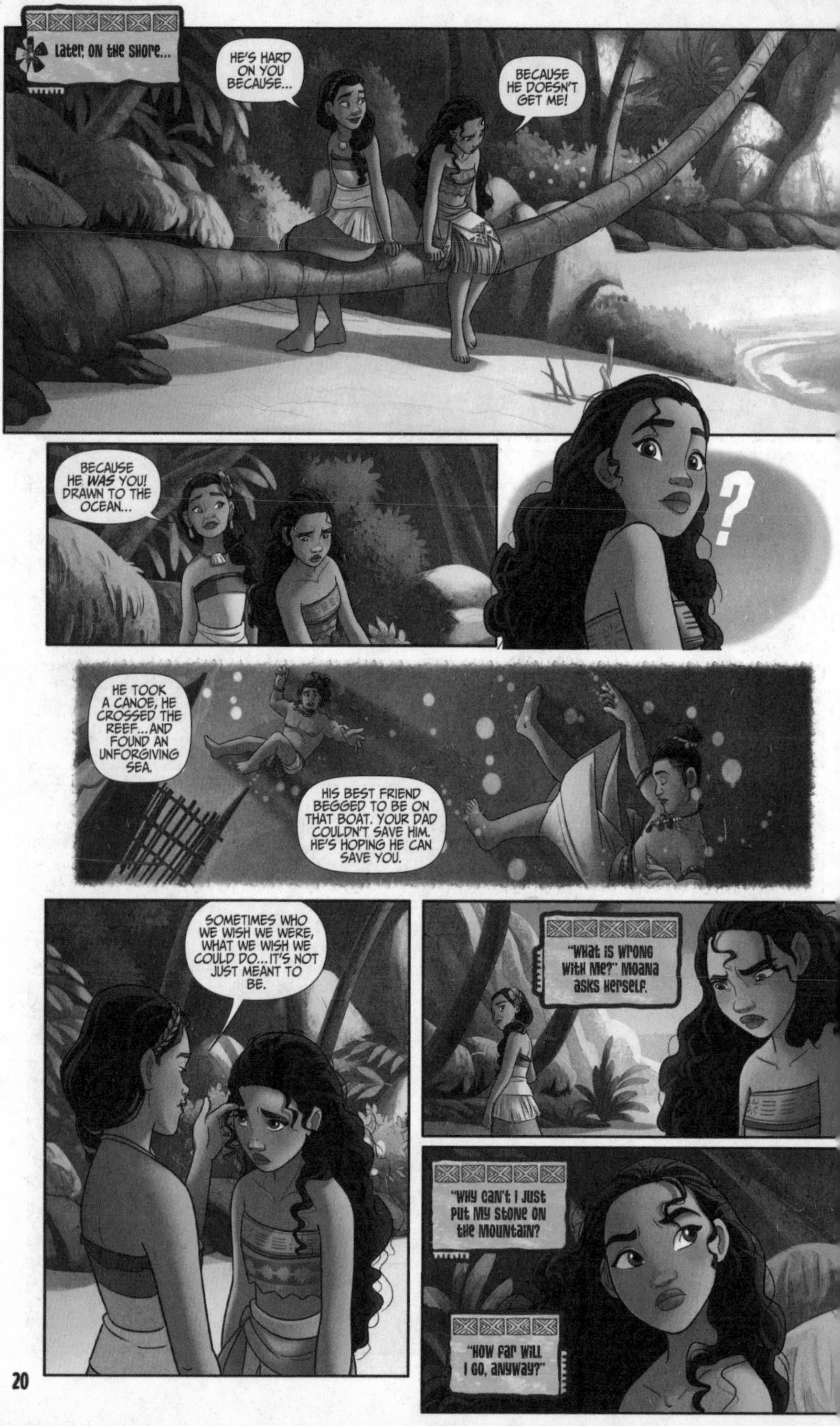

Later, on the shore...
HE'S HARD ON YOU BECAUSE...
BECAUSE HE DOESN'T GET ME!
BECAUSE HE WAS YOU! DRAWN TO THE OCEAN...
?
HE TOOK A CANOE, HE CROSSED THE REEF...AND FOUND AN UNFORGIVING SEA.
HIS BEST FRIEND BEGGED TO BE ON THAT BOAT. YOUR DAD COULDN'T SAVE HIM. HE'S HOPING HE CAN SAVE YOU.
SOMETIMES WHO WE WISH WE WERE, WHAT WE WISH WE COULD DO...IT'S NOT JUST MEANT TO BE.
"What is wrong with me?" Moana asks herself.
"Why can't I just put my stone on the mountain?
"How far will I go, anyway?"

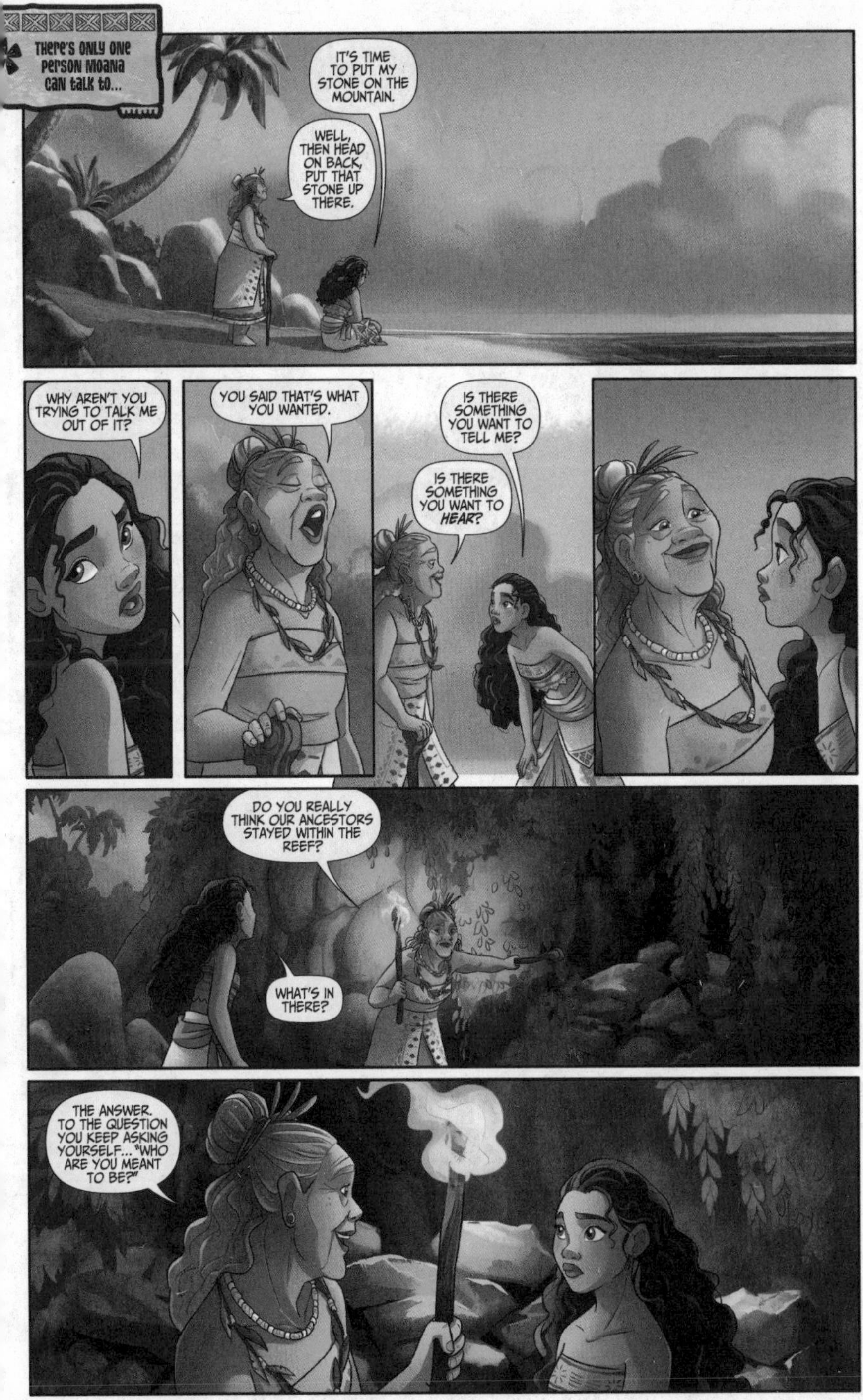
There's only one person Moana can talk to...
IT'S TIME TO PUT MY STONE ON THE MOUNTAIN.
WELL, THEN HEAD ON BACK, PUT THAT STONE UP THERE.
WHY AREN'T YOU TRYING TO TALK ME OUT OF IT?
YOU SAID THAT'S WHAT YOU WANTED.
IS THERE SOMETHING YOU WANT TO TELL ME?
IS THERE SOMETHING YOU WANT TO HEAR?
DO YOU REALLY THINK OUR ANCESTORS STAYED WITHIN THE REEF?
WHAT'S IN THERE?
THE ANSWER. TO THE QUESTION YOU KEEP ASKING YOURSELF... "WHO ARE YOU MEANT TO BE?"

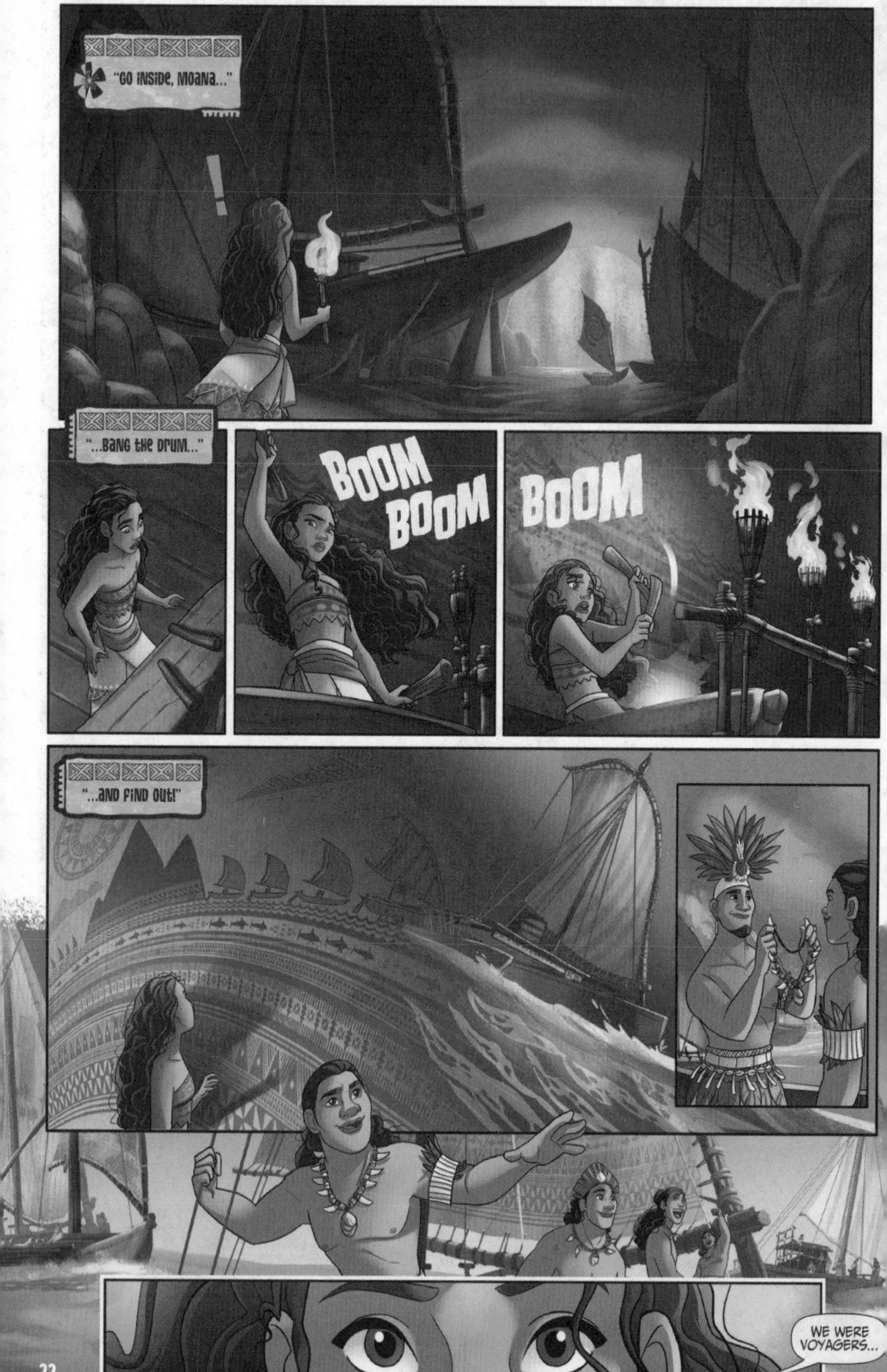
"GO INSIDE, MOANA..."
!
"...BANG THE DRUM..."
BOOM
BOOM
BOOM
"...AND FIND OUT!"
WE WERE VOYAGERS...

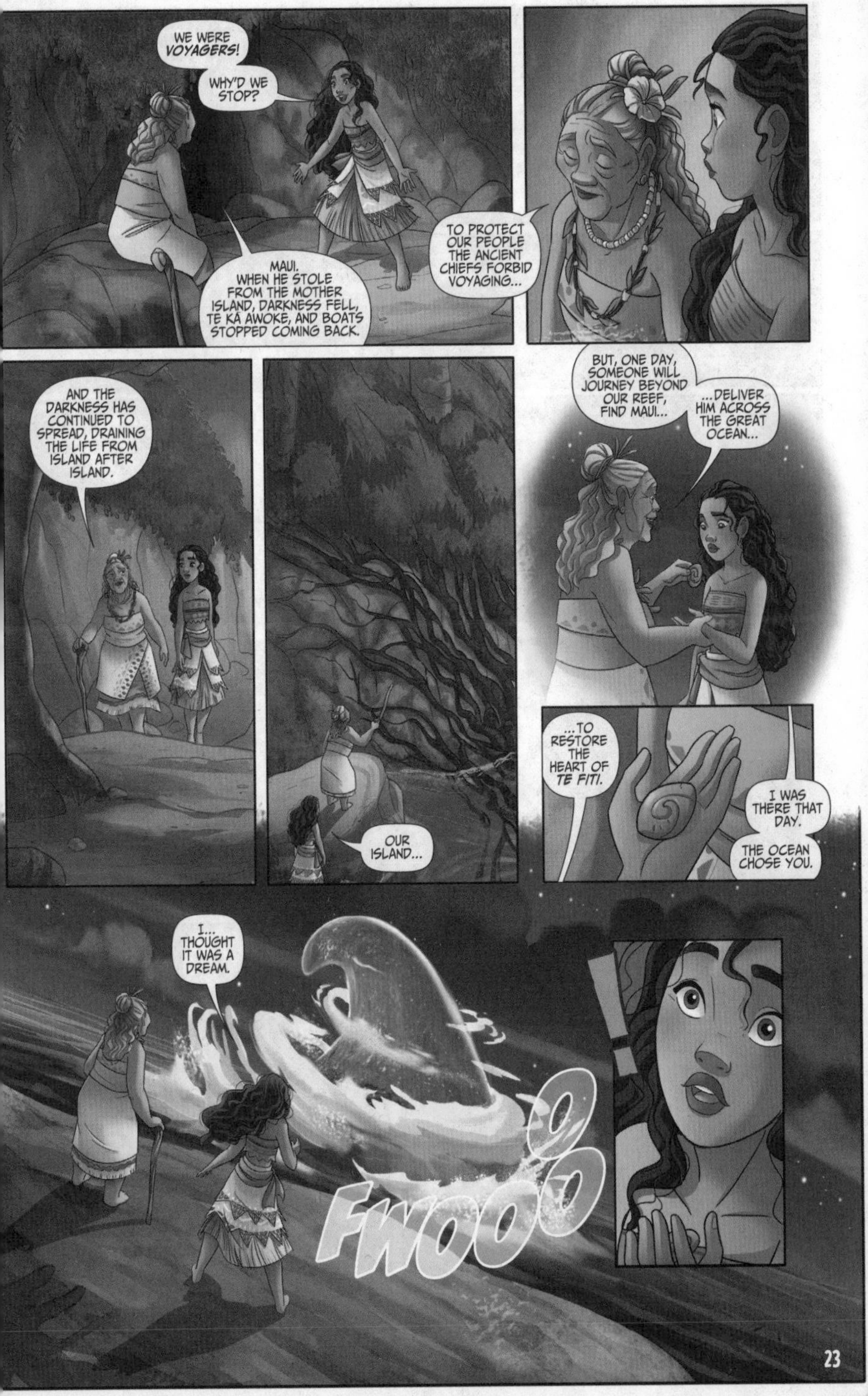
WE WERE VOYAGERS!
WHY'D WE STOP?
MAUI. WHEN HE STOLE FROM THE MOTHER ISLAND, DARKNESS FELL, TE KĀ AWOKE, AND BOATS STOPPED COMING BACK.
TO PROTECT OUR PEOPLE THE ANCIENT CHIEFS FORBID VOYAGING...
AND THE DARKNESS HAS CONTINUED TO SPREAD, DRAINING THE LIFE FROM ISLAND AFTER ISLAND.
OUR ISLAND...
BUT, ONE DAY, SOMEONE WILL JOURNEY BEYOND OUR REEF, FIND MAUI...
...DELIVER HIM ACROSS THE GREAT OCEAN...
...TO RESTORE THE HEART OF TE FITI.
I WAS THERE THAT DAY.
THE OCEAN CHOSE YOU.
I... THOUGHT IT WAS A DREAM.
FWOOOSH
!

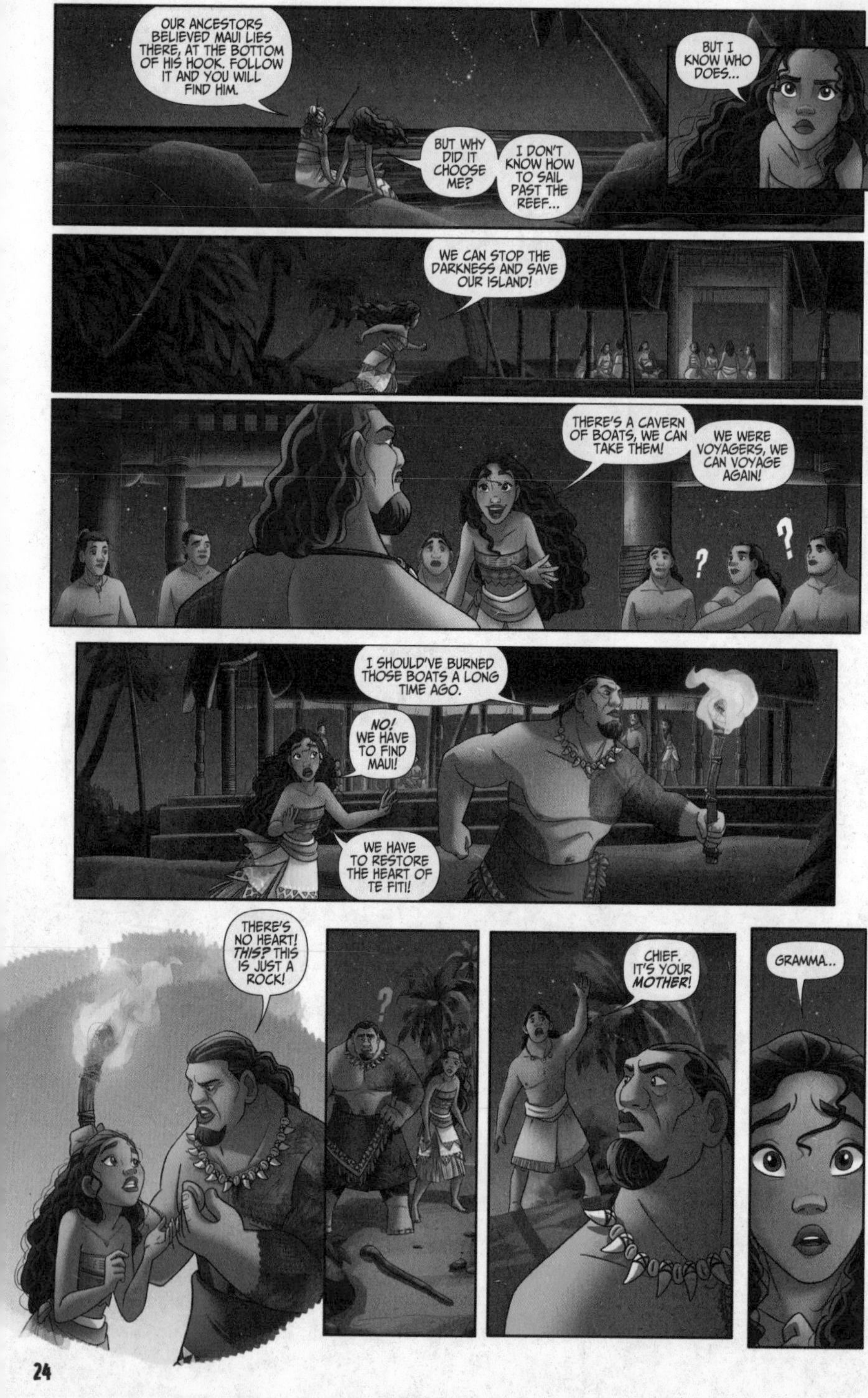
OUR ANCESTORS BELIEVED MAUI LIES THERE, AT THE BOTTOM OF HIS HOOK. FOLLOW IT AND YOU WILL FIND HIM.
BUT WHY DID IT CHOOSE ME?
I DON'T KNOW HOW TO SAIL PAST THE REEF...
BUT I KNOW WHO DOES...
WE CAN STOP THE DARKNESS AND SAVE OUR ISLAND!
THERE'S A CAVERN OF BOATS, WE CAN TAKE THEM!
WE WERE VOYAGERS, WE CAN VOYAGE AGAIN!
?
?
I SHOULD'VE BURNED THOSE BOATS A LONG TIME AGO.
NO! WE HAVE TO FIND MAUI!
WE HAVE TO RESTORE THE HEART OF TE FITI!
THERE'S NO HEART! THIS? THIS IS JUST A ROCK!
?
CHIEF. IT'S YOUR MOTHER!
GRAMMA...

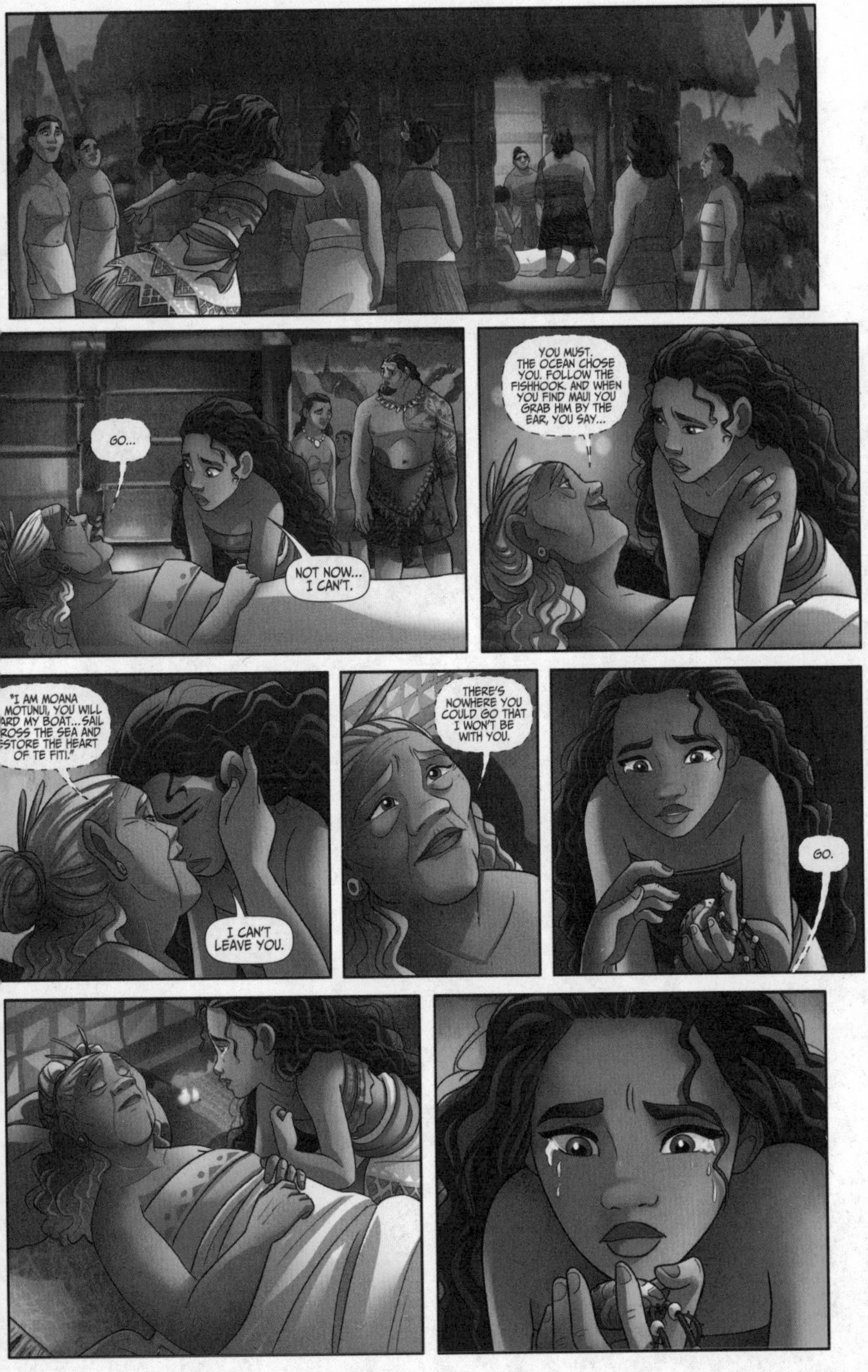
GO...
NOT NOW... I CAN'T.
YOU MUST. THE OCEAN CHOSE YOU. FOLLOW THE FISHHOOK. AND WHEN YOU FIND MAUI YOU GRAB HIM BY THE EAR, YOU SAY...
"I AM MOANA MOTUNUI, YOU WILL ARD MY BOAT...SAIL ROSS THE SEA AND ESTORE THE HEART OF TE FITI."
I CAN'T LEAVE YOU.
THERE'S NOWHERE YOU COULD GO THAT I WON'T BE WITH YOU.
GO.

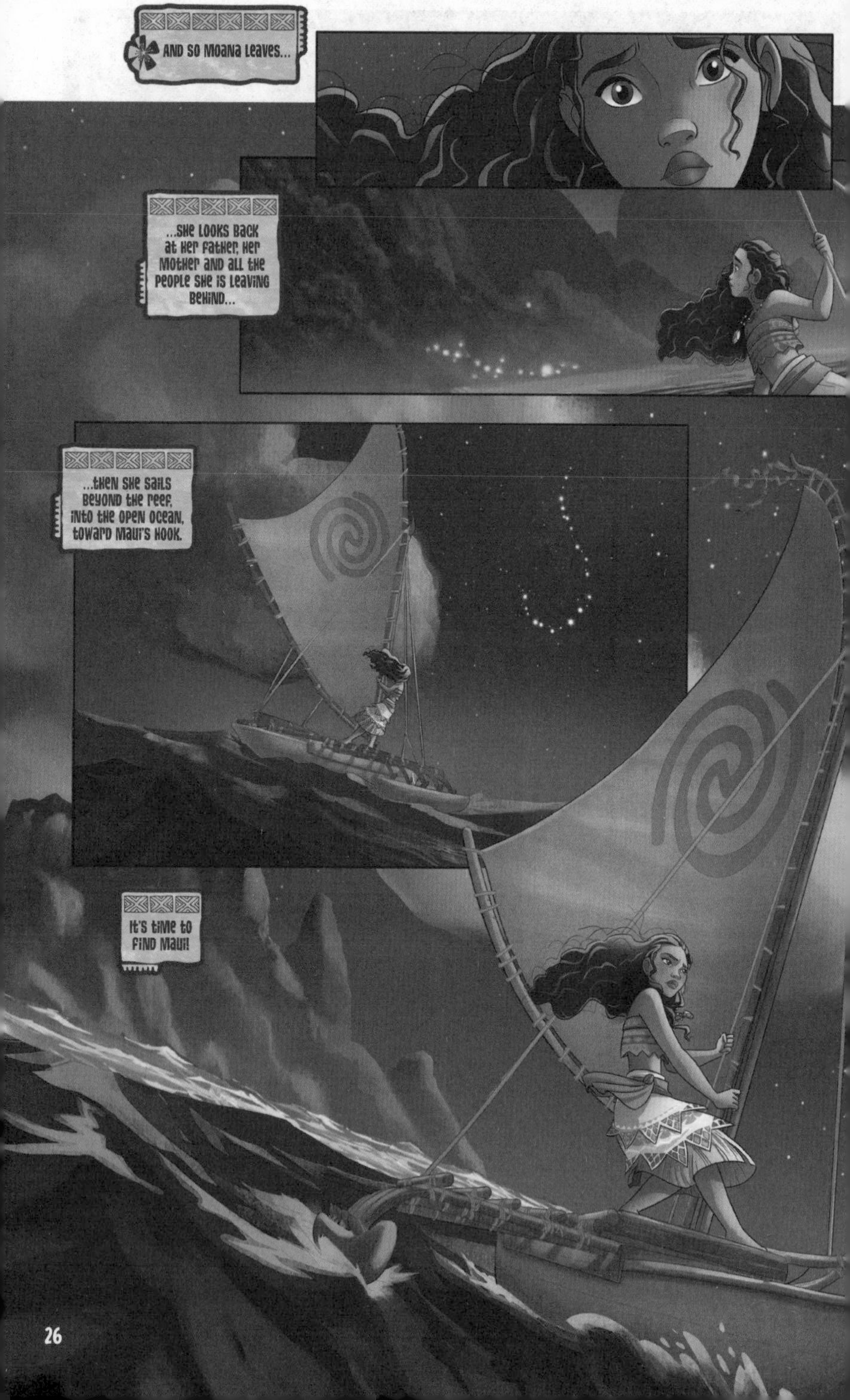
AND SO MOANA LEAVES...
...SHE LOOKS BACK AT HER FATHER, HER MOTHER AND ALL THE PEOPLE SHE IS LEAVING BEHIND...
...THEN SHE SAILS BEYOND THE REEF, INTO THE OPEN OCEAN, TOWARD MAUI'S HOOK.
IT'S TIME TO FIND MAUI!

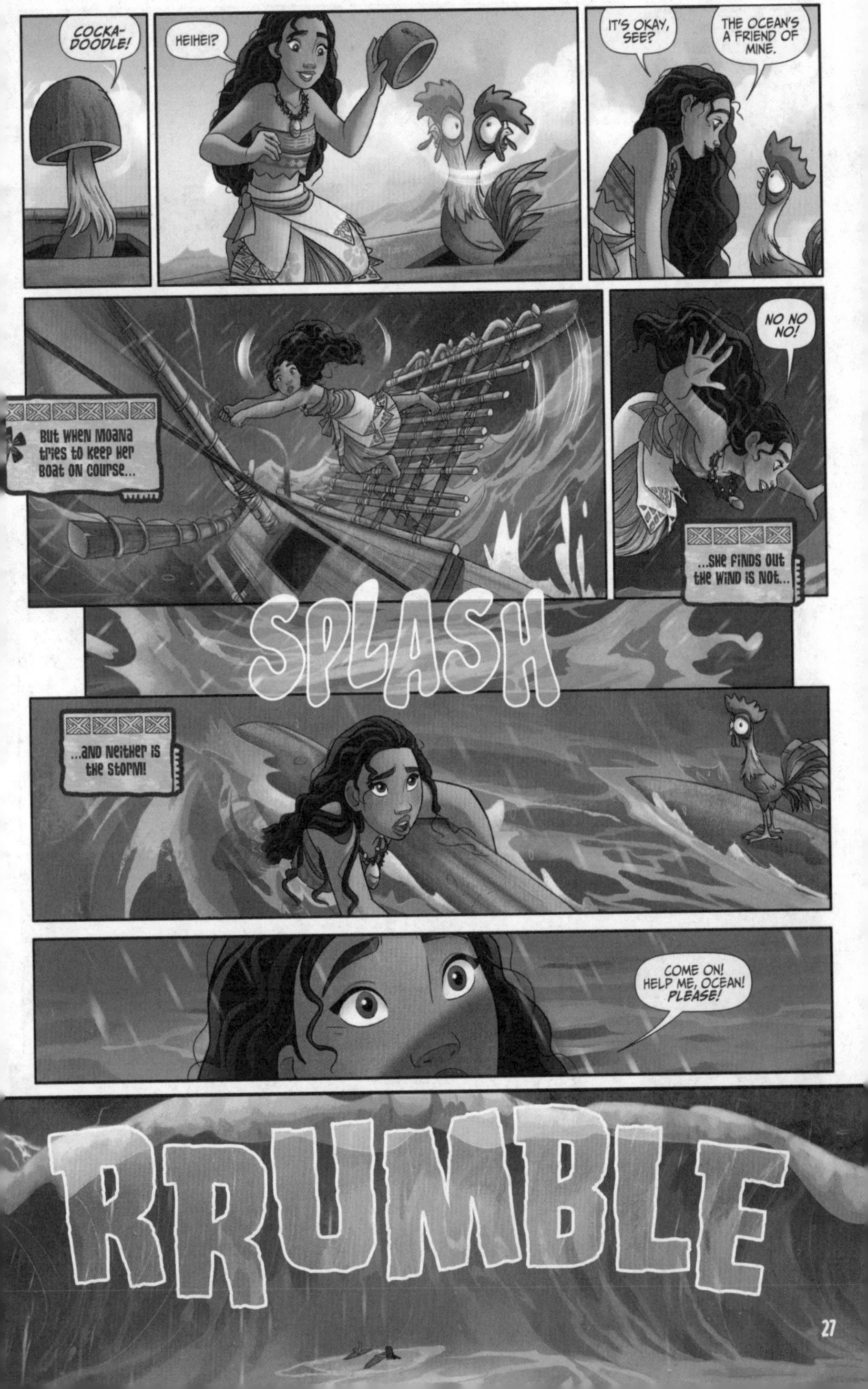
COCKA-DOODLE!
HEIHEI?
IT'S OKAY, SEE?
THE OCEAN'S A FRIEND OF MINE.
But when Moana tries to keep her boat on course...
NO NO NO!
...she finds out the wind is not...
SPLASH
...and neither is the storm!
COME ON! HELP ME, OCEAN! PLEASE!
RRUMBLE

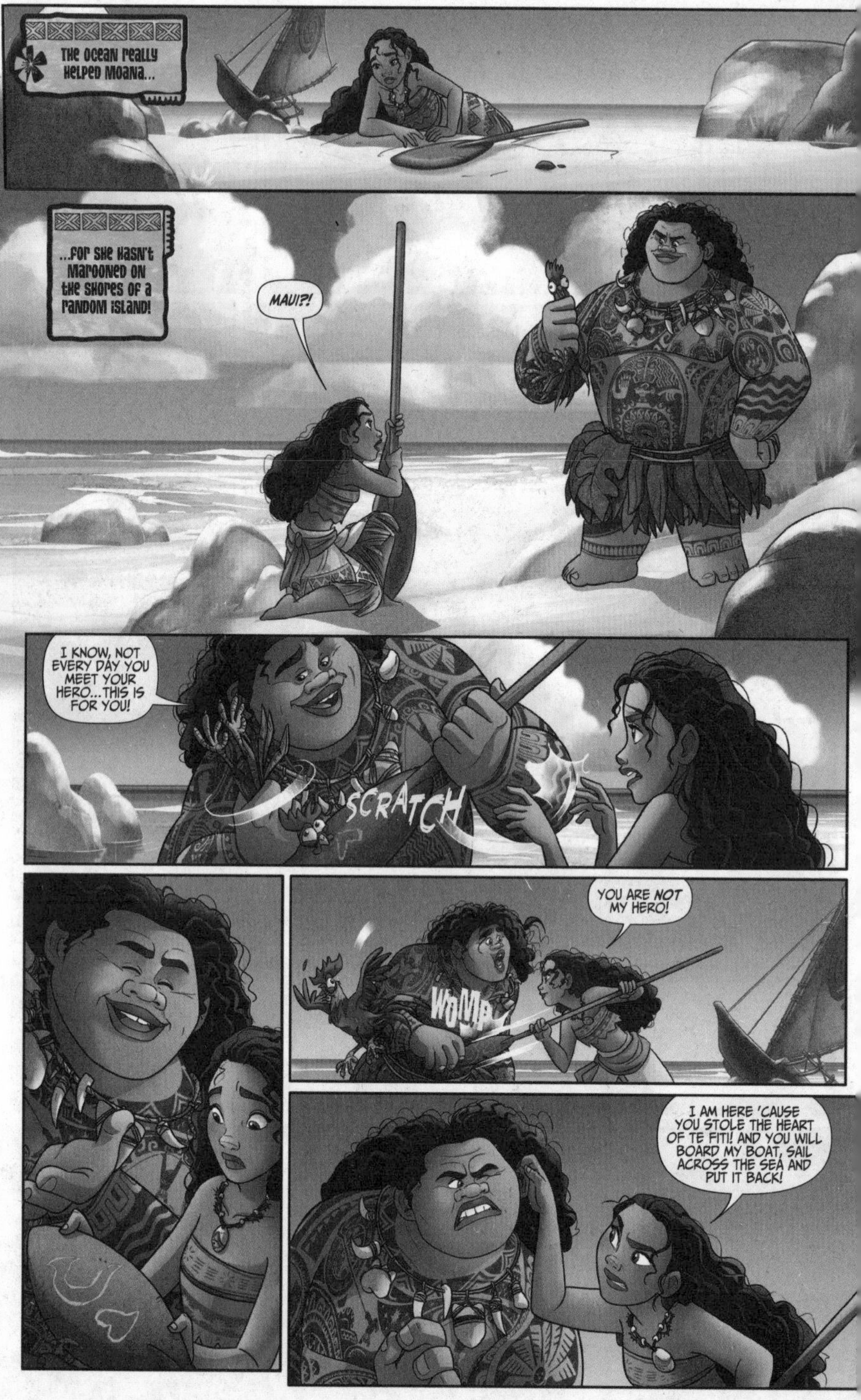
THE OCEAN REALLY HELPED MOANA...
...FOR SHE HASN'T MAROONED ON THE SHORES OF A RANDOM ISLAND!
MAUI!?!
I KNOW, NOT EVERY DAY YOU MEET YOUR HERO...THIS IS FOR YOU!
SCRATCH
YOU ARE NOT MY HERO!
WOMP
I AM HERE 'CAUSE YOU STOLE THE HEART OF TE FITI! AND YOU WILL BOARD MY BOAT, SAIL ACROSS THE SEA AND PUT IT BACK!

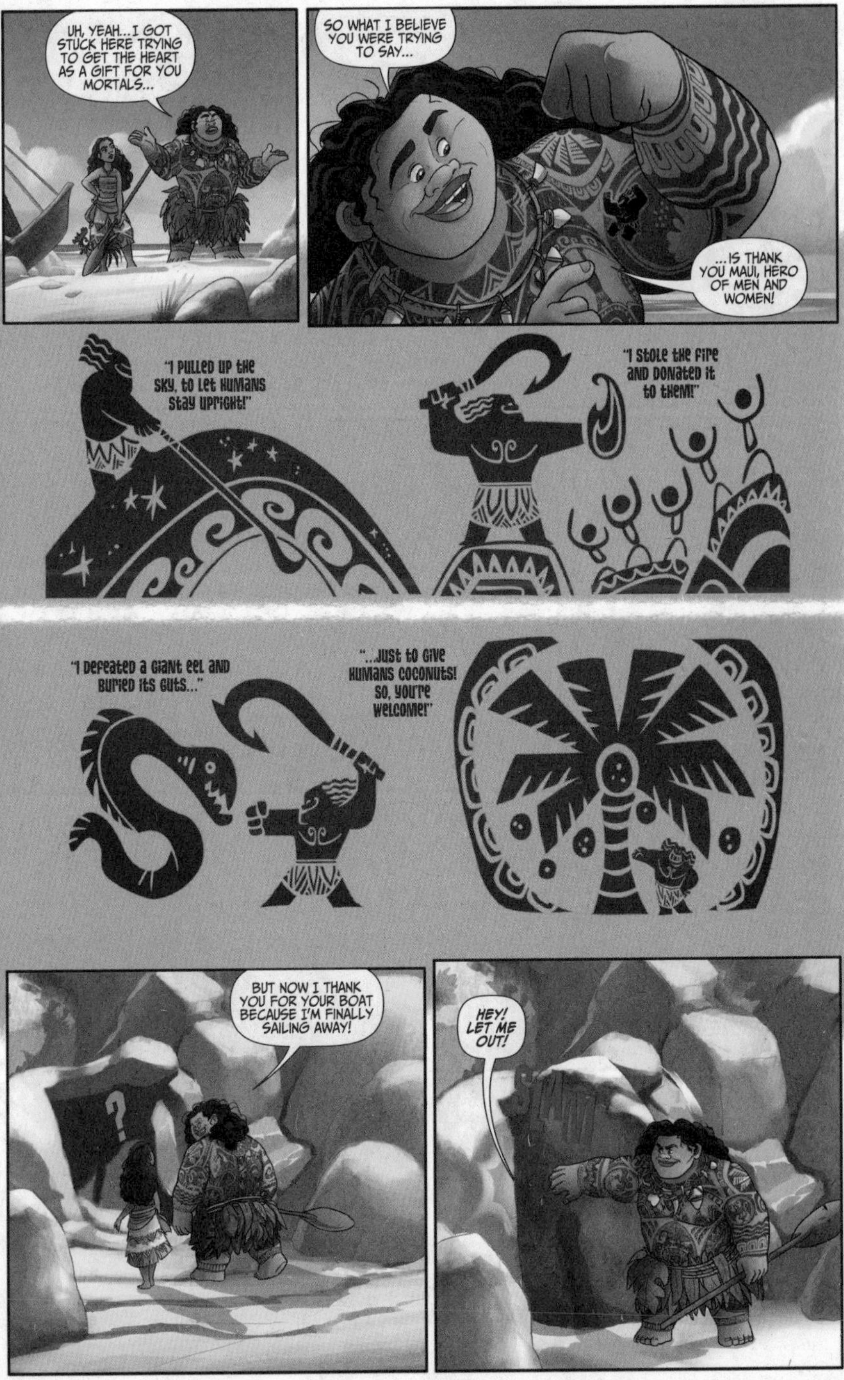
UH, YEAH... I GOT STUCK HERE TRYING TO GET THE HEART AS A GIFT FOR YOU MORTALS...
SO WHAT I BELIEVE YOU WERE TRYING TO SAY...
...IS THANK YOU MAUI, HERO OF MEN AND WOMEN!
"I PULLED UP THE SKY, TO LET HUMANS STAY UPRIGHT!"
"I STOLE THE FIRE AND DONATED IT TO THEM!"
"I DEFEATED A GIANT EEL AND BURIED ITS GUTS..."
"...JUST TO GIVE HUMANS COCONUTS! SO, YOU'RE WELCOME!"
BUT NOW I THANK YOU FOR YOUR BOAT BECAUSE I'M FINALLY SAILING AWAY!
HEY! LET ME OUT!

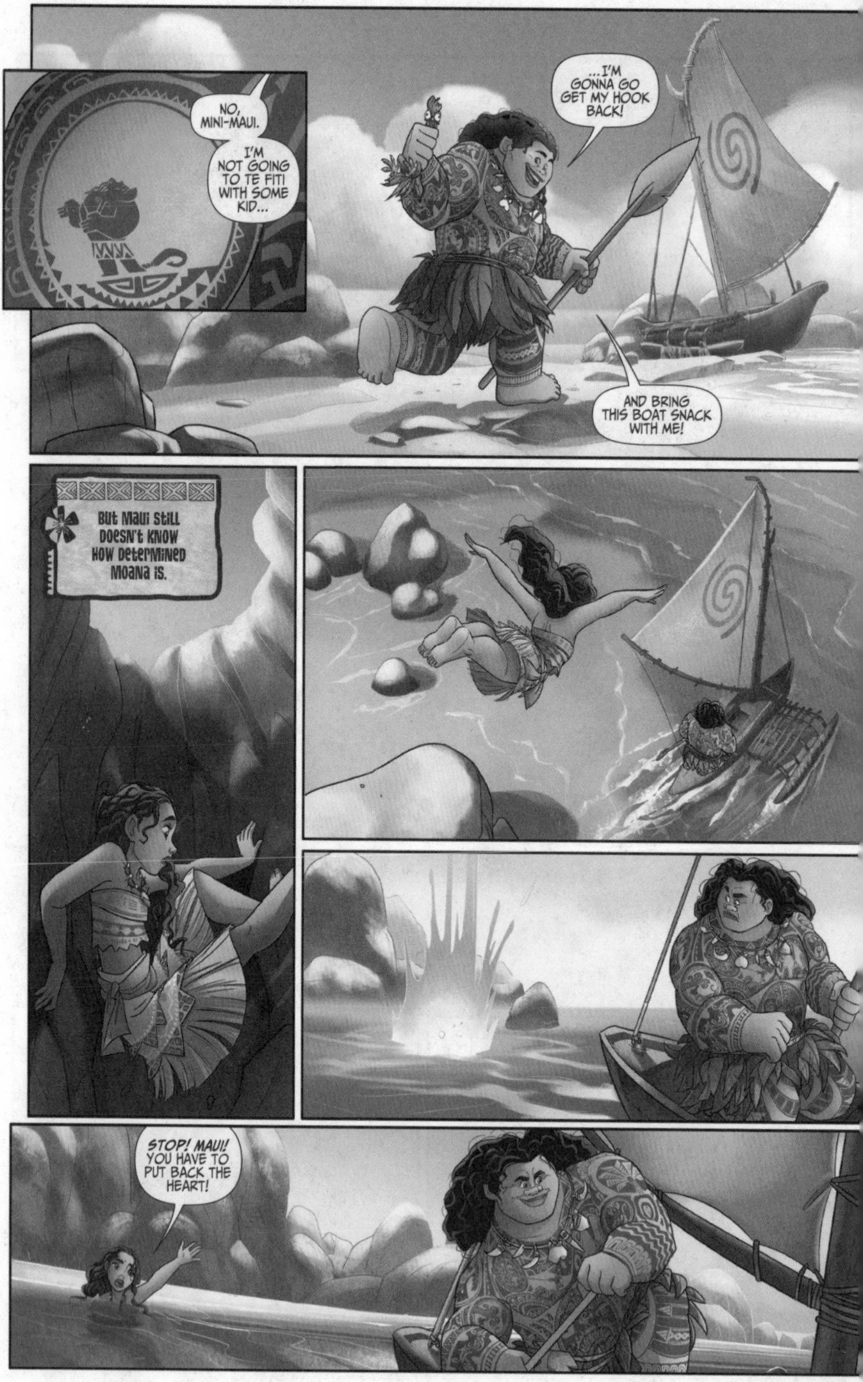
NO, MINI-MAUI.
I'M NOT GOING TO TE FITI WITH SOME KID...
...I'M GONNA GO GET MY HOOK BACK!
AND BRING THIS BOAT SNACK WITH ME!
But Maui still doesn't know how determined Moana is.
STOP! MAUI! YOU HAVE TO PUT BACK THE HEART!

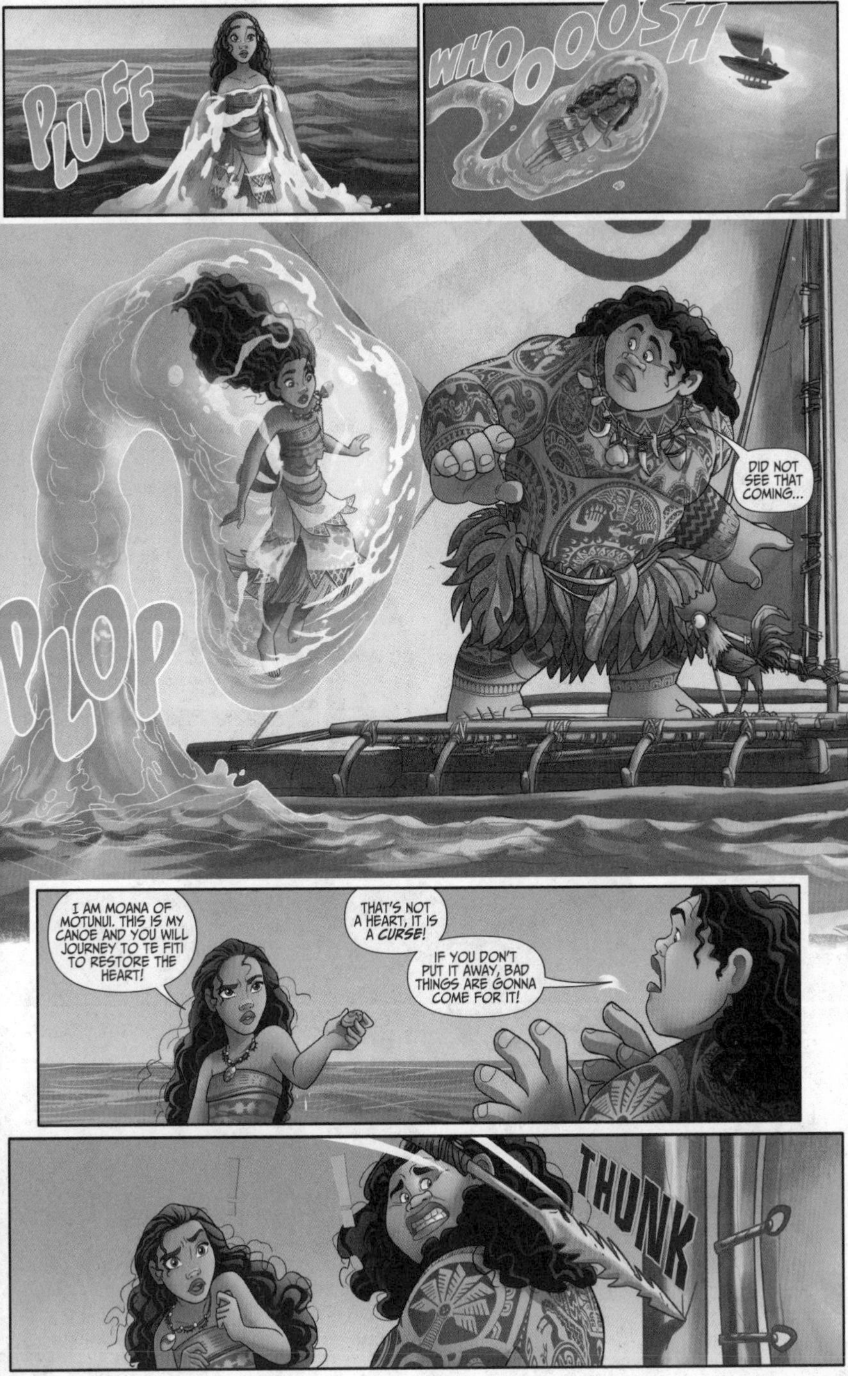
PLUFF
WHOOOOOSH
PLOP
DID NOT SEE THAT COMING...
I AM MOANA OF MOTUNUI. THIS IS MY CANOE AND YOU WILL JOURNEY TO TE FITI TO RESTORE THE HEART!
THAT'S NOT A HEART, IT IS A *CURSE*!
IF YOU DON'T PUT IT AWAY, BAD THINGS ARE GONNA COME FOR IT!
THUNK

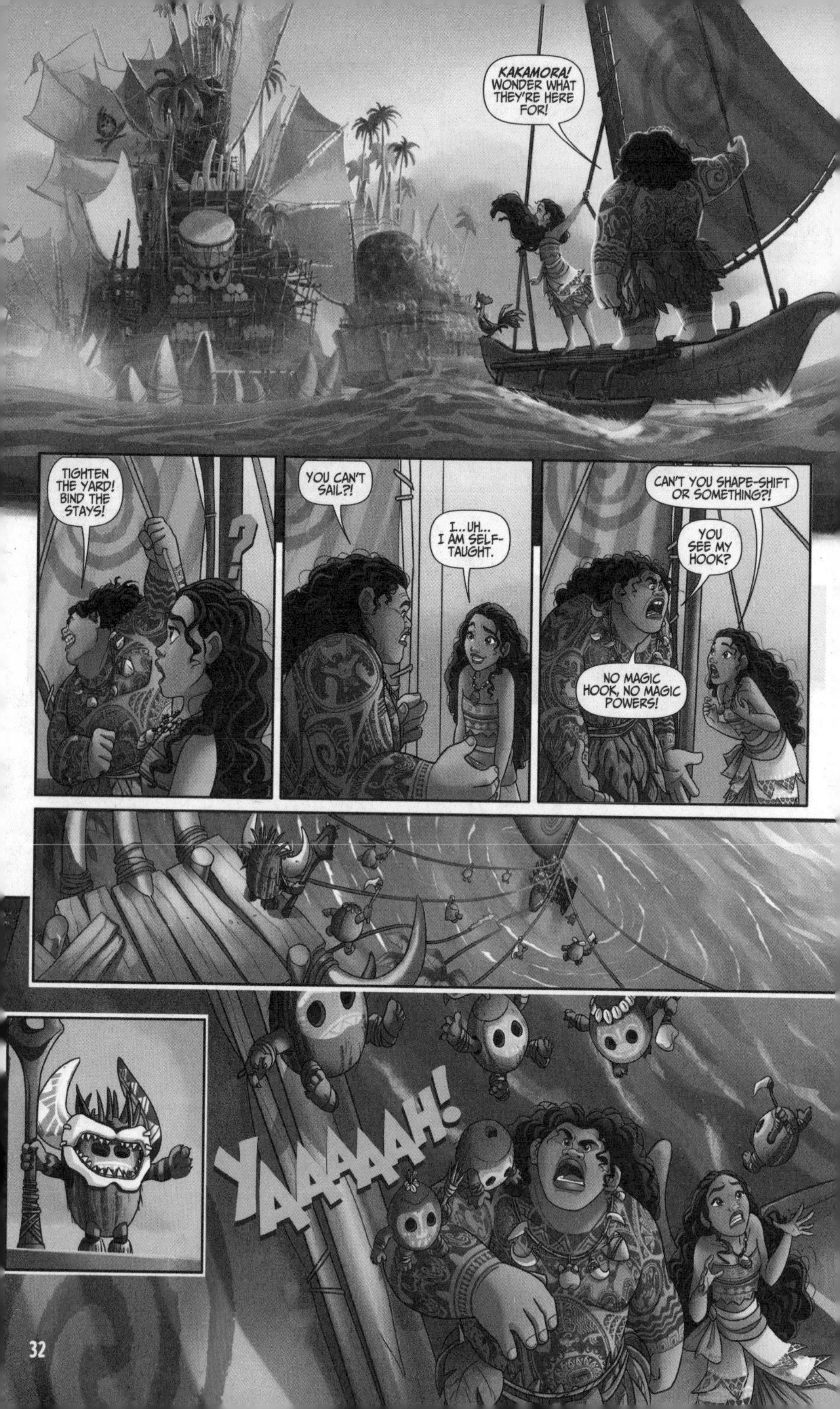
KAKAMORA! WONDER WHAT THEY'RE HERE FOR!
TIGHTEN THE YARD! BIND THE STAYS!
?
YOU CAN'T SAIL?!
I...UH... I AM SELF-TAUGHT.
CAN'T YOU SHAPE-SHIFT OR SOMETHING?!
YOU SEE MY HOOK?
NO MAGIC HOOK, NO MAGIC POWERS!
YAAAAAH!

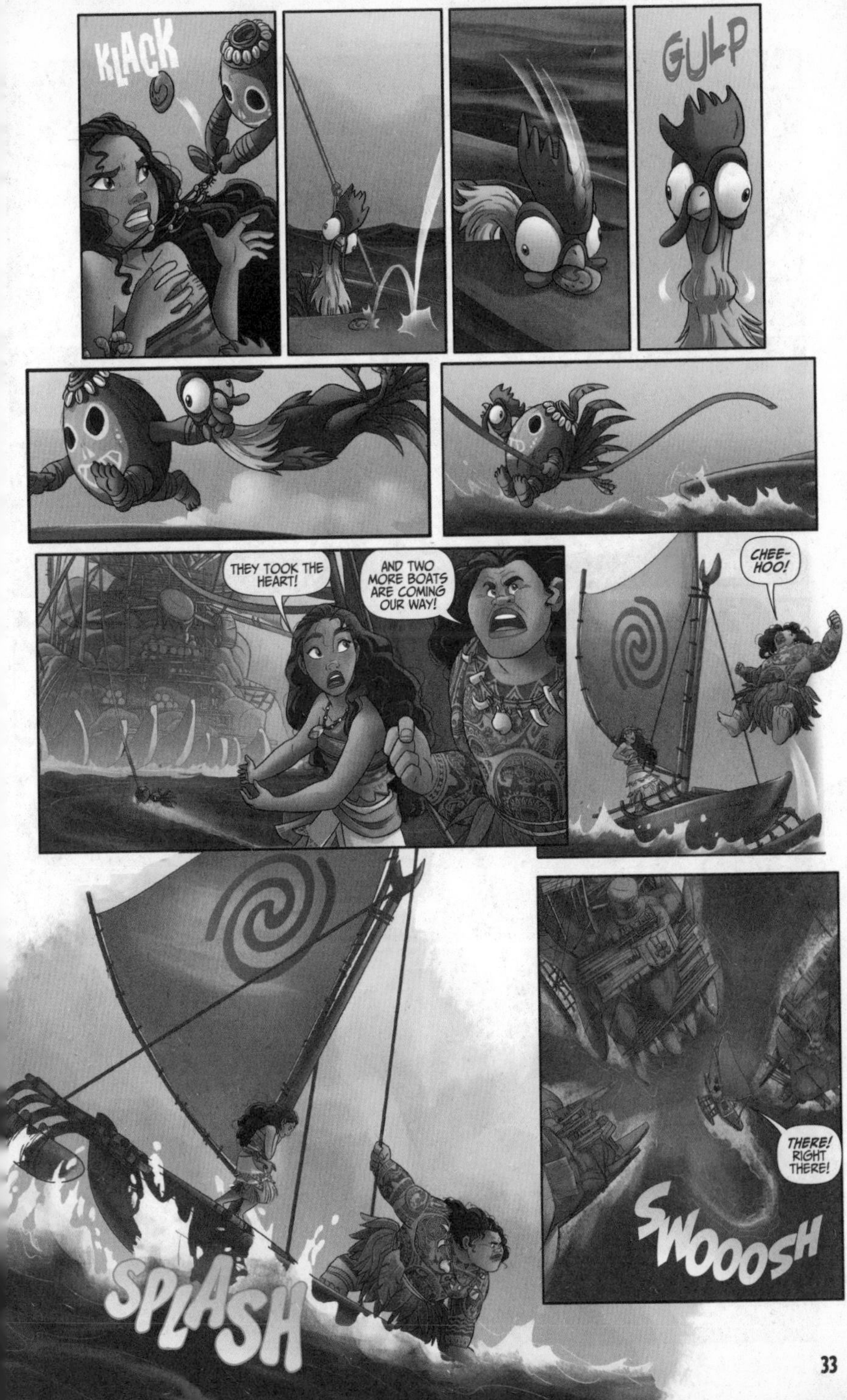
KLACK
GULP
THEY TOOK THE HEART!
AND TWO MORE BOATS ARE COMING OUR WAY!
CHEE-HOO!
SPLASH
THERE! RIGHT THERE!
SWOOOSH

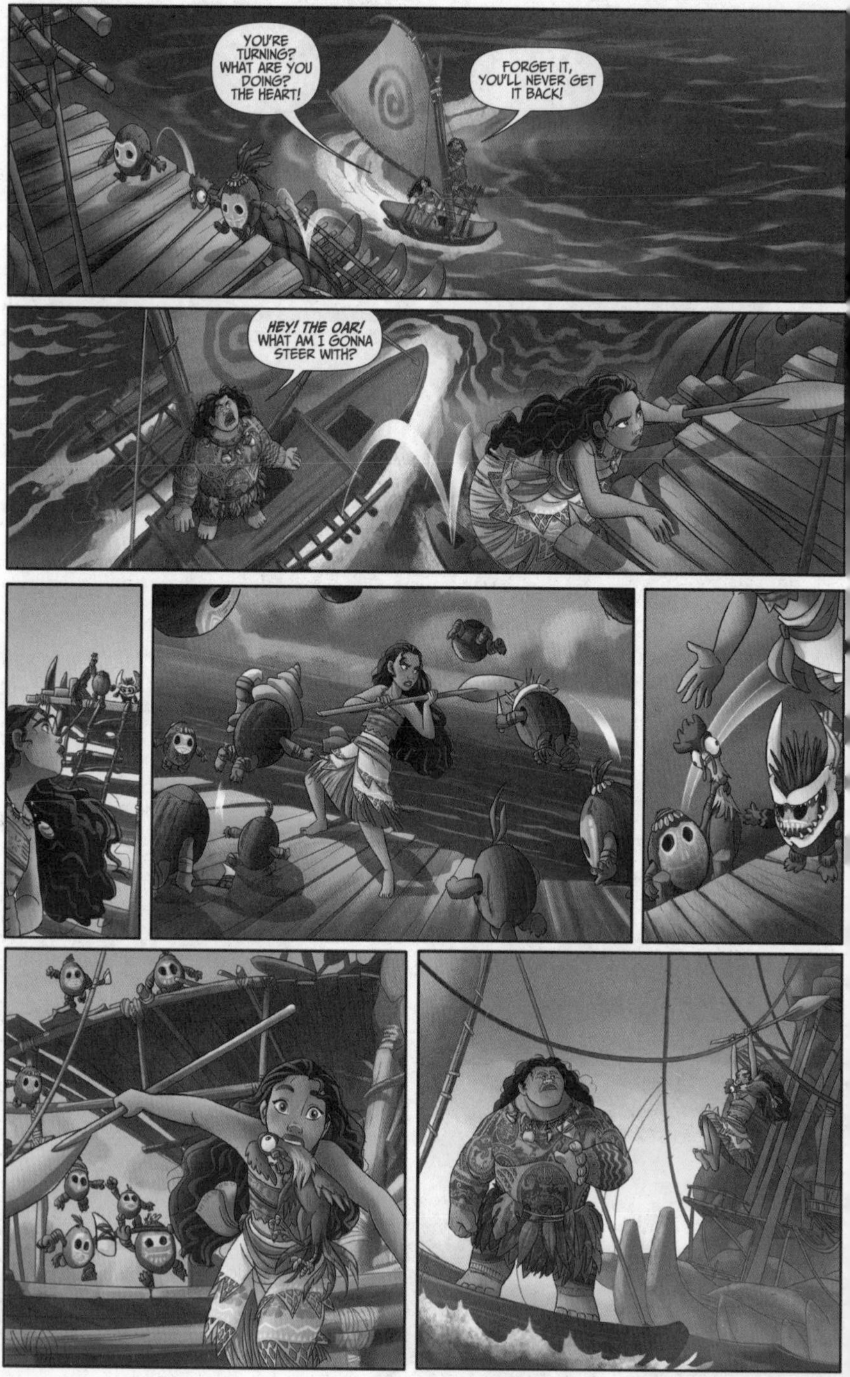
YOU'RE TURNING? WHAT ARE YOU DOING? THE HEART!
FORGET IT, YOU'LL NEVER GET IT BACK!
HEY! THE OAR! WHAT AM I GONNA STEER WITH?

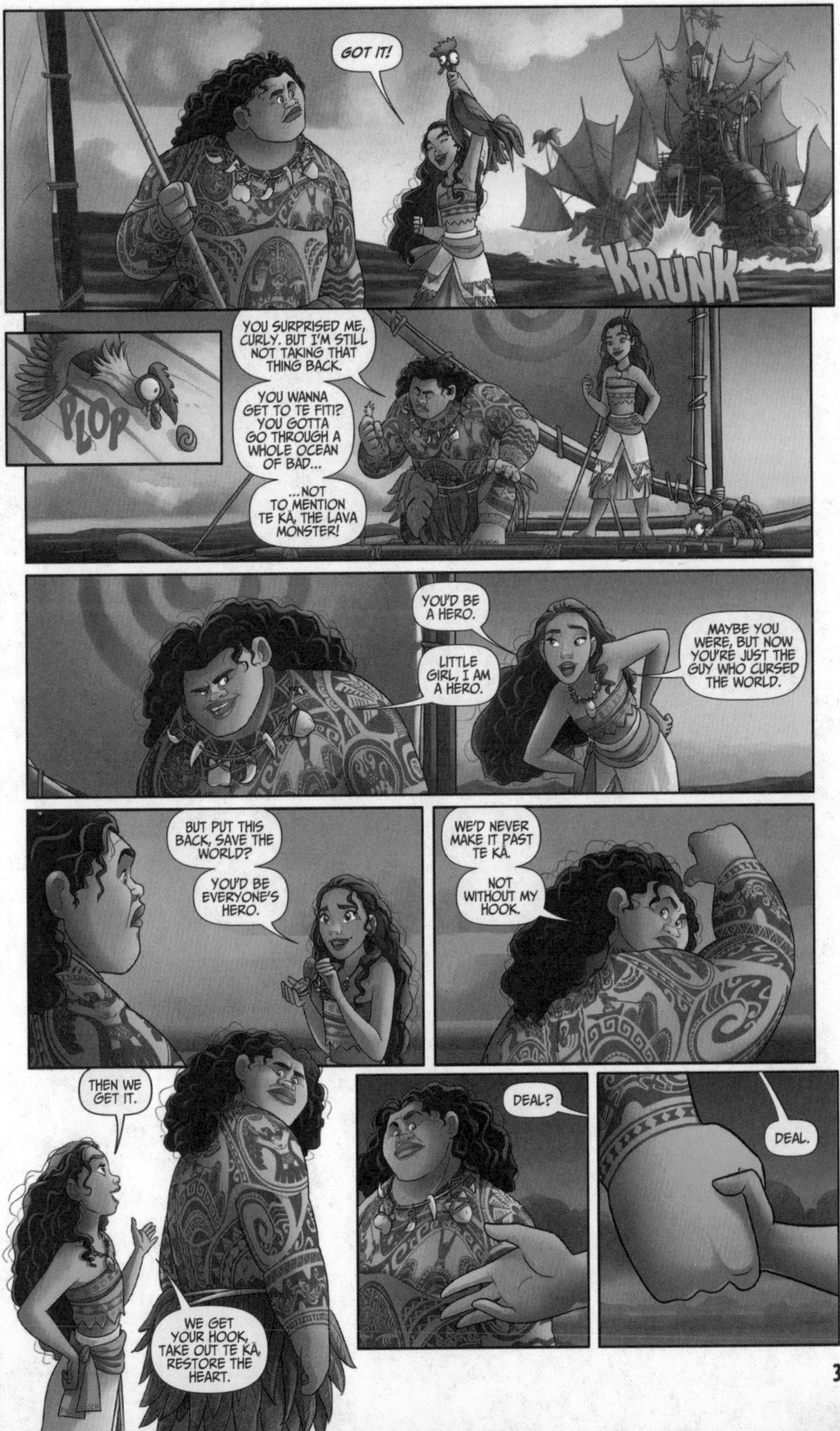
GOT IT!
KRUNK
PLOP
YOU SURPRISED ME, CURLY. BUT I'M STILL NOT TAKING THAT THING BACK.
YOU WANNA GET TO TE FITI? YOU GOTTA GO THROUGH A WHOLE OCEAN OF BAD...
...NOT TO MENTION TE KĀ, THE LAVA MONSTER!
YOU'D BE A HERO.
LITTLE GIRL, I AM A HERO.
MAYBE YOU WERE, BUT NOW YOU'RE JUST THE GUY WHO CURSED THE WORLD.
BUT PUT THIS BACK, SAVE THE WORLD?
YOU'D BE EVERYONE'S HERO.
WE'D NEVER MAKE IT PAST TE KĀ.
NOT WITHOUT MY HOOK.
THEN WE GET IT.
WE GET YOUR HOOK, TAKE OUT TE KĀ, RESTORE THE HEART.
DEAL?
DEAL.

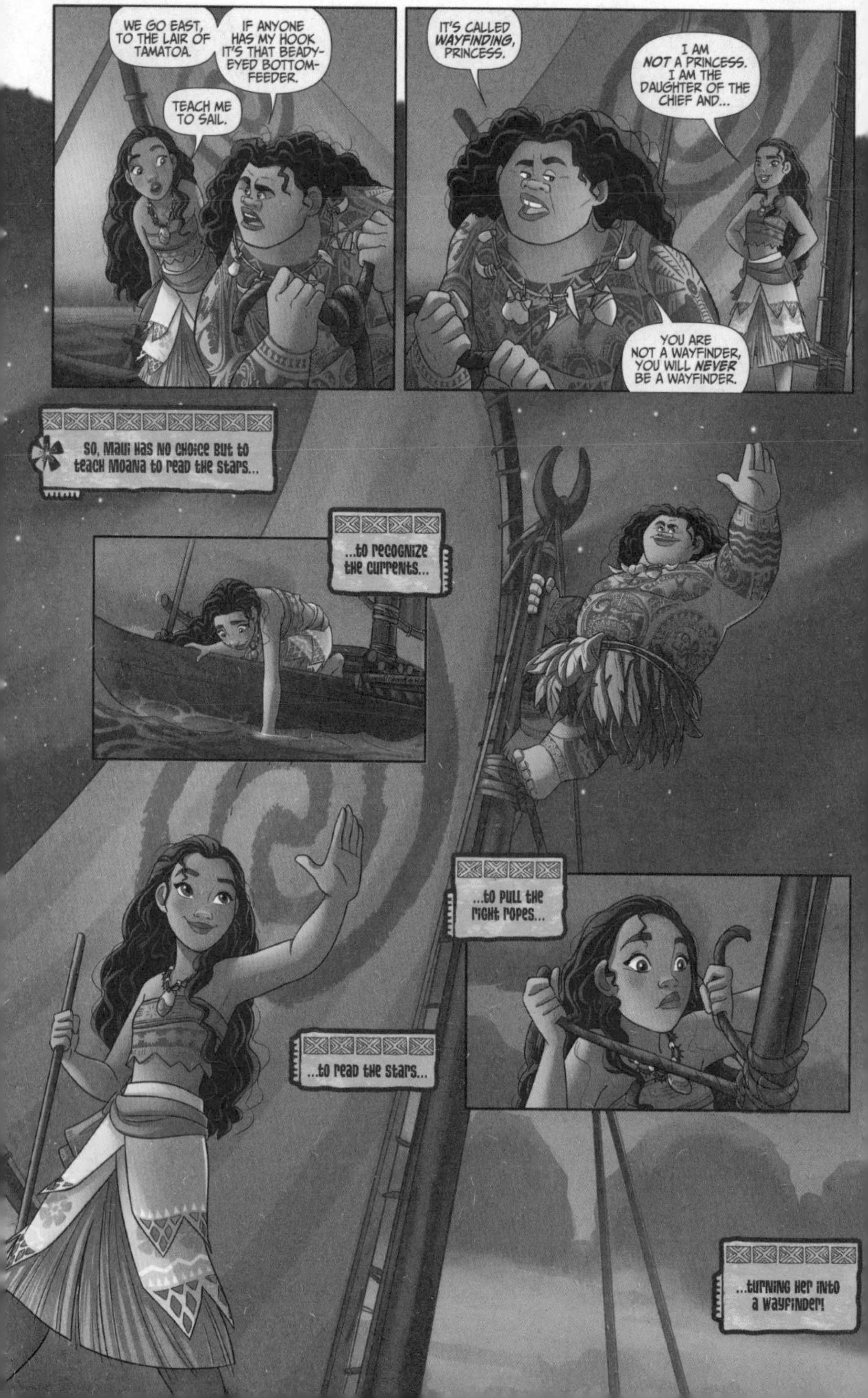
WE GO EAST, TO THE LAIR OF TAMATOA.
IF ANYONE HAS MY HOOK IT'S THAT BEADY-EYED BOTTOM-FEEDER.
TEACH ME TO SAIL.
IT'S CALLED *WAYFINDING*, PRINCESS.
I AM *NOT* A PRINCESS. I AM THE DAUGHTER OF THE CHIEF AND...
YOU ARE NOT A WAYFINDER, YOU WILL *NEVER* BE A WAYFINDER.
SO, MAUI HAS NO CHOICE BUT TO TEACH MOANA TO READ THE STARS...
...TO RECOGNIZE THE CURRENTS...
...TO PULL THE RIGHT ROPES...
...TO READ THE STARS...
...TURNING HER INTO A WAYFINDER!

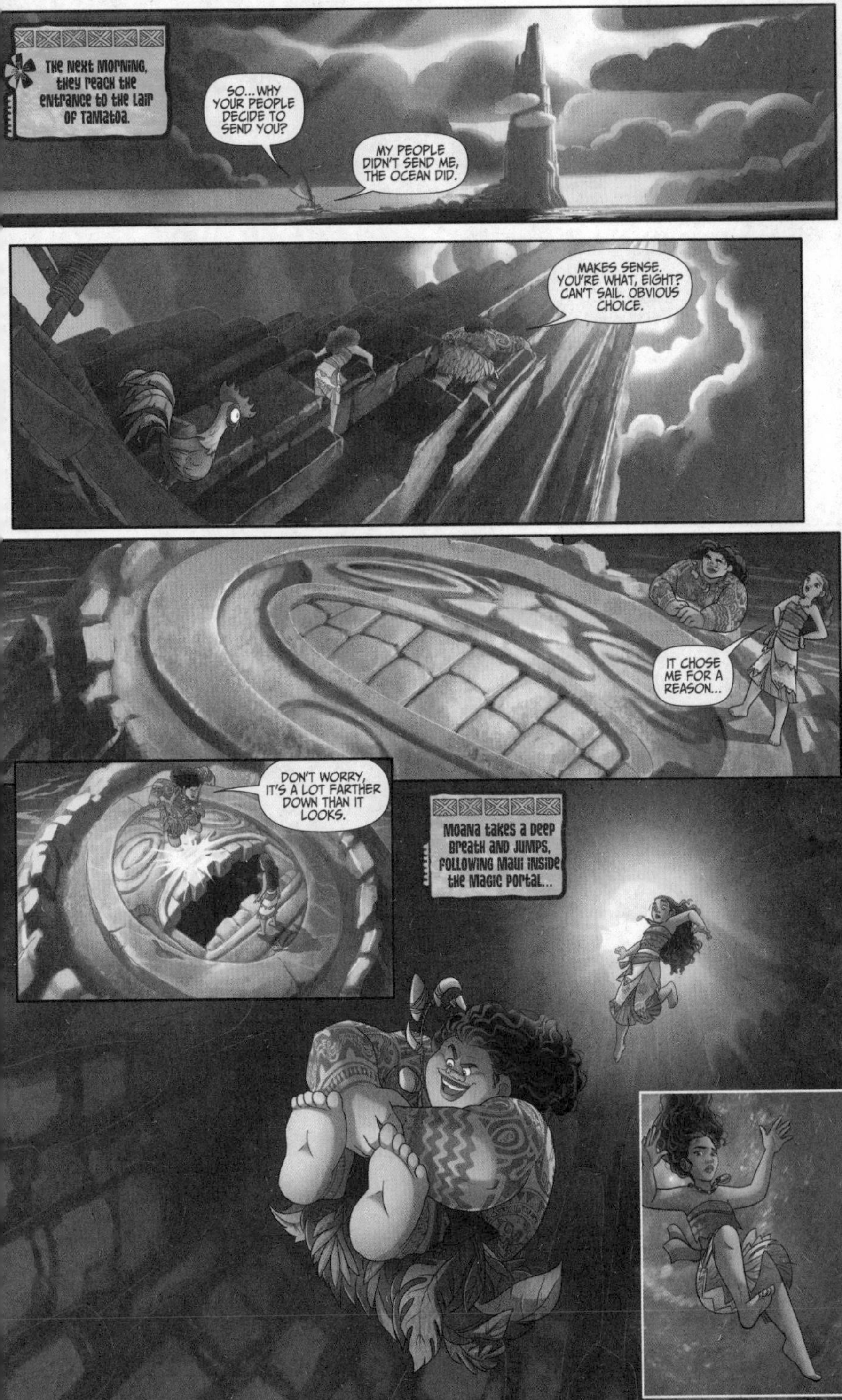
The Next Morning, they reach the entrance to the Lair of Tamatoa.
SO...WHY YOUR PEOPLE DECIDE TO SEND YOU?
MY PEOPLE DIDN'T SEND ME, THE OCEAN DID.
MAKES SENSE. YOU'RE WHAT, EIGHT? CAN'T SAIL. OBVIOUS CHOICE.
IT CHOSE ME FOR A REASON...
DON'T WORRY, IT'S A LOT FARTHER DOWN THAN IT LOOKS.
Moana takes a deep breath and jumps, following Maui inside the Magic Portal...

...FINDING HERSELF IN LALOTAI, THE LAND OF MONSTERS!

RRROARR

FWOOSH

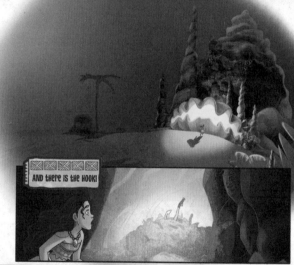

AND THERE IS THE HOOK!

STAY HERE.

WHAT? NO!

LISTEN, FOR A THOUSAND YEARS I'VE ONLY BEEN THINKING OF GETTING MY HOOK. AND IT'S NOT GETTING SCREWED UP BY A MORTAL WHO HAS NO BUSINESS HERE EXCEPT...

...MAYBE AS A BAIT!

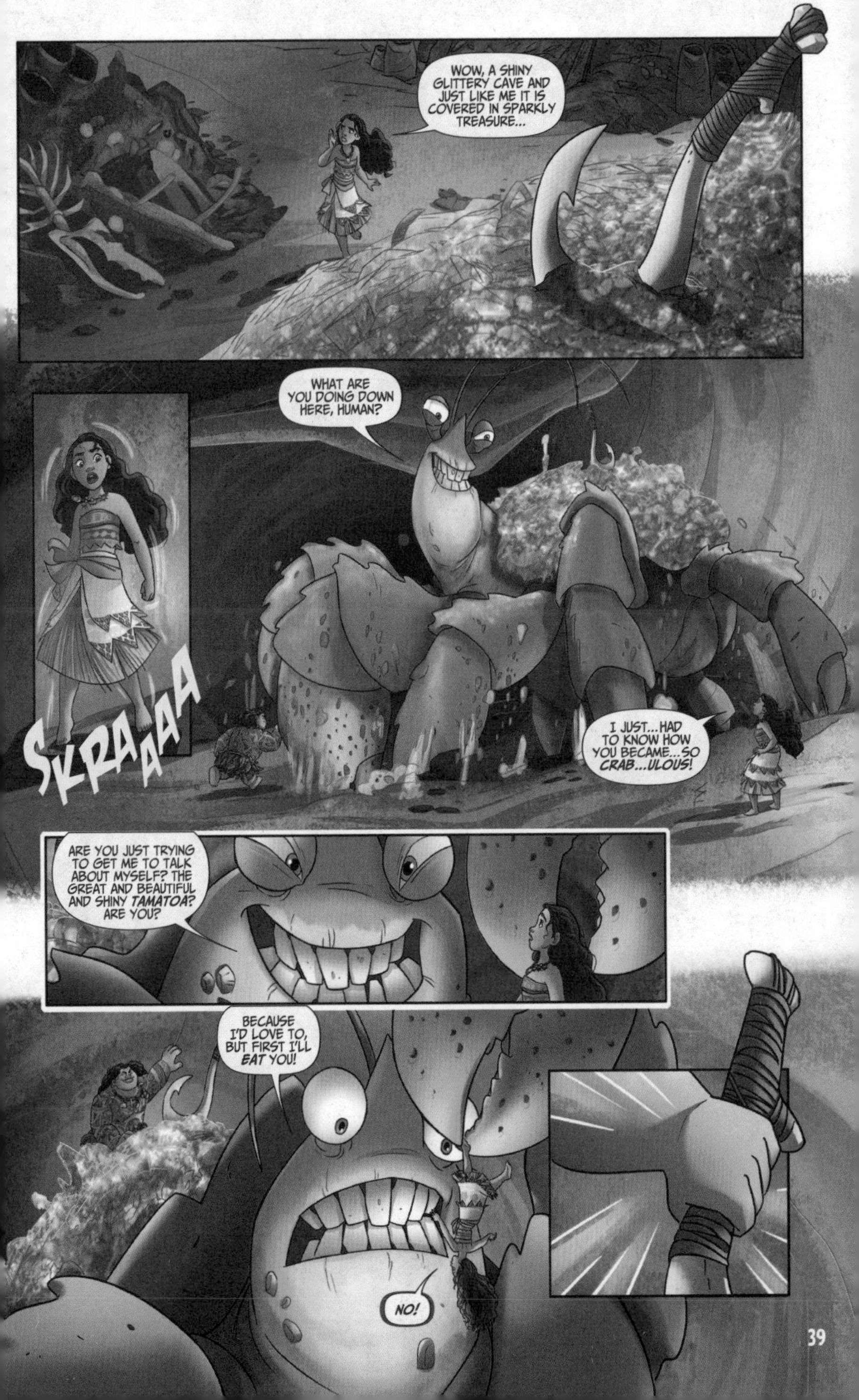
WOW, A SHINY GLITTERY CAVE AND JUST LIKE ME IT IS COVERED IN SPARKLY TREASURE...
WHAT ARE YOU DOING DOWN HERE, HUMAN?
SKRAAAA
I JUST...HAD TO KNOW HOW YOU BECAME...SO *CRAB...ULOUS!*
ARE YOU JUST TRYING TO GET ME TO TALK ABOUT MYSELF? THE GREAT AND BEAUTIFUL AND SHINY *TAMATOA?* ARE YOU?
BECAUSE I'D LOVE TO, BUT FIRST I'LL *EAT* YOU!
NO!

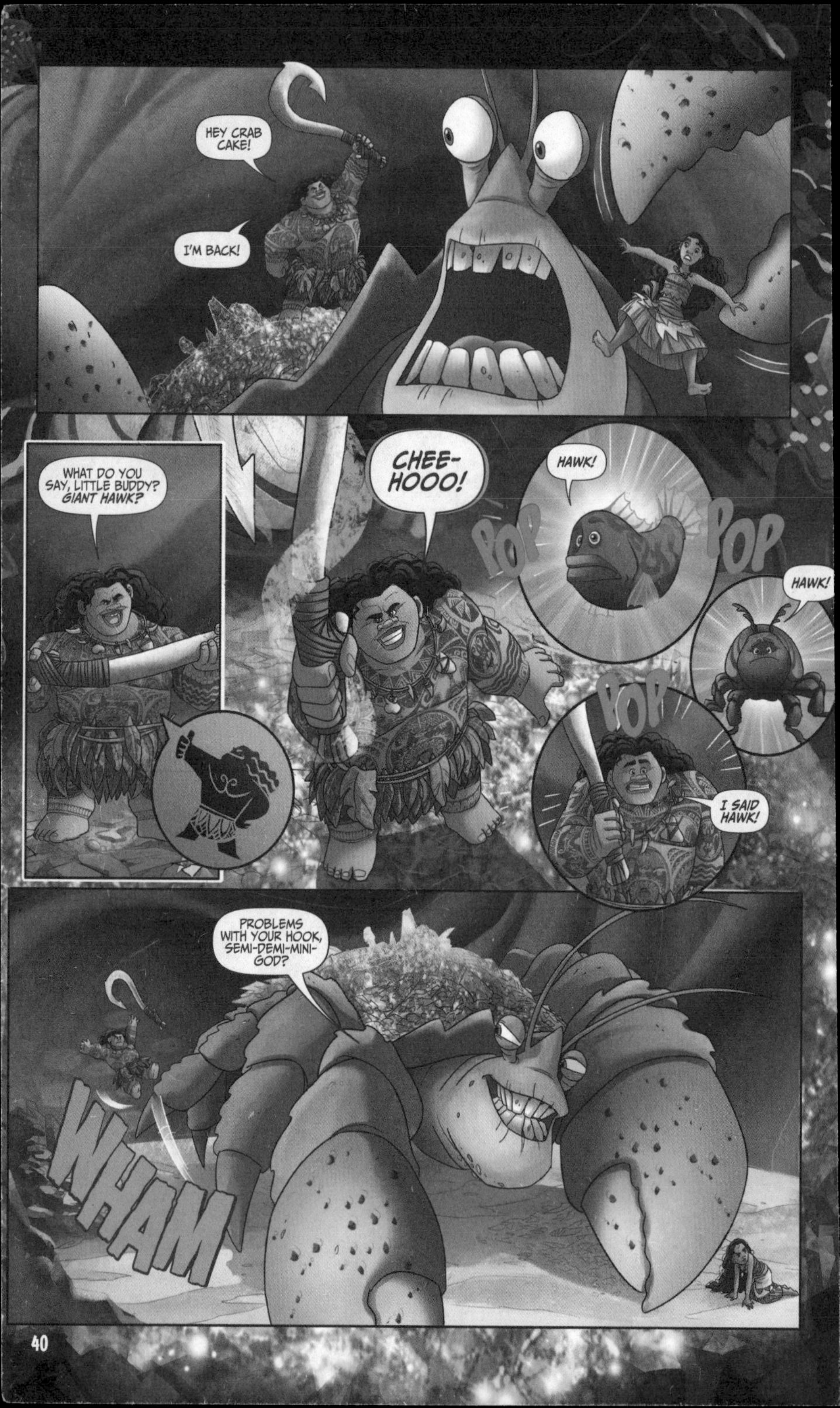
HEY CRAB CAKE!
I'M BACK!
WHAT DO YOU SAY, LITTLE BUDDY? GIANT HAWK?
CHEE-HOOO!
HAWK!
POP
POP
HAWK!
POP
I SAID HAWK!
PROBLEMS WITH YOUR HOOK, SEMI-DEMI-MINI-GOD?
WHAM

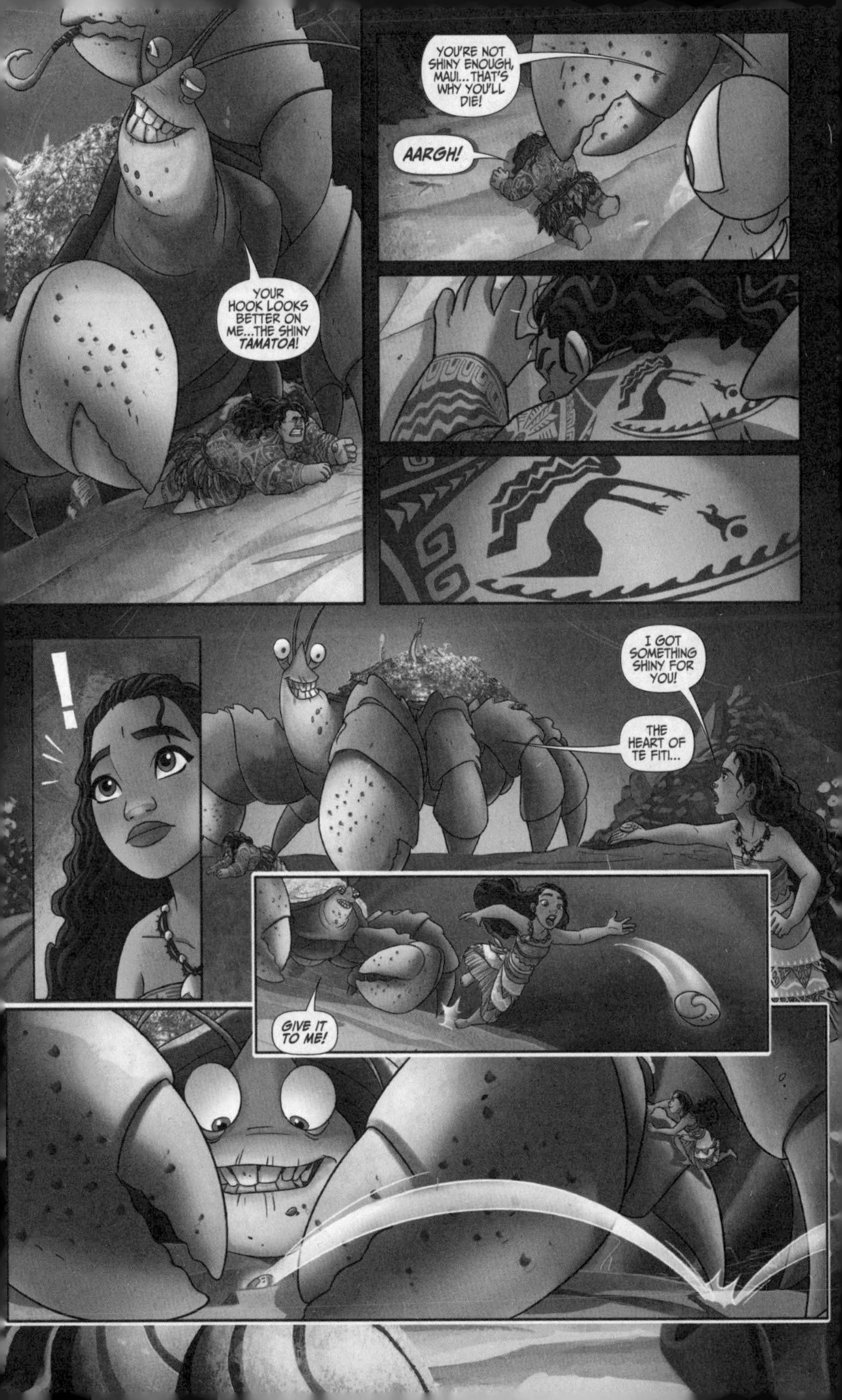
YOUR HOOK LOOKS BETTER ON ME...THE SHINY *TAMATOA!*
YOU'RE NOT SHINY ENOUGH, MAUI...THAT'S WHY YOU'LL DIE!
AARGH!
!
I GOT SOMETHING SHINY FOR YOU!
THE HEART OF TE FITI...
GIVE IT TO ME!

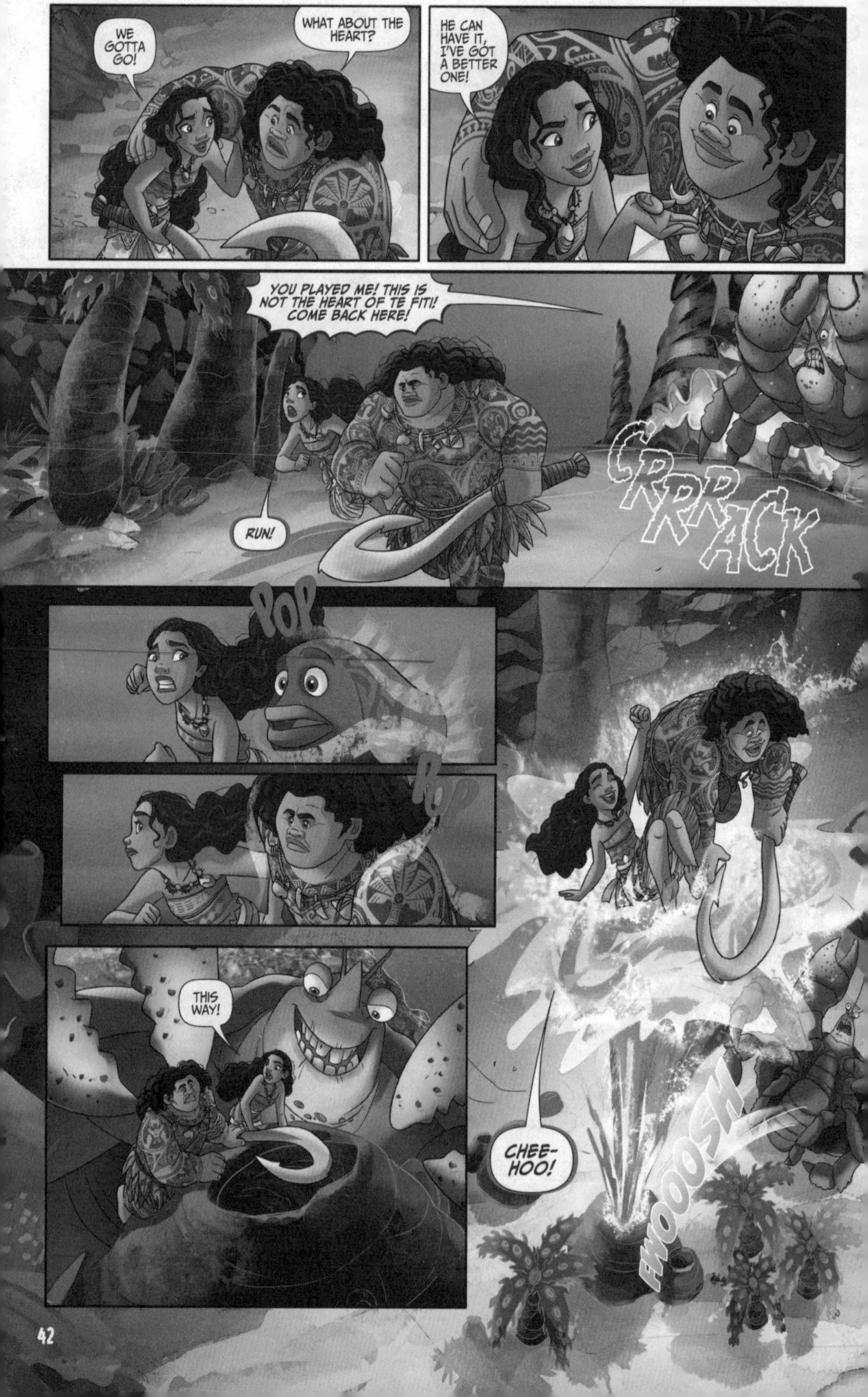

WE GOTTA GO!
WHAT ABOUT THE HEART?
HE CAN HAVE IT, I'VE GOT A BETTER ONE!
YOU PLAYED ME! THIS IS NOT THE HEART OF TE FITI! COME BACK HERE!
RUN!
CRRRACK
POP
POP
THIS WAY!
CHEE-HOO!
FWOOOSH

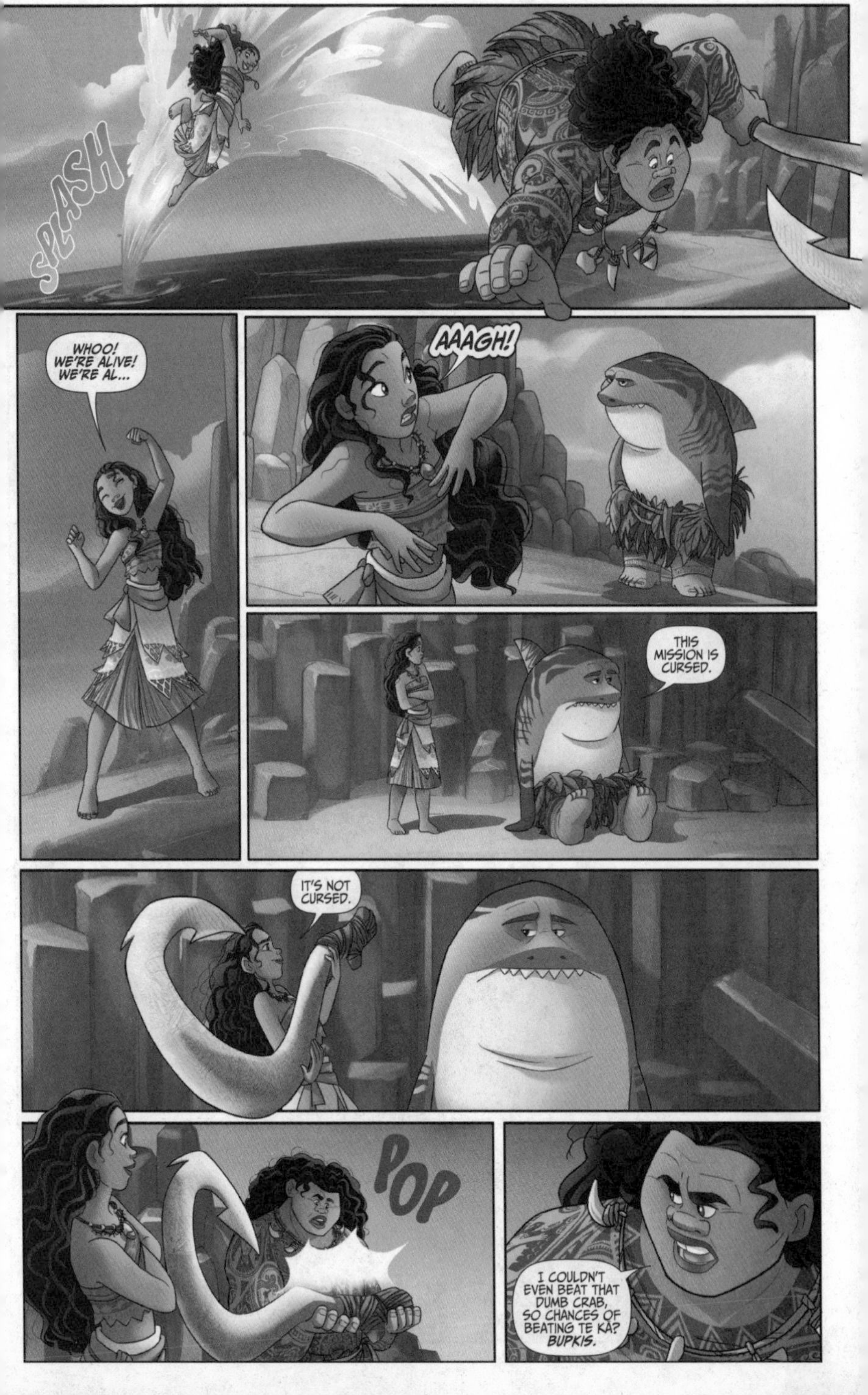
SPLASH
WHOO! WE'RE ALIVE! WE'RE AL...
AAAGH!
THIS MISSION IS CURSED.
IT'S NOT CURSED.
POP
I COULDN'T EVEN BEAT THAT DUMB CRAB, SO CHANCES OF BEATING TE KĀ? *BUPKIS.*

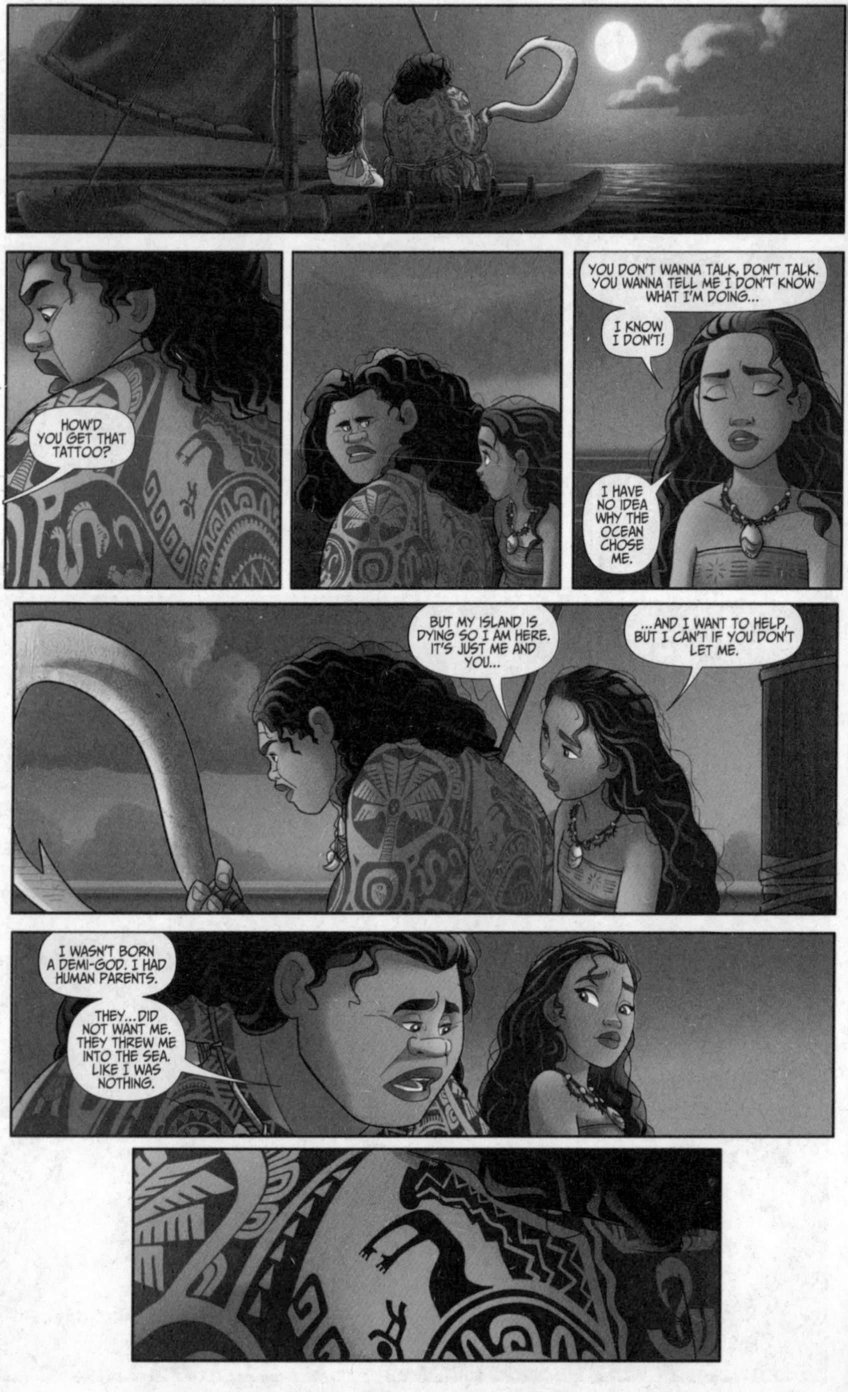
HOW'D YOU GET THAT TATTOO?
YOU DON'T WANNA TALK, DON'T TALK. YOU WANNA TELL ME I DON'T KNOW WHAT I'M DOING...
I KNOW I DON'T!
I HAVE NO IDEA WHY THE OCEAN CHOSE ME.
BUT MY ISLAND IS DYING SO I AM HERE. IT'S JUST ME AND YOU...
...AND I WANT TO HELP, BUT I CAN'T IF YOU DON'T LET ME.
I WASN'T BORN A DEMI-GOD. I HAD HUMAN PARENTS.
THEY...DID NOT WANT ME. THEY THREW ME INTO THE SEA. LIKE I WAS NOTHING.

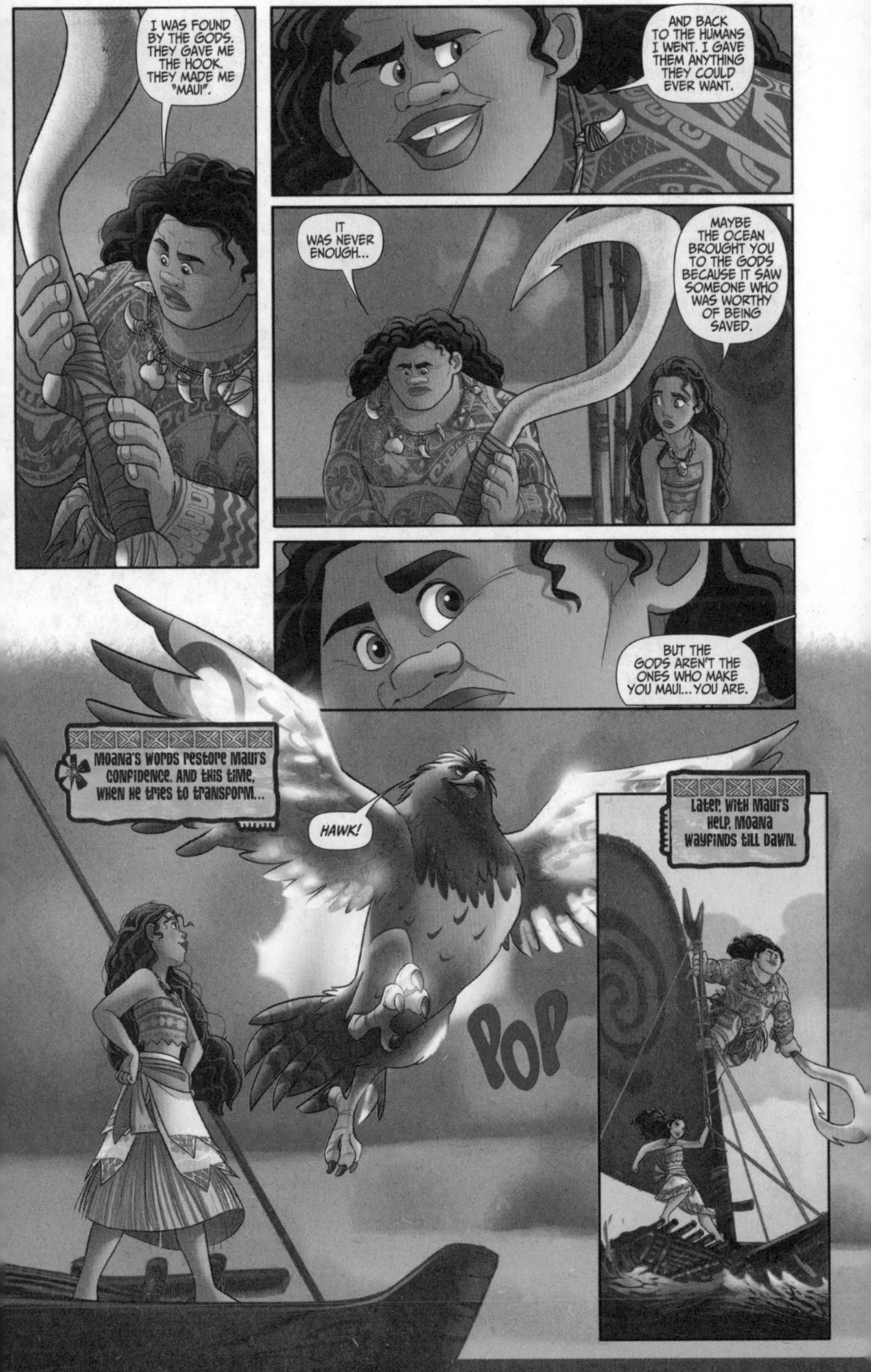

I WAS FOUND BY THE GODS. THEY GAVE ME THE HOOK. THEY MADE ME "MAUI".
AND BACK TO THE HUMANS I WENT. I GAVE THEM ANYTHING THEY COULD EVER WANT.
IT WAS NEVER ENOUGH...
MAYBE THE OCEAN BROUGHT YOU TO THE GODS BECAUSE IT SAW SOMEONE WHO WAS WORTHY OF BEING SAVED.
BUT THE GODS AREN'T THE ONES WHO MAKE YOU MAUI...YOU ARE.
Moana's words restore Maui's confidence. And this time, when he tries to transform...
HAWK!
POP
Later, with Maui's help, Moana wayfinds till dawn.

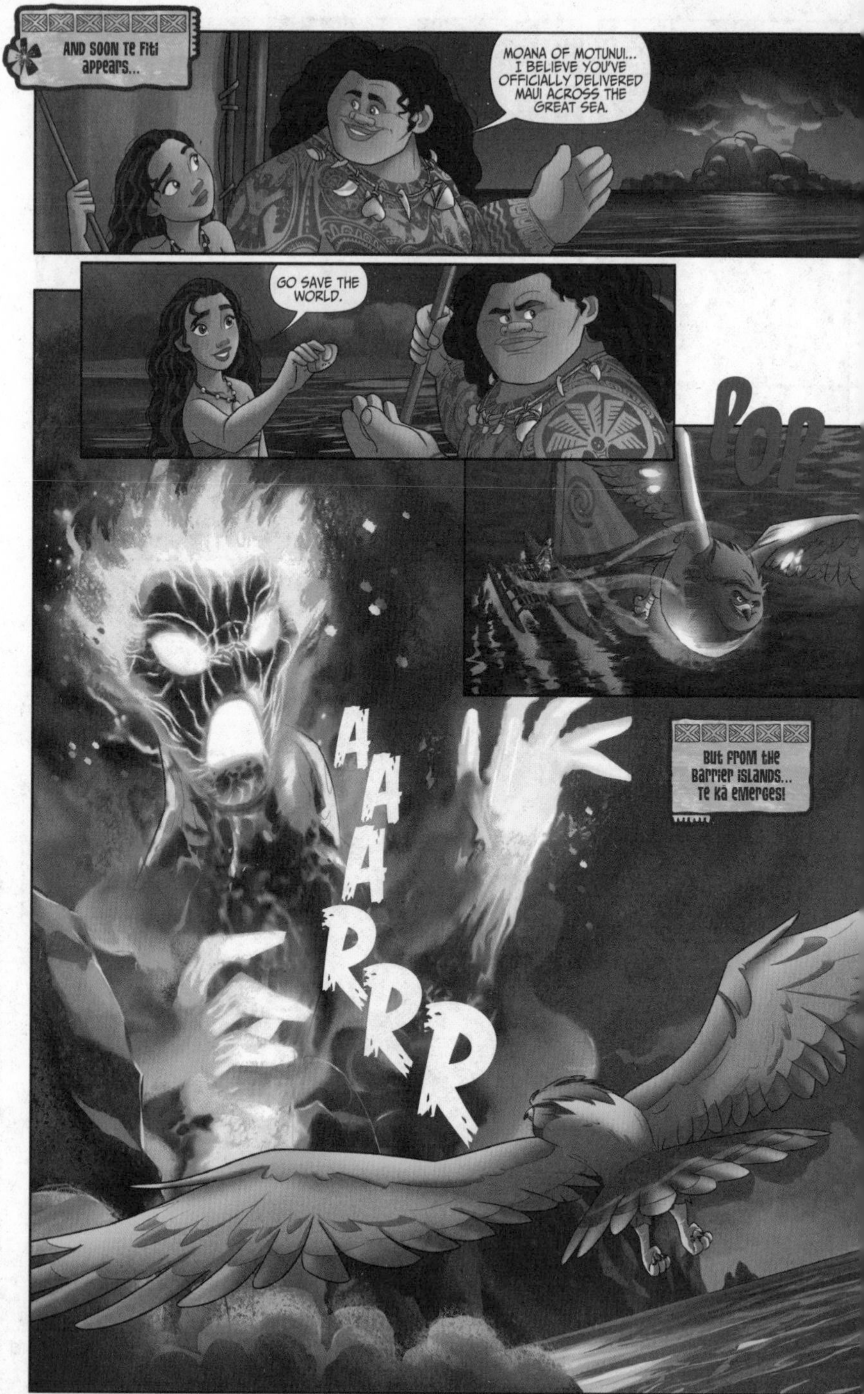
AND SOON TE FITI appears...
MOANA OF MOTUNUI... I BELIEVE YOU'VE OFFICIALLY DELIVERED MAUI ACROSS THE GREAT SEA.
GO SAVE THE WORLD.
POP
But from the Barrier islands... Te Ka emerges!
AAARRR

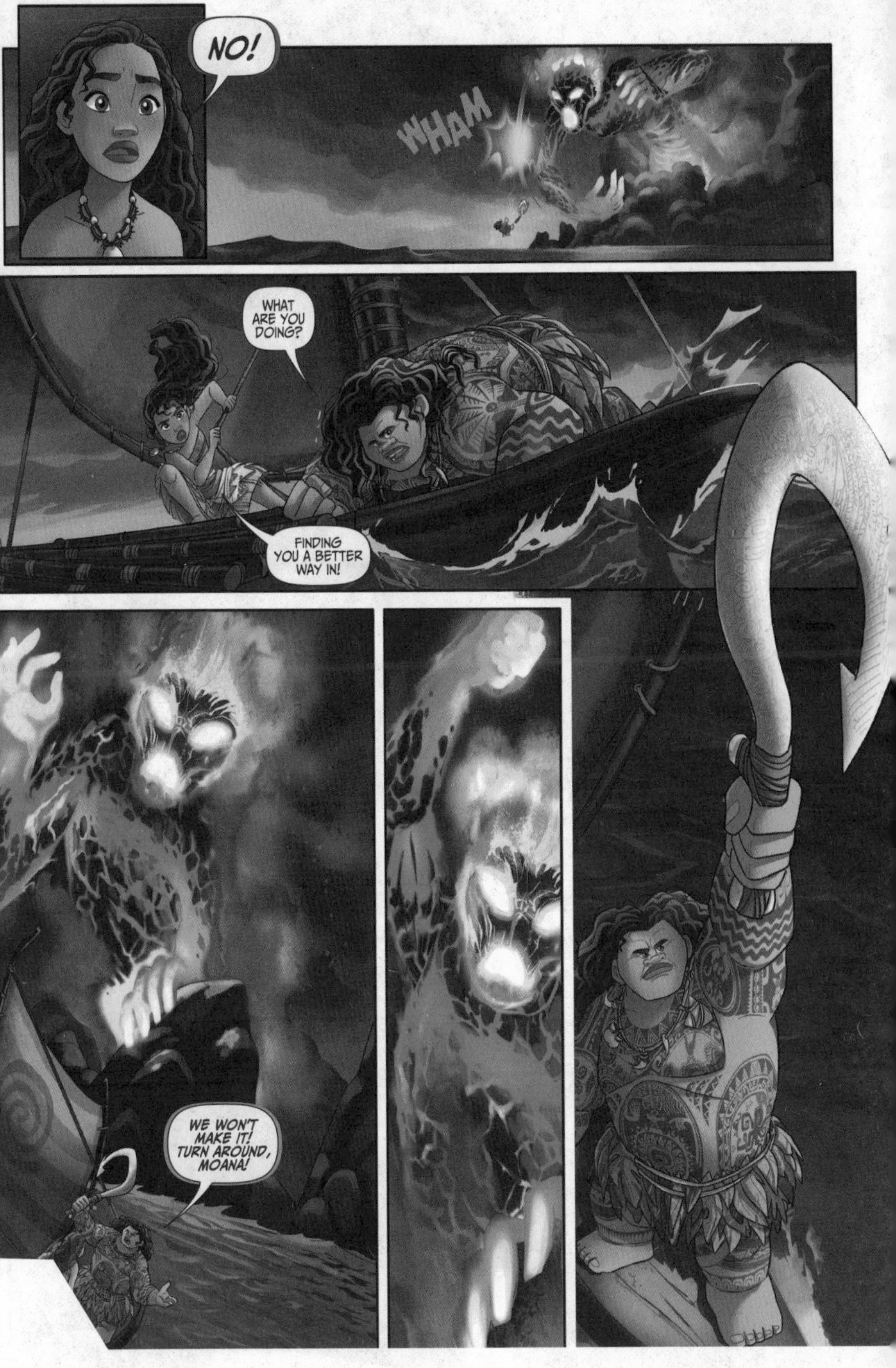
NO!
WHAM
WHAT ARE YOU DOING?
FINDING YOU A BETTER WAY IN!
WE WON'T MAKE IT! TURN AROUND, MOANA!

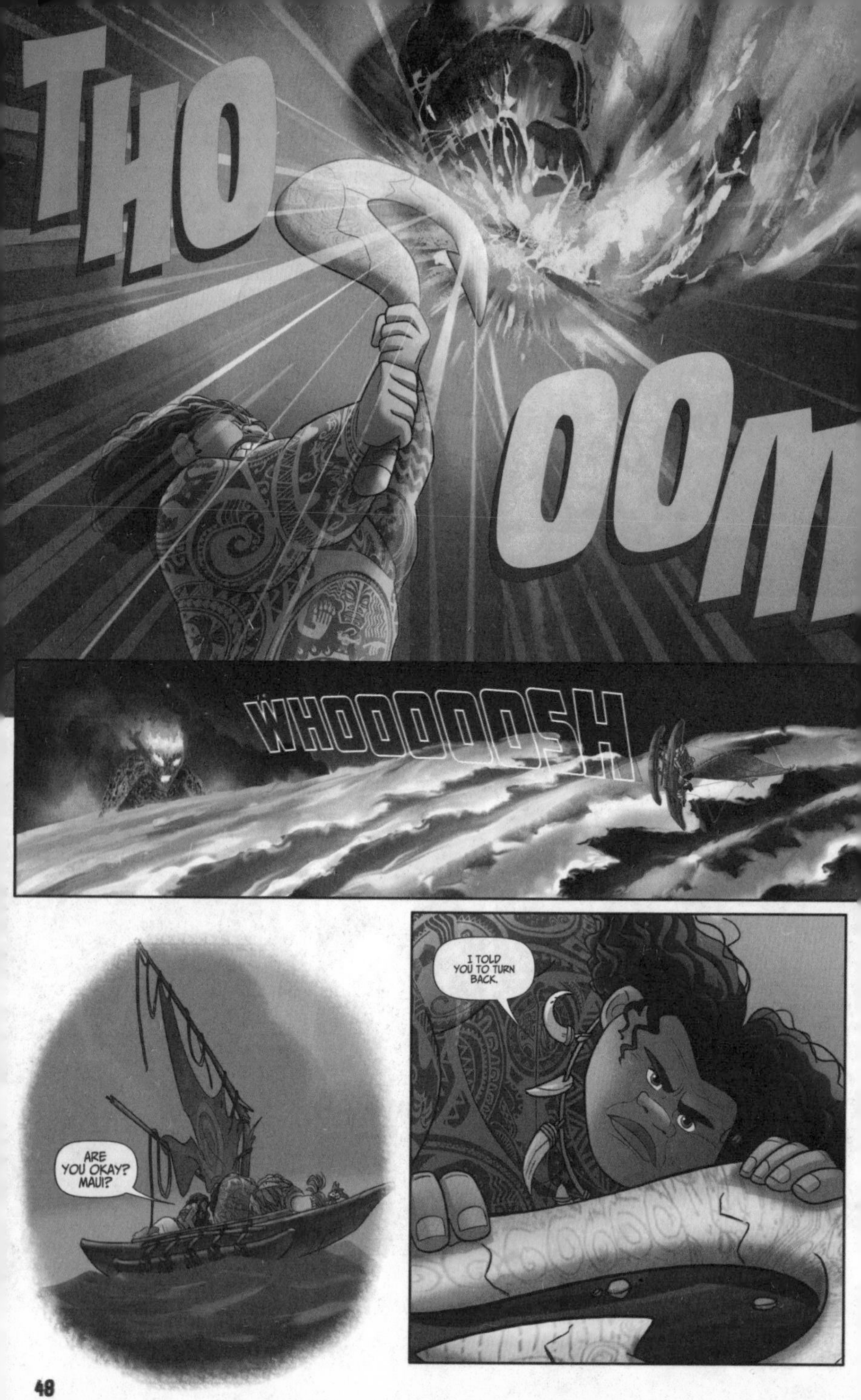
THO
OOM
WHOOOOOSH
ARE YOU OKAY? MAUI?
I TOLD YOU TO TURN BACK.

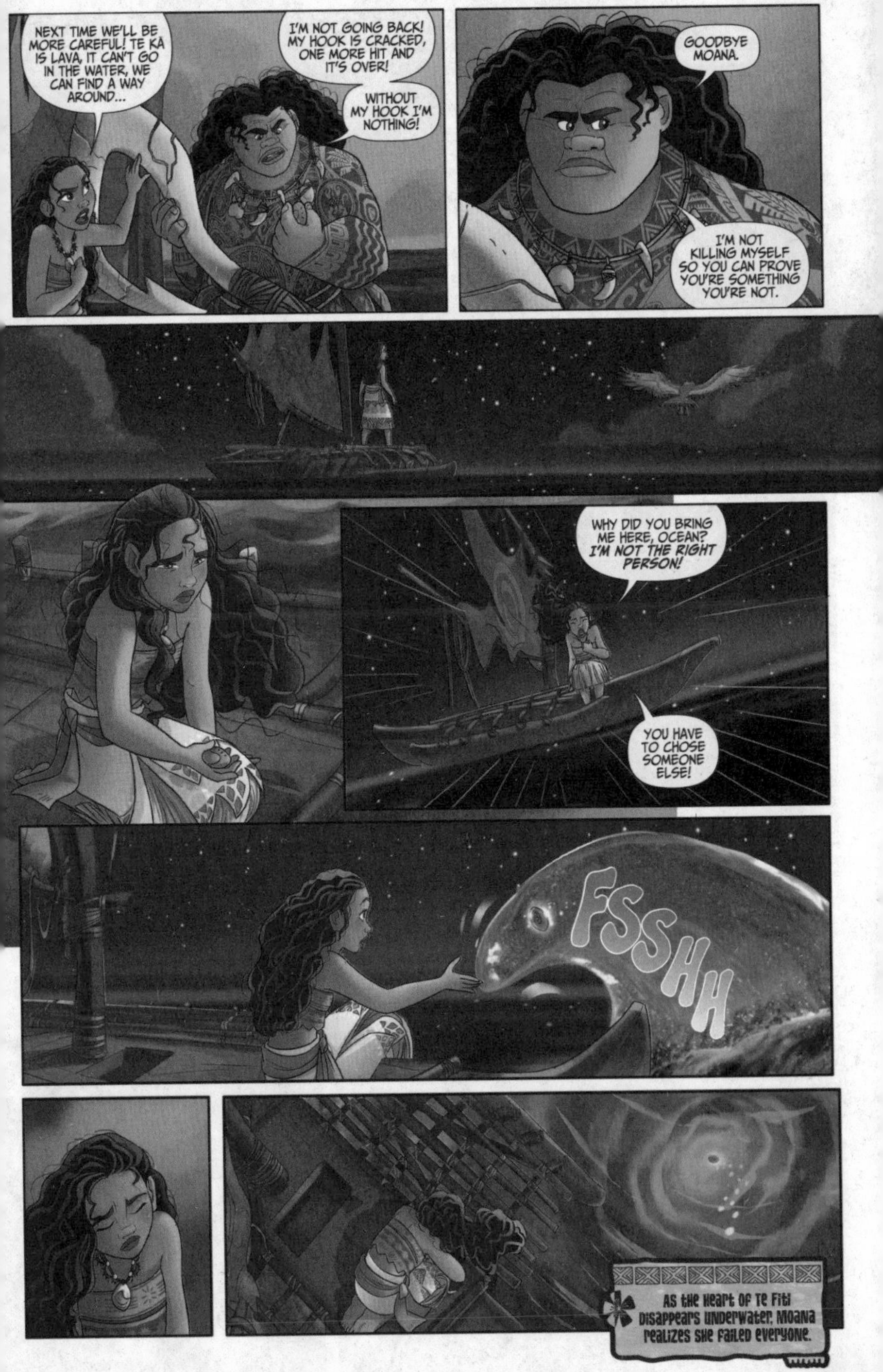

NEXT TIME WE'LL BE MORE CAREFUL! TE KĀ IS LAVA, IT CAN'T GO IN THE WATER, WE CAN FIND A WAY AROUND...
I'M NOT GOING BACK! MY HOOK IS CRACKED, ONE MORE HIT AND IT'S OVER!
WITHOUT MY HOOK I'M NOTHING!
GOODBYE MOANA.
I'M NOT KILLING MYSELF SO YOU CAN PROVE YOU'RE SOMETHING YOU'RE NOT.
WHY DID YOU BRING ME HERE, OCEAN? I'M NOT THE RIGHT PERSON!
YOU HAVE TO CHOSE SOMEONE ELSE!
FSSHH
As the Heart of Te Fiti disappears underwater, Moana realizes she failed everyone.

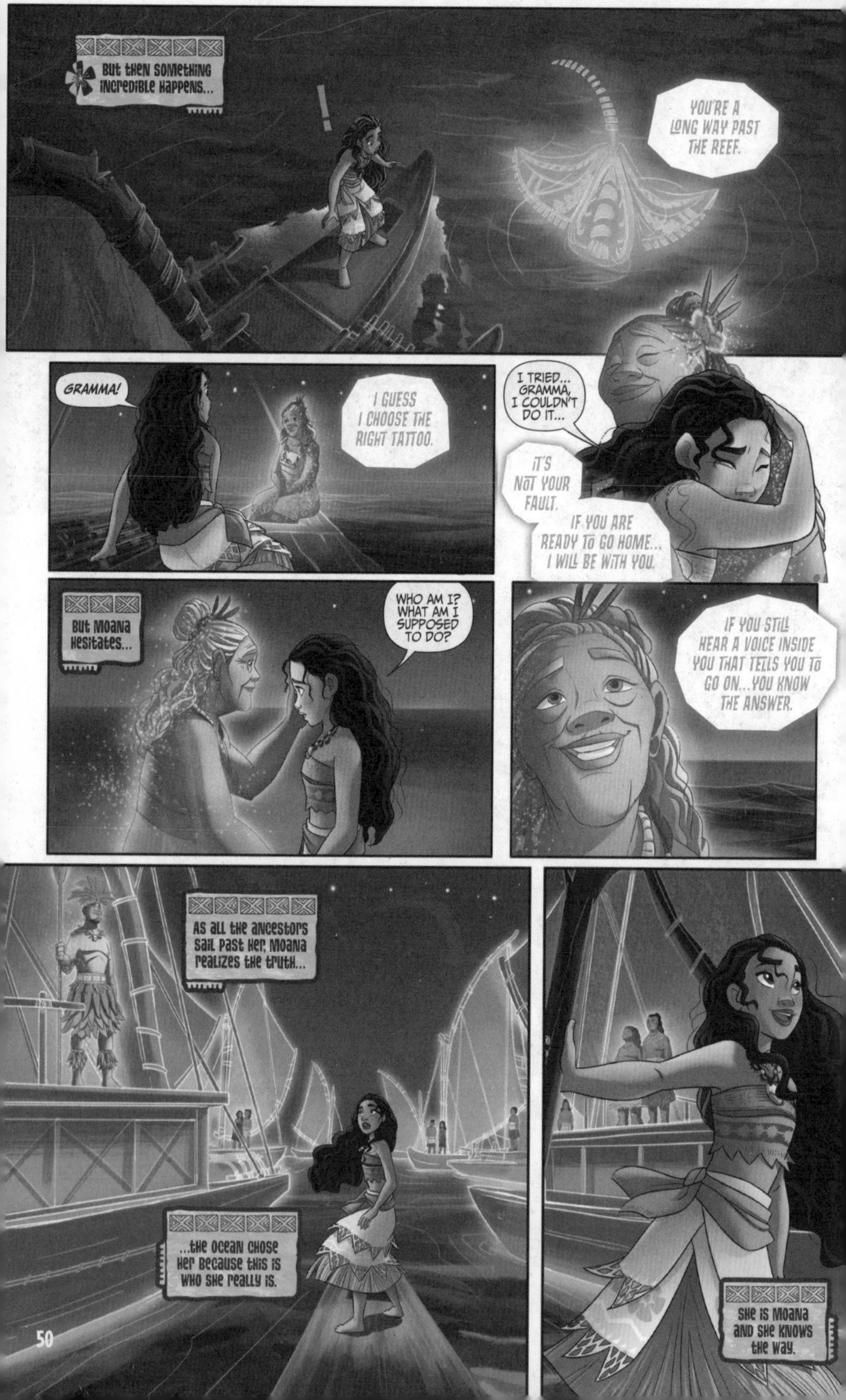
But then something incredible happens...
YOU'RE A LONG WAY PAST THE REEF.
GRAMMA!
I GUESS I CHOOSE THE RIGHT TATTOO.
I TRIED... GRAMMA, I COULDN'T DO IT...
IT'S NOT YOUR FAULT.
IF YOU ARE READY TO GO HOME... I WILL BE WITH YOU.
But Moana hesitates...
WHO AM I? WHAT AM I SUPPOSED TO DO?
IF YOU STILL HEAR A VOICE INSIDE YOU THAT TELLS YOU TO GO ON...YOU KNOW THE ANSWER.
As all the ancestors sail past her, Moana realizes the truth...
...the ocean chose her because this is who she really is.
She is Moana and she knows the way.

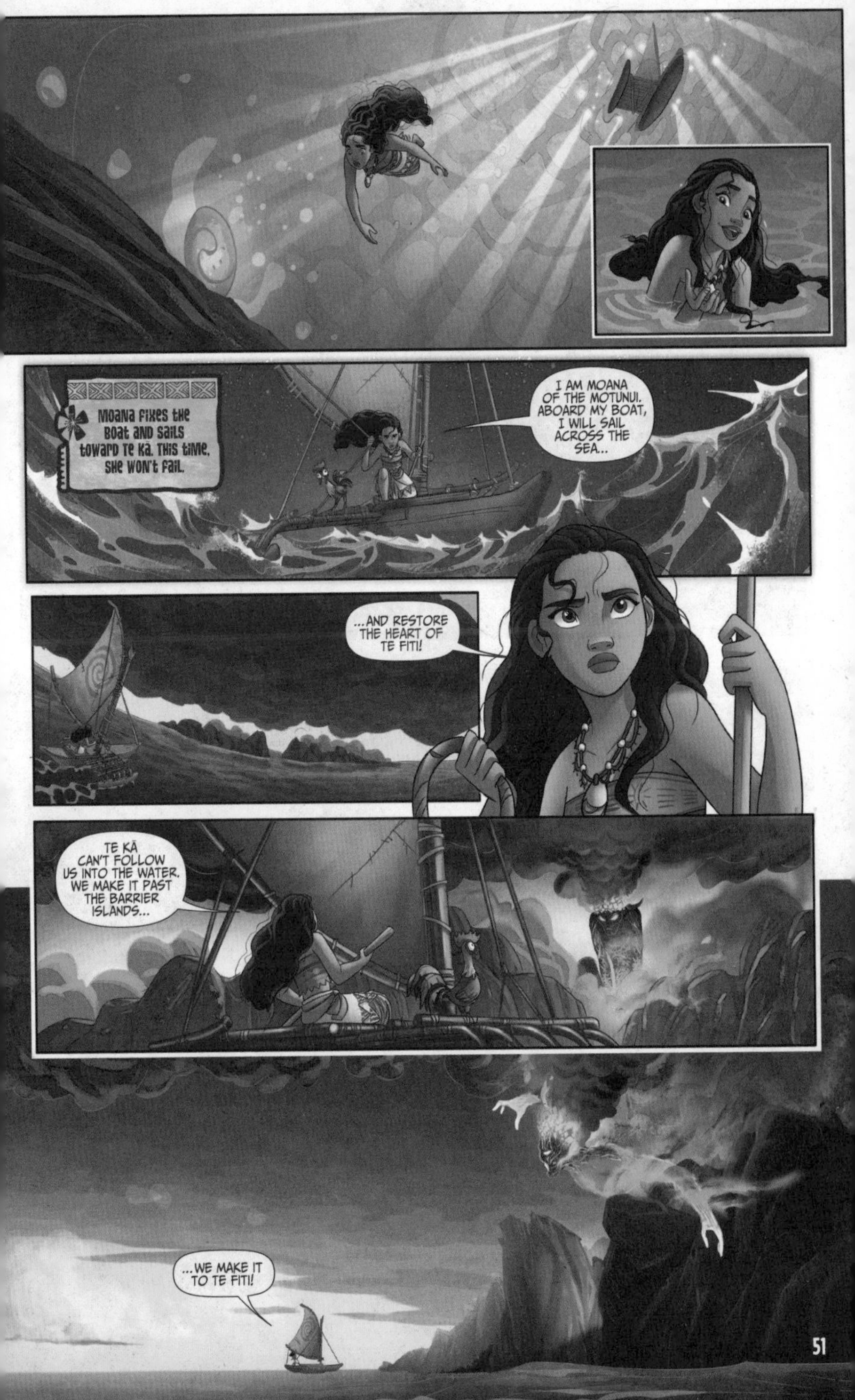
Moana fixes the boat and sails toward Te Kā. This time, she won't fail.
I AM MOANA OF THE MOTUNUI. ABOARD MY BOAT, I WILL SAIL ACROSS THE SEA...
...AND RESTORE THE HEART OF TE FITI!
TE KĀ CAN'T FOLLOW US INTO THE WATER. WE MAKE IT PAST THE BARRIER ISLANDS...
...WE MAKE IT TO TE FITI!

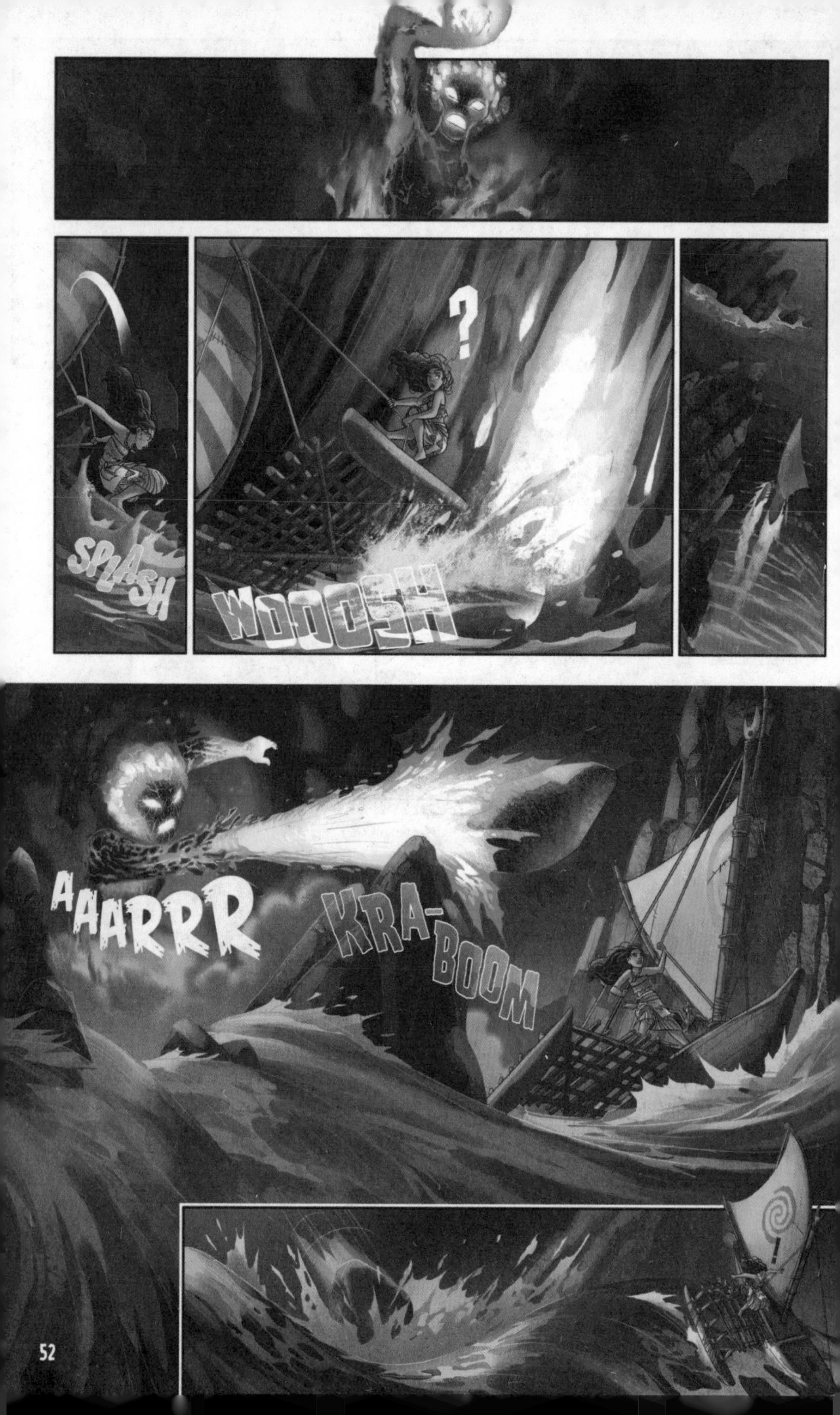
SPLASH
?
WOOOSH
AAARRR
KRA-BOOM
!

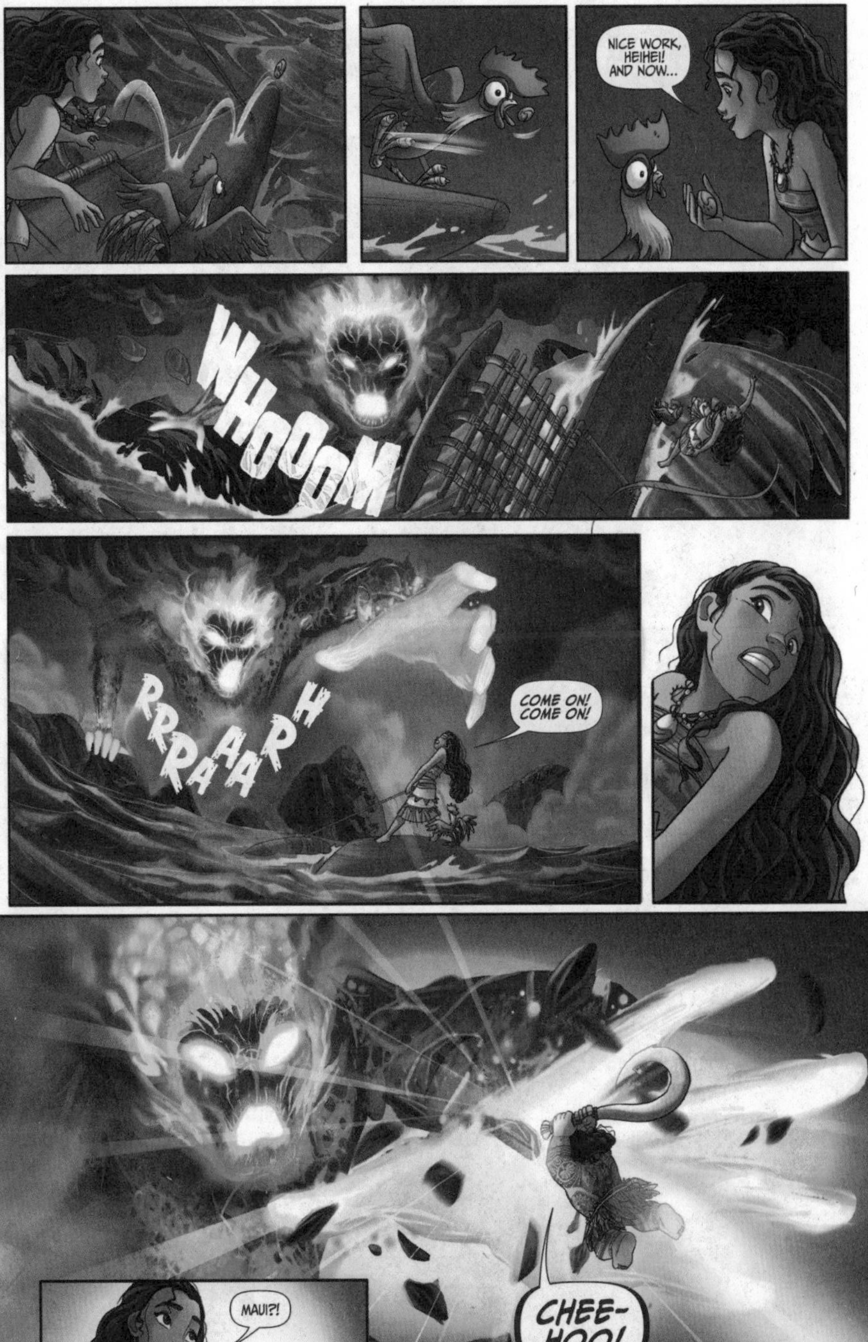
NICE WORK, HEIHEI! AND NOW...
WHOOOOM
RRRAAAARH
COME ON! COME ON!
CHEE-HOO!
MAUI?!

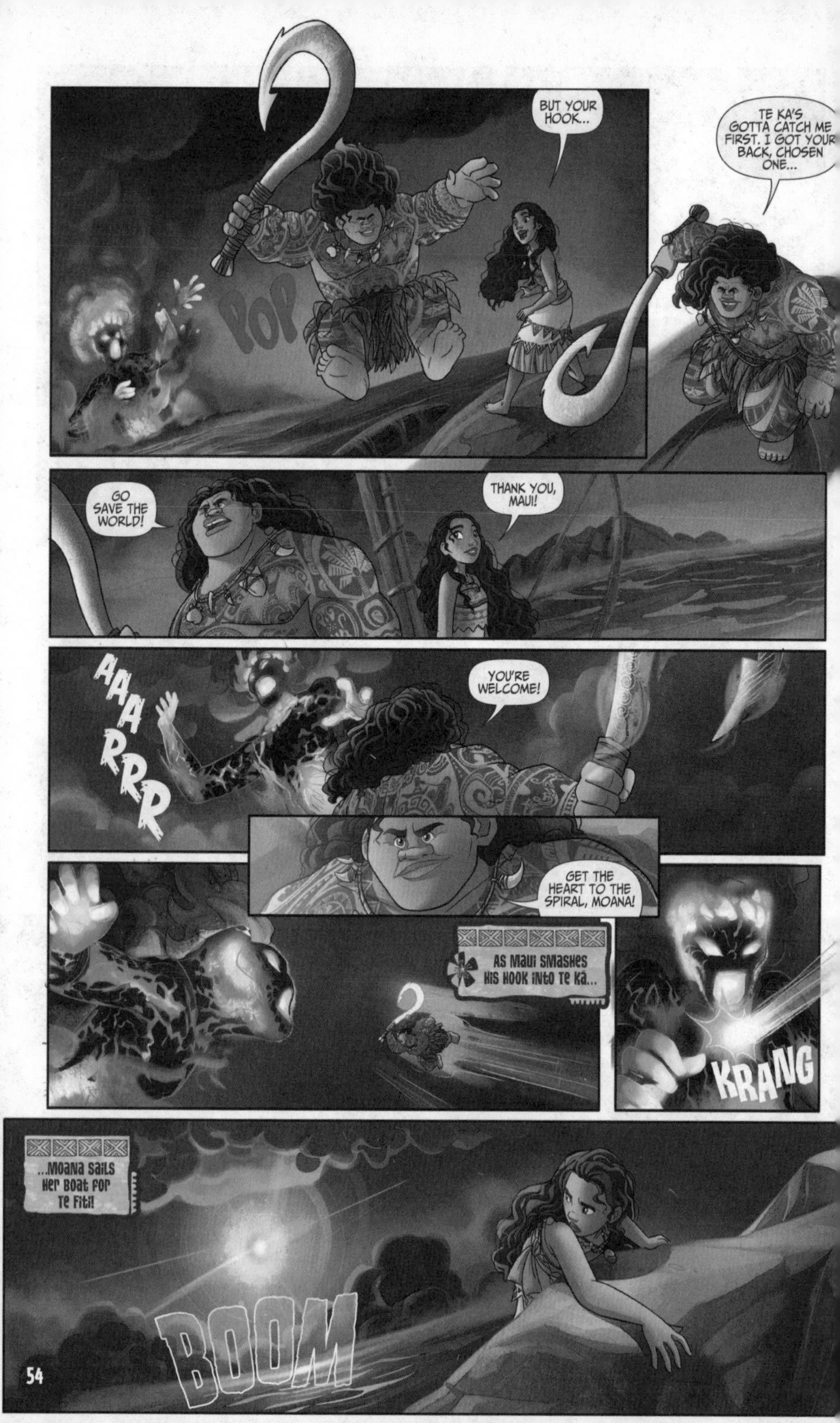

BUT YOUR HOOK...
POP
TE KA'S GOTTA CATCH ME FIRST. I GOT YOUR BACK, CHOSEN ONE...
GO SAVE THE WORLD!
THANK YOU, MAUI!
AAARRR
YOU'RE WELCOME!
GET THE HEART TO THE SPIRAL, MOANA!
AS MAUI SMASHES HIS HOOK INTO TE KA...
KRANG
...MOANA SAILS HER BOAT FOR TE FITI!
BOOM

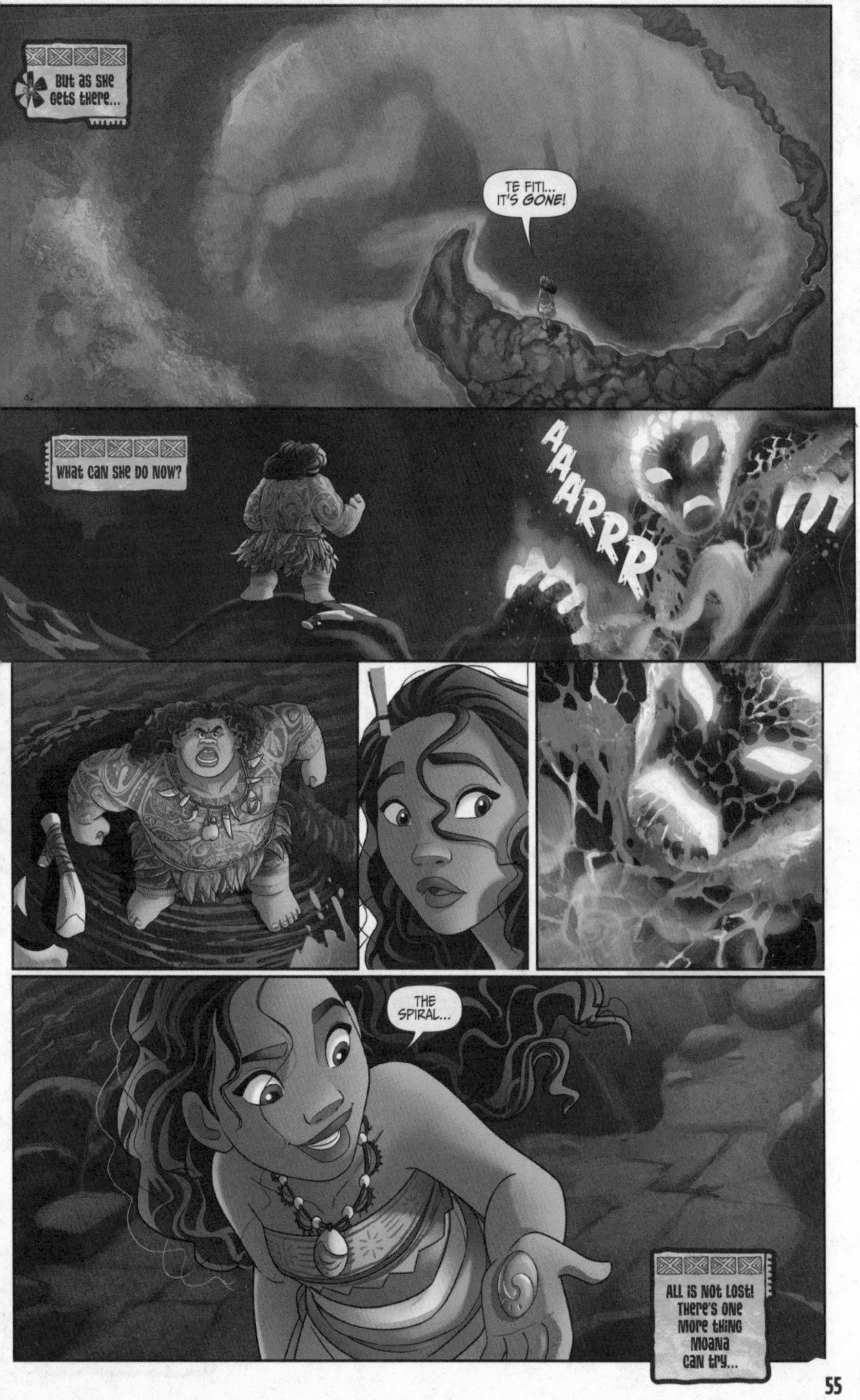

But as she gets there...
TE FITI... IT'S GONE!
What can she do now?
AAARRR
THE SPIRAL...
All is not lost! There's one more thing Moana can try...

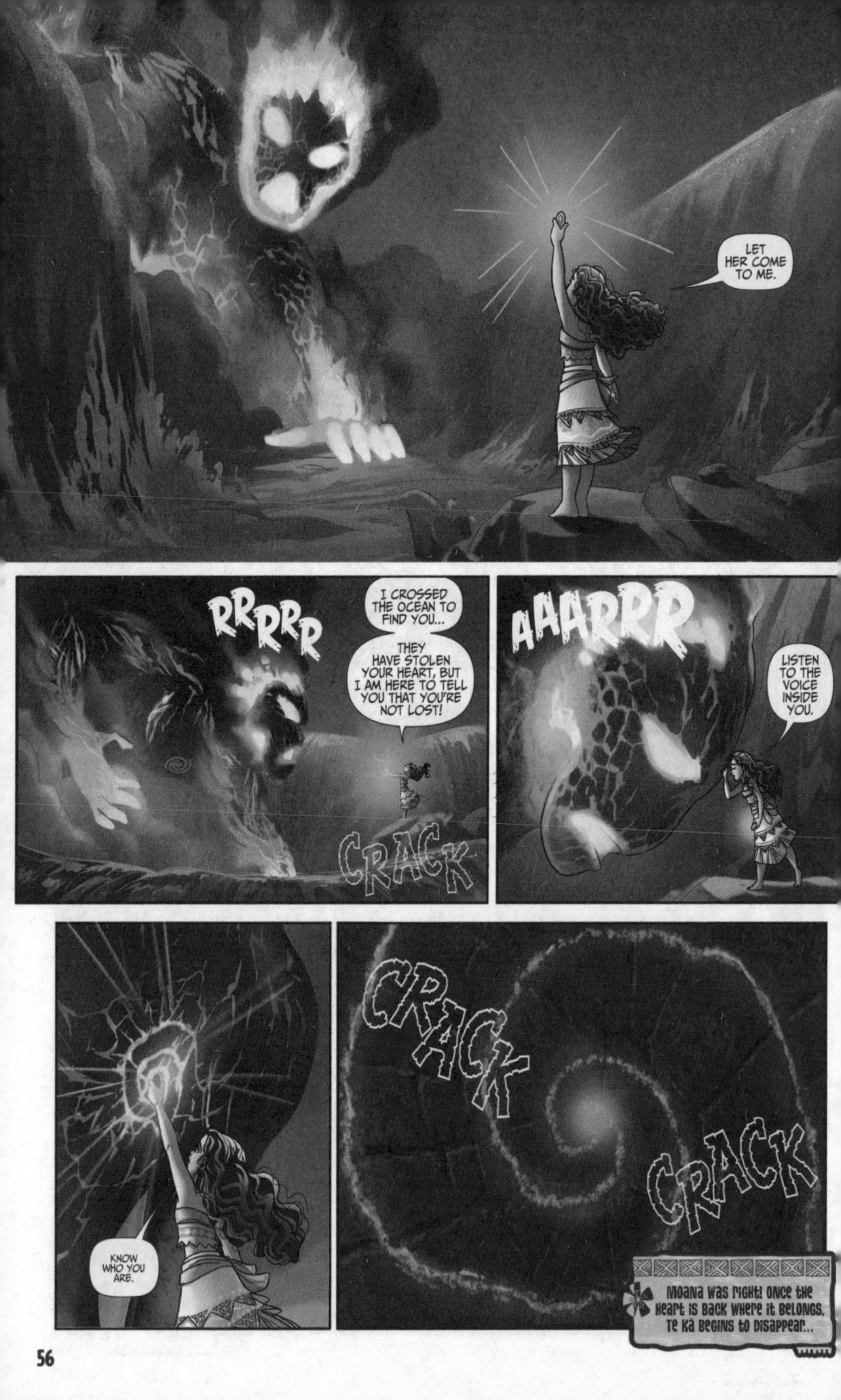
LET HER COME TO ME.
RRRRR
I CROSSED THE OCEAN TO FIND YOU...
THEY HAVE STOLEN YOUR HEART, BUT I AM HERE TO TELL YOU THAT YOU'RE NOT LOST!
CRACK
AAARRR
LISTEN TO THE VOICE INSIDE YOU.
KNOW WHO YOU ARE.
CRACK
CRACK
Moana was right! Once the Heart is back where it belongs, Te Kā begins to disappear...

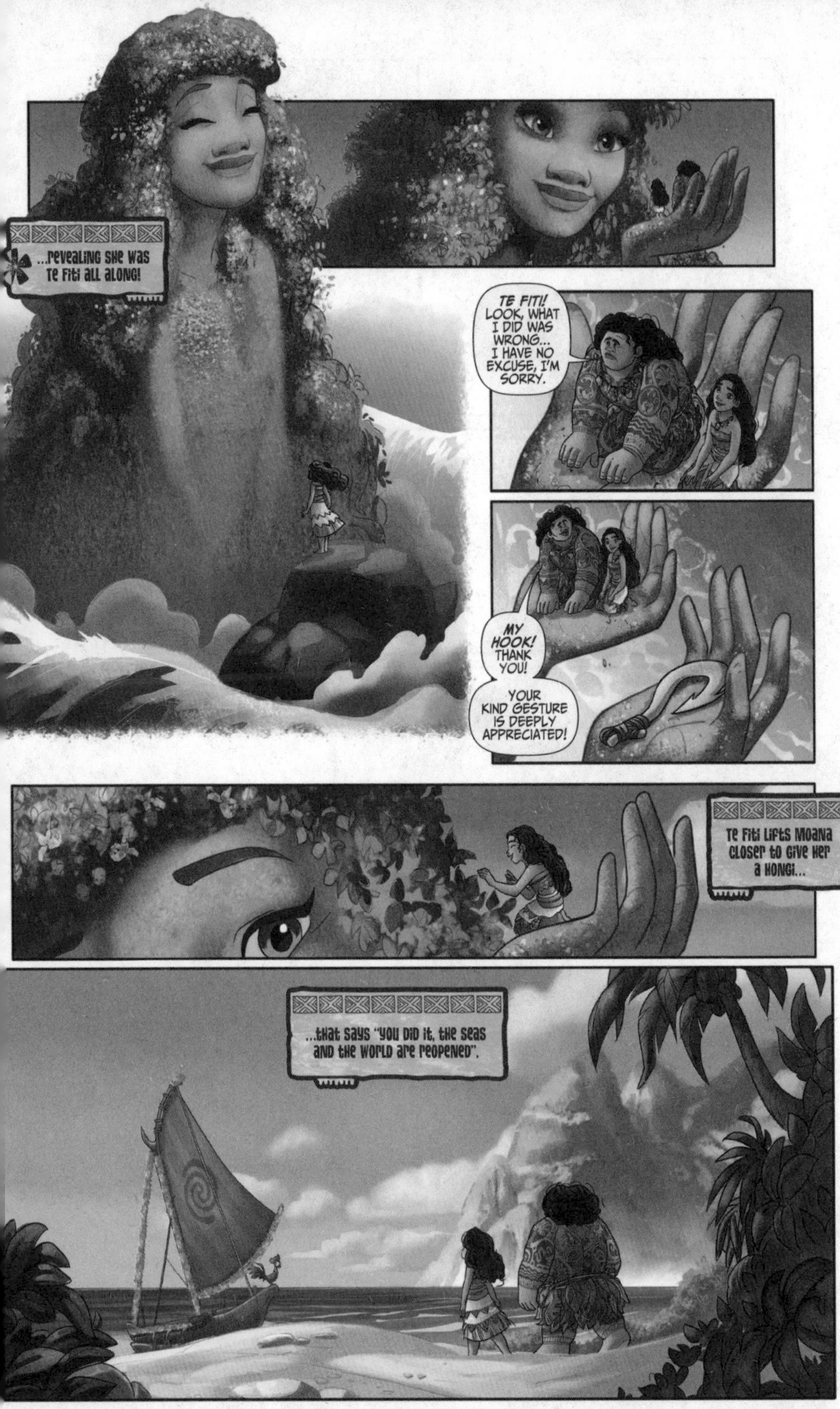
...revealing she was Te Fiti all along!
TE FITI! LOOK, WHAT I DID WAS WRONG... I HAVE NO EXCUSE, I'M SORRY.
MY HOOK! THANK YOU!
YOUR KIND GESTURE IS DEEPLY APPRECIATED!
Te Fiti lifts Moana closer to give her a hongi...
...that says "you did it, the seas and the world are reopened".

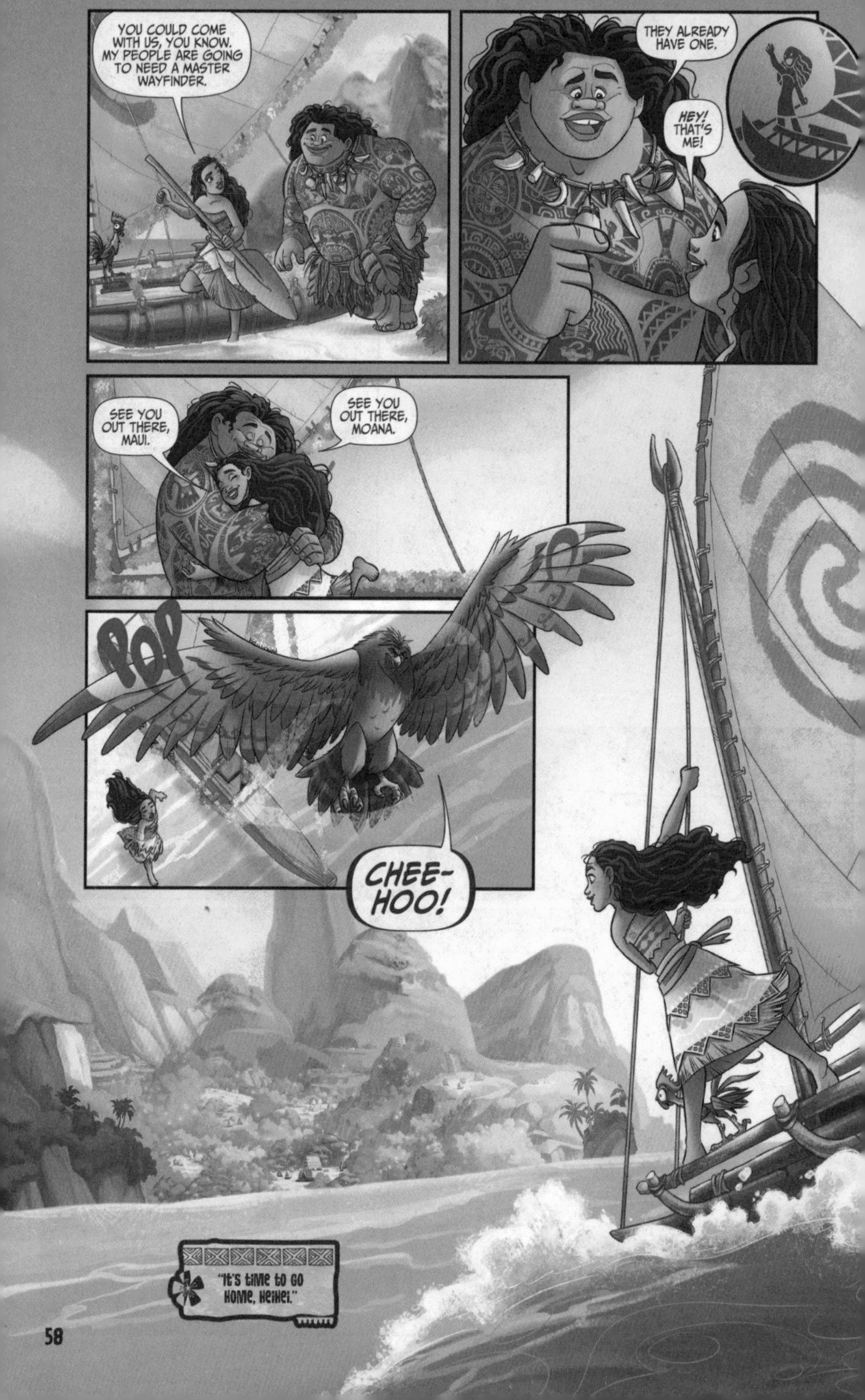
YOU COULD COME WITH US, YOU KNOW. MY PEOPLE ARE GOING TO NEED A MASTER WAYFINDER.
THEY ALREADY HAVE ONE.
HEY! THAT'S ME!
SEE YOU OUT THERE, MAUI.
SEE YOU OUT THERE, MOANA.
POP
CHEE-HOO!
"It's time to go home, Heihei."

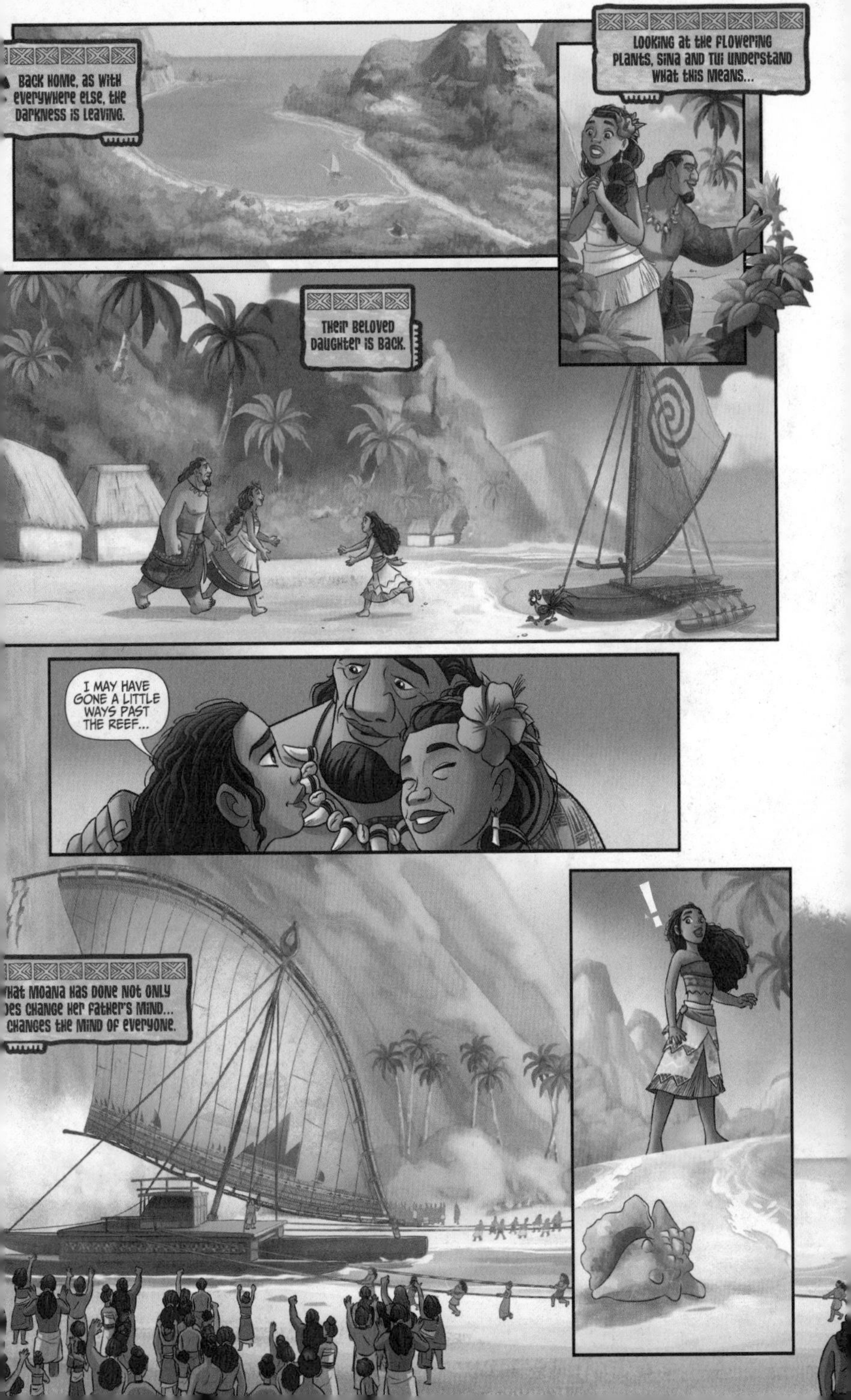
Back home, as with everywhere else, the Darkness is leaving.
Looking at the flowering plants, Sina and Tui understand what this means...
Their beloved daughter is back.
I MAY HAVE GONE A LITTLE WAYS PAST THE REEF...
!
hat Moana has done not only oes change her father's mind... changes the mind of everyone.

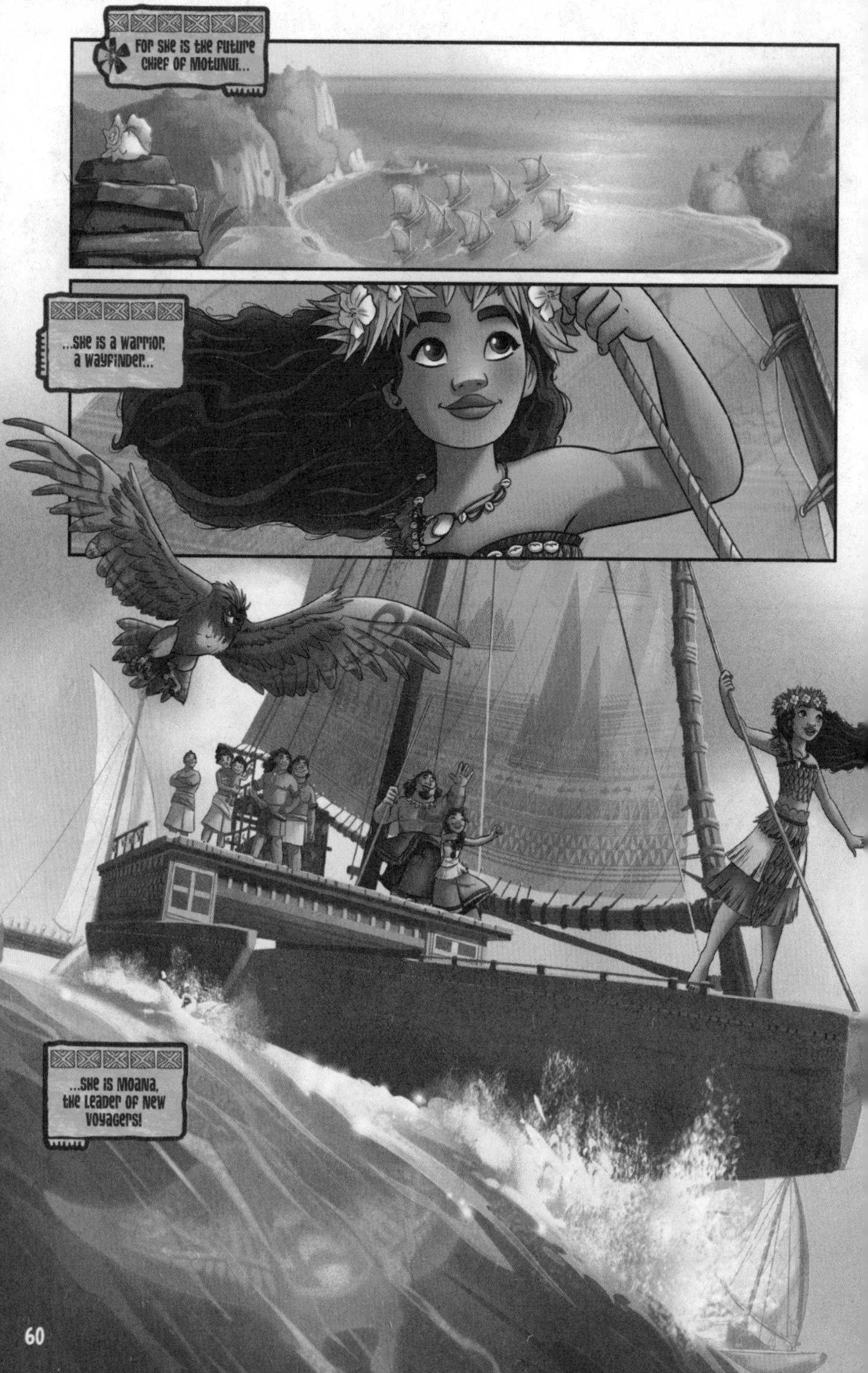
For she is the future chief of Motunui...
...she is a warrior, a wayfinder...
...she is Moana, the leader of new voyagers!

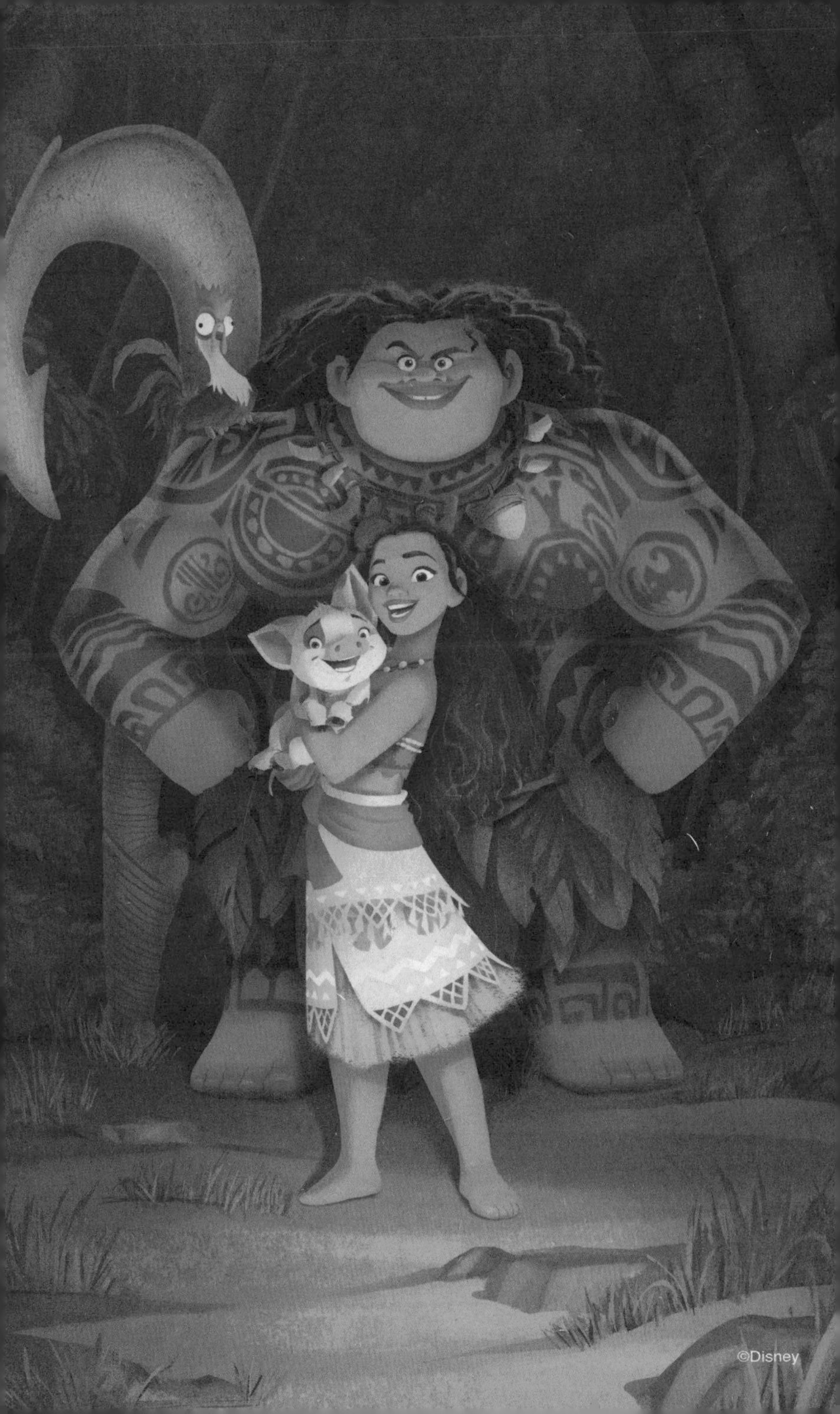

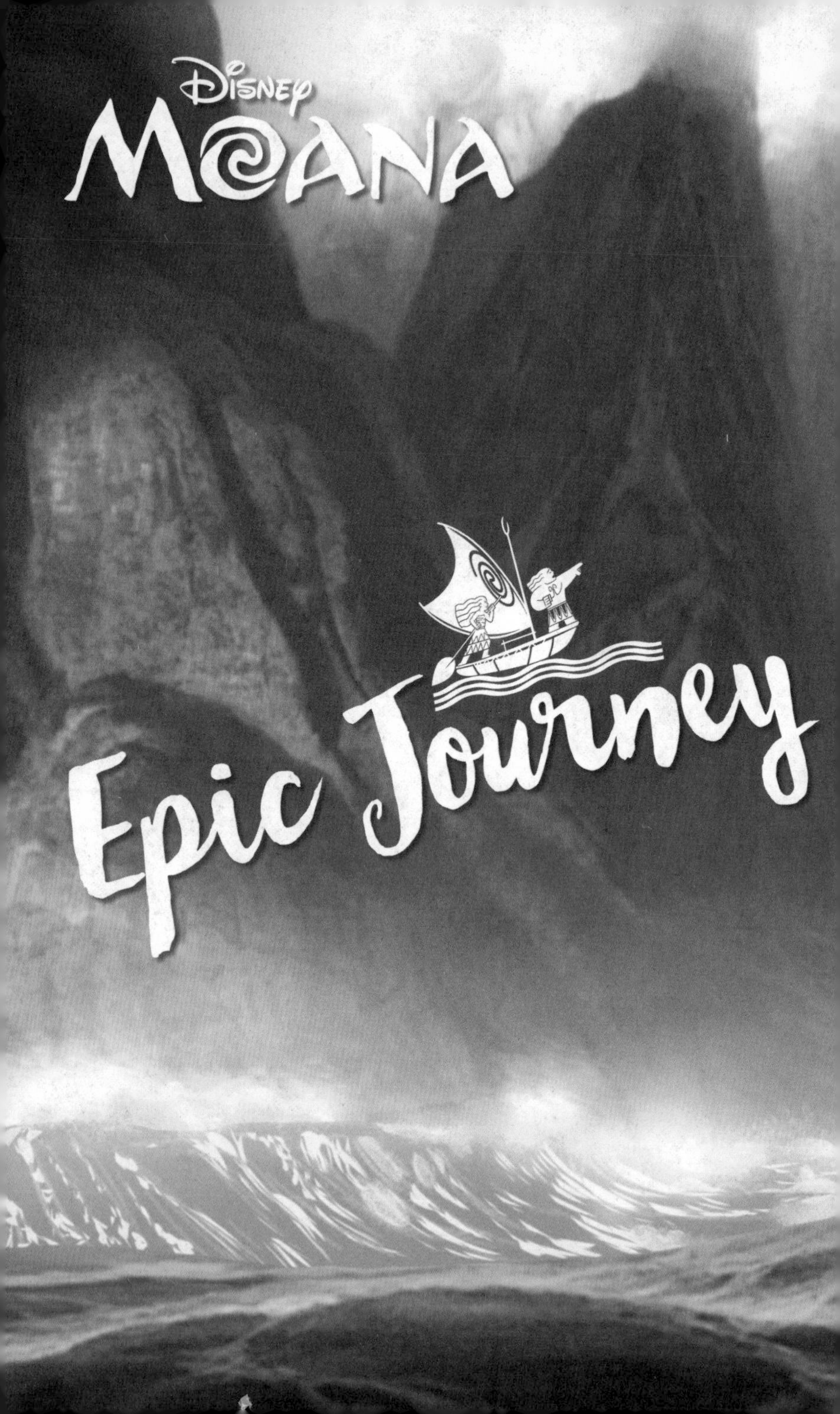
Disney
Moana
Epic Journey

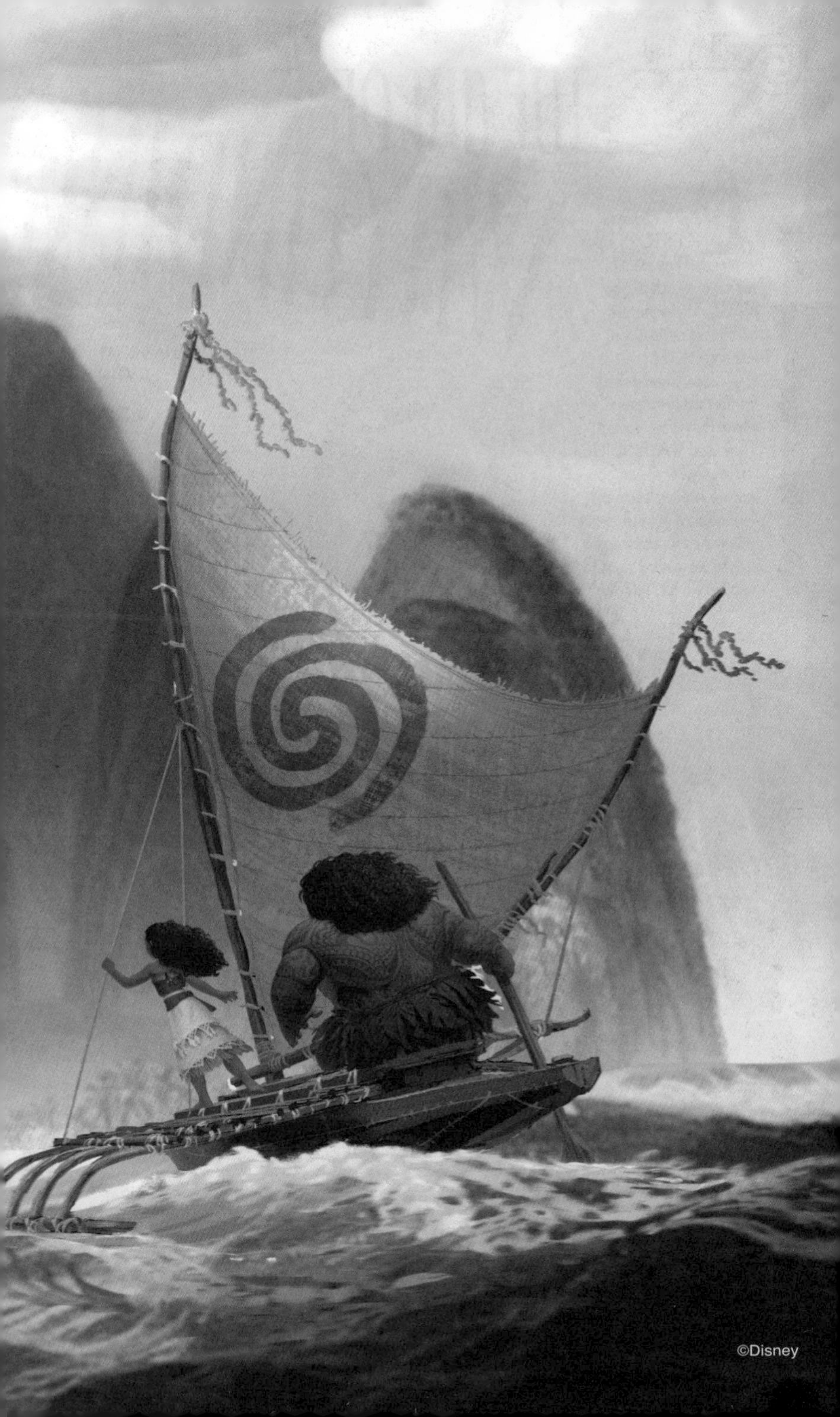

THE ART OF WAYFINDING

Long ago, Moana's ANCESTORS were voyagers. They would set sail in search of new islands without the use of modern navigational instruments, like compasses, to help them. So how did they know where they were going? They used WAYFINDING techniques. While on her journey Moana learns that wayfinding is not just about sails and knots and learns how to use natural signs to help her FIND HER WAY.

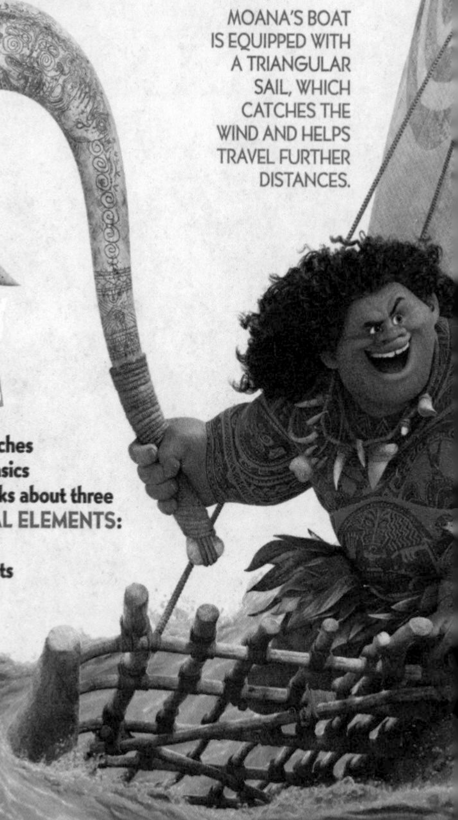

MOANA'S BOAT IS EQUIPPED WITH A TRIANGULAR SAIL, WHICH CATCHES THE WIND AND HELPS TRAVEL FURTHER DISTANCES.

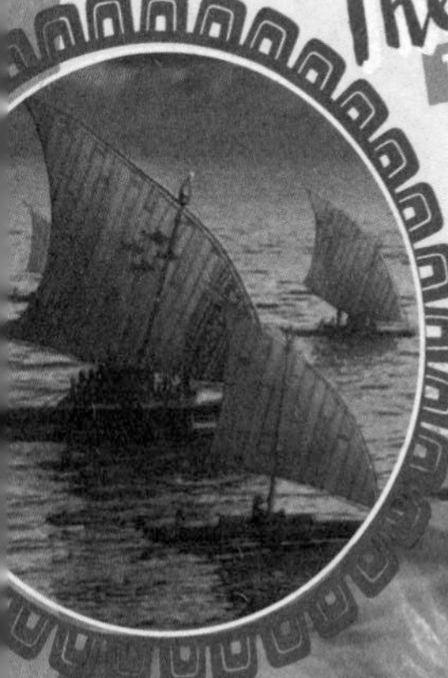

The Basics

THE FIRST THREE ELEMENTS

When Maui teaches Moana the basics of wayfinding he talks about three important NATURAL ELEMENTS:

1) the sun
2) the ocean currents
3) the stars

1

STARS

Wayfinders use the position of the STARS AND CONSTELLATIONS to help them navigate AT NIGHT.

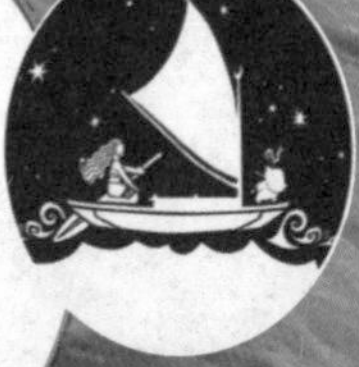

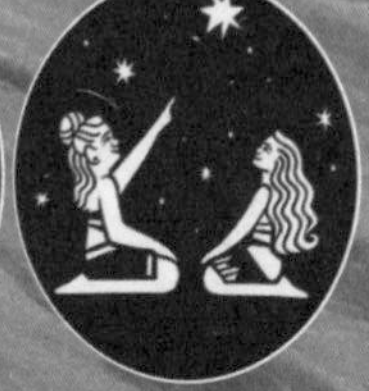

The Basics
OTHER ELEMENTS

Other important elements that can help a master wayfinder find the right direction are:

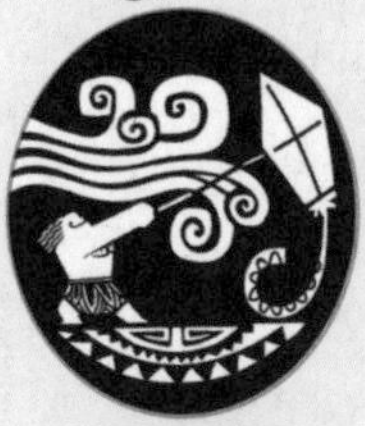

CLOUDS
Their different **SHAPES** and **MOVEMENTS** show how the weather and the wind will change.

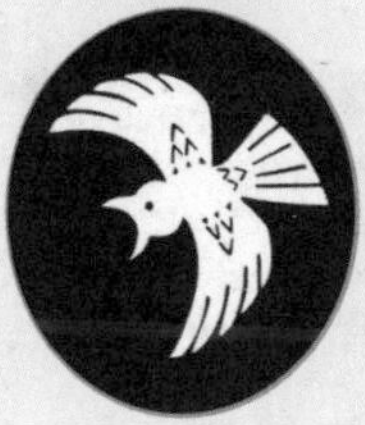

BIRDS
They come out to fish and then return to their home islands, so their presence usually means that **LAND** is close.

3

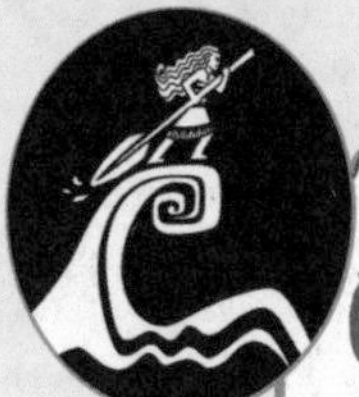

OCEAN CURRENTS

WAYFINDERS read the ocean currents and know which ones can **HELP THEM** get to where they are trying **TO GO.**

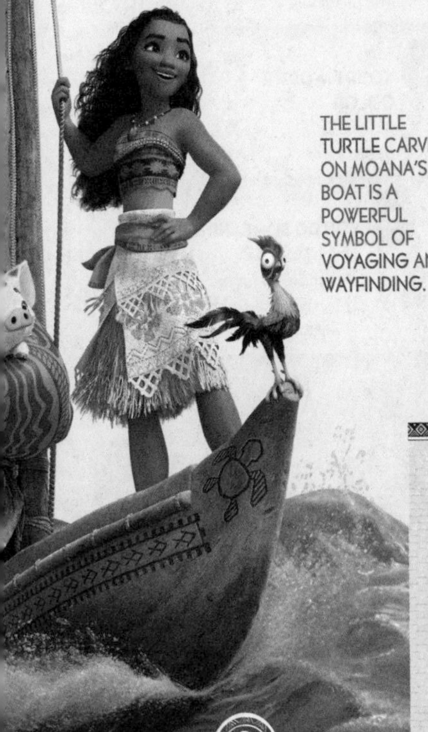

THE LITTLE TURTLE CARVED ON MOANA'S BOAT IS A POWERFUL SYMBOL OF VOYAGING AND WAYFINDING.

VAKA TAURUA

Ancient Polynesian Wayfinders often used **DOUBLE HULLED CANOES** made of two hulls connected by lashed crossbeams. **SAILS** were usually made of **PANDANUS.**

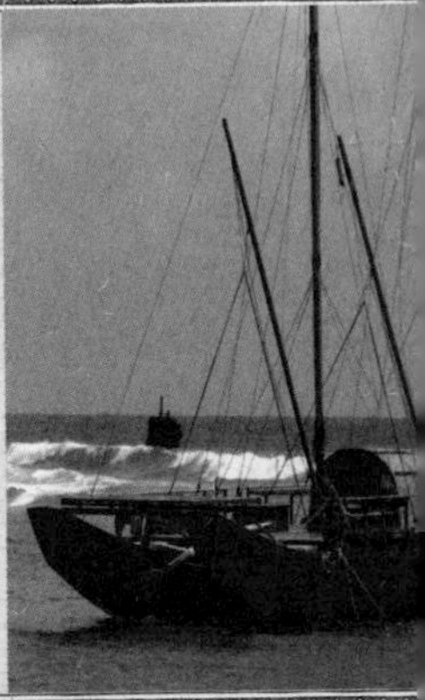

2

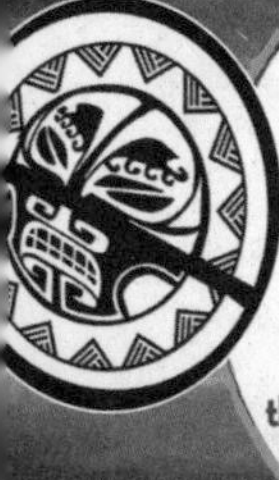

SUN

During the **DAY**, navigators let the sun guide them. **SUNRISE** and **SUNSET** are the most accurate times to set a course because, when the sun is on the **HORIZON.**

HERO QUIZ

Maui and Moana are different, but they become good friends and great WAYFINDING PARTNERS. ANSWER the following questions to find out how much you have in common with each of them!

1 YOUR LUCKY CHARM:
A) It's important, but you don't rely on it to reach your goals.
B) Without it you feel lost.

2 A NEW ADVENTURE:
A) You dive into it and hope everything will be okay.
B) You need to know all the details before you set off.

3 SOMEONE GIVES YOU GOOD ADVICE:
A) You listen carefully and decide whether to follow it or not.
B) You don't listen to it, because you already know what to do.

4 YOU ARE:
A) Curious and determined.
B) Strong and easy-going.

5 AT SCHOOL:
A) You are a bit shy.
B) Everyone loves your sense of humor.

6 YOUR FAVORITE COLOR:
A) Red.
B) Black.

7 YOU DO SOMETHING WRONG:
A) You immediately try to make up for it.
B) You hope the others will forget about it.

8 YOU ACCOMPLISH YOUR GOALS THROUGH:
A) Hard work.
B) Good luck and charm.

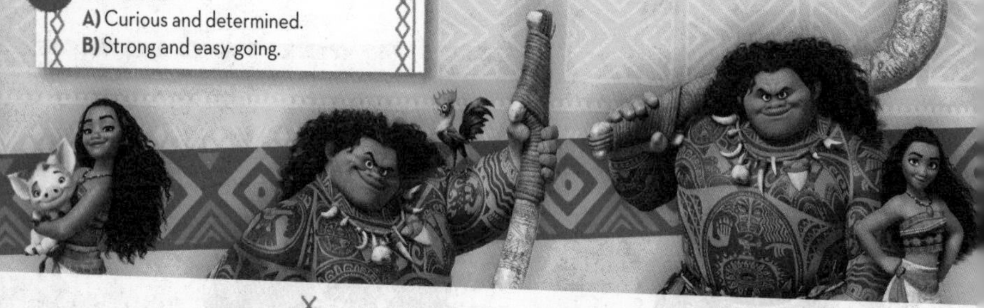

Mostly A's:
YOU'RE LIKE MOANA

You're spontaneous, vibrant, and determined and you're not afraid of following your dreams. Sometimes you get things wrong and feel inadequate, but you always give your best and should be proud of what you are! You really care about the happiness of your family and friends and everyone appreciates your efforts.

Mostly B's:
YOU'RE LIKE MAUI

Your charisma and kindness impress everyone and you always look really self-confident, even when you are not. You don't trust everyone you meet, but when you find a true friend, you are ready to do everything for him/her. When you fail, you feel ashamed, but remember that your mistakes help you improve yourself and make you become even more awesome.

Same number of A's and B's:
YOU ARE LIKE MAUI & MOANA

You are strong and independent, and you love traveling the world to discover new places. You dream of living big adventures with your friends, and you never get tired of learning something new from both good and bad experiences. People appreciate your easygoing attitude, which helps you feel welcome wherever you go.

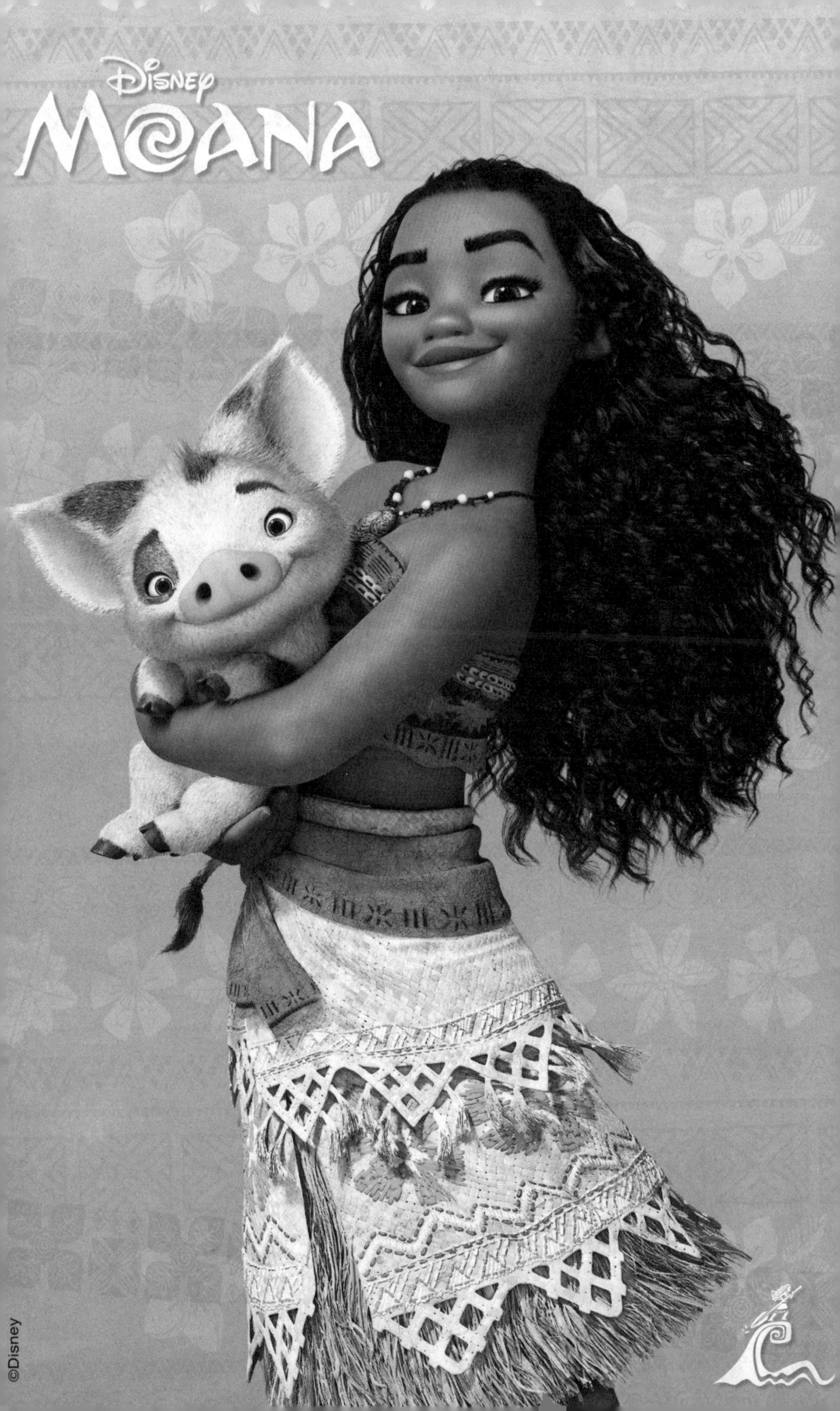
Disney
MOANA

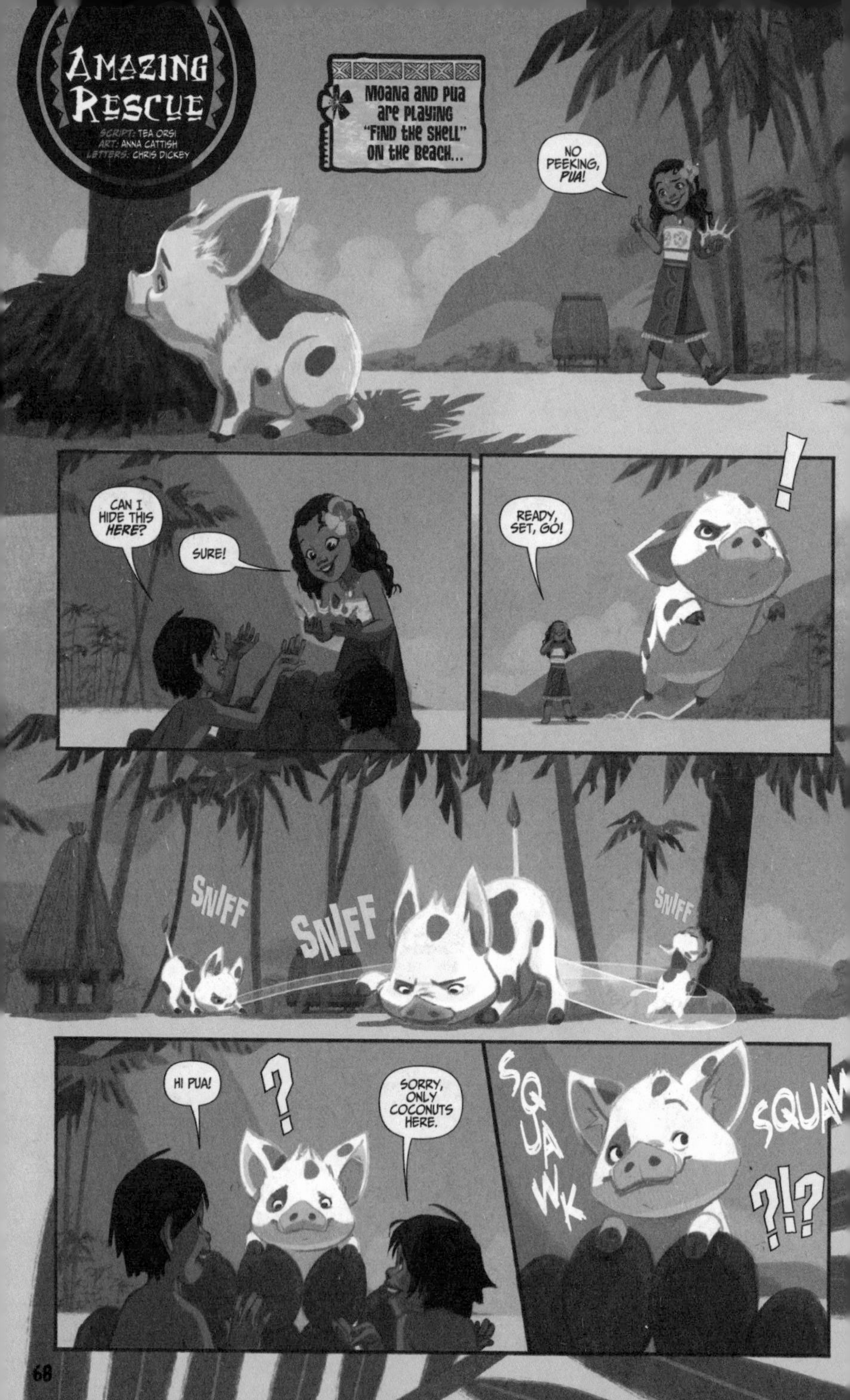
AMAZING RESCUE
SCRIPT: TEA ORSI
ART: ANNA CATTISH
LETTERS: CHRIS DICKEY
MOANA AND PUA ARE PLAYING "FIND THE SHELL" ON THE BEACH...
NO PEEKING, PUA!
CAN I HIDE THIS HERE?
SURE!
READY, SET, GO!
!
SNIFF
SNIFF
SNIFF
HI PUA!
?
SORRY, ONLY COCONUTS HERE.
SQUAWK
SQUAW
?!?

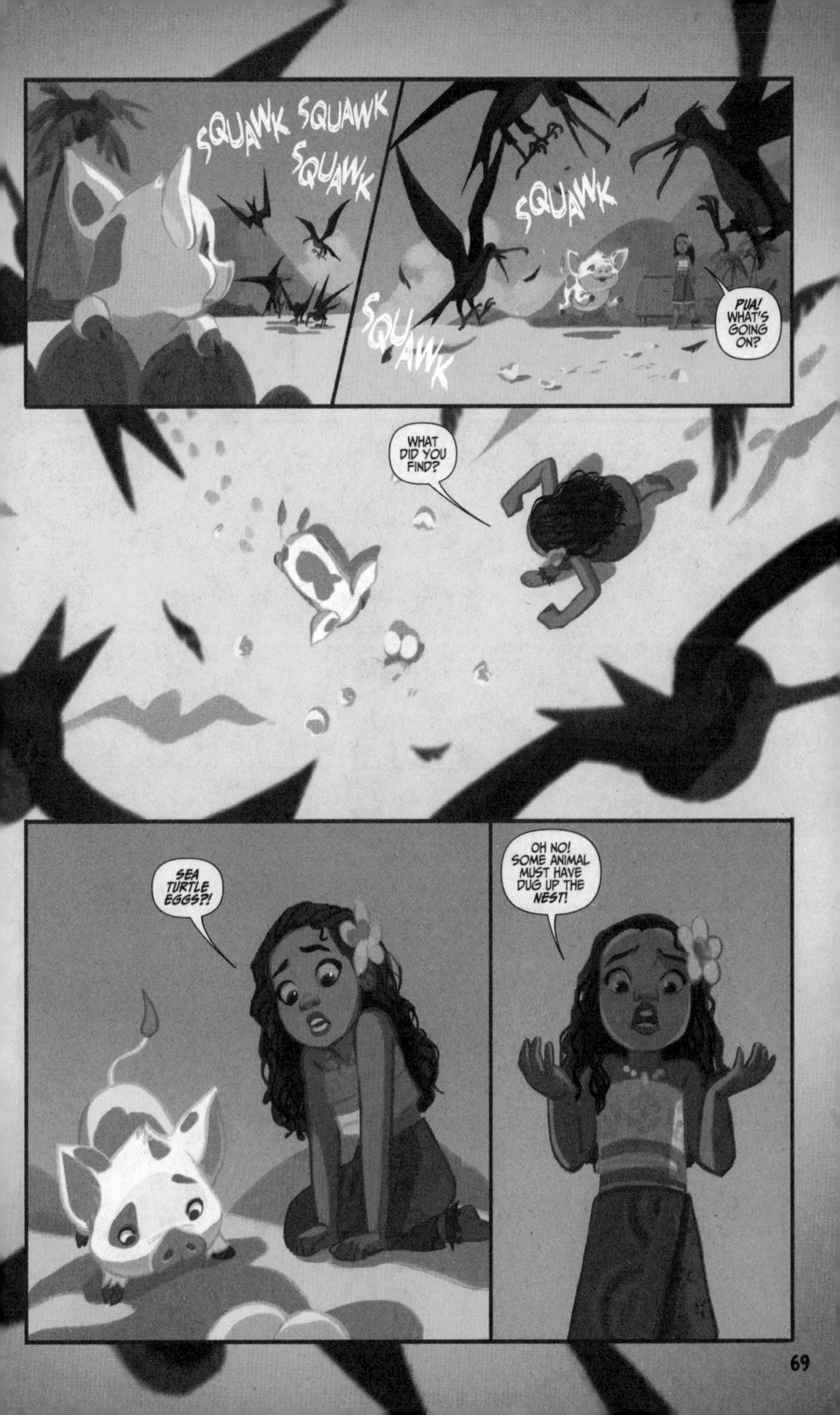
SQUAWK SQUAWK
SQUAWK
SQUAWK
SQUAWK
PUA! WHAT'S GOING ON?
WHAT DID YOU FIND?
SEA TURTLE EGGS?!
OH NO! SOME ANIMAL MUST HAVE DUG UP THE NEST!

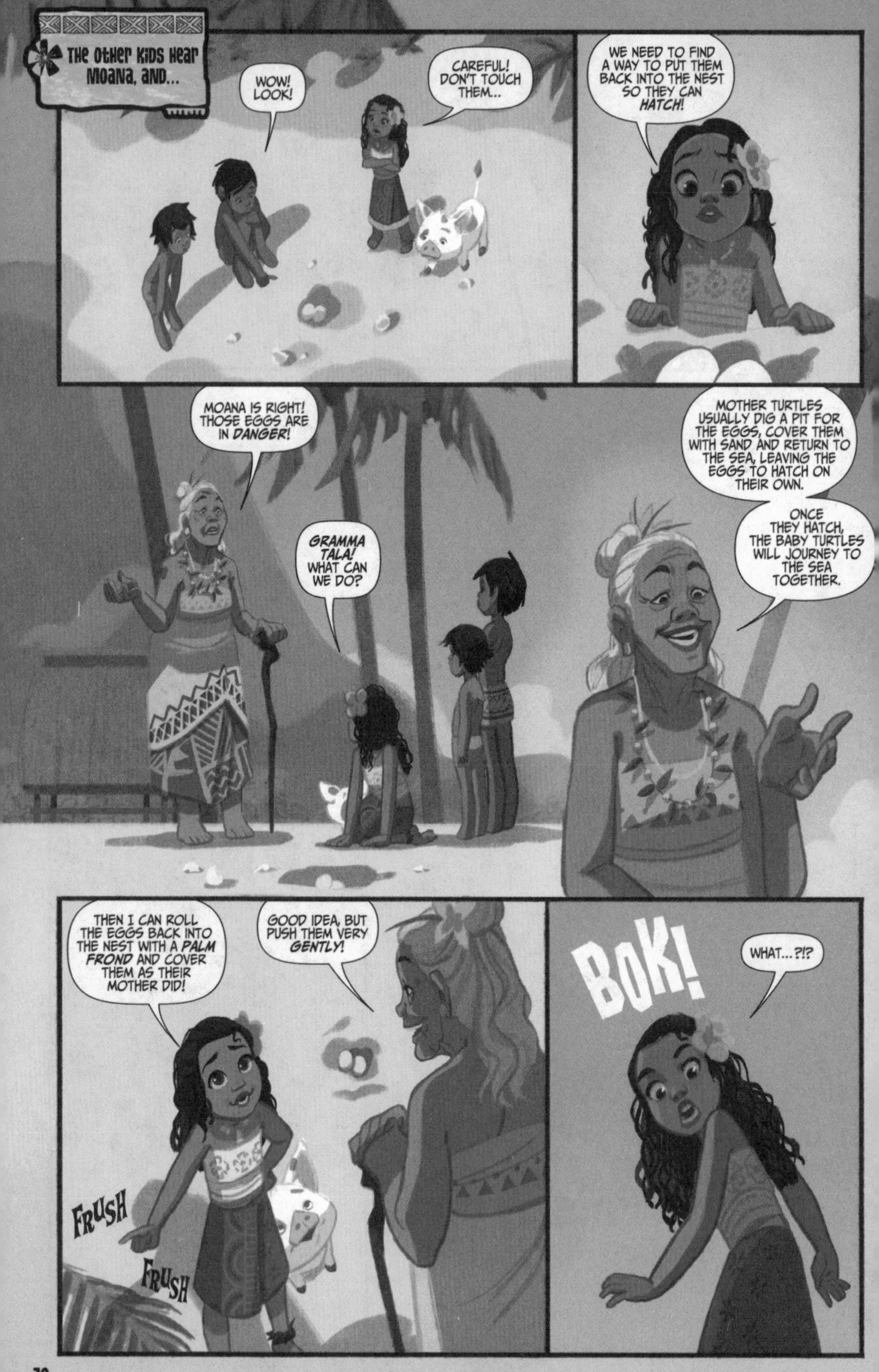
The other kids hear Moana, and...
WOW! LOOK!
CAREFUL! DON'T TOUCH THEM...
WE NEED TO FIND A WAY TO PUT THEM BACK INTO THE NEST SO THEY CAN *HATCH*!
MOANA IS RIGHT! THOSE EGGS ARE IN *DANGER*!
GRAMMA TALA! WHAT CAN WE DO?
MOTHER TURTLES USUALLY DIG A PIT FOR THE EGGS, COVER THEM WITH SAND AND RETURN TO THE SEA, LEAVING THE EGGS TO HATCH ON THEIR OWN.
ONCE THEY HATCH, THE BABY TURTLES WILL JOURNEY TO THE SEA TOGETHER.
THEN I CAN ROLL THE EGGS BACK INTO THE NEST WITH A *PALM FROND* AND COVER THEM AS THEIR MOTHER DID!
GOOD IDEA, BUT PUSH THEM VERY *GENTLY*!
FRUSH
FRUSH
BOK!
WHAT...?!?

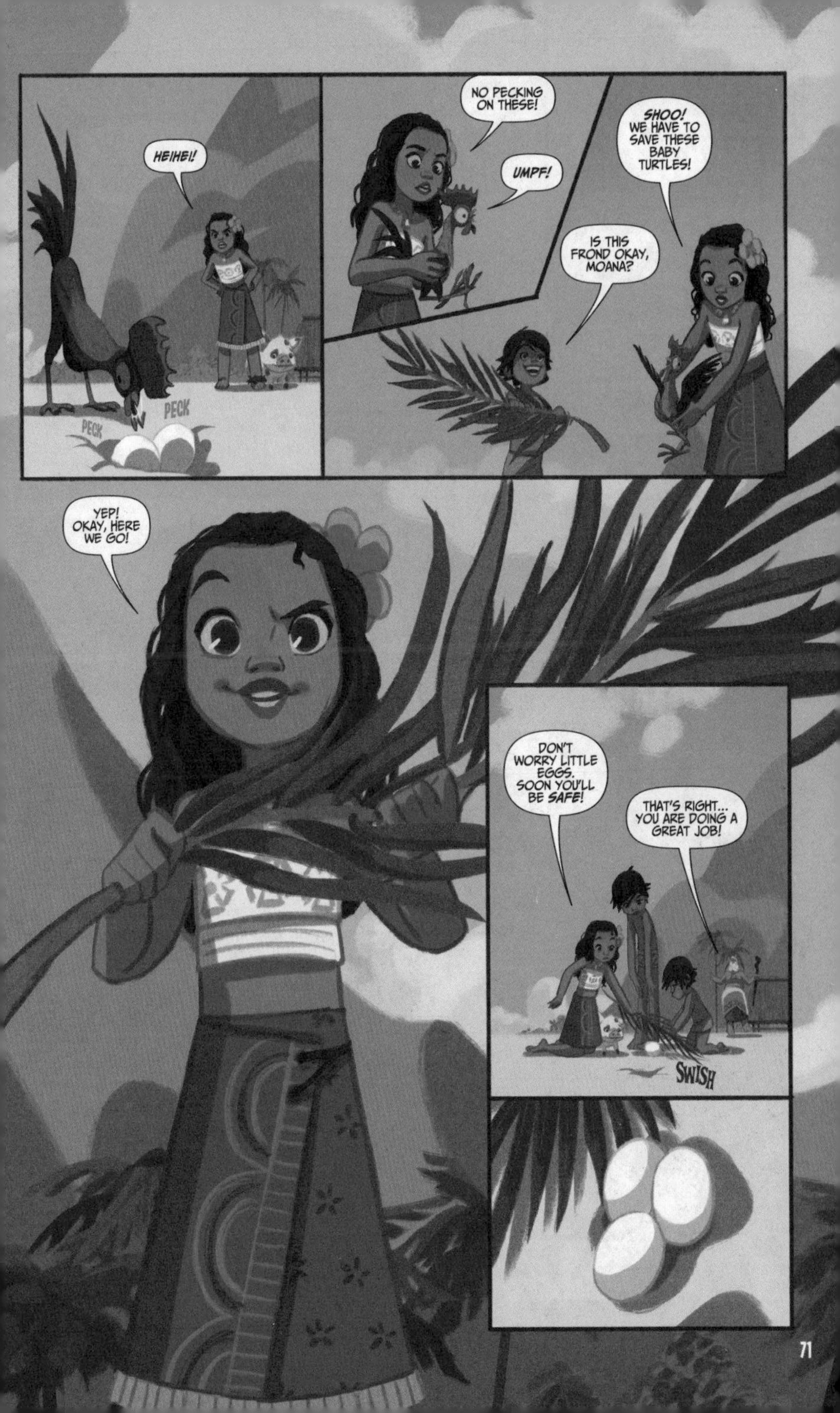
HEIHEI!
PECK
PECK
NO PECKING ON THESE!
UMPF!
SHOO! WE HAVE TO SAVE THESE BABY TURTLES!
IS THIS FROND OKAY, MOANA?
YEP! OKAY, HERE WE GO!
DON'T WORRY LITTLE EGGS. SOON YOU'LL BE SAFE!
THAT'S RIGHT... YOU ARE DOING A GREAT JOB!
SWISH

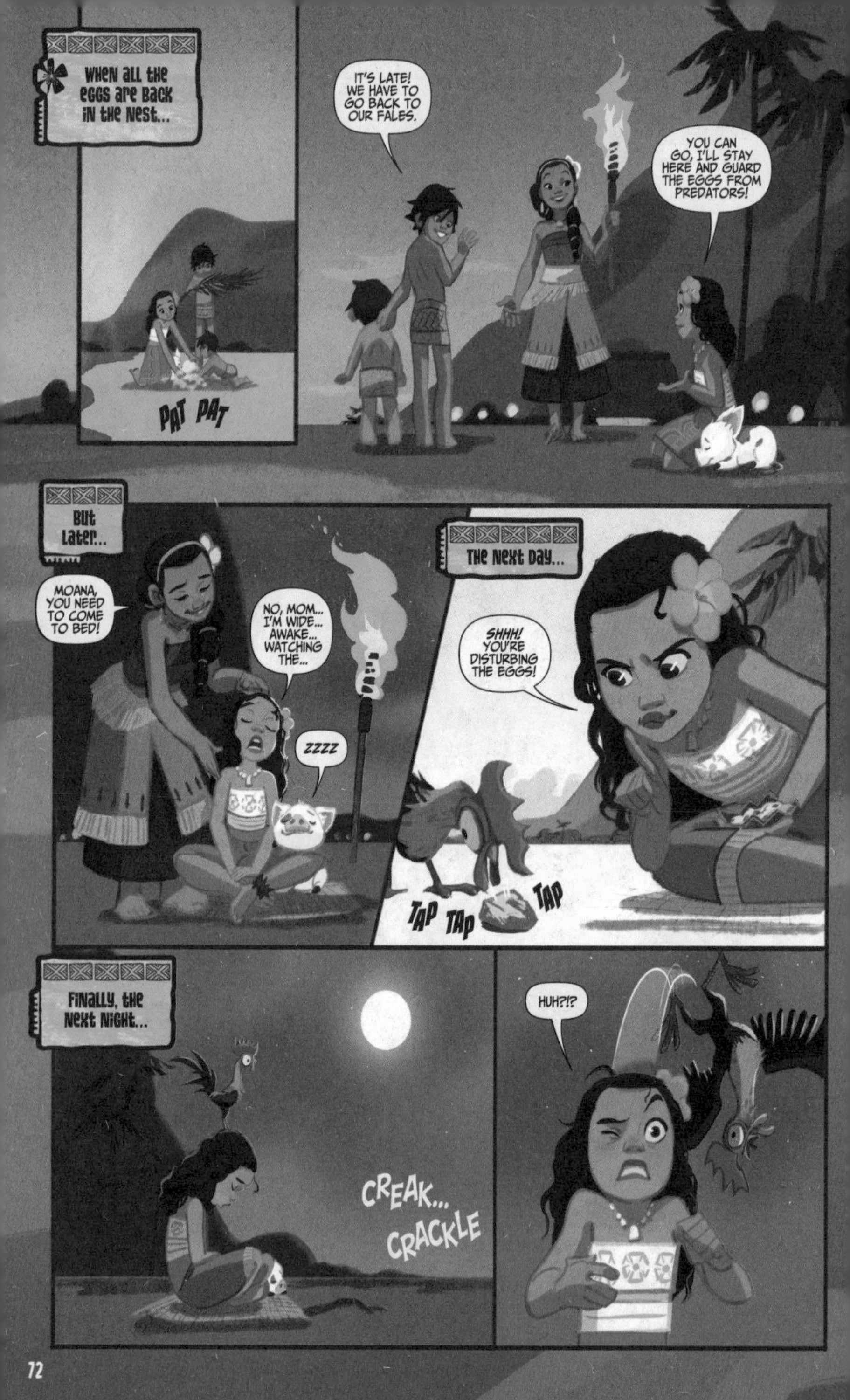
When all the eggs are back in the nest...
PAT PAT
IT'S LATE! WE HAVE TO GO BACK TO OUR FALES.
YOU CAN GO, I'LL STAY HERE AND GUARD THE EGGS FROM PREDATORS!
But later...
MOANA, YOU NEED TO COME TO BED!
NO, MOM... I'M WIDE... AWAKE... WATCHING THE...
ZZZZ
The next day...
SHHH! YOU'RE DISTURBING THE EGGS!
TAP TAP TAP
Finally, the next night...
CREAK... CRACKLE
HUH?!?

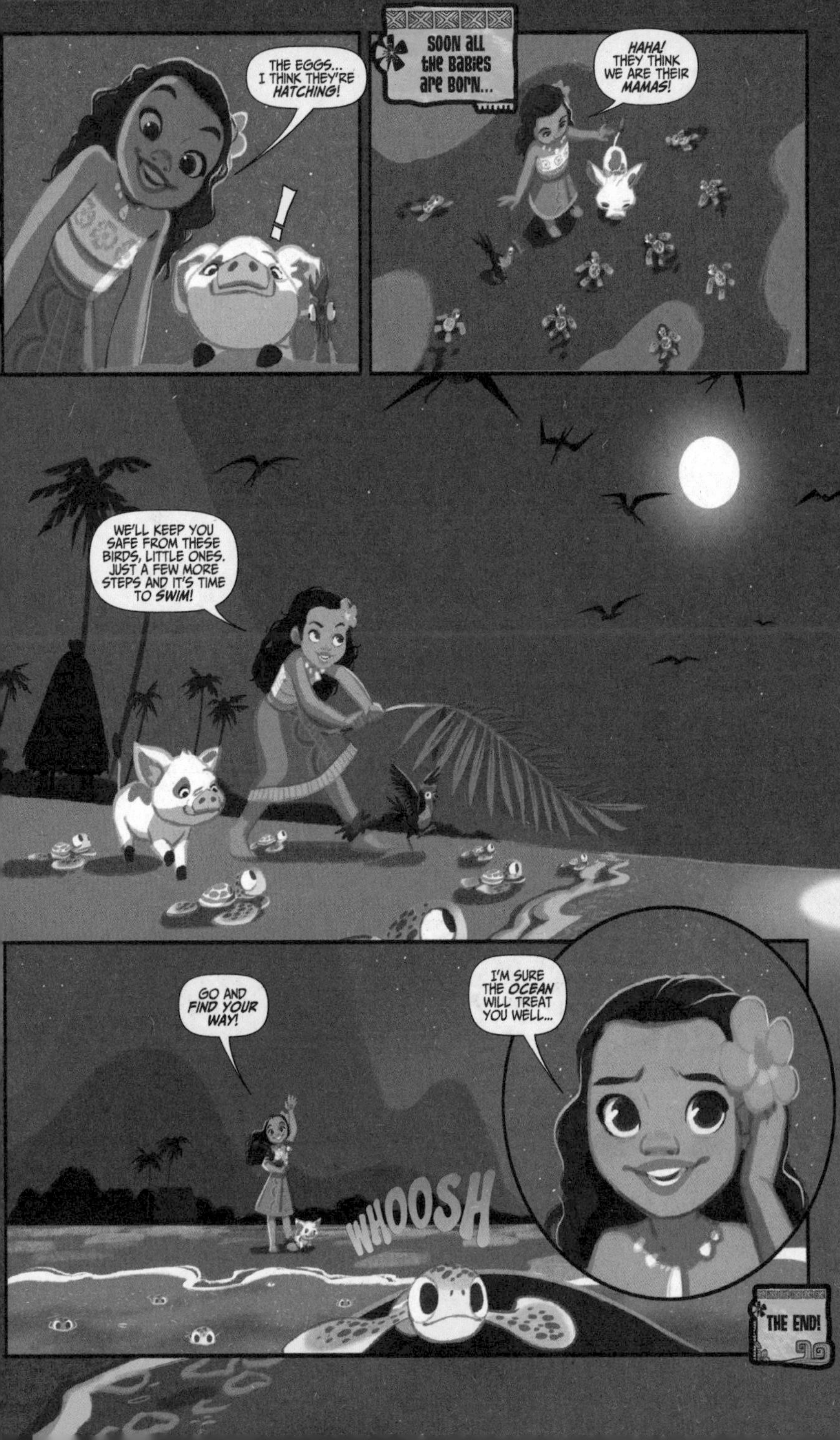

THE EGGS... I THINK THEY'RE *HATCHING!*
!
SOON ALL THE BABIES ARE BORN...
HAHA! THEY THINK WE ARE THEIR *MAMAS!*
WE'LL KEEP YOU SAFE FROM THESE BIRDS, LITTLE ONES. JUST A FEW MORE STEPS AND IT'S TIME TO *SWIM!*
GO AND *FIND YOUR WAY!*
WHOOSH
I'M SURE THE *OCEAN* WILL TREAT YOU WELL...
THE END!

Disney Moana

In the Beginning

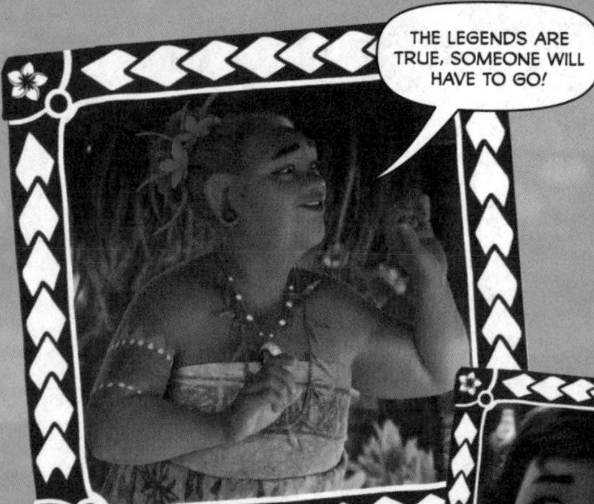
THE LEGENDS ARE TRUE, SOMEONE WILL HAVE TO GO!

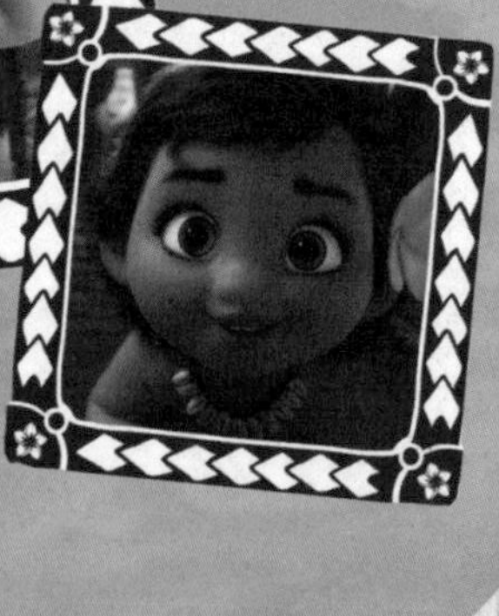

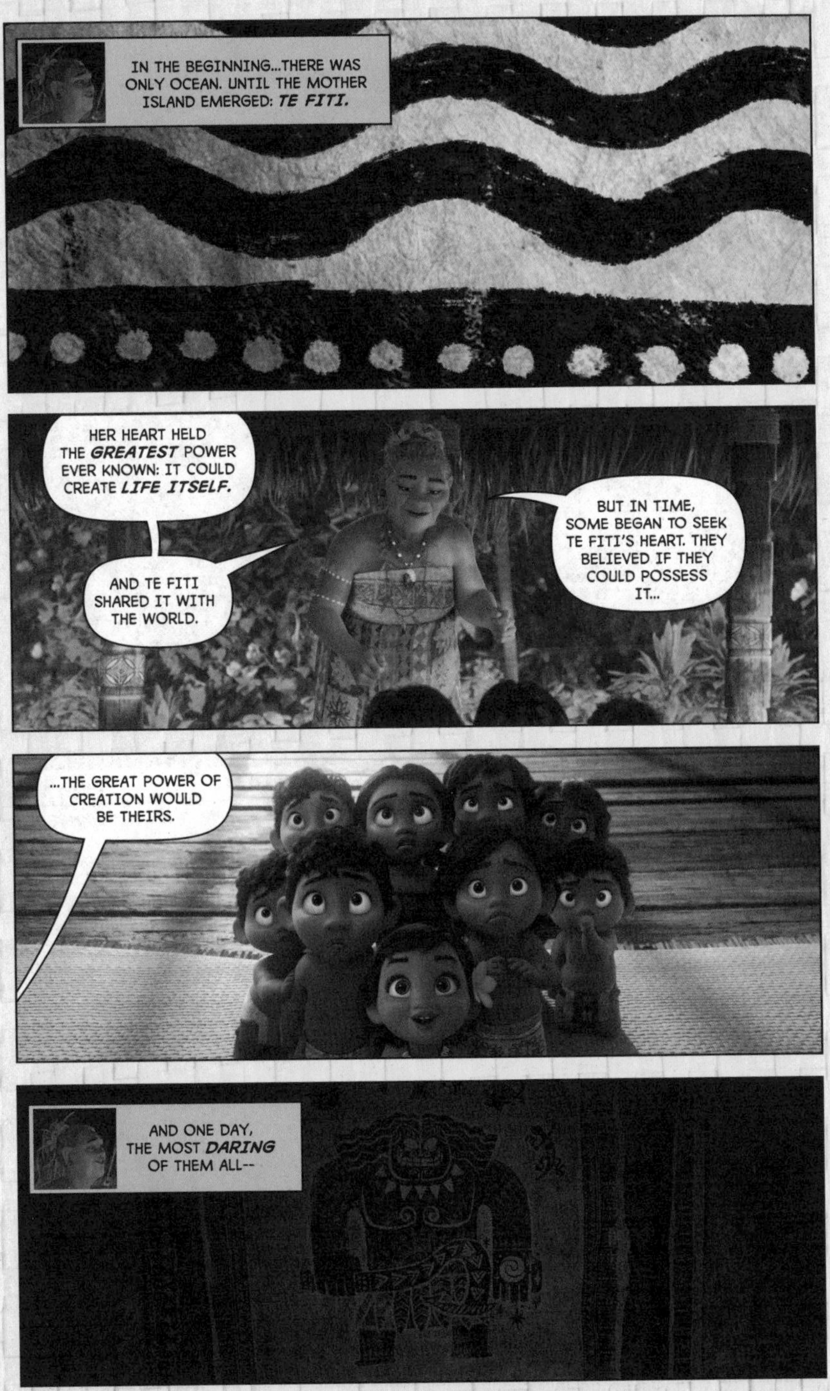
IN THE BEGINNING...THERE WAS ONLY OCEAN. UNTIL THE MOTHER ISLAND EMERGED: *TE FITI.*
HER HEART HELD THE ***GREATEST*** POWER EVER KNOWN: IT COULD CREATE ***LIFE ITSELF.***
AND TE FITI SHARED IT WITH THE WORLD.
BUT IN TIME, SOME BEGAN TO SEEK TE FITI'S HEART. THEY BELIEVED IF THEY COULD POSSESS IT...
...THE GREAT POWER OF CREATION WOULD BE THEIRS.
AND ONE DAY, THE MOST ***DARING*** OF THEM ALL--

--VOYAGED ACROSS THE VAST OCEAN TO TAKE IT.

HE WAS A *DEMIGOD* OF THE WIND AND SEA. A SHAPESHIFTER, A TRICKSTER...

...A WARRIOR WHO WIELDED A *MAGICAL FISHHOOK.* AND HIS NAME... WAS *MAUI.*

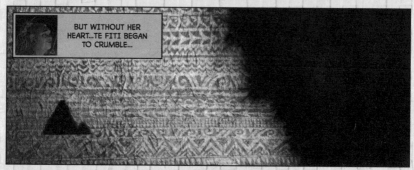

BUT WITHOUT HER HEART...TE FITI BEGAN TO CRUMBLE...

...GIVING BIRTH TO A *TERRIBLE DARKNESS.*

MAUI TRIED TO ESCAPE, BUT WAS CONFRONTED BY ANOTHER WHO SOUGHT THE HEART:

TE KA, A DEMON OF EARTH AND FIRE!

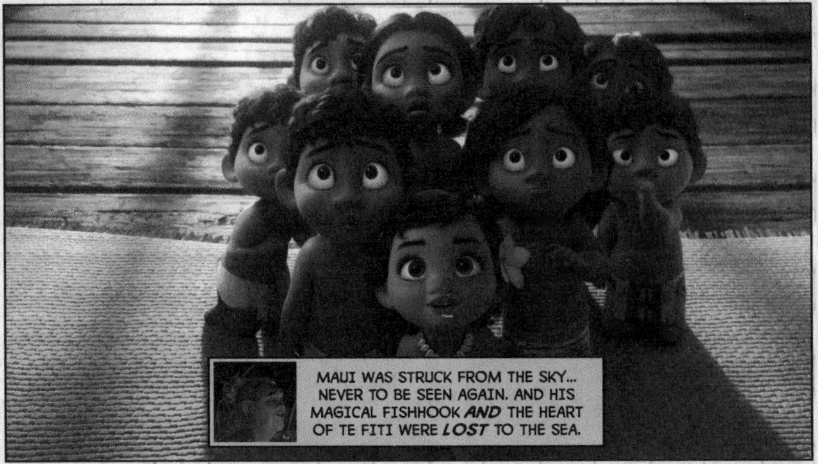
MAUI WAS STRUCK FROM THE SKY... NEVER TO BE SEEN AGAIN. AND HIS MAGICAL FISHHOOK *AND* THE HEART OF TE FITI WERE *LOST* TO THE SEA.

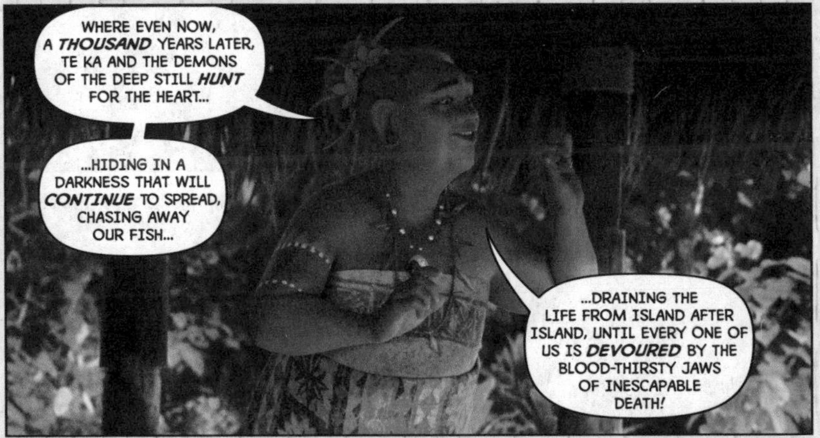
WHERE EVEN NOW, A *THOUSAND* YEARS LATER, TE KA AND THE DEMONS OF THE DEEP STILL *HUNT* FOR THE HEART...
...HIDING IN A DARKNESS THAT WILL *CONTINUE* TO SPREAD, CHASING AWAY OUR FISH...
...DRAINING THE LIFE FROM ISLAND AFTER ISLAND, UNTIL EVERY ONE OF US IS *DEVOURED* BY THE BLOOD-THIRSTY JAWS OF INESCAPABLE DEATH!

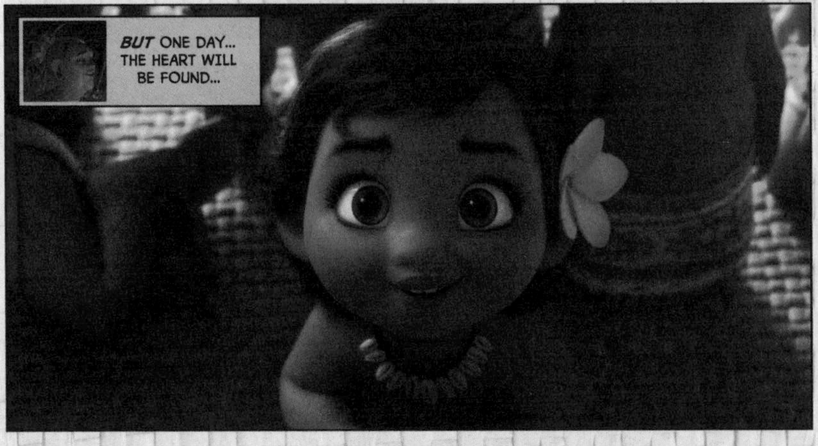
BUT ONE DAY... THE HEART WILL BE FOUND...

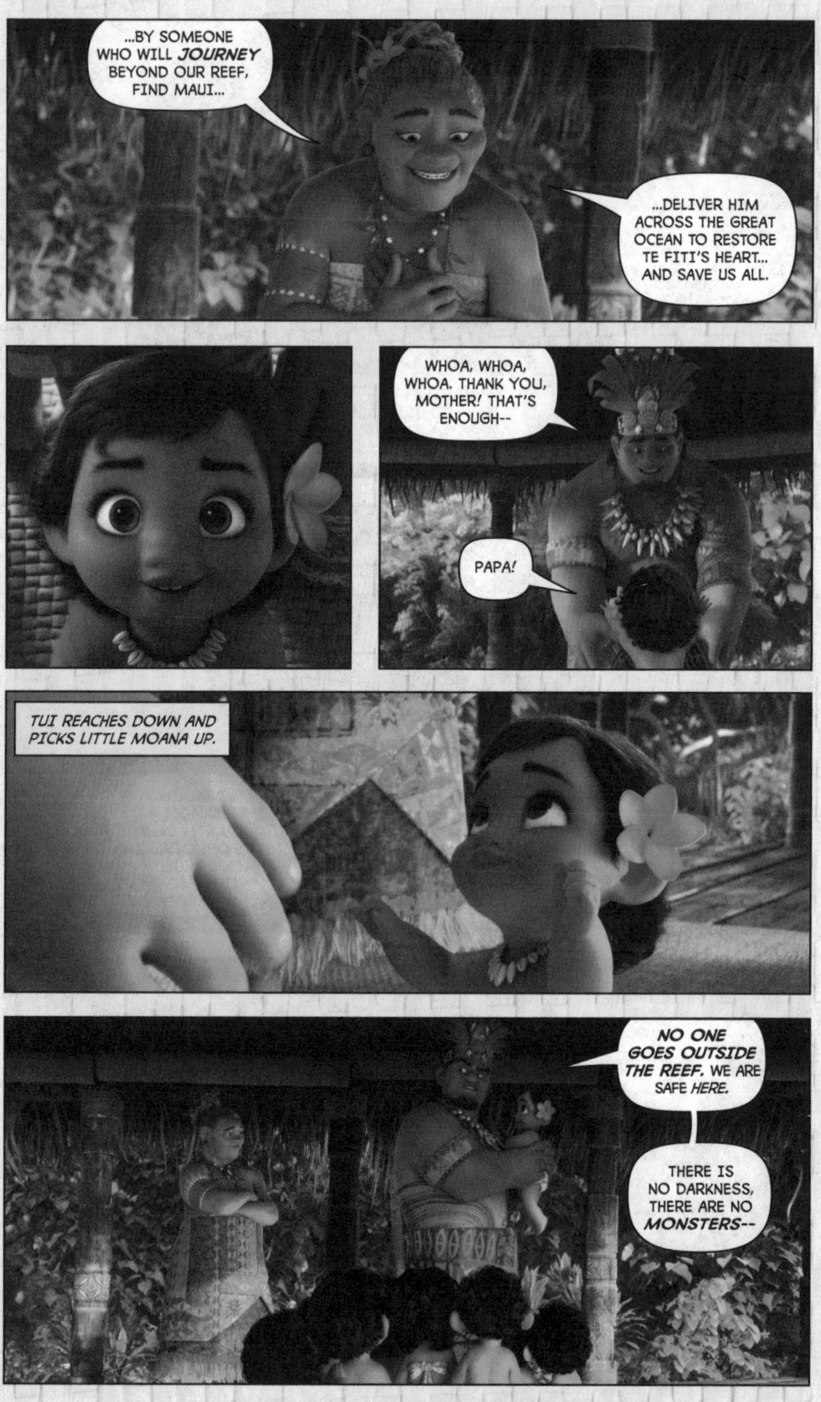
...BY SOMEONE WHO WILL JOURNEY BEYOND OUR REEF, FIND MAUI...
...DELIVER HIM ACROSS THE GREAT OCEAN TO RESTORE TE FITI'S HEART... AND SAVE US ALL.
WHOA, WHOA, WHOA. THANK YOU, MOTHER! THAT'S ENOUGH--
PAPA!
TUI REACHES DOWN AND PICKS LITTLE MOANA UP.
NO ONE GOES OUTSIDE THE REEF. WE ARE SAFE HERE.
THERE IS NO DARKNESS, THERE ARE NO MONSTERS--

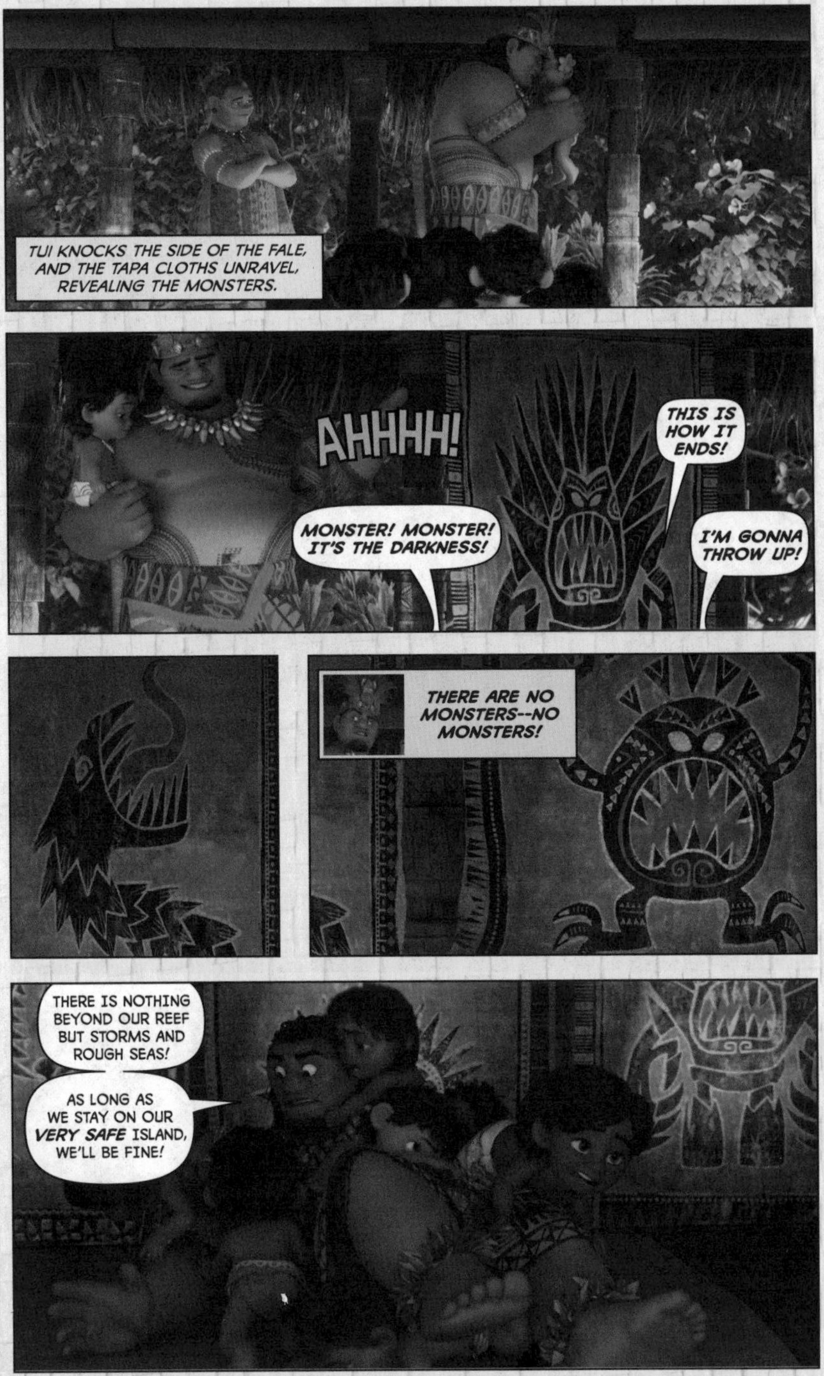

TUI KNOCKS THE SIDE OF THE FALE, AND THE TAPA CLOTHS UNRAVEL, REVEALING THE MONSTERS.
AHHHH!
MONSTER! MONSTER! IT'S THE DARKNESS!
THIS IS HOW IT ENDS!
I'M GONNA THROW UP!
THERE ARE NO MONSTERS--NO MONSTERS!
THERE IS NOTHING BEYOND OUR REEF BUT STORMS AND ROUGH SEAS!
AS LONG AS WE STAY ON OUR *VERY SAFE* ISLAND, WE'LL BE FINE!

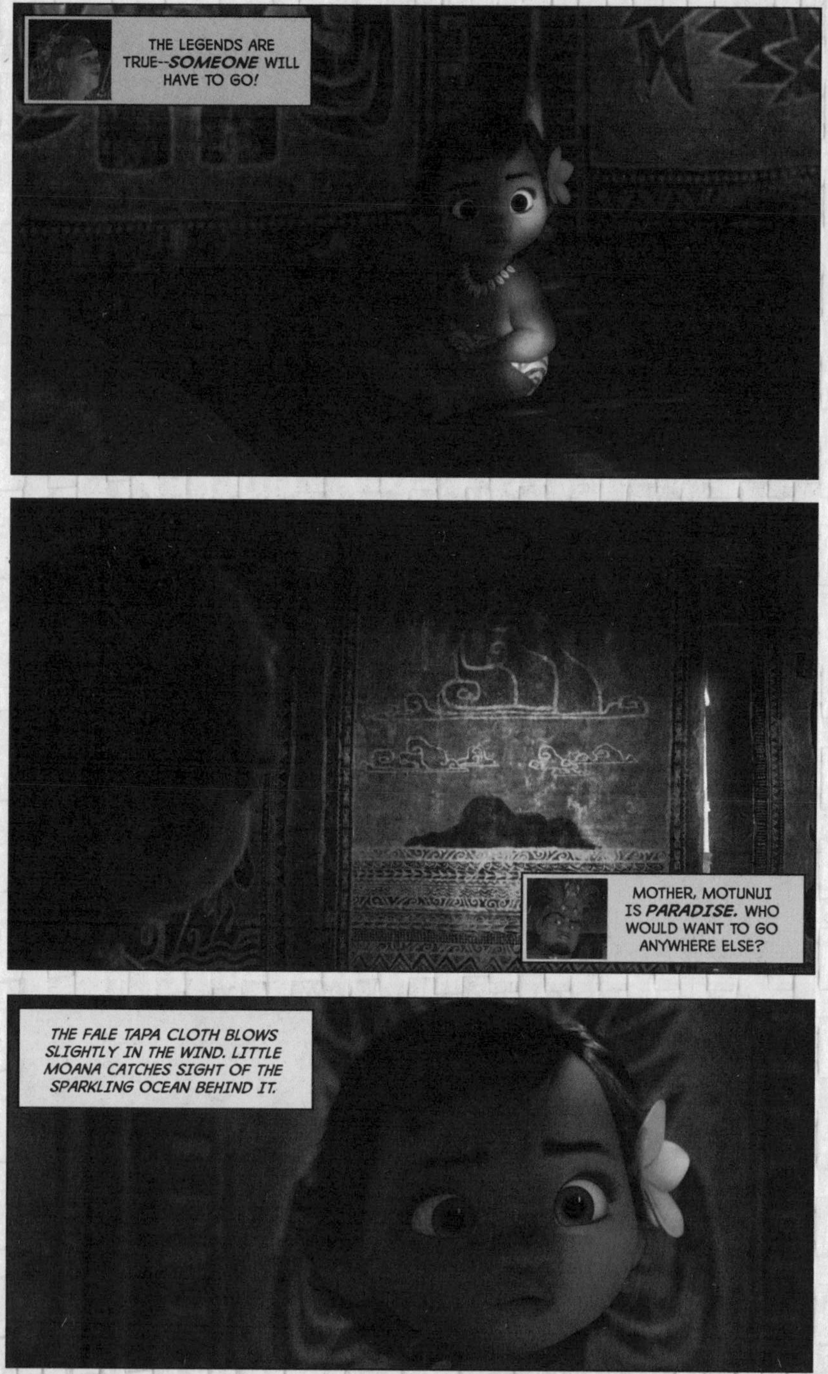
THE LEGENDS ARE TRUE--SOMEONE WILL HAVE TO GO!
MOTHER, MOTUNUI IS PARADISE. WHO WOULD WANT TO GO ANYWHERE ELSE?
THE FALE TAPA CLOTH BLOWS SLIGHTLY IN THE WIND. LITTLE MOANA CATCHES SIGHT OF THE SPARKLING OCEAN BEHIND IT.

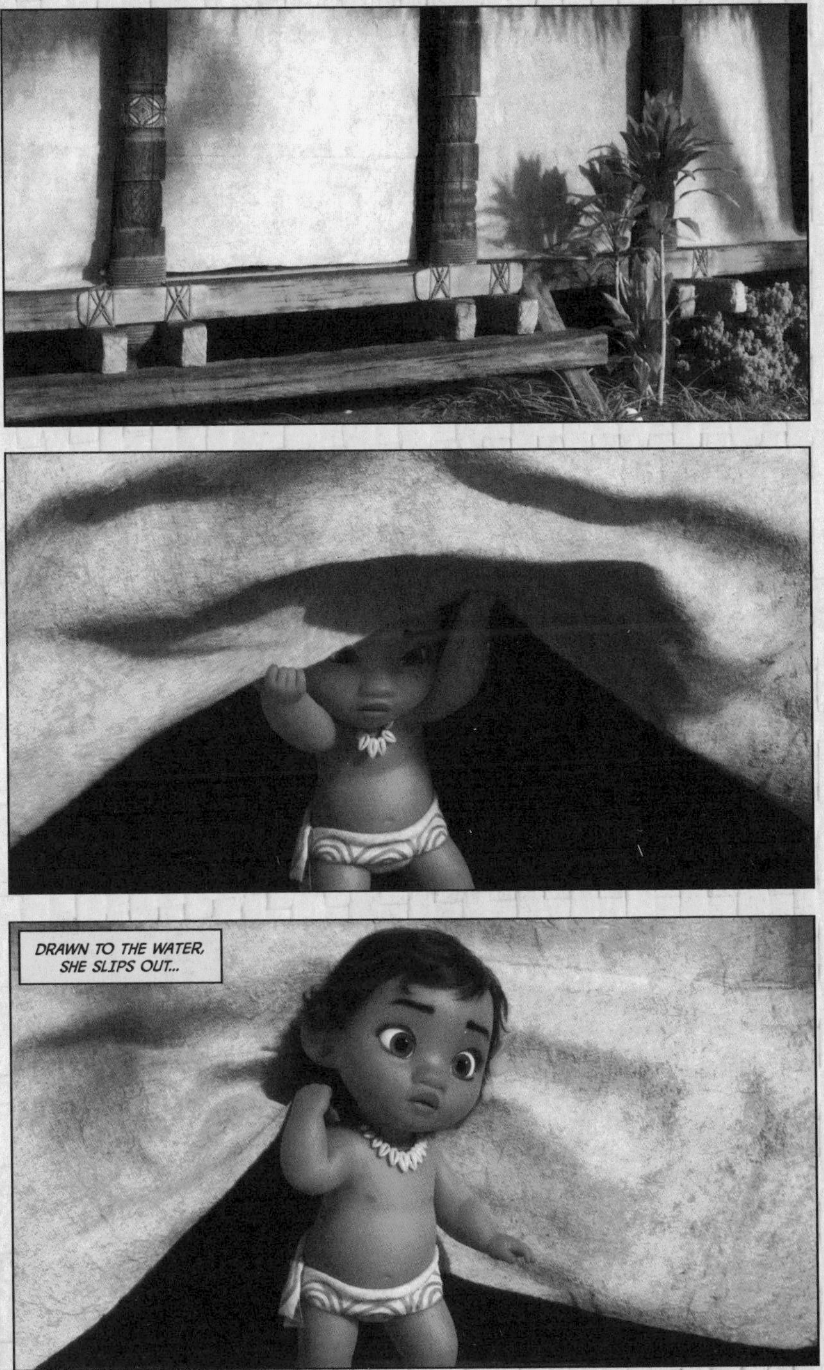
DRAWN TO THE WATER, SHE SLIPS OUT...

DISNEY

MOANA

Moana Meets the Ocean

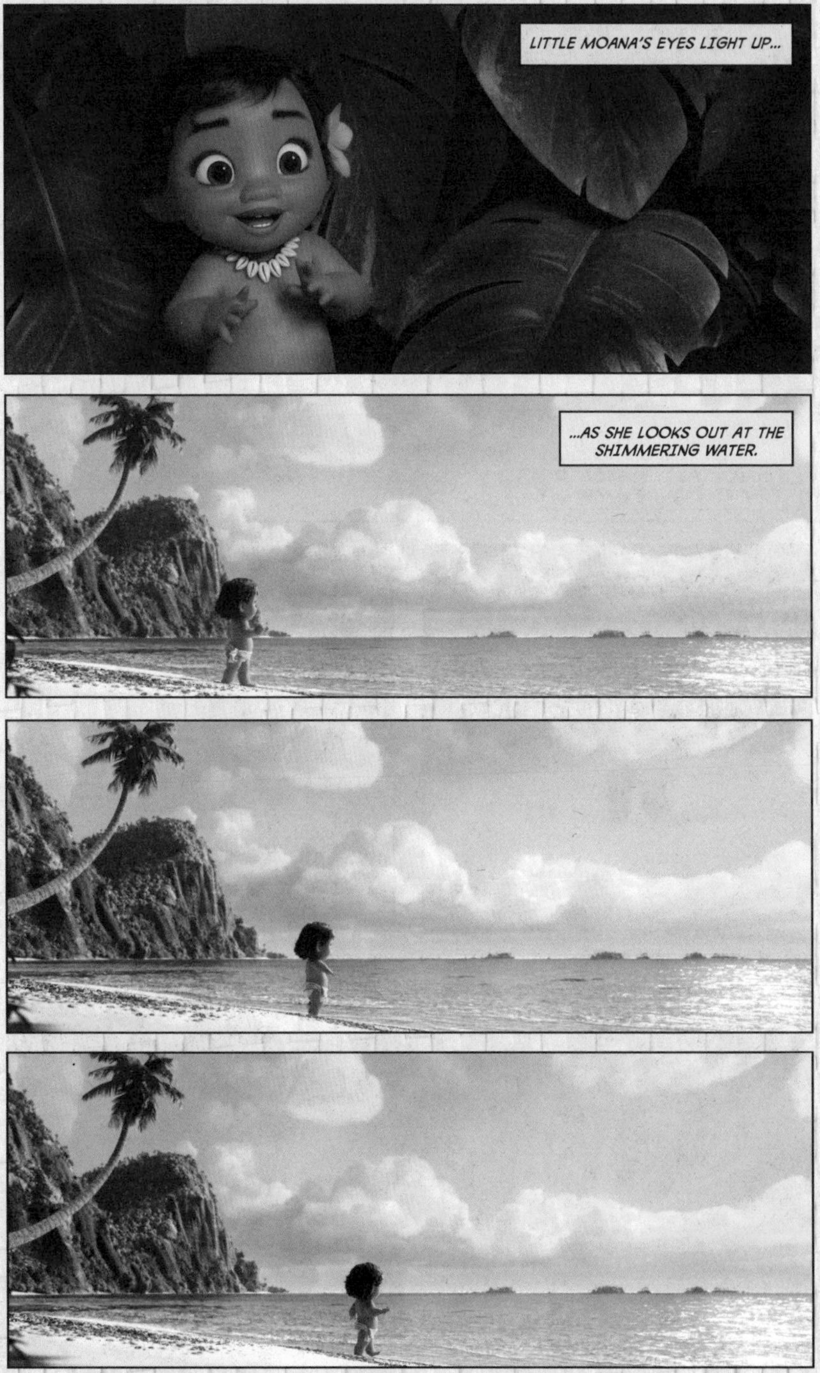
LITTLE MOANA'S EYES LIGHT UP...
...AS SHE LOOKS OUT AT THE SHIMMERING WATER.

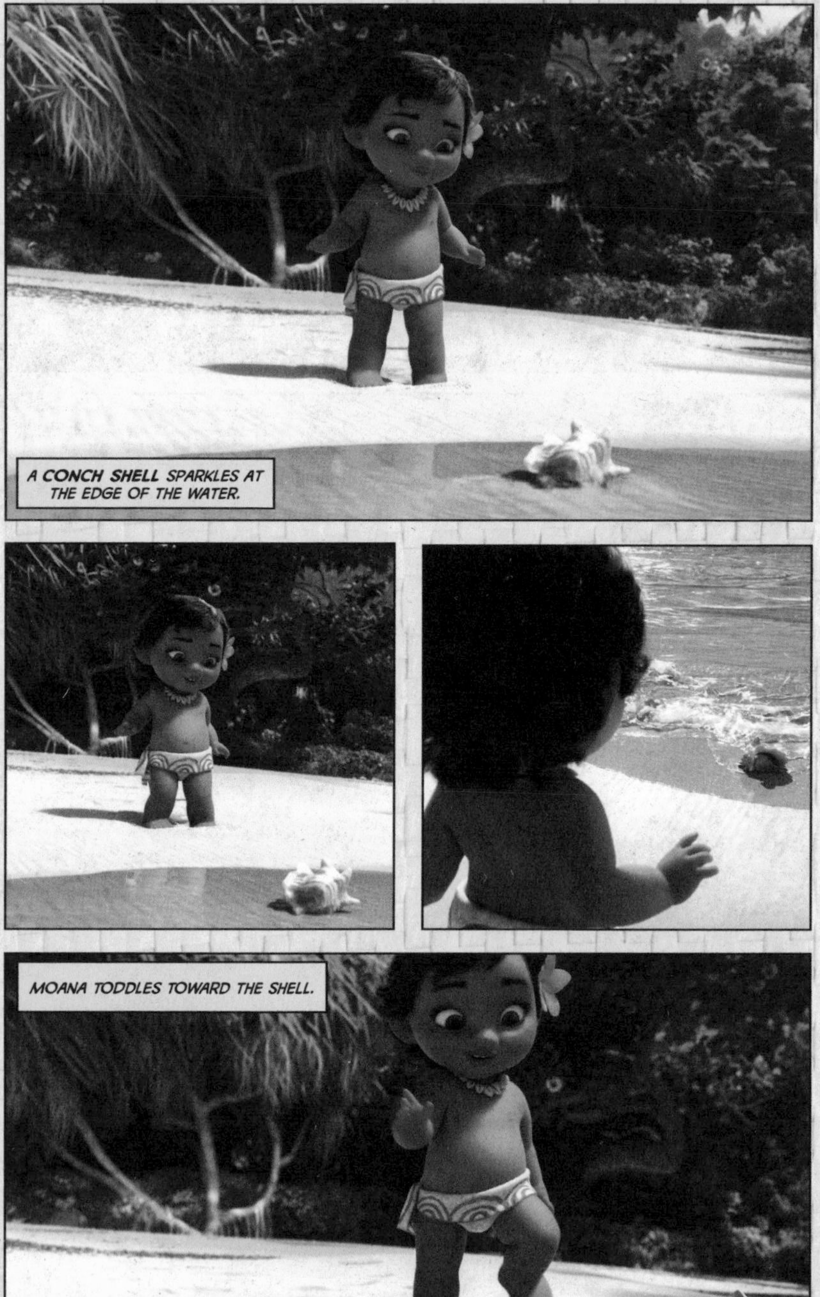
A **CONCH SHELL** SPARKLES AT THE EDGE OF THE WATER.
MOANA TODDLES TOWARD THE SHELL.

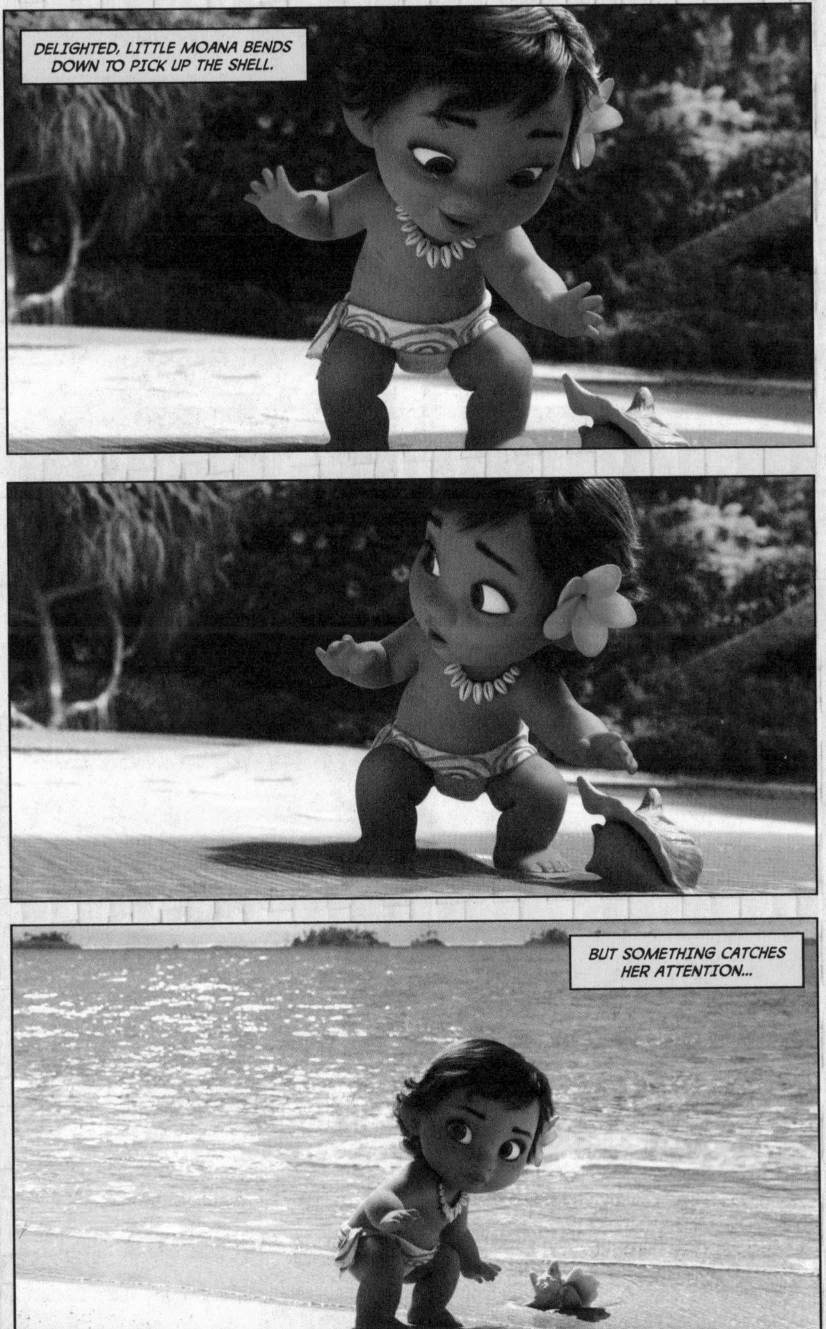
DELIGHTED, LITTLE MOANA BENDS DOWN TO PICK UP THE SHELL.
BUT SOMETHING CATCHES HER ATTENTION...

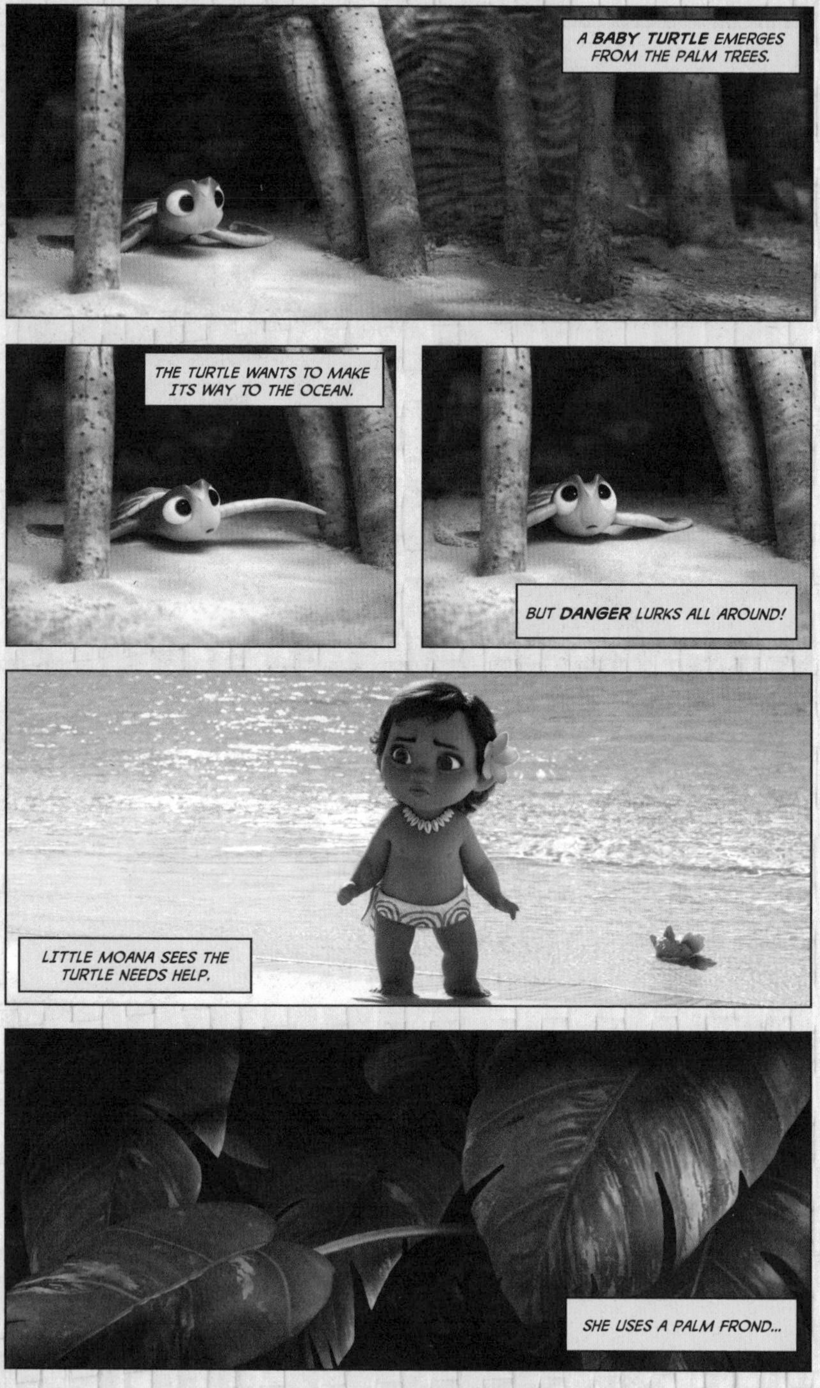
A BABY TURTLE EMERGES FROM THE PALM TREES.
THE TURTLE WANTS TO MAKE ITS WAY TO THE OCEAN.
BUT DANGER LURKS ALL AROUND!
LITTLE MOANA SEES THE TURTLE NEEDS HELP.
SHE USES A PALM FROND...

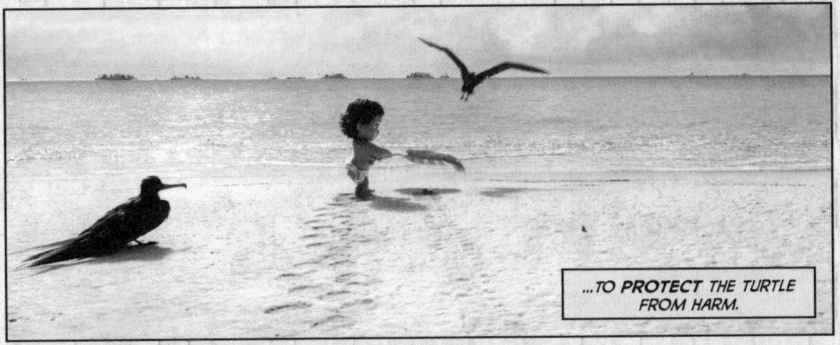
...TO PROTECT THE TURTLE FROM HARM.

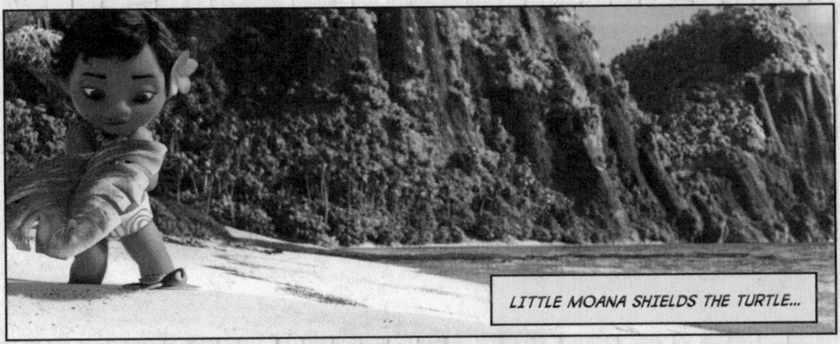
LITTLE MOANA SHIELDS THE TURTLE...

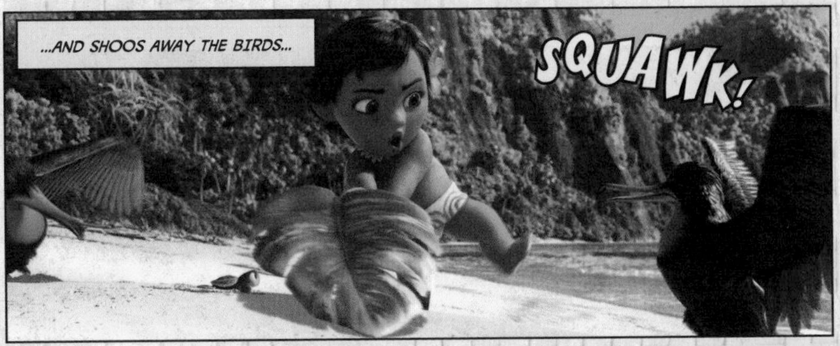
...AND SHOOS AWAY THE BIRDS...
SQUAWK!

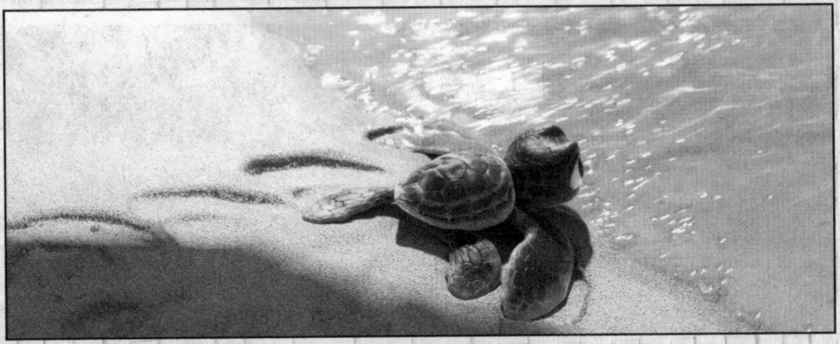

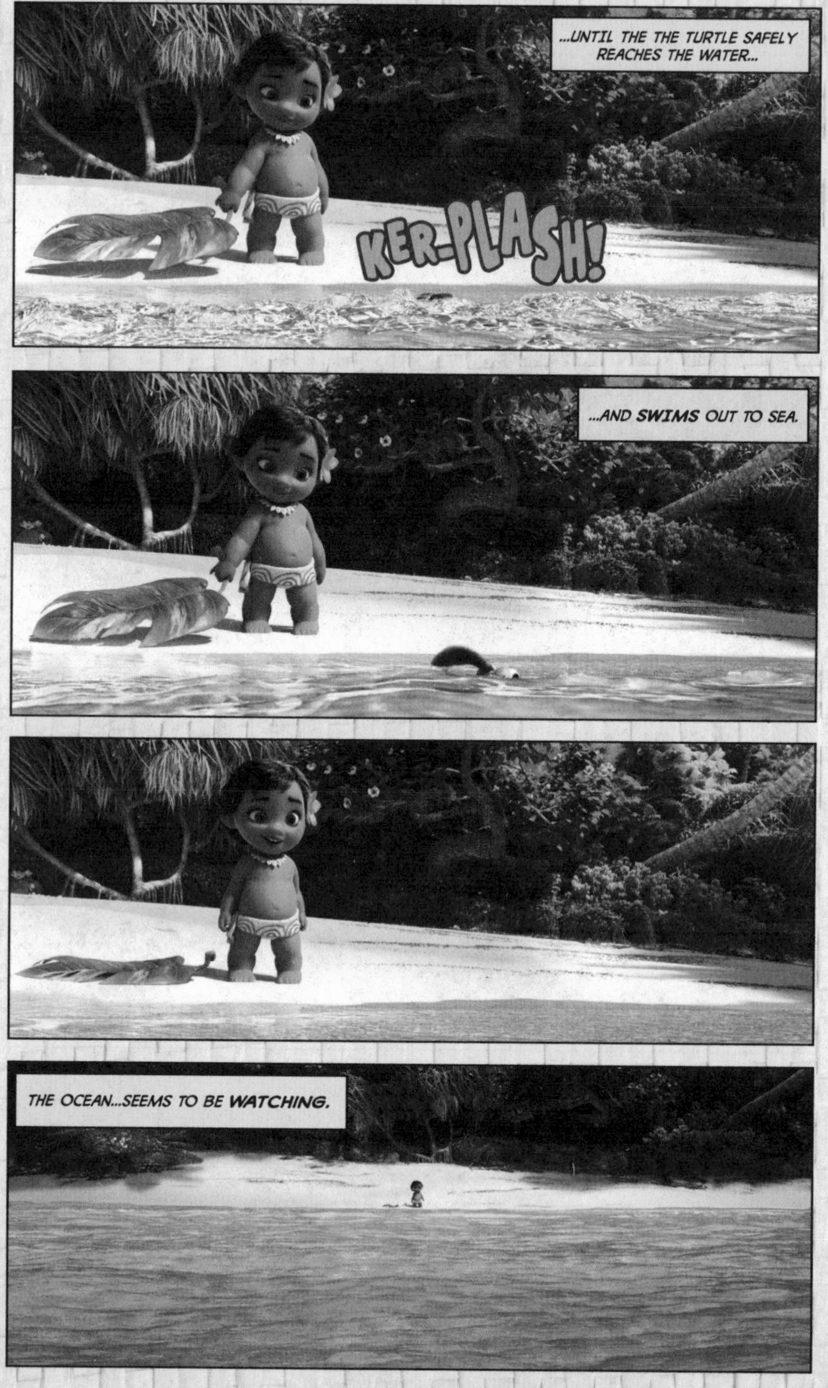
...UNTIL THE THE TURTLE SAFELY REACHES THE WATER...
KER-PLASH!
...AND SWIMS OUT TO SEA.
THE OCEAN...SEEMS TO BE WATCHING.

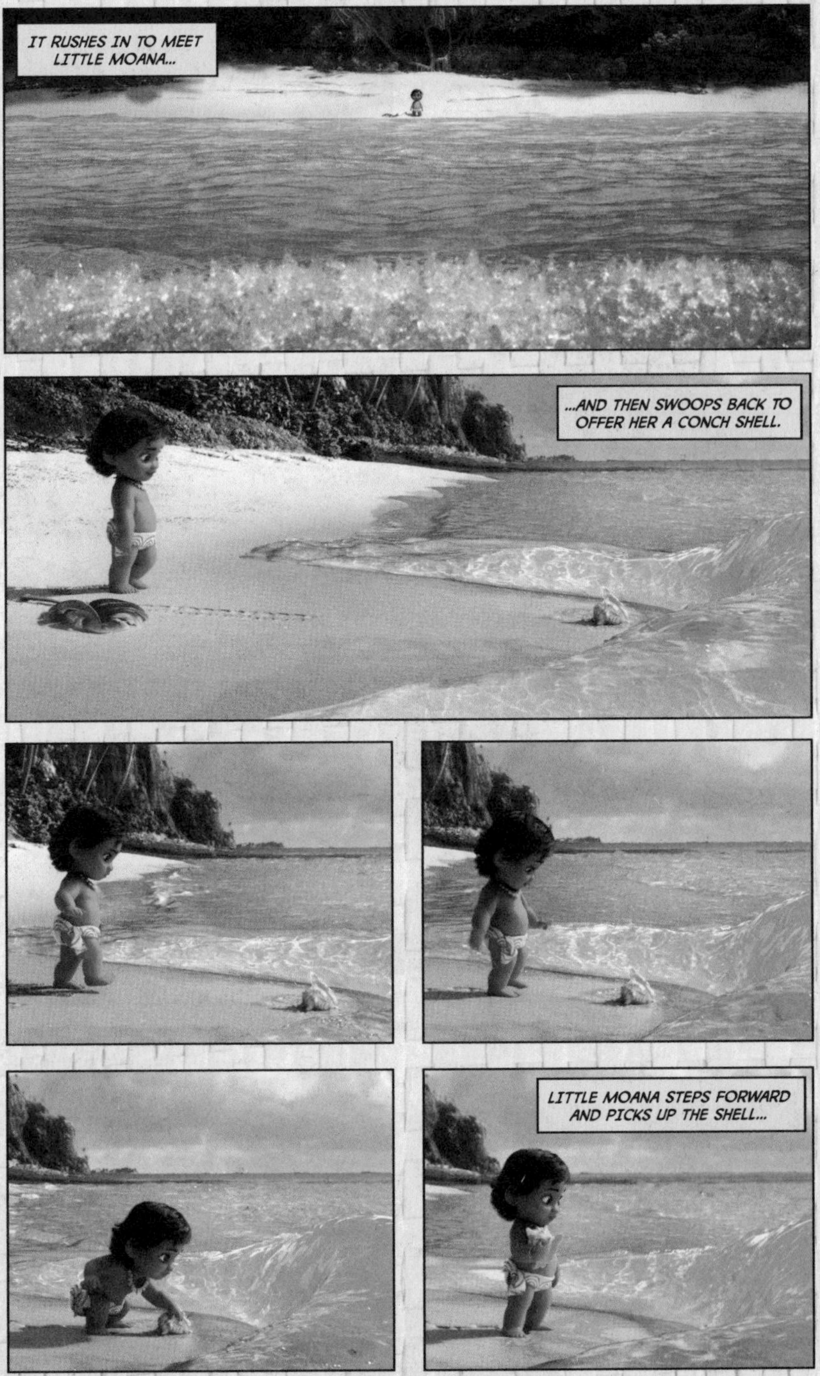
IT RUSHES IN TO MEET LITTLE MOANA...
...AND THEN SWOOPS BACK TO OFFER HER A CONCH SHELL.
LITTLE MOANA STEPS FORWARD AND PICKS UP THE SHELL...

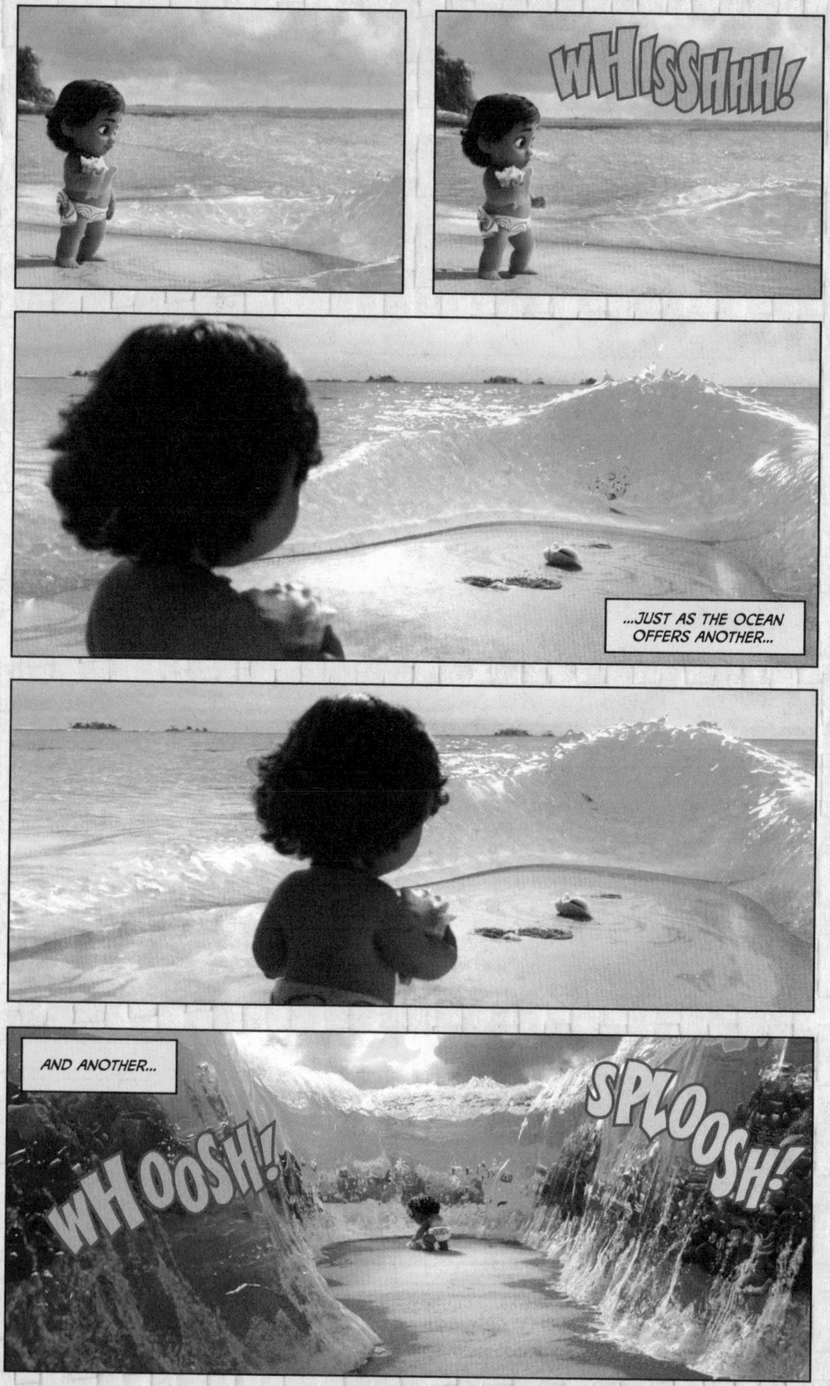
WHISSHHH!
...JUST AS THE OCEAN OFFERS ANOTHER...
AND ANOTHER...
WHOOSH!
SPLOOSH!

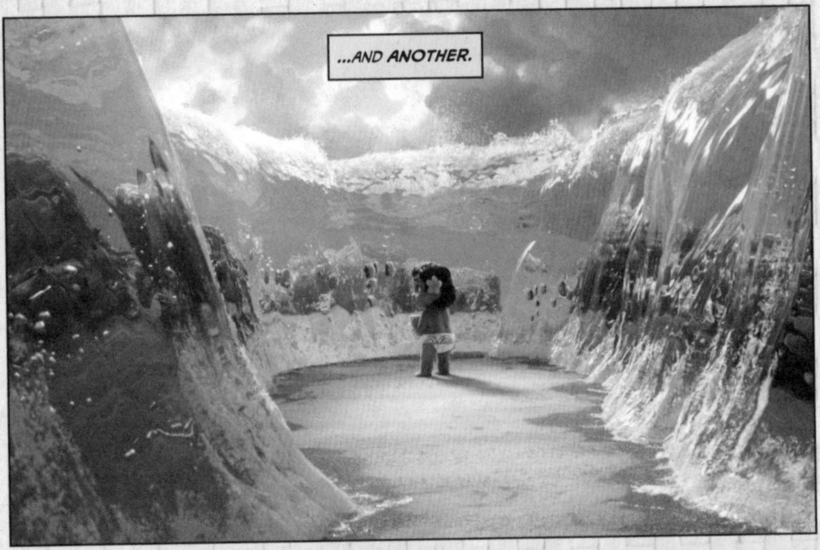
...AND ANOTHER.

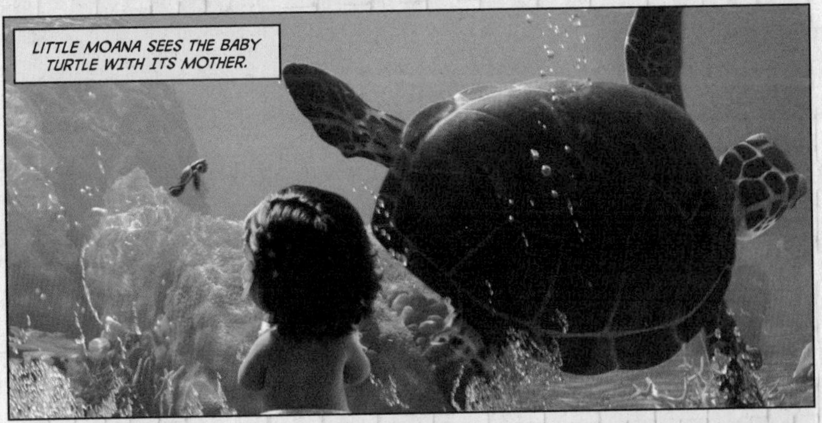
LITTLE MOANA SEES THE BABY TURTLE WITH ITS MOTHER.

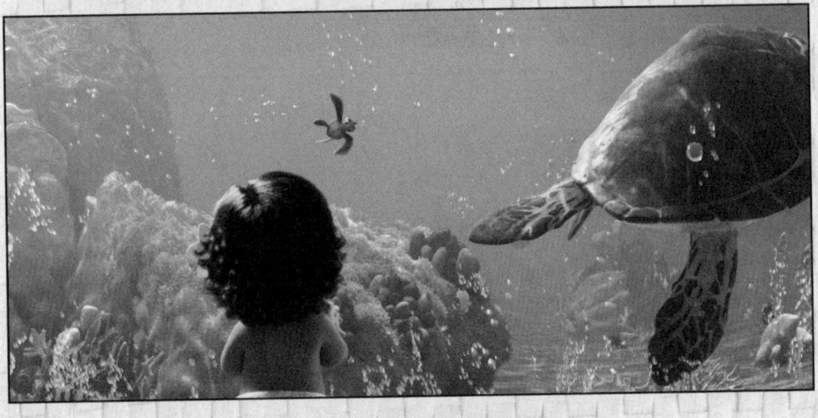

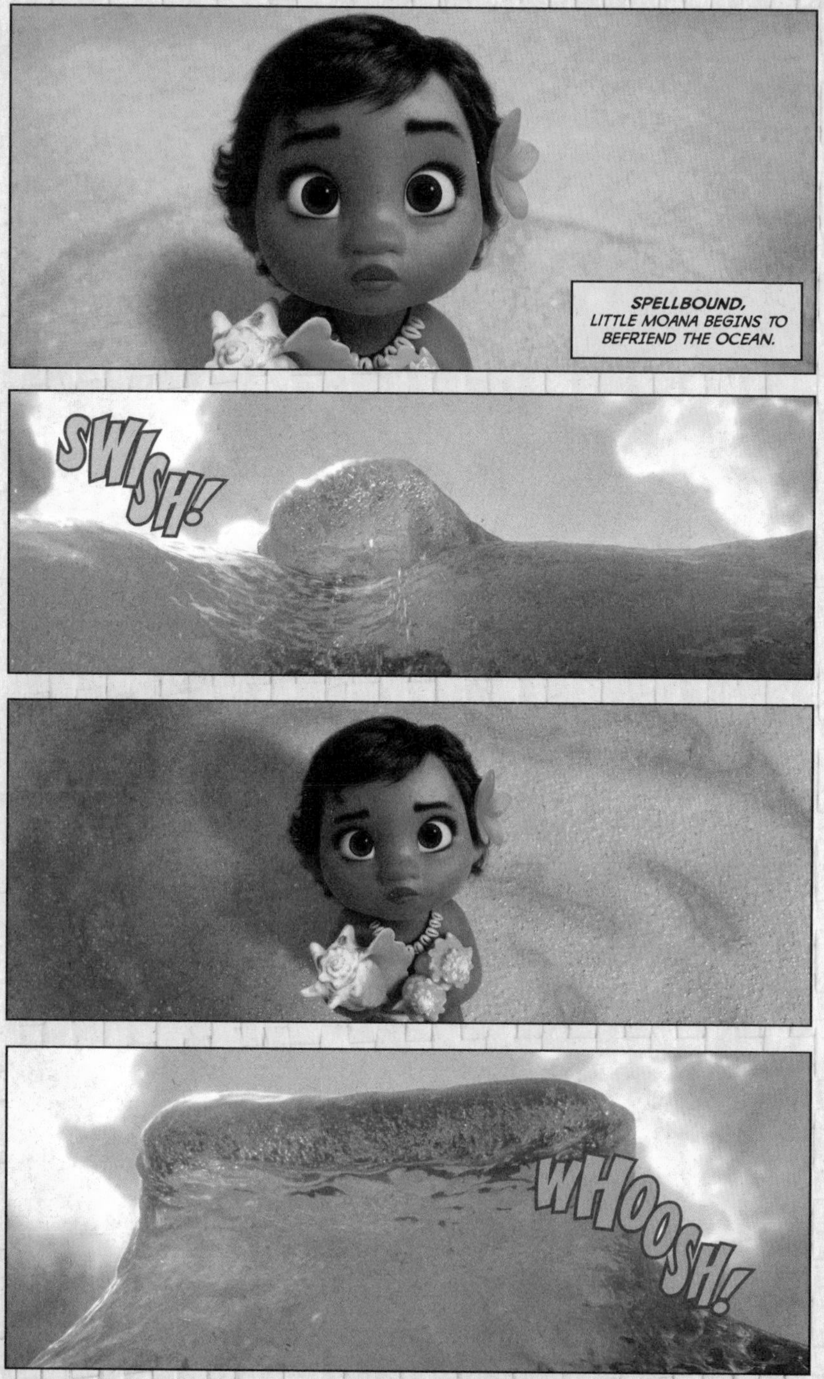
SPELLBOUND,
LITTLE MOANA BEGINS TO
BEFRIEND THE OCEAN.
SWISH!
WHOOSH!

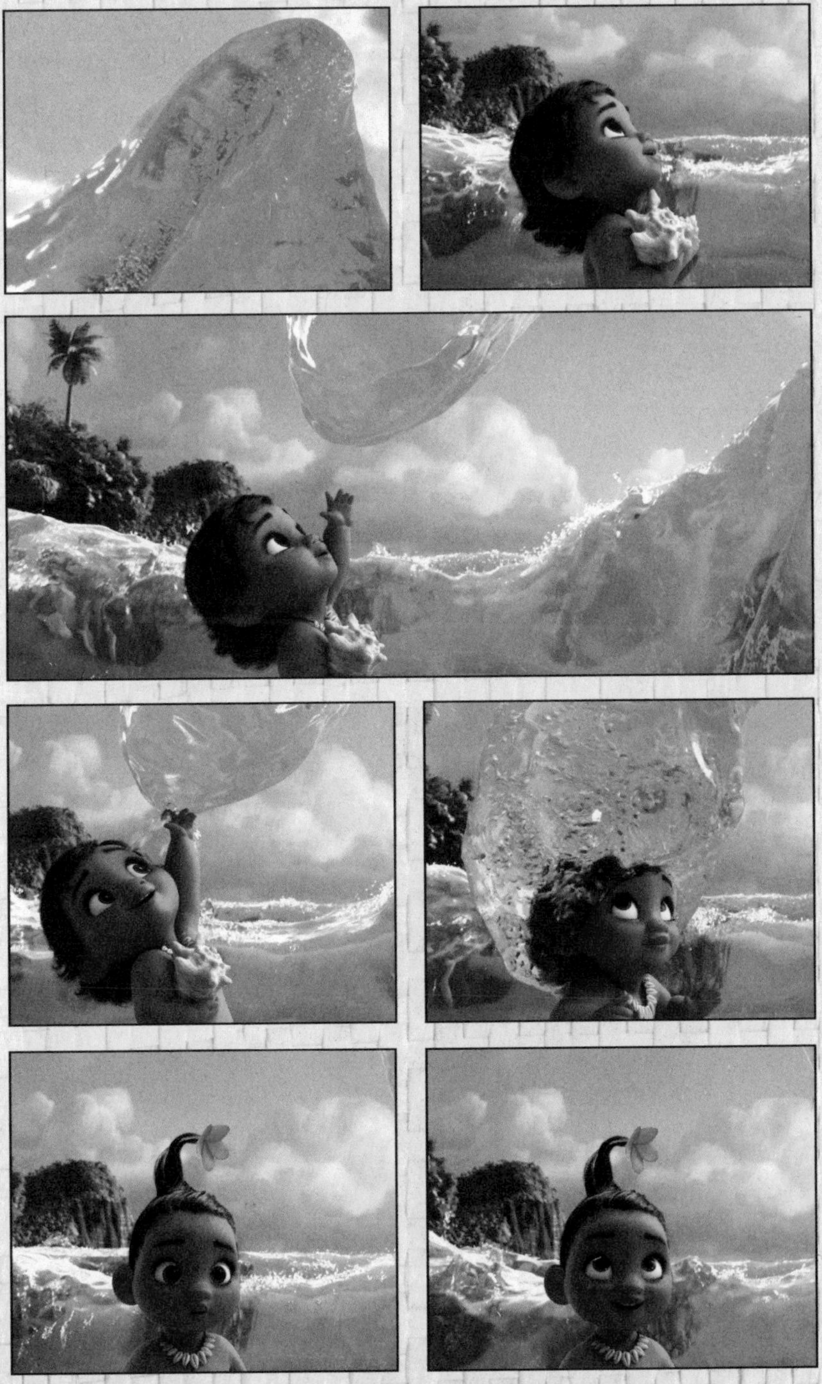

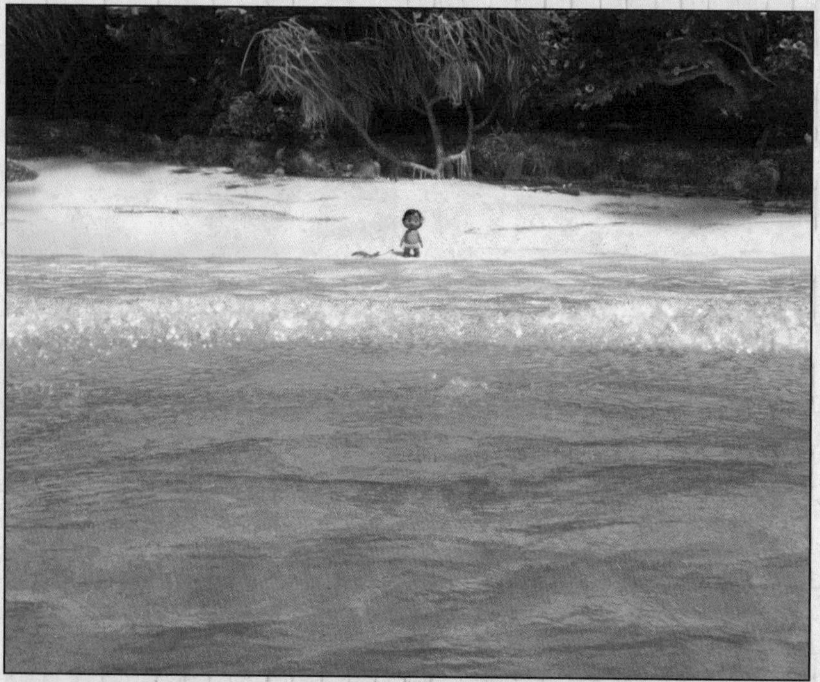

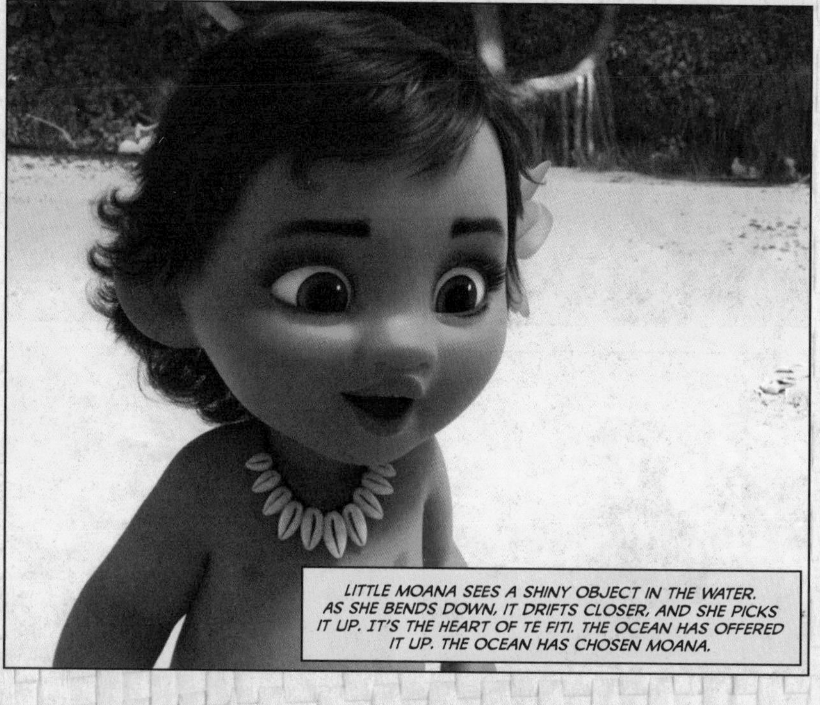
LITTLE MOANA SEES A SHINY OBJECT IN THE WATER. AS SHE BENDS DOWN, IT DRIFTS CLOSER, AND SHE PICKS IT UP. IT'S THE HEART OF TE FITI. THE OCEAN HAS OFFERED IT UP. THE OCEAN HAS CHOSEN MOANA.

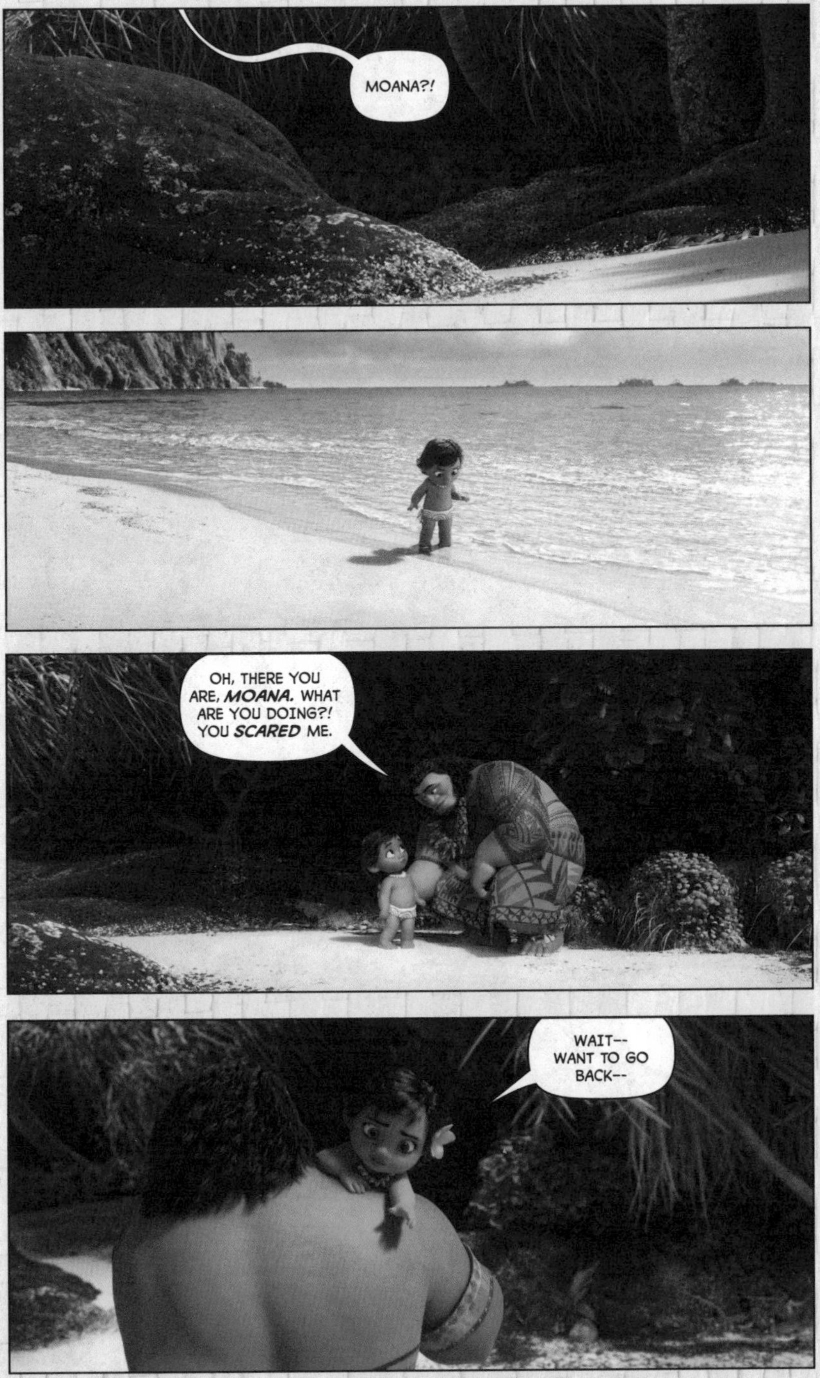
MOANA?!
OH, THERE YOU ARE, MOANA. WHAT ARE YOU DOING?! YOU SCARED ME.
WAIT-- WANT TO GO BACK--

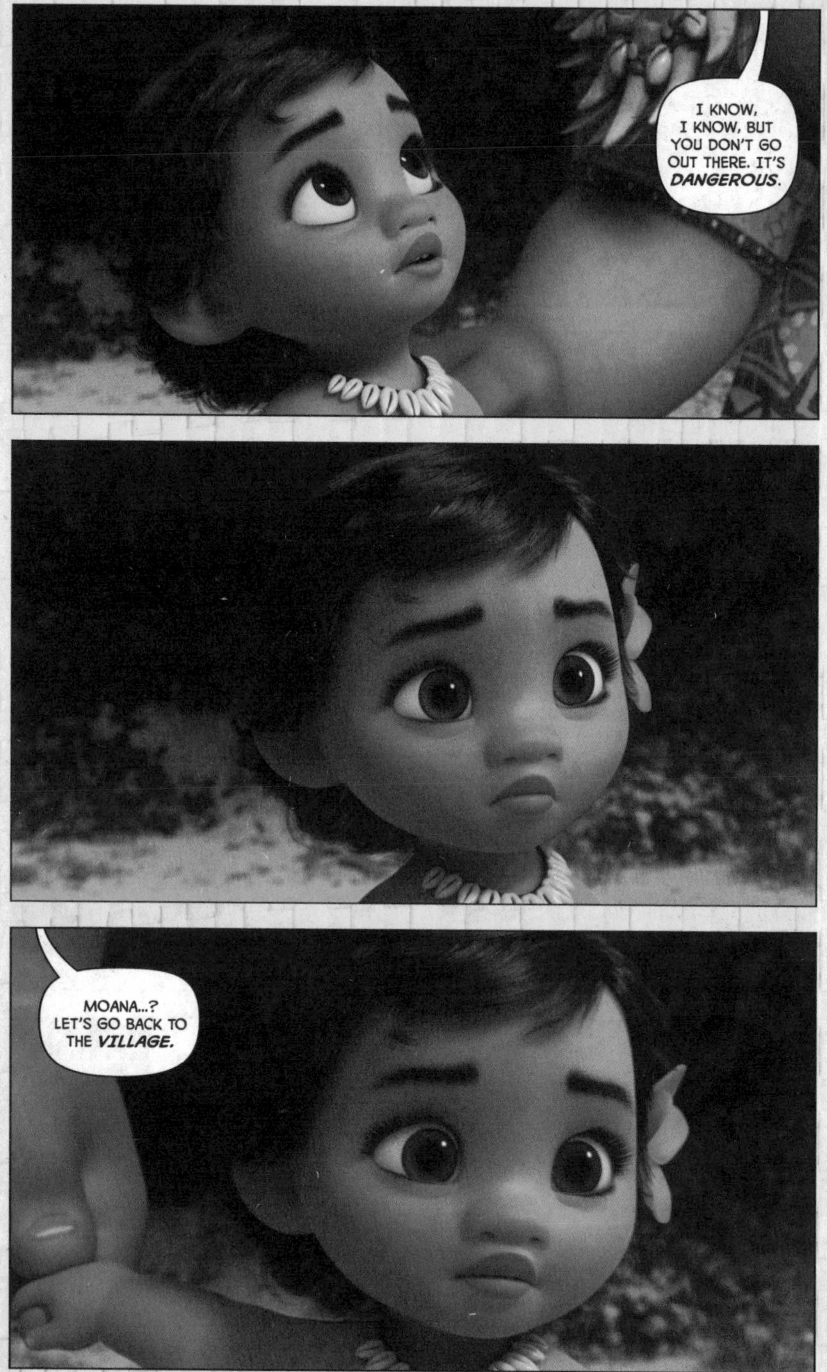
I KNOW, I KNOW, BUT YOU DON'T GO OUT THERE. IT'S *DANGEROUS*.
MOANA...? LET'S GO BACK TO THE *VILLAGE.*

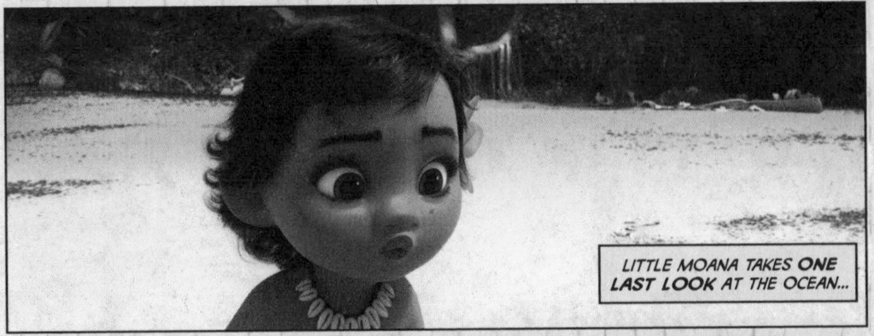
LITTLE MOANA TAKES ONE LAST LOOK AT THE OCEAN...

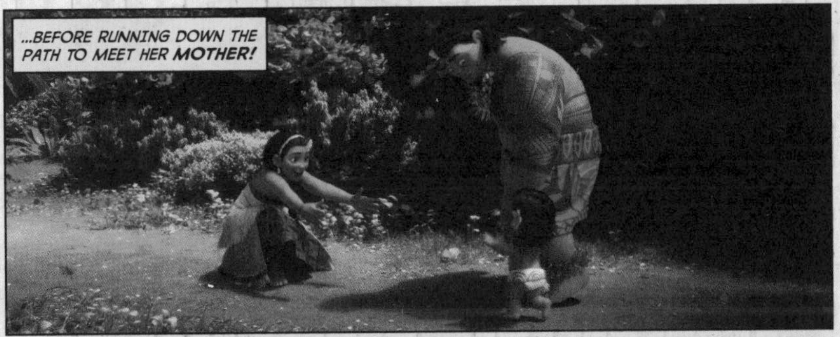
...BEFORE RUNNING DOWN THE PATH TO MEET HER MOTHER!

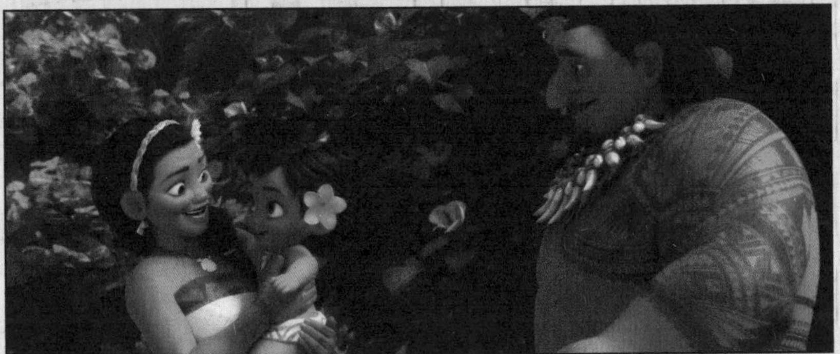

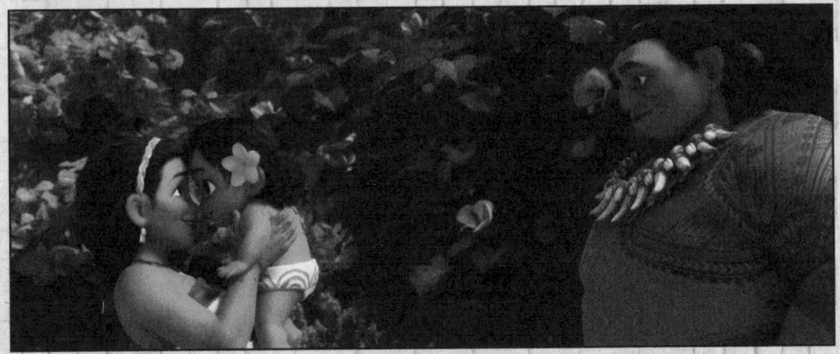

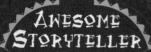

AWESOME STORYTELLER

SCRIPT: TEA ORSI
ART: ANNA CATTISH
LETTERS: CHRIS DICKEY

Little Moana wants to listen to her favorite story once again...

GRAMMA?!?

HUH?!? WHERE'S GRAMMA TALA?

WHAT DO WE DO?

I KNOW!

I CAN TELL IT!

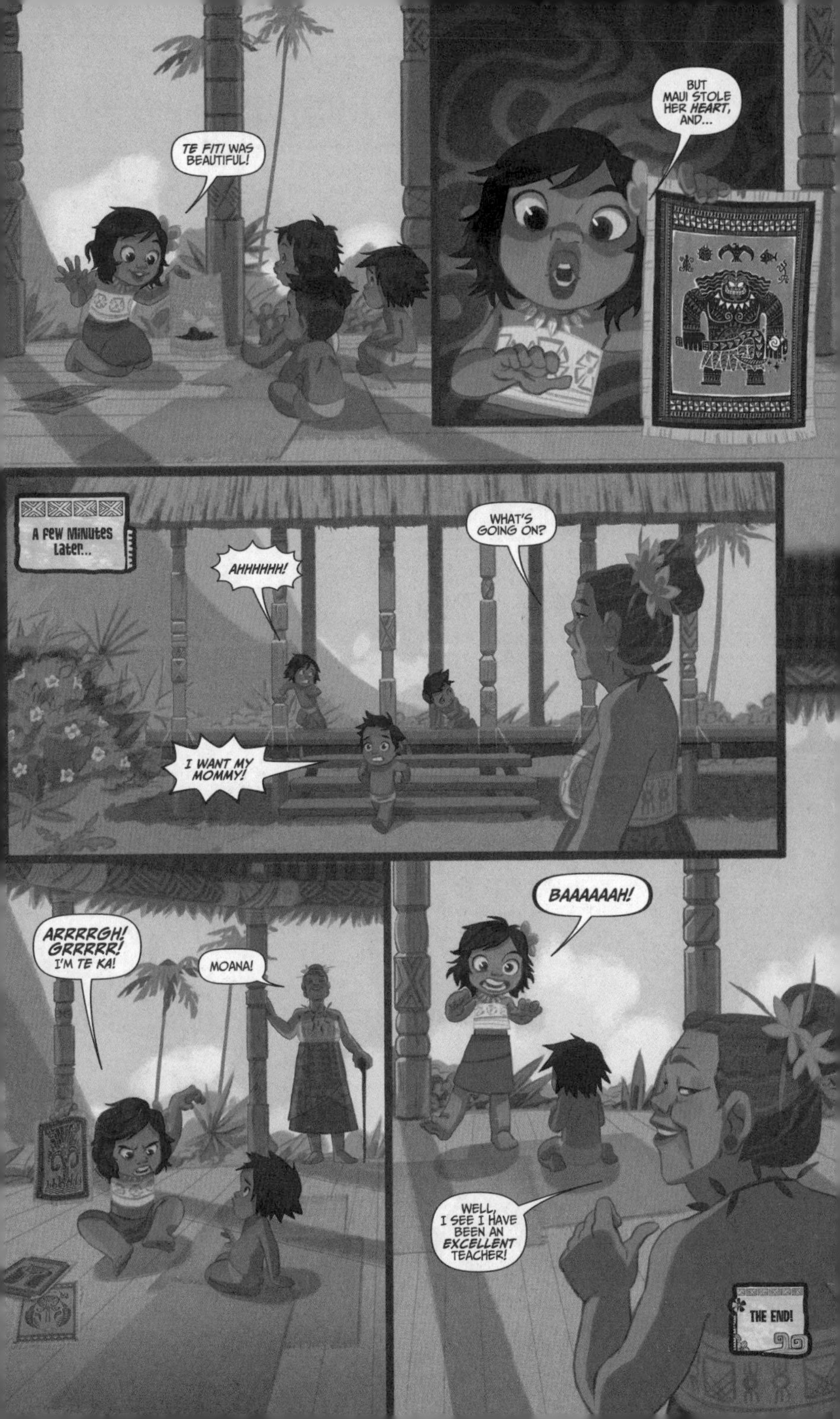
TE FITI WAS BEAUTIFUL!
BUT MAUI STOLE HER HEART, AND...
A FEW MINUTES LATER...
AHHHHHH!
WHAT'S GOING ON?
I WANT MY MOMMY!
ARRRRGH! GRRRRR! I'M TE KA!
MOANA!
BAAAAAAH!
WELL, I SEE I HAVE BEEN AN EXCELLENT TEACHER!
THE END!

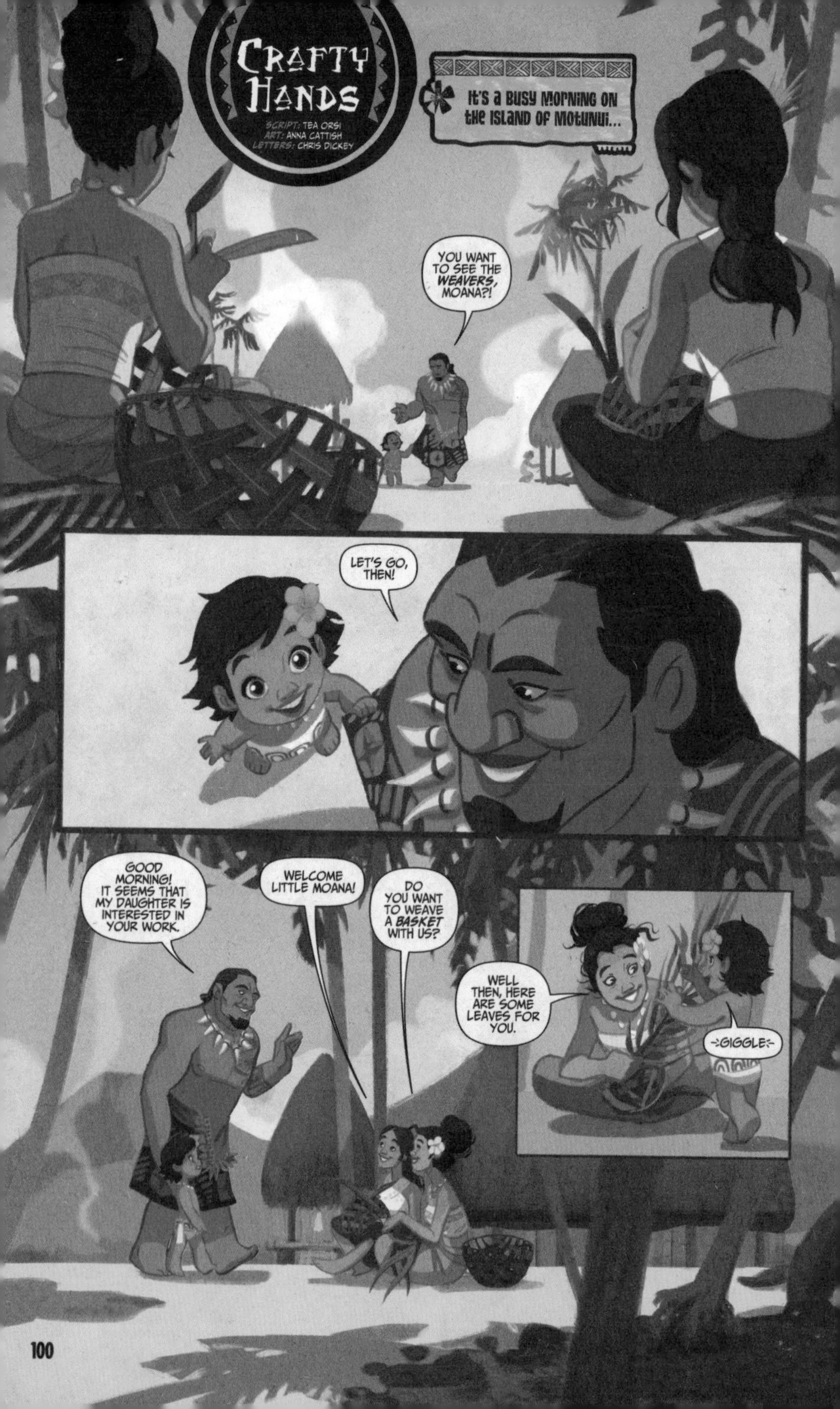

CRAFTY HANDS
SCRIPT: TEA ORSI
ART: ANNA CATTISH
LETTERS: CHRIS DICKEY
IT'S A BUSY MORNING ON THE ISLAND OF MOTUNUI...
YOU WANT TO SEE THE WEAVERS, MOANA?!
LET'S GO, THEN!
GOOD MORNING! IT SEEMS THAT MY DAUGHTER IS INTERESTED IN YOUR WORK.
WELCOME LITTLE MOANA!
DO YOU WANT TO WEAVE A BASKET WITH US?
WELL THEN, HERE ARE SOME LEAVES FOR YOU.
-GIGGLE-

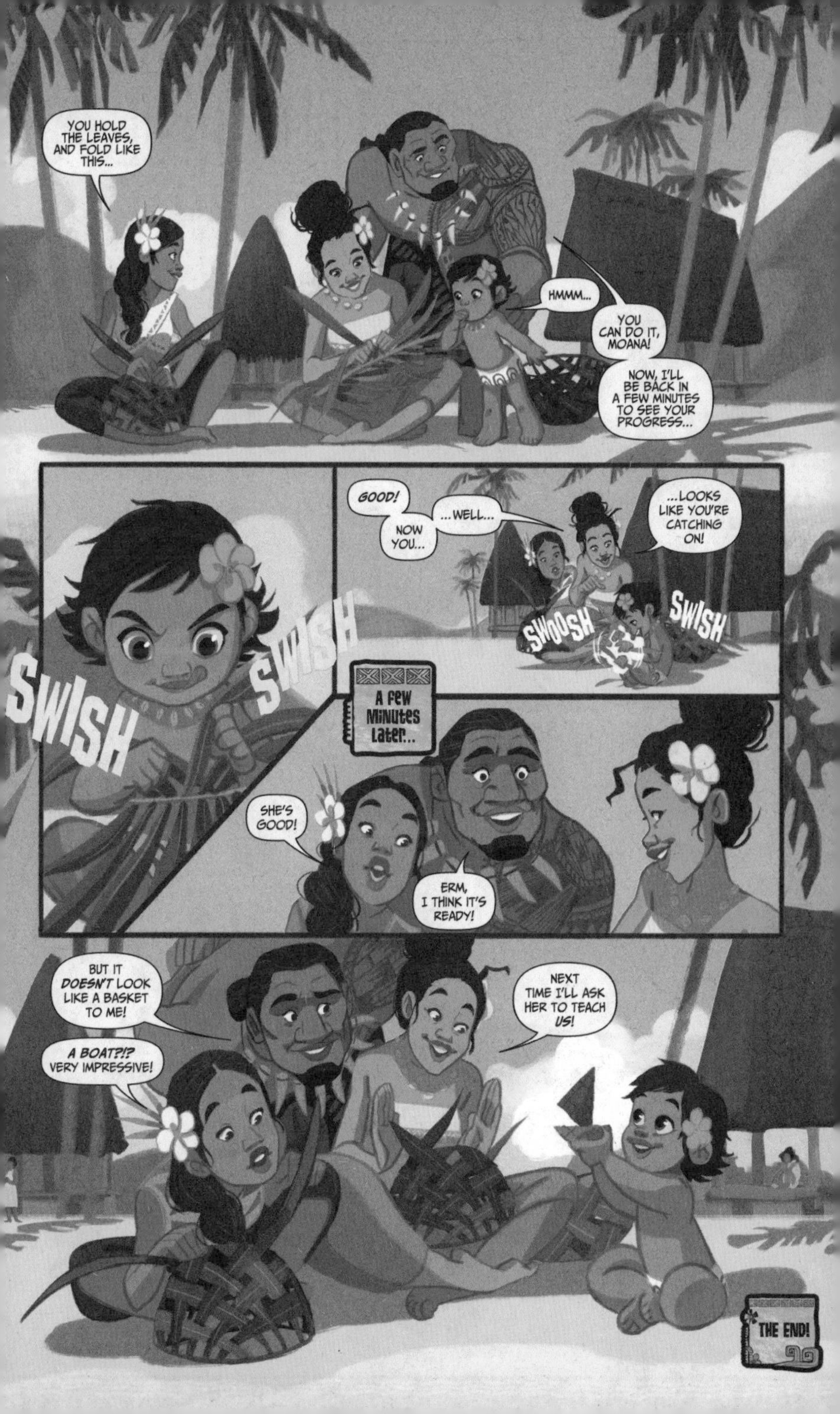
YOU HOLD THE LEAVES, AND FOLD LIKE THIS...
HMMM...
YOU CAN DO IT, MOANA!
NOW, I'LL BE BACK IN A FEW MINUTES TO SEE YOUR PROGRESS...
SWISH
SWISH
GOOD!
NOW YOU...
...WELL...
...LOOKS LIKE YOU'RE CATCHING ON!
SWOOSH
SWISH
A Few Minutes Later...
SHE'S GOOD!
ERM, I THINK IT'S READY!
BUT IT DOESN'T LOOK LIKE A BASKET TO ME!
A BOAT?!? VERY IMPRESSIVE!
NEXT TIME I'LL ASK HER TO TEACH US!
THE END!

MAKE A BEAUTIFUL HEAD HEI

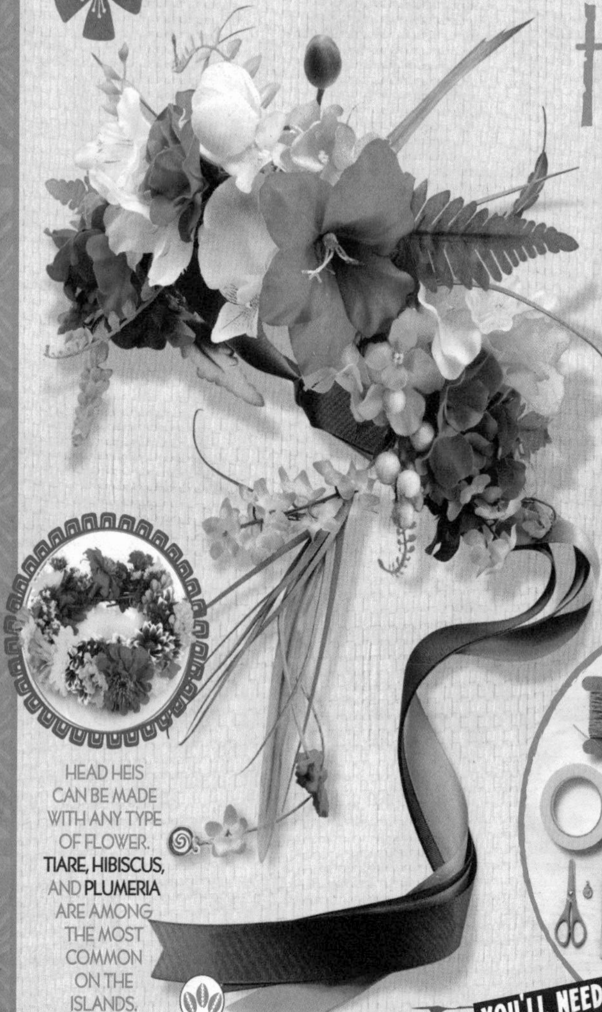

Head heis are wrapped and worn by Tahitians and other Pacific Islanders on special occasions. To make one, you just need colorful FLOWERS, SOME LEAVES, a bit of STRING, and a lot of CREATIVITY.

HEAD HEIS CAN BE MADE WITH ANY TYPE OF FLOWER. **TIARE, HIBISCUS,** AND **PLUMERIA** ARE AMONG THE MOST COMMON ON THE ISLANDS.

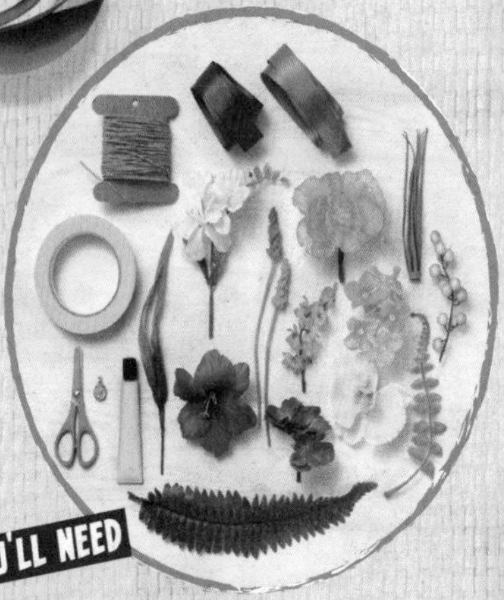

YOU'LL NEED

- Fabric Flowers, Berries, and Leaves
- Green Satin Ribbon
- Green Ribbon
- Paper String
- Green Rafia
- Scissors
- Paper Tape
- Glue
- Tiny Metal Medal

INSPIRED BY THE SEA

Decorate your crown by gluing some little shells among the flowers and leaves.

IT'S YOUR TURN! Follow the steps below and make your own hei using multicolored fabric flowers.

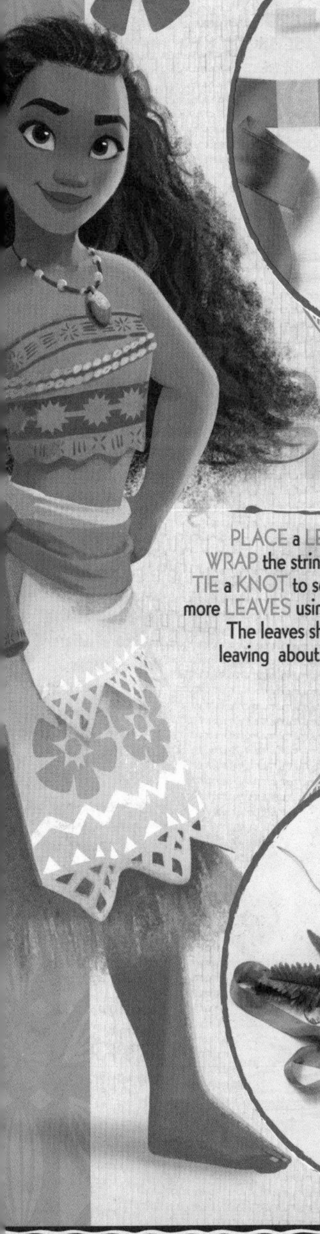

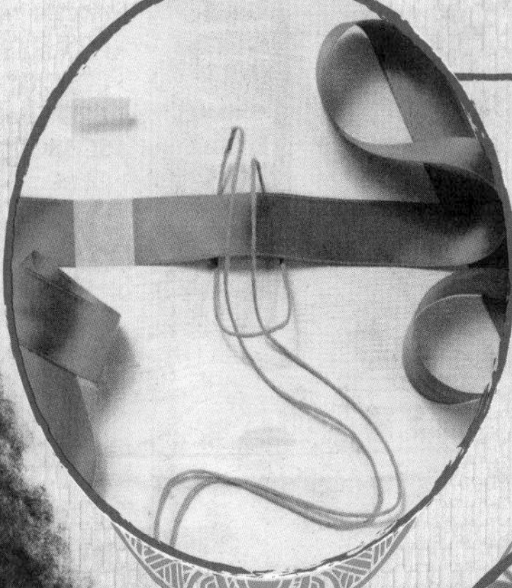

STEP 1

CUT a piece of green ribbon (about 170 cm) and TAPE one of its ends to the table. Then, CUT a piece of STRING, twice as long as the ribbon, and TIE it around the ribbon at about 60-65 cm from the taped end.

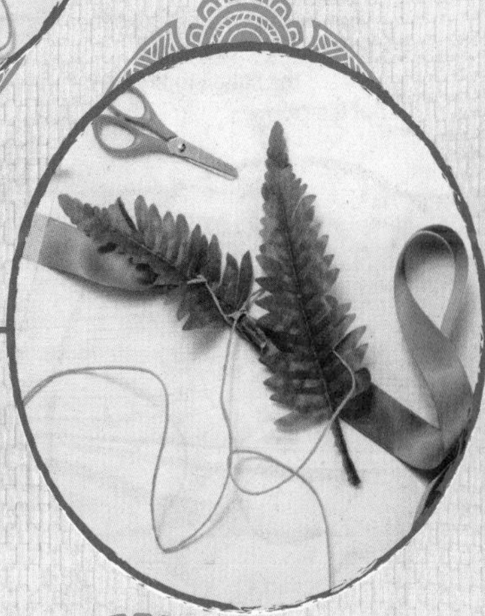

STEP 2

PLACE a LEAF on the ribbon and WRAP the string twice around it, then TIE a KNOT to secure it. ADD and TIE more LEAVES using the same technique. The leaves should cover the ribbon, leaving about 40 cm from each end.

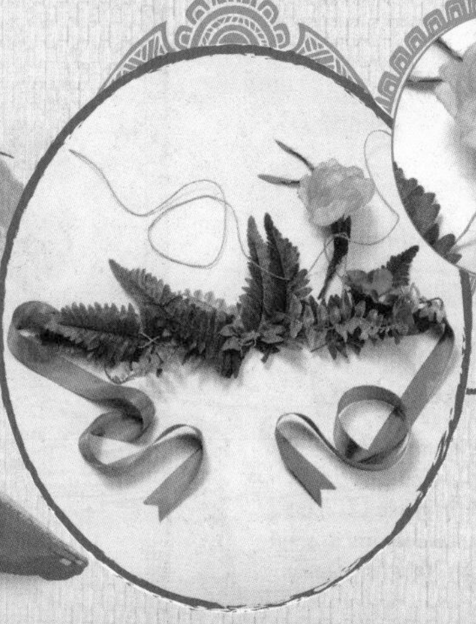

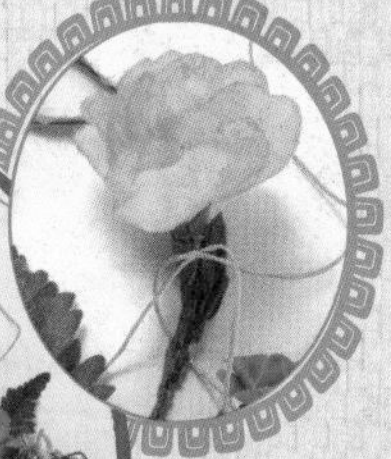

WRAP THE PAPER STRING AROUND THE FLOWERS' STEMS TO SECURE THEM TO THE CROWN.

STEP 3

Start ADDING IN flowers and berries by TYING them onto the leaves. Remember that the biggest flowers should ideally be placed at about 2/3 of the ribbon.

Extra Idea

Paper flowers look great too. Here's how to make them!

- GREEN TAPE
- FLORIST'S WIRE
- COLORED CREPE PAPER
- SCISSORS
- GLUE
- PETAL AND LEAF TEMPLATES

STEP 4

Now tie the ends of your ribbon into a KNOT or two and GLUE the ribbon to the back of the crown.

STEP 5

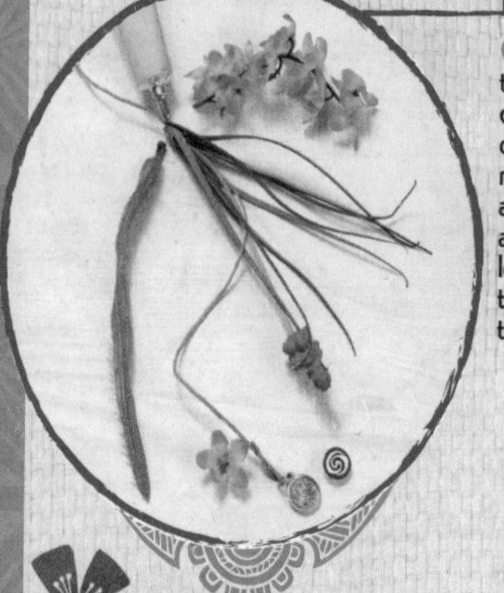

GLUE some rafia to another piece of string. INSERT one end into the medal, GLUE on a little flower and some tiny leaves, and TIE this decoration to the crown.

PISTIL

CUT one strip of yellow paper (about 2.5 x 8 cm) and one red (2 x 10 cm). CUT FRINGES all along them. PUT glue on the wire and WRAP the yellow fringe around its top. GLUE ON the red fringe and wrap it too, going a bit more down.

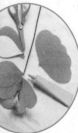

PETALS

Using the petal template, CUT OUT five petals from a piece of differently colored paper. GLUE them onto one another as shown and then on the stem, around the pistil.

FLOWERS

WRAP some green tape around the base of the petals, then add the leaf that you cut out using the template and keep WRAPPING the tape around it and the stem. OPEN the petals to obtain a nice flower.

Blossoms Everywhere!

Pacific Islanders also wear flowers behind their EARS or braid them into LEIS, the floral wreaths they use to greet visitors and returning family.

Your Head Hei is ready to be worn!

WATER OR LAND?

Moana is torn between her love for her island and her calling to the sea. **TAKE** this quiz to find out if you are more suited to **WATER** or **LAND**.

3

A souvenir from nature...

A A beautiful shell.
B A nice leaf.

1

You are at the seaside and you can't wait to...

A Swim all day long.
B Play on the water edge.

4

In your opinion, the most exciting sport is...

A Windsurfing.
B Roller skating.

6

Which color do you like better?

A Green.
B Blue.

2

Your family is planning a trip and you ask them to go...

A Camping in the mountains.
B Camping near the lake.

5

You'd really like to bump into...

A A tortoise.
B A colorful fish.

7

You are more likely to crave...

A A fresh fruit smoothie.
B A big tasty sandwich.

A Water

The sound of the current makes you happy and free. No matter if you are sailing on the sea or enjoying a day at the lake, water really suits you! Like Moana, you always **FEEL** at home when you're close to it.

B Land

Walking in the forest, hiking on the mountains, visiting a new city...how exciting! Like Moana, you enjoy all the amazing things around you, **BUT** you prefer to feel the steady ground under your feet.

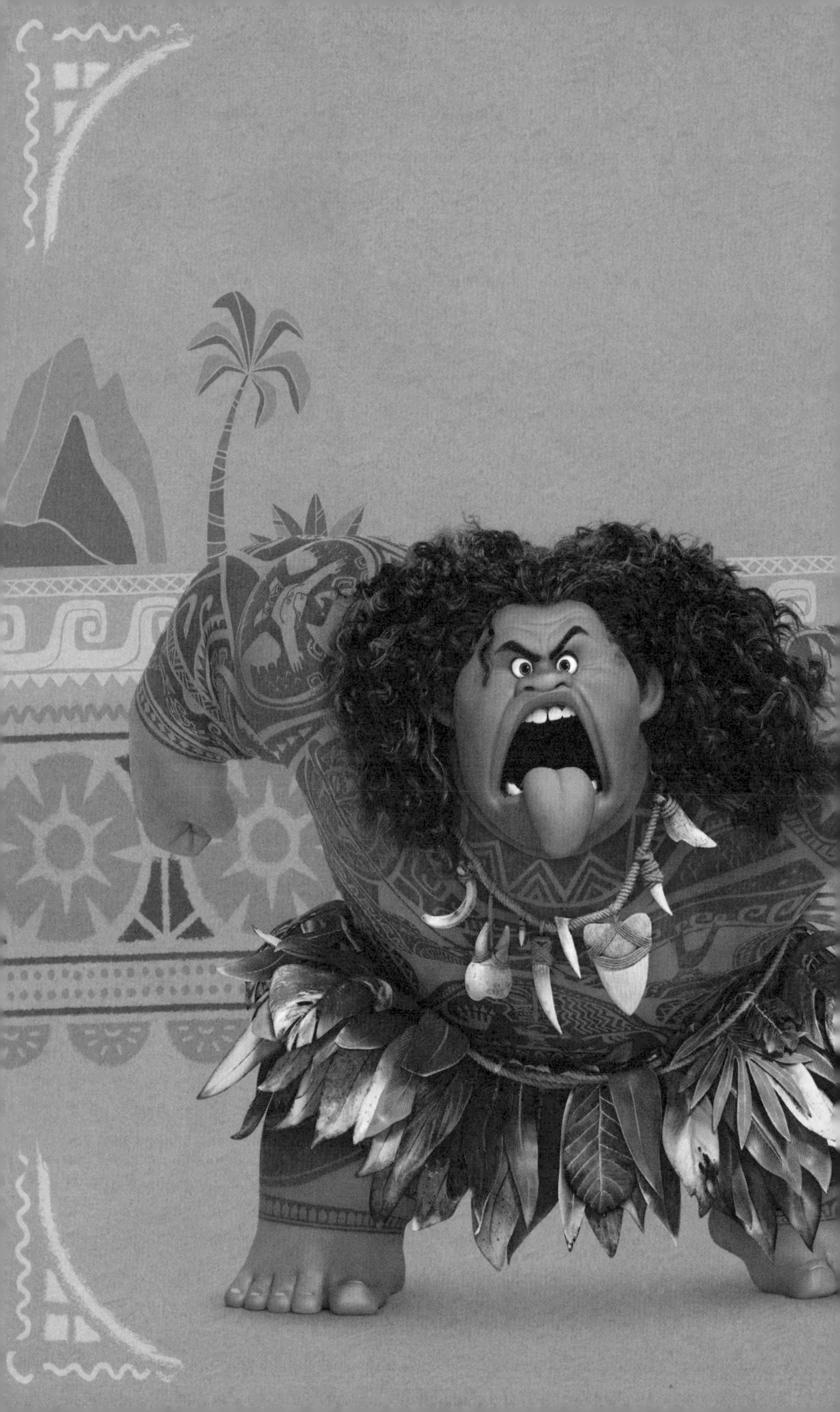

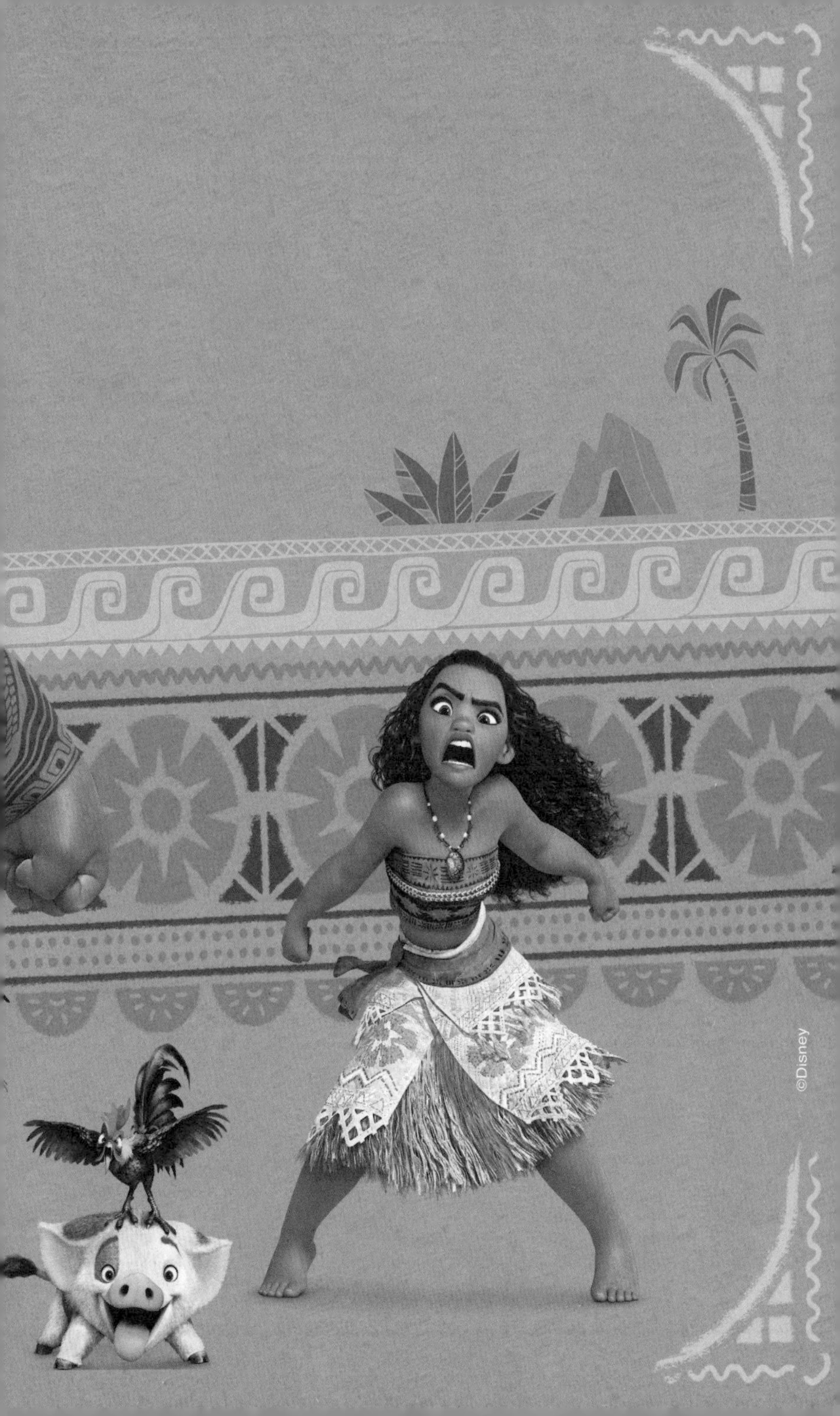

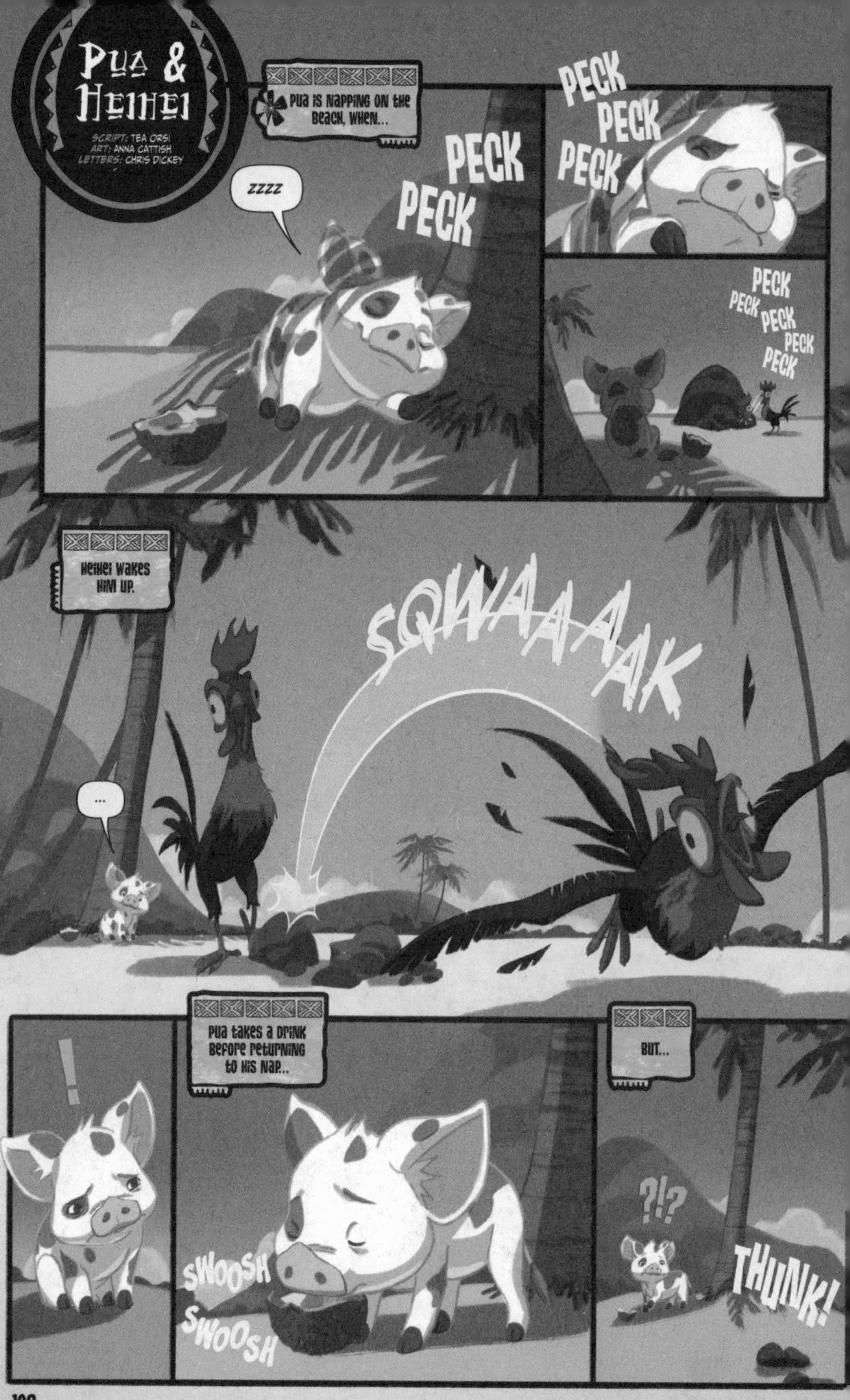
Pua &
Heihei
SCRIPT: TEA ORSI
ART: ANNA CATTISH
LETTERS: CHRIS DICKEY
Pua is napping on the beach, when...
ZZZZ
PECK
PECK
PECK
PECK
PECK
PECK
PECK
PECK
PECK
PECK
Heihei wakes him up.
SQWAAAAAK
...
!
Pua takes a drink before returning to his nap...
SWOOSH
SWOOSH
But...
?!?
THUNK!

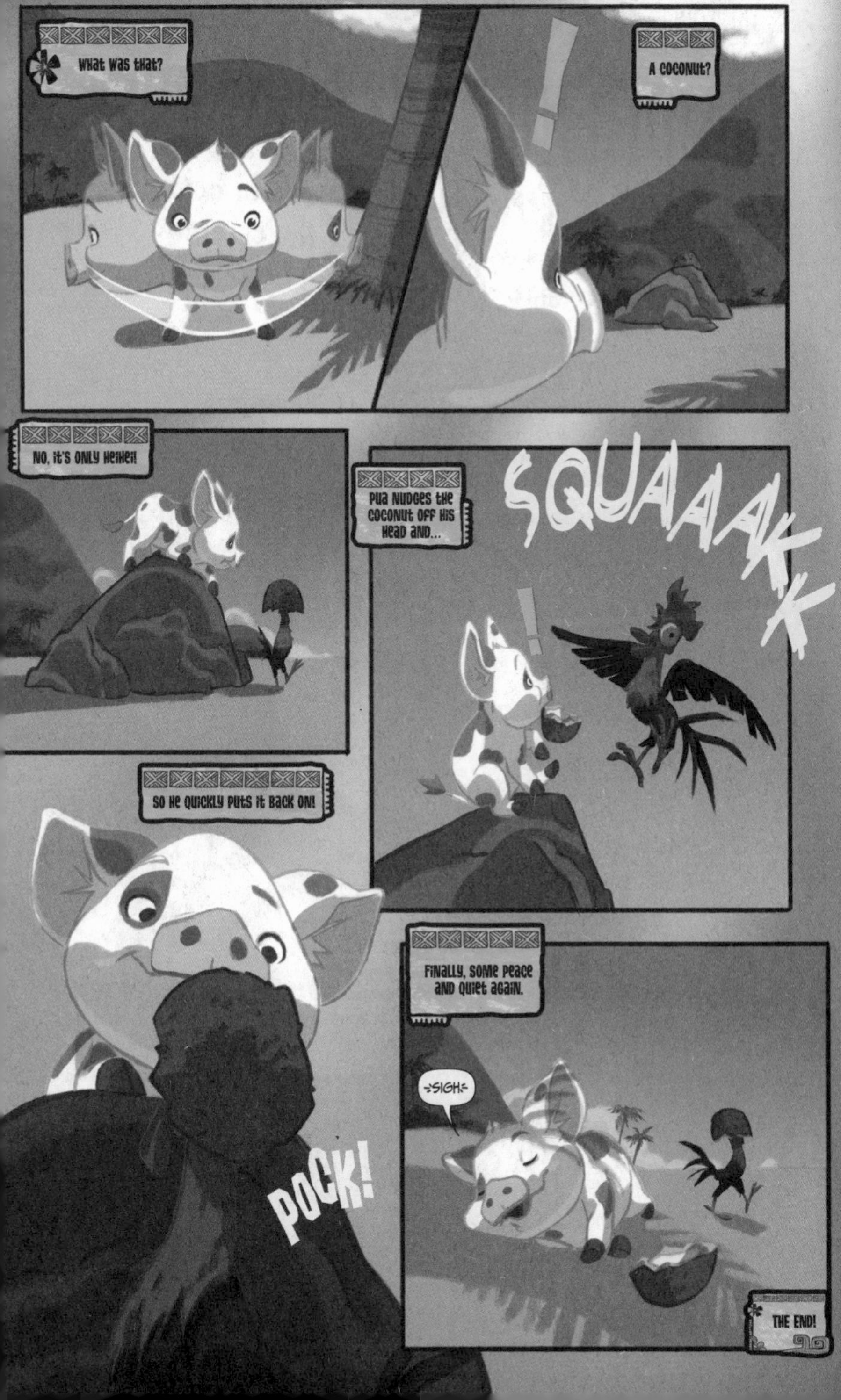
What was that?
A COCONUT?
!
NO, IT'S ONLY HEIHEI!
PUA NUDGES THE COCONUT OFF HIS HEAD AND...
SQUAAAKK
!
SO HE QUICKLY PUTS IT BACK ON!
POCK!
FINALLY, SOME PEACE AND QUIET AGAIN.
SIGH
THE END!

CONSIDER THE COCONUT

The villagers of Motunui really know how to conserve and use all parts of the coconut. Here are some of its amazing uses!

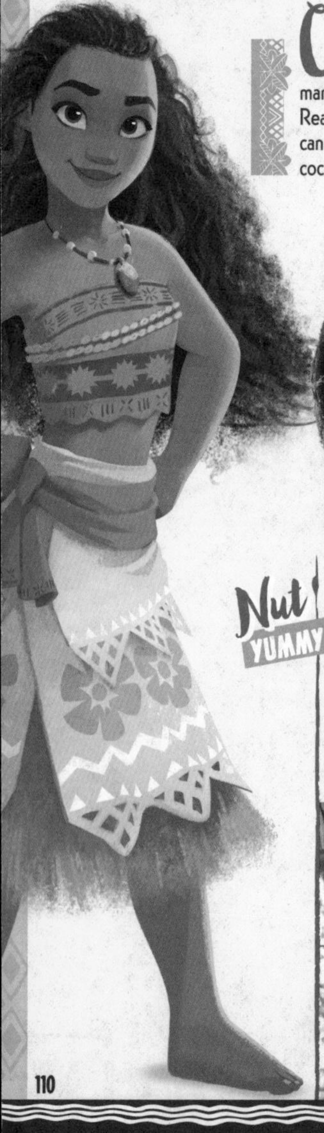

Coconut trees are essential for Pacific Islanders who have many uses for the coconuts. Read on to find out what they can make out of different coconut PARTS!

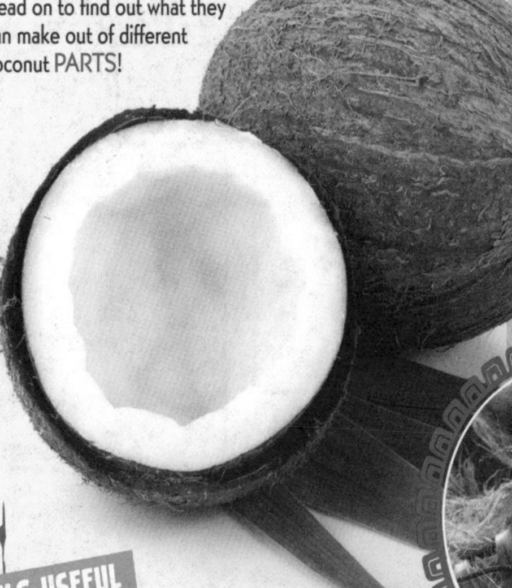

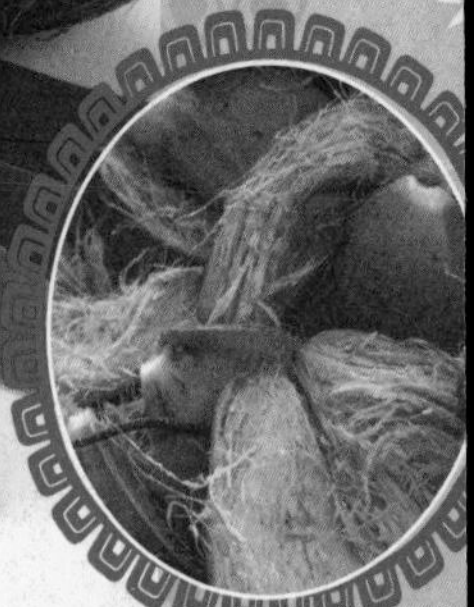

Nut
YUMMY & USEFUL

The coconut is **ENTIRELY EDIBLE** at a certain stage of ripeness. Its **FLESH** can be dried and turned into flour, or crushed to make **OIL** or **MILK**.

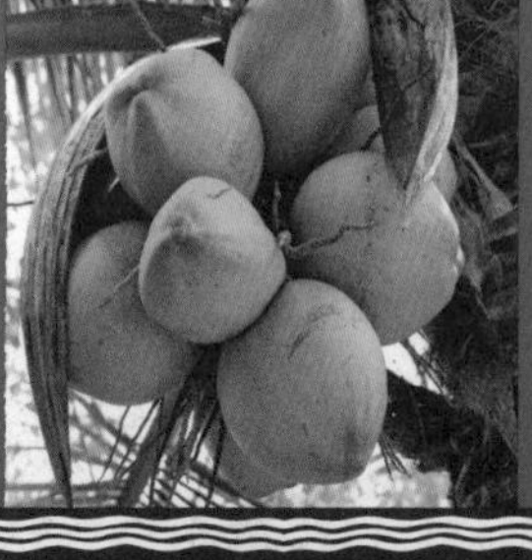

Fibers

Coconut fiber is also called COIR and comes from the husk of coconut. Ropes and cordage made from coir can be weaved to create fishing nets.

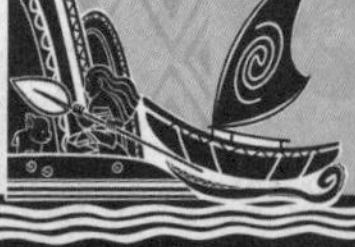

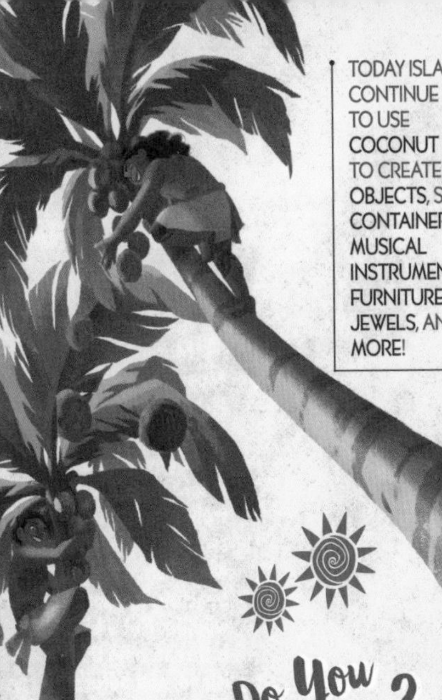

Fun Fact
CONSERVATION

Conservation is a daily part of life for Pacific Islanders as they make **MAXIMUM USE** of **NATURAL RESOURCES.**

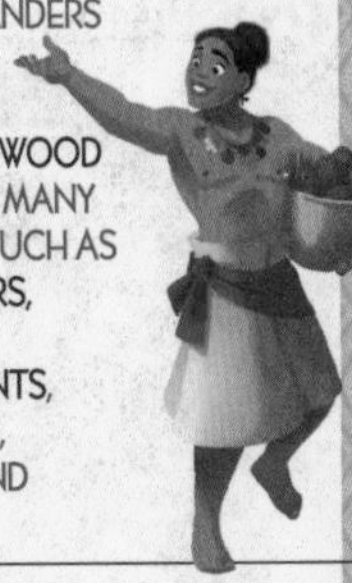

TODAY ISLANDERS CONTINUE TO USE **COCONUT WOOD** TO CREATE MANY **OBJECTS**, SUCH AS **CONTAINERS, MUSICAL INSTRUMENTS, FURNITURE, JEWELS, AND MORE!**

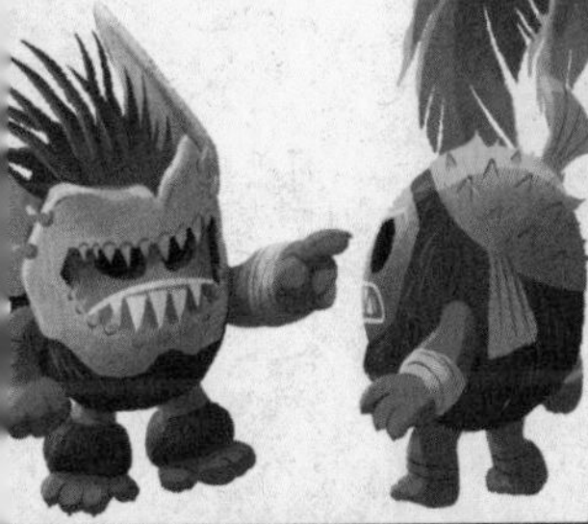

Do You Know?

Fresh coconuts can hold up to one liter of coconut water, which is very refreshing and lightly sweet.

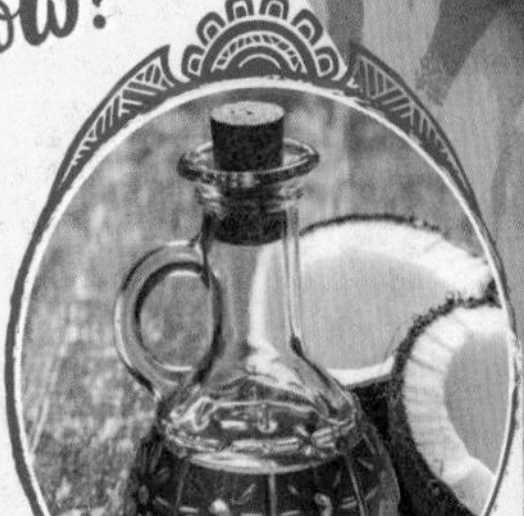

THE KAKAMORA

The Kakamora area group of small **COCONUT-ARMORED BANDITS**, who live on several islands of flotsam collected from the ocean; we see their arms and legs but never their faces or eyes—instead, they **DRAW THEIR FACES** and expressions onto the front of their coconuts. They want to take the heart of Te Fiti from Moana.

COCONUTS ARE STILL USED TODAY FOR **THATCHING HOUSES, WEAVING BASKETS, MAKING TRADITIONAL ACCESSORIES**, AND FOR COOKING.

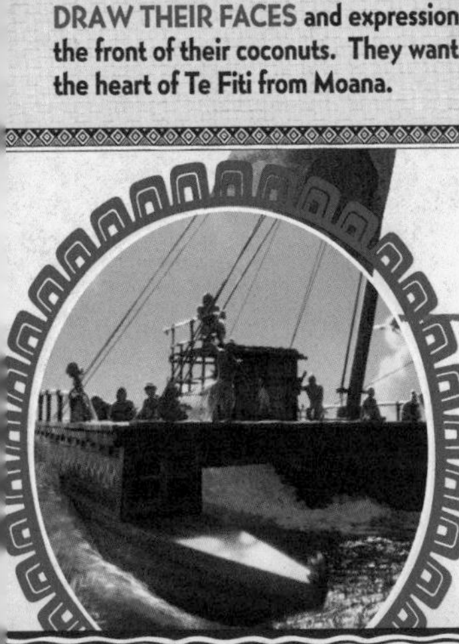

A bit of History

Coconuts travel well, so...ancient Pacific voyagers carried them on the boats during the great oceanic **MIGRATIONS**, about 2,000 years ago and then replanted them on the islands they discovered. This is why coconut became a symbol of their **CONQUEST** of the **PACIFIC OCEAN.**

MOTUNUI

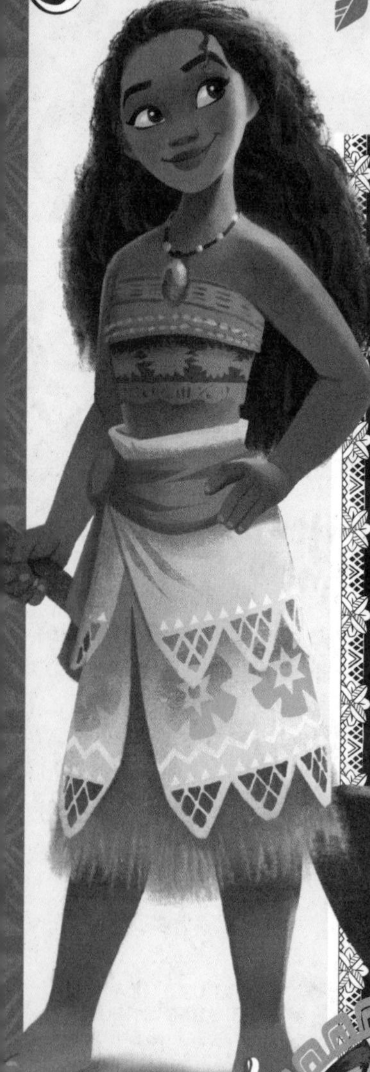

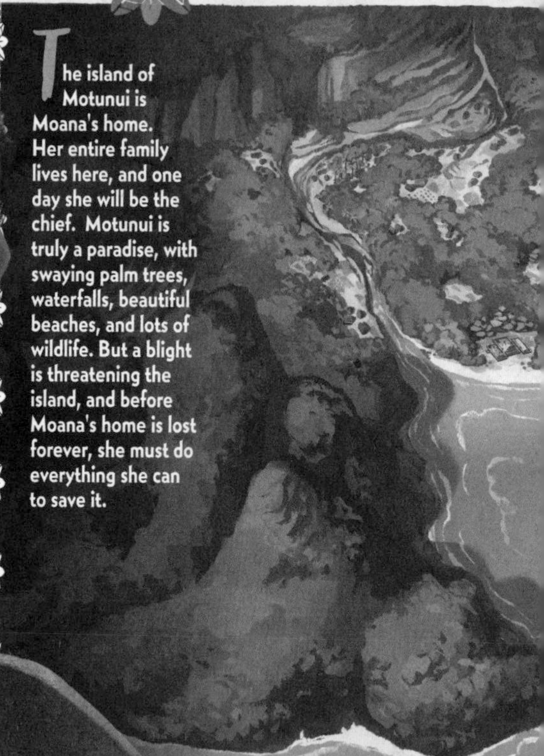

The island of Motunui is Moana's home. Her entire family lives here, and one day she will be the chief. Motunui is truly a paradise, with swaying palm trees, waterfalls, beautiful beaches, and lots of wildlife. But a blight is threatening the island, and before Moana's home is lost forever, she must do everything she can to save it.

The Beach

The beach is one of Moana's FAVORITE places, because there she can be close to the OCEAN.

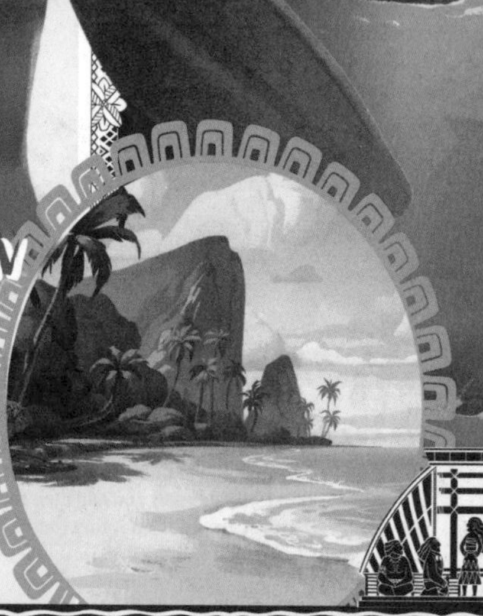

SLAND

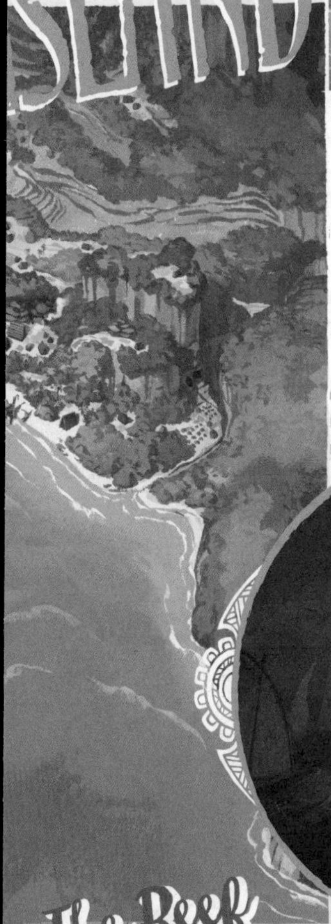

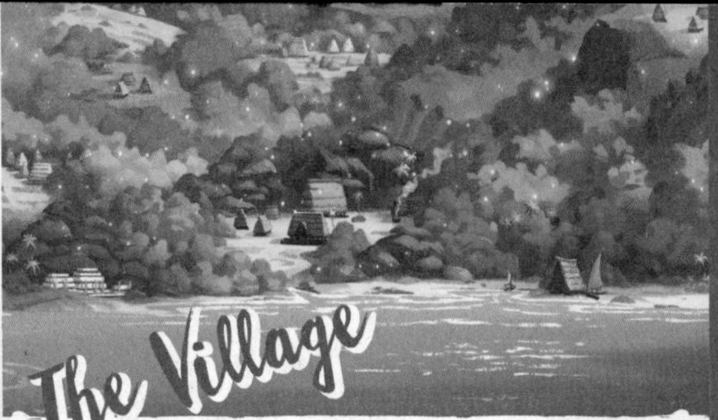

The Village

Residents of Motunui live, work, and commune in the village. Their houses are called "FALES" and are built on a raised rock platform. The roof is thatched with coconut palm fronds, and the interior and exterior are decorated with braided coconut fiber or bark cloth. Dried coconut LEAVES are placed on the floors and then covered with finely woven mats for extra softness.

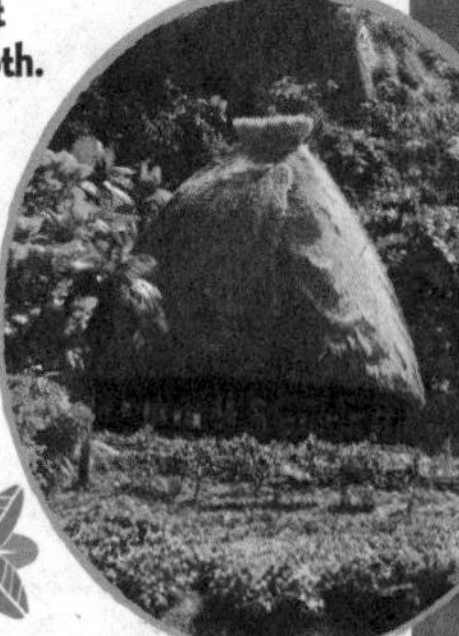

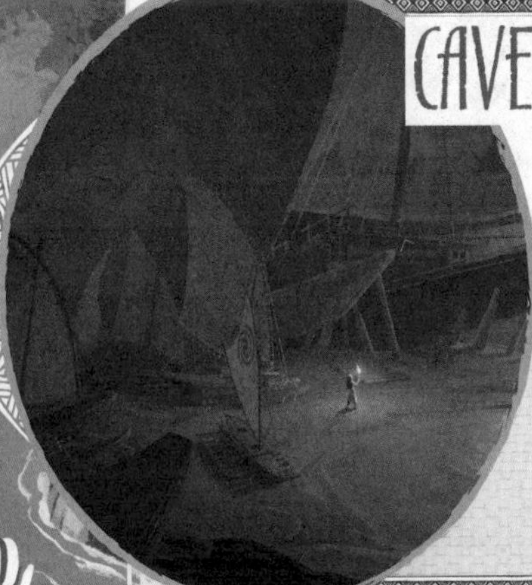

CAVERN OF THE WAYFINDERS

Gramma Tala takes Moana to the CAVERN OF ANCESTORS, a secret place she never knew about. Hidden inside the cave there are many LARGE SAILING CANOES, which belonged to Moana's ancestors who were VOYAGERS.

The Reef

The REEF that surrounds the island is the BARRIER that the people of Motunui are forbidden to cross. Despite her father's warning, Moana longs to EXPLORE beyond the reef.

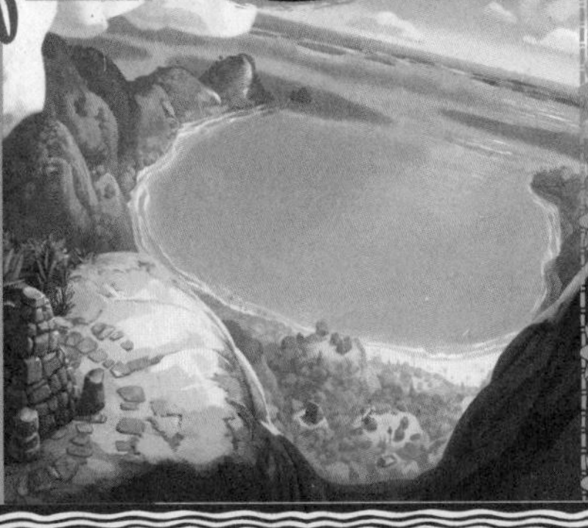

Disney

MOANA

The Wayfinders

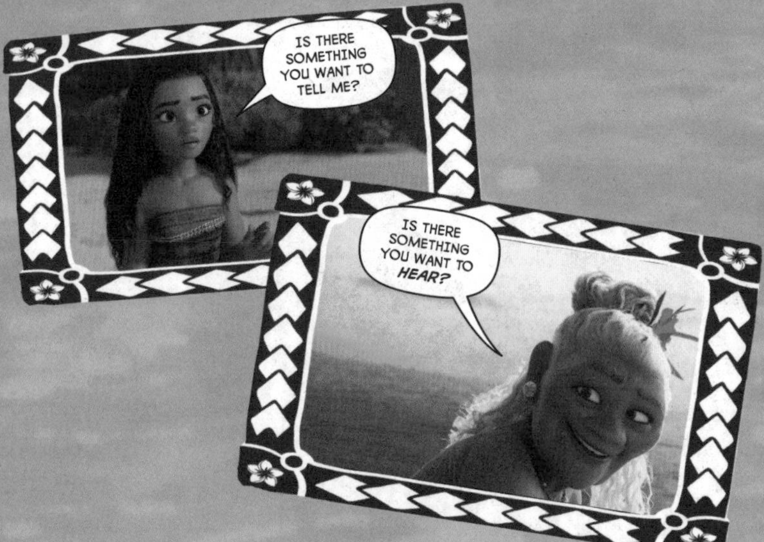
IS THERE SOMETHING YOU WANT TO TELL ME?
IS THERE SOMETHING YOU WANT TO *HEAR?*

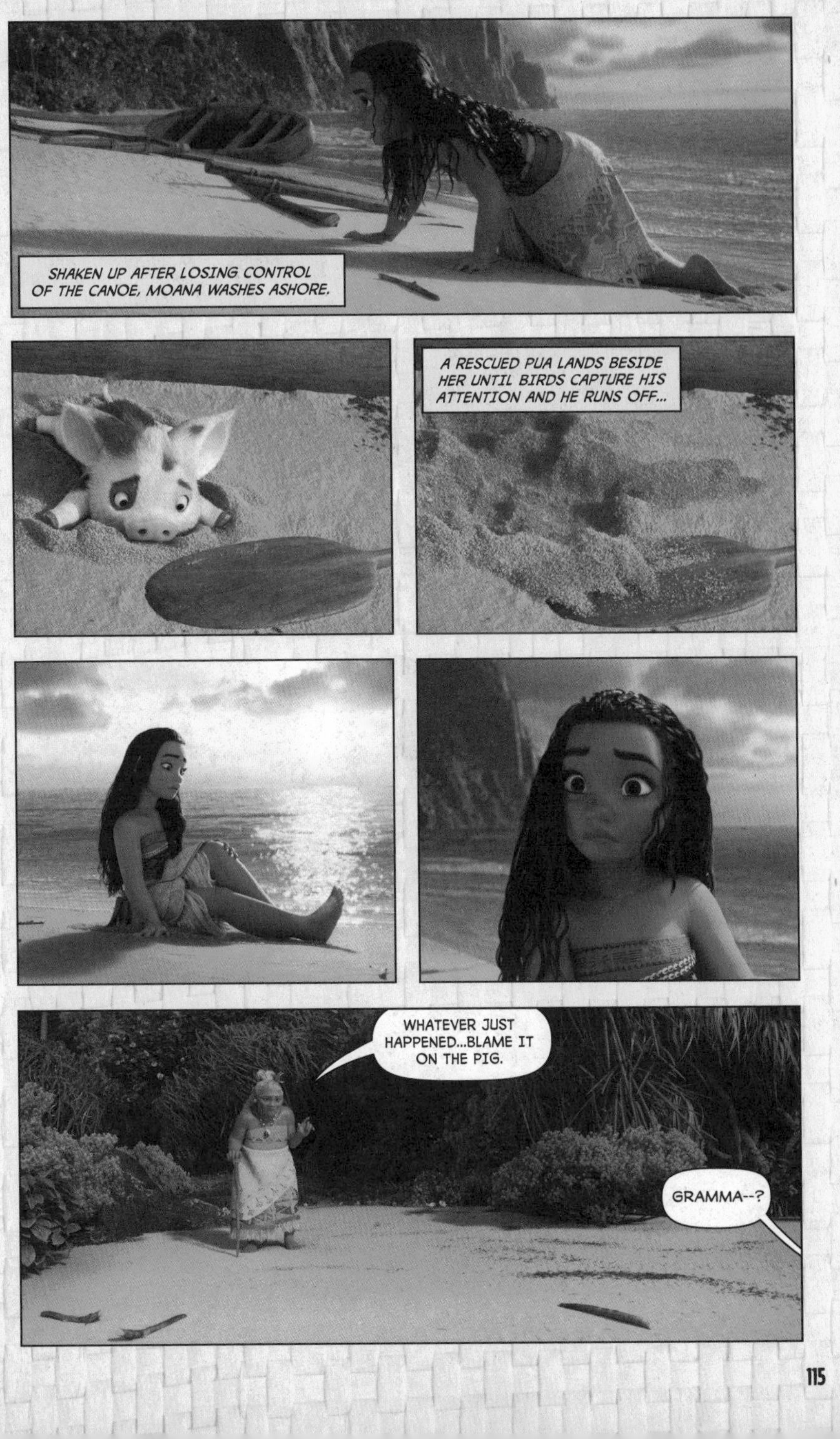
SHAKEN UP AFTER LOSING CONTROL OF THE CANOE, MOANA WASHES ASHORE.
A RESCUED PUA LANDS BESIDE HER UNTIL BIRDS CAPTURE HIS ATTENTION AND HE RUNS OFF...
WHATEVER JUST HAPPENED...BLAME IT ON THE PIG.
GRAMMA--?

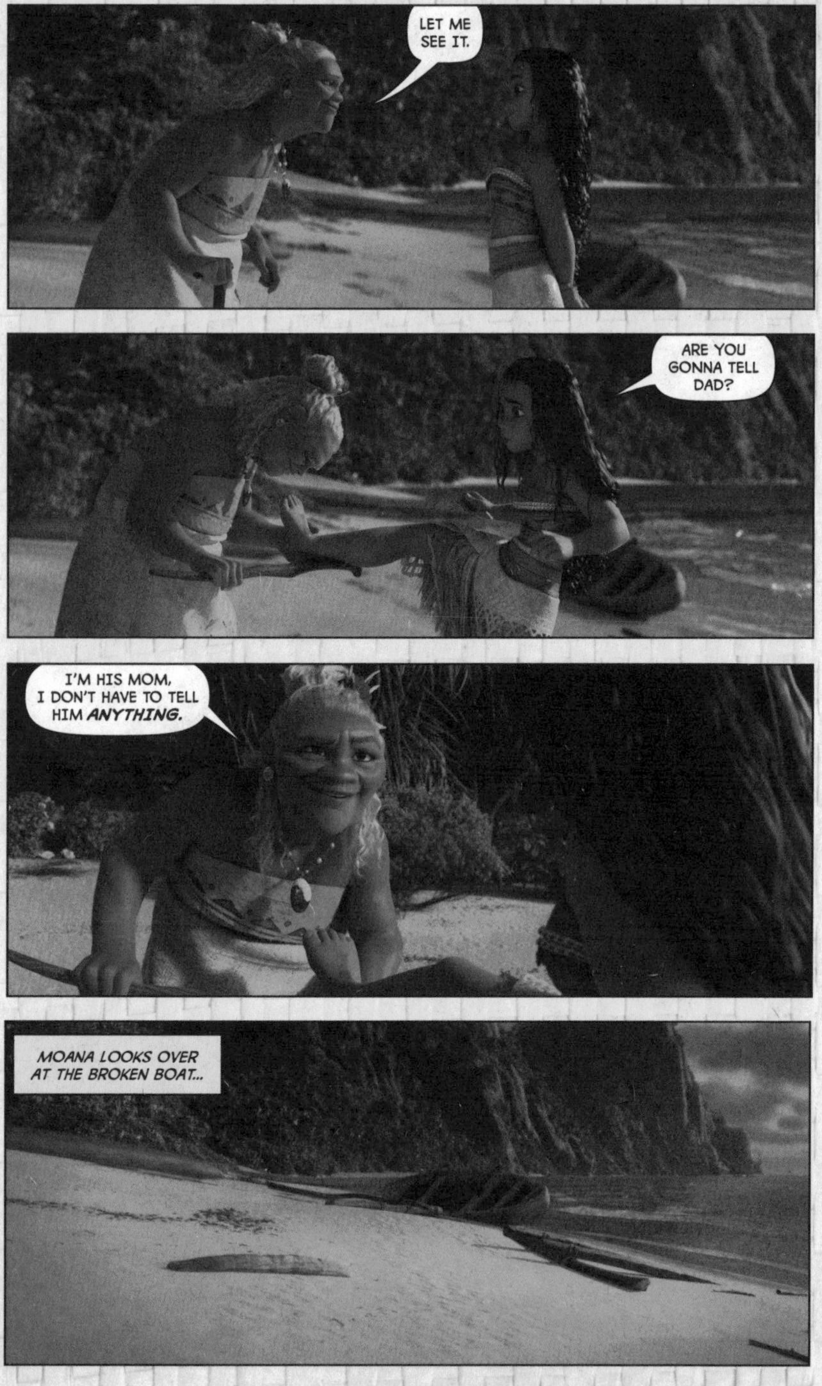
LET ME SEE IT.
ARE YOU GONNA TELL DAD?
I'M HIS MOM, I DON'T HAVE TO TELL HIM ANYTHING.
MOANA LOOKS OVER AT THE BROKEN BOAT...

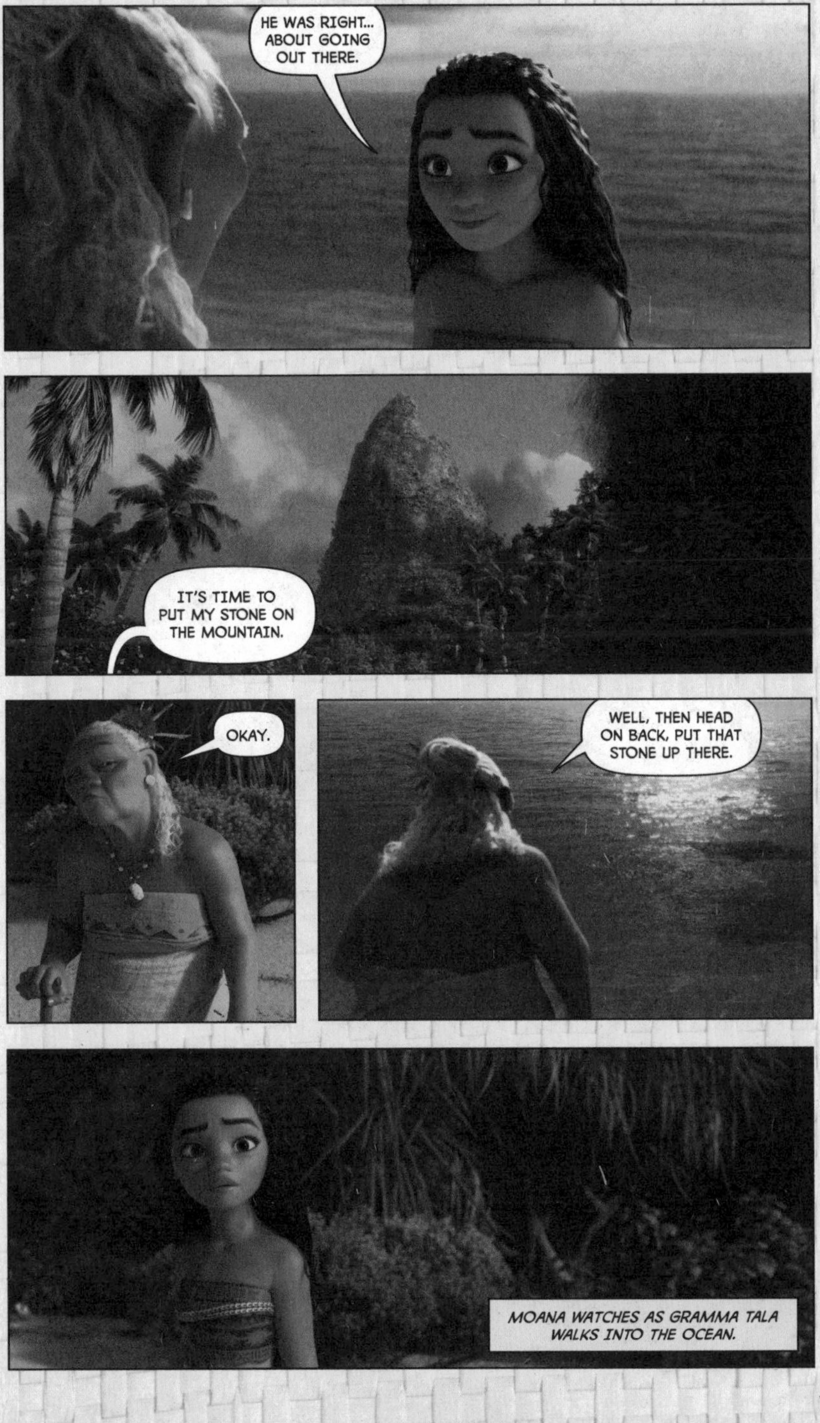
HE WAS RIGHT... ABOUT GOING OUT THERE.
IT'S TIME TO PUT MY STONE ON THE MOUNTAIN.
OKAY.
WELL, THEN HEAD ON BACK, PUT THAT STONE UP THERE.
MOANA WATCHES AS GRAMMA TALA WALKS INTO THE OCEAN.

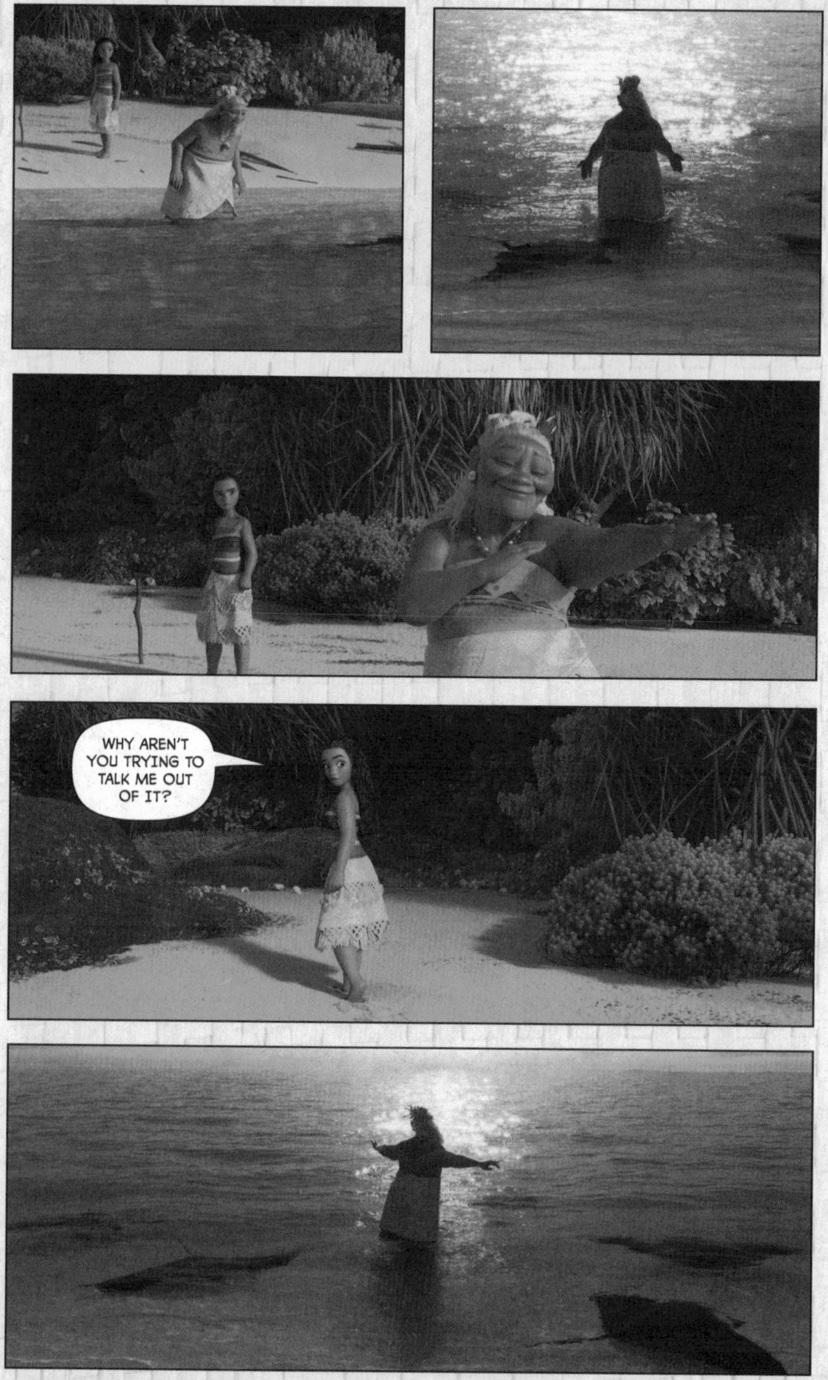
WHY AREN'T YOU TRYING TO TALK ME OUT OF IT?

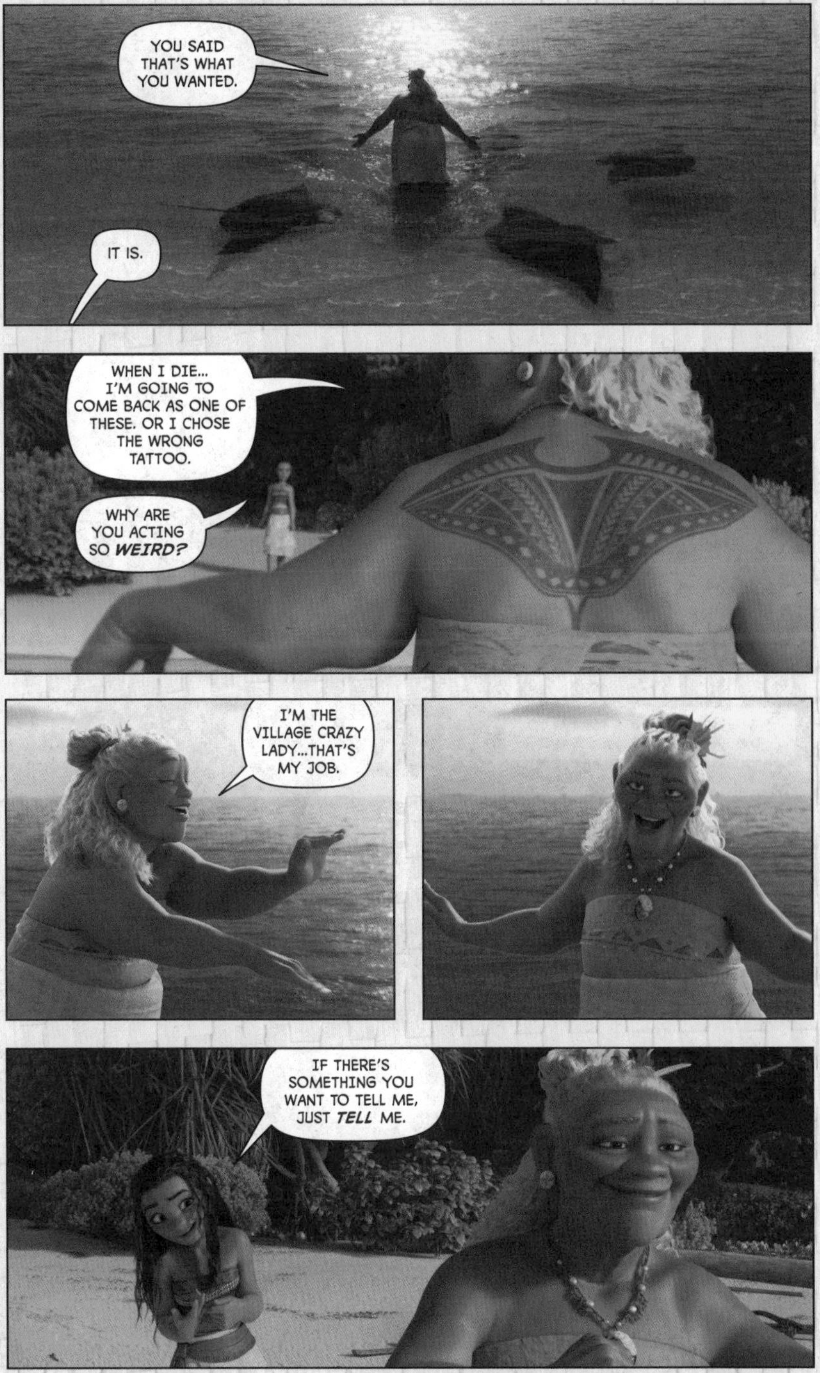
YOU SAID THAT'S WHAT YOU WANTED.
IT IS.
WHEN I DIE... I'M GOING TO COME BACK AS ONE OF THESE. OR I CHOSE THE WRONG TATTOO.
WHY ARE YOU ACTING SO *WEIRD?*
I'M THE VILLAGE CRAZY LADY...THAT'S MY JOB.
IF THERE'S SOMETHING YOU WANT TO TELL ME, JUST *TELL* ME.

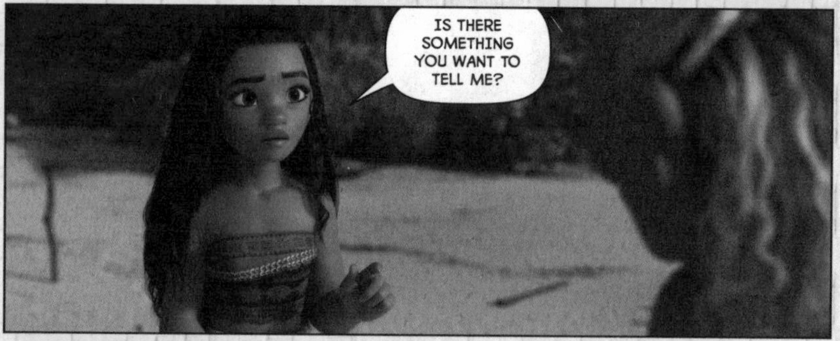
IS THERE SOMETHING YOU WANT TO TELL ME?

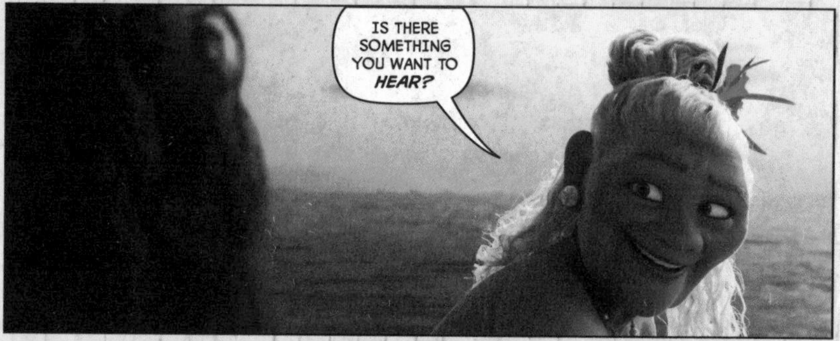
IS THERE SOMETHING YOU WANT TO ***HEAR?***

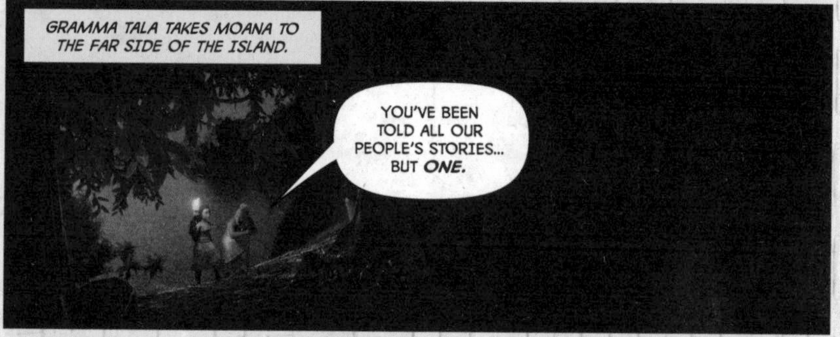
GRAMMA TALA TAKES MOANA TO THE FAR SIDE OF THE ISLAND.
YOU'VE BEEN TOLD ALL OUR PEOPLE'S STORIES... BUT ***ONE.***

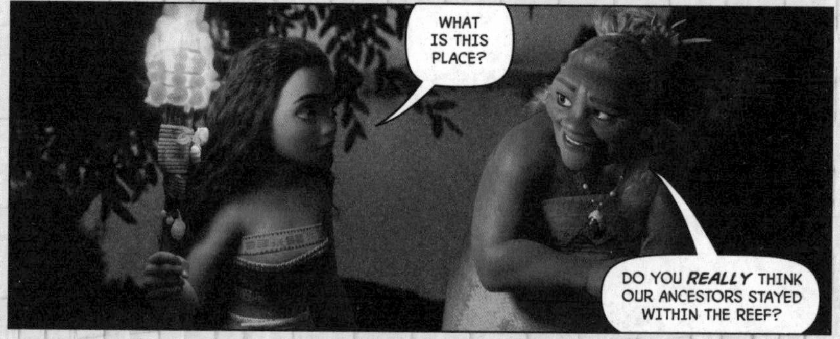
WHAT IS THIS PLACE?
DO YOU ***REALLY*** THINK OUR ANCESTORS STAYED WITHIN THE REEF?

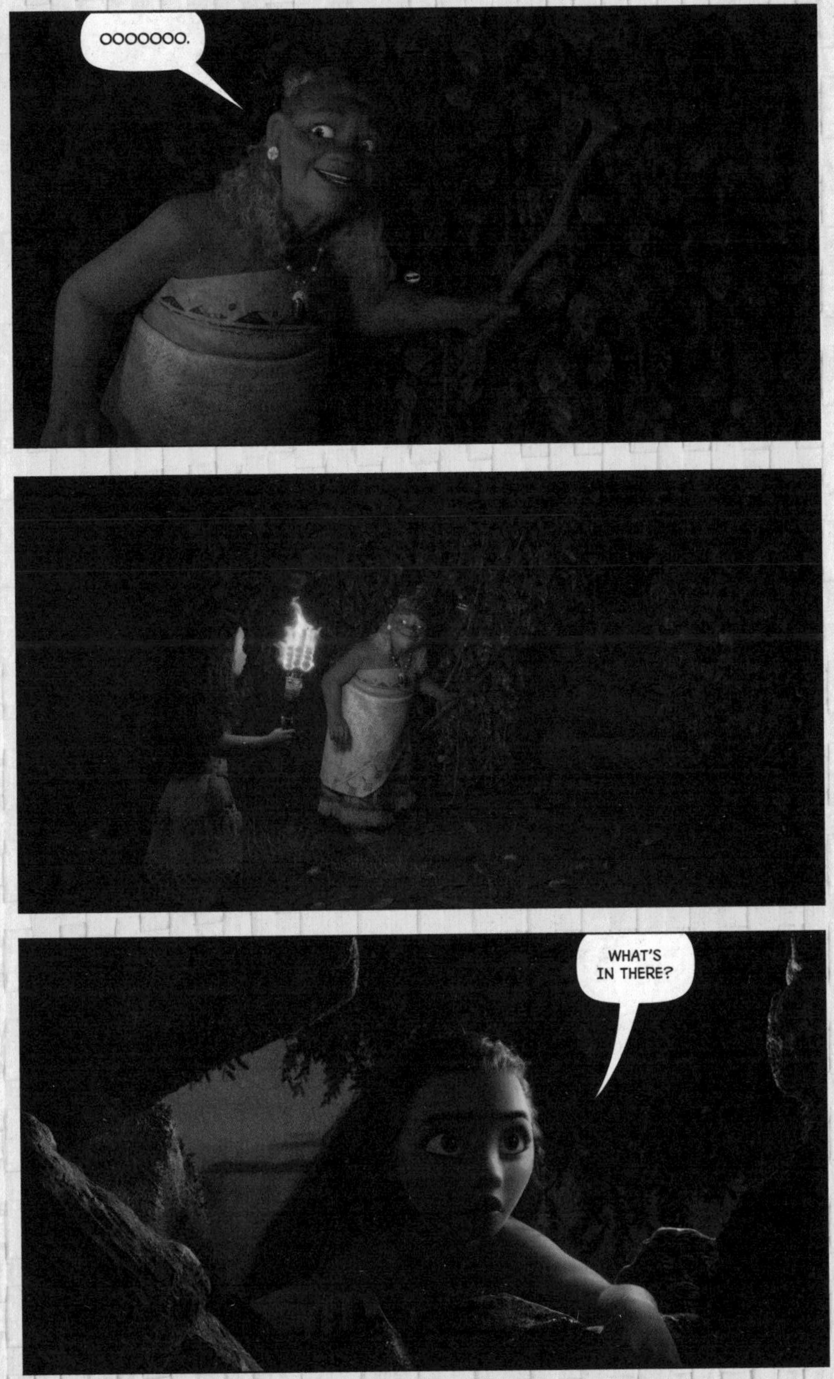
OOOOOOO.
WHAT'S IN THERE?

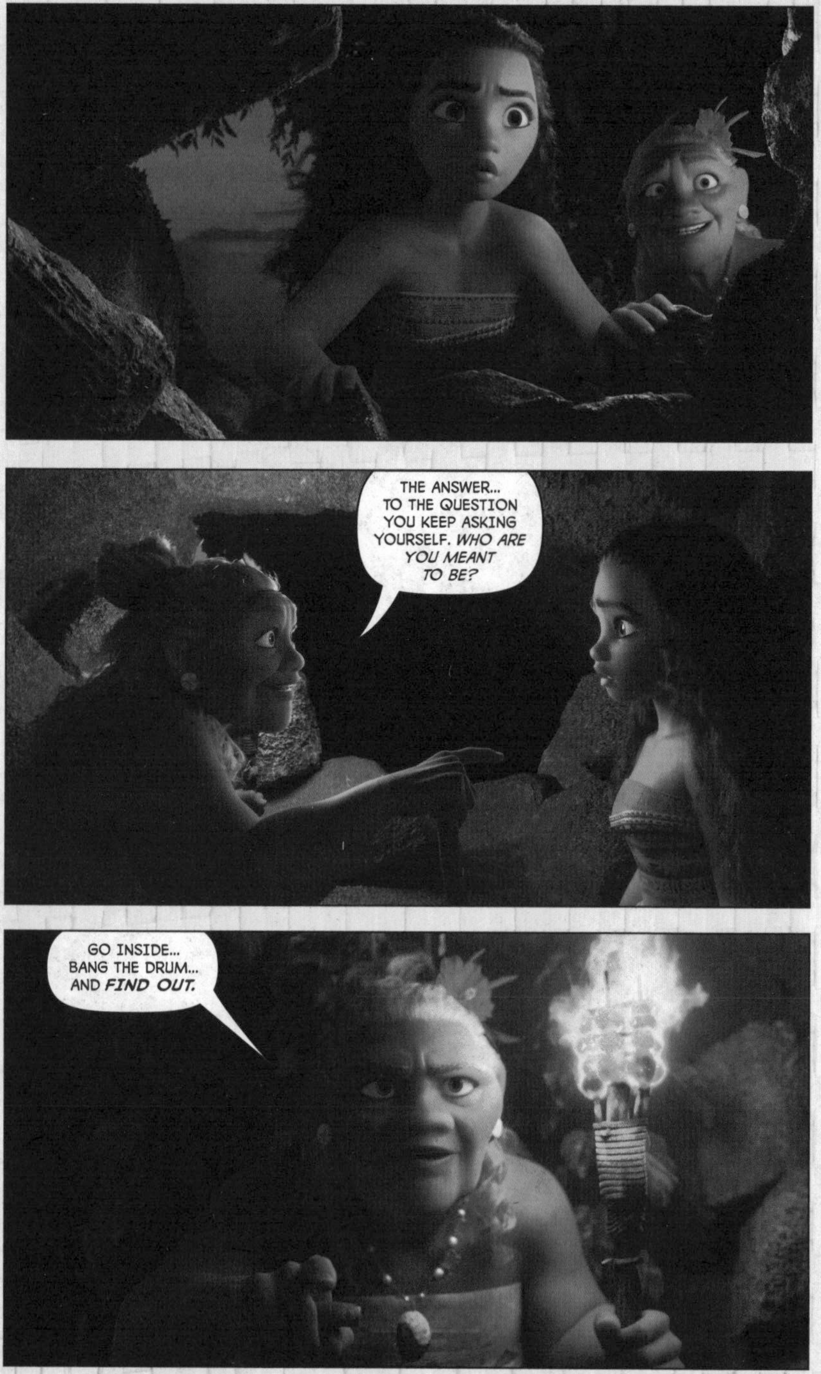
THE ANSWER... TO THE QUESTION YOU KEEP ASKING YOURSELF. *WHO ARE YOU MEANT TO BE?*
GO INSIDE... BANG THE DRUM... AND *FIND OUT.*

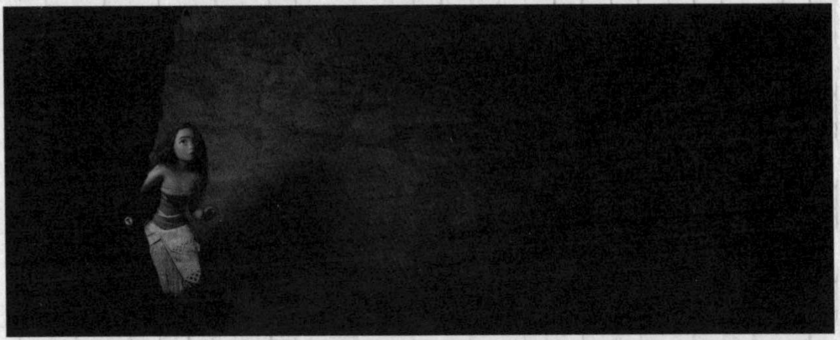

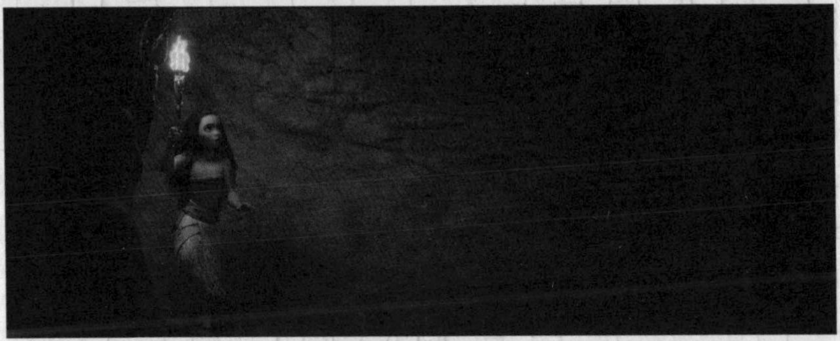

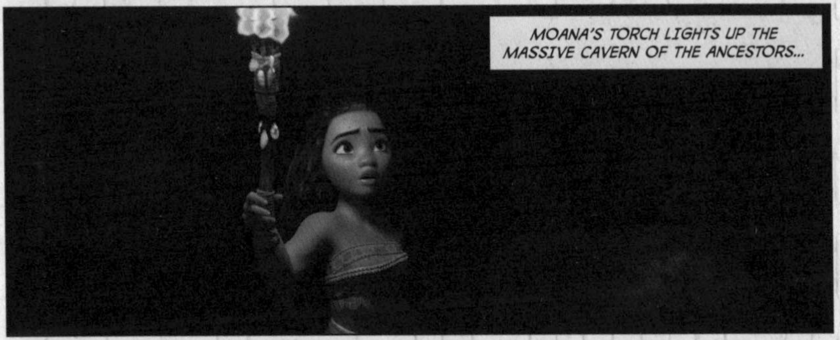
MOANA'S TORCH LIGHTS UP THE MASSIVE CAVERN OF THE ANCESTORS...

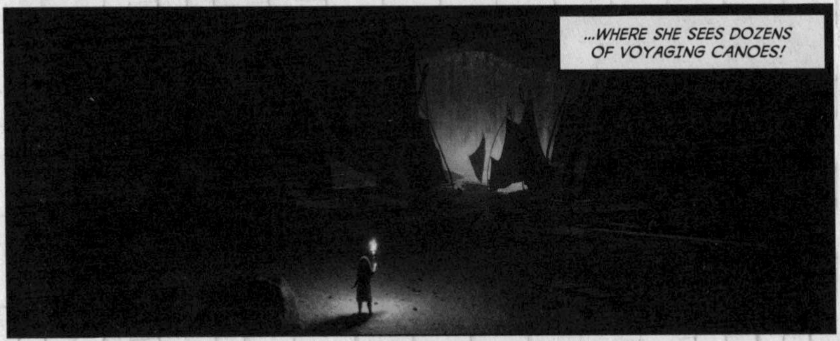
...WHERE SHE SEES DOZENS OF VOYAGING CANOES!

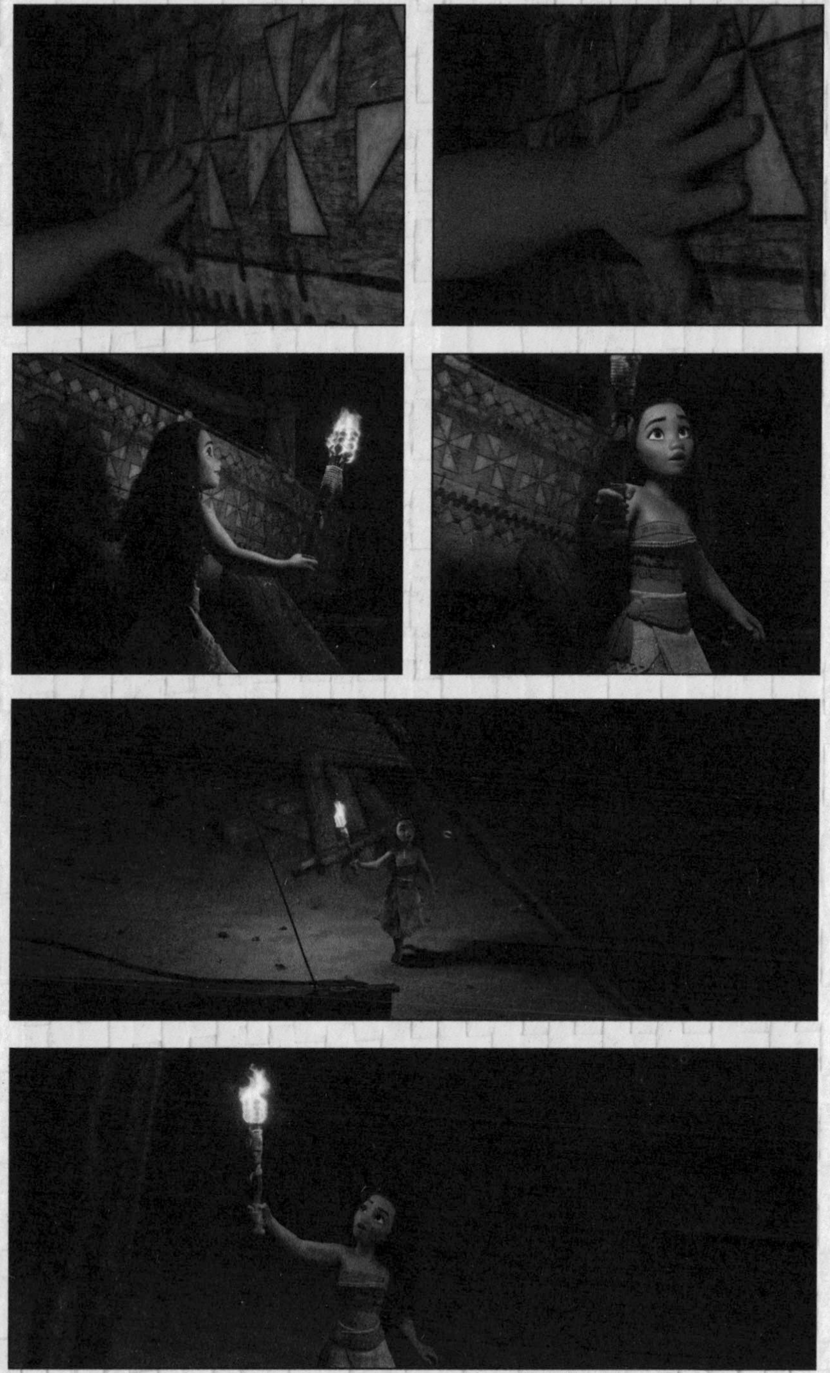

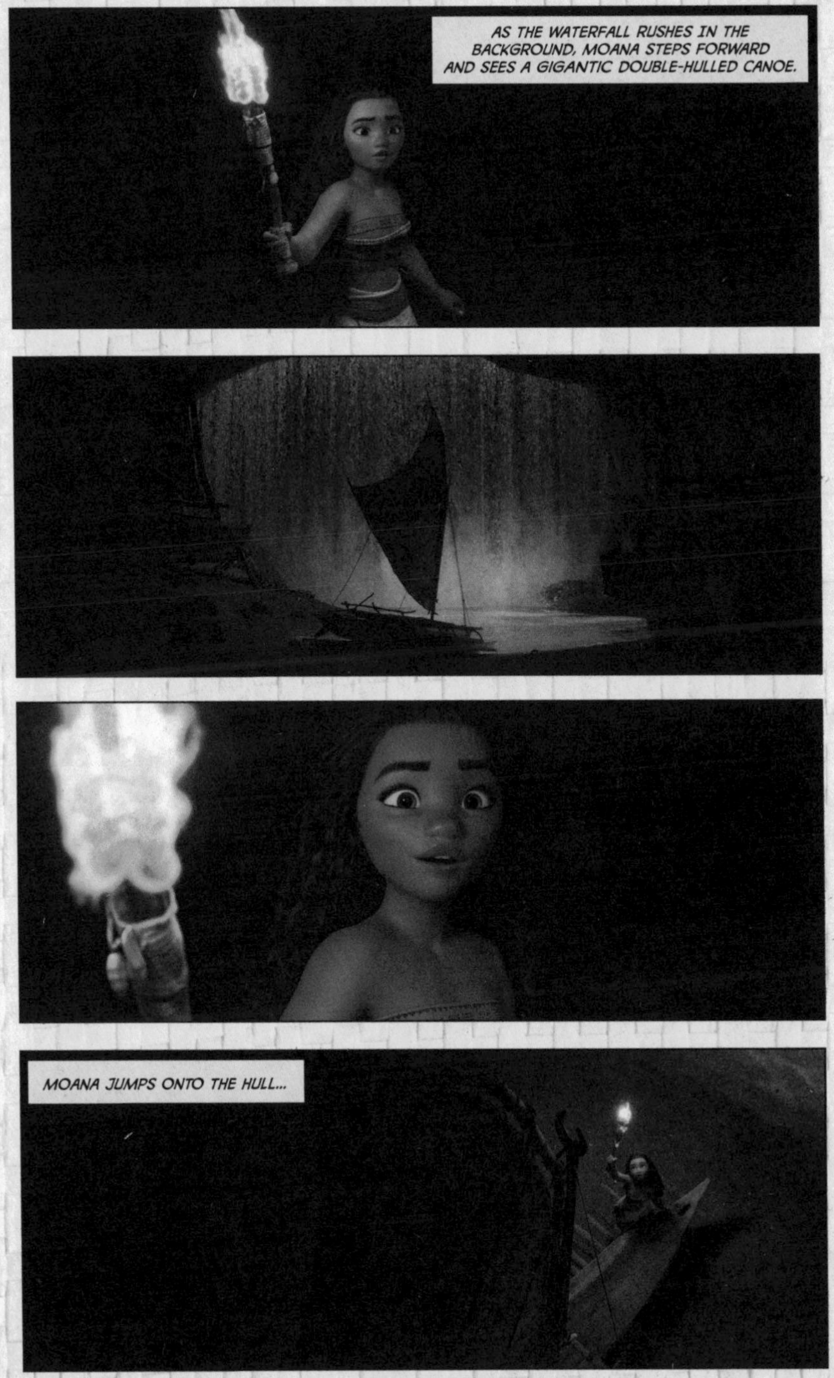
AS THE WATERFALL RUSHES IN THE BACKGROUND, MOANA STEPS FORWARD AND SEES A GIGANTIC DOUBLE-HULLED CANOE.
MOANA JUMPS ONTO THE HULL...

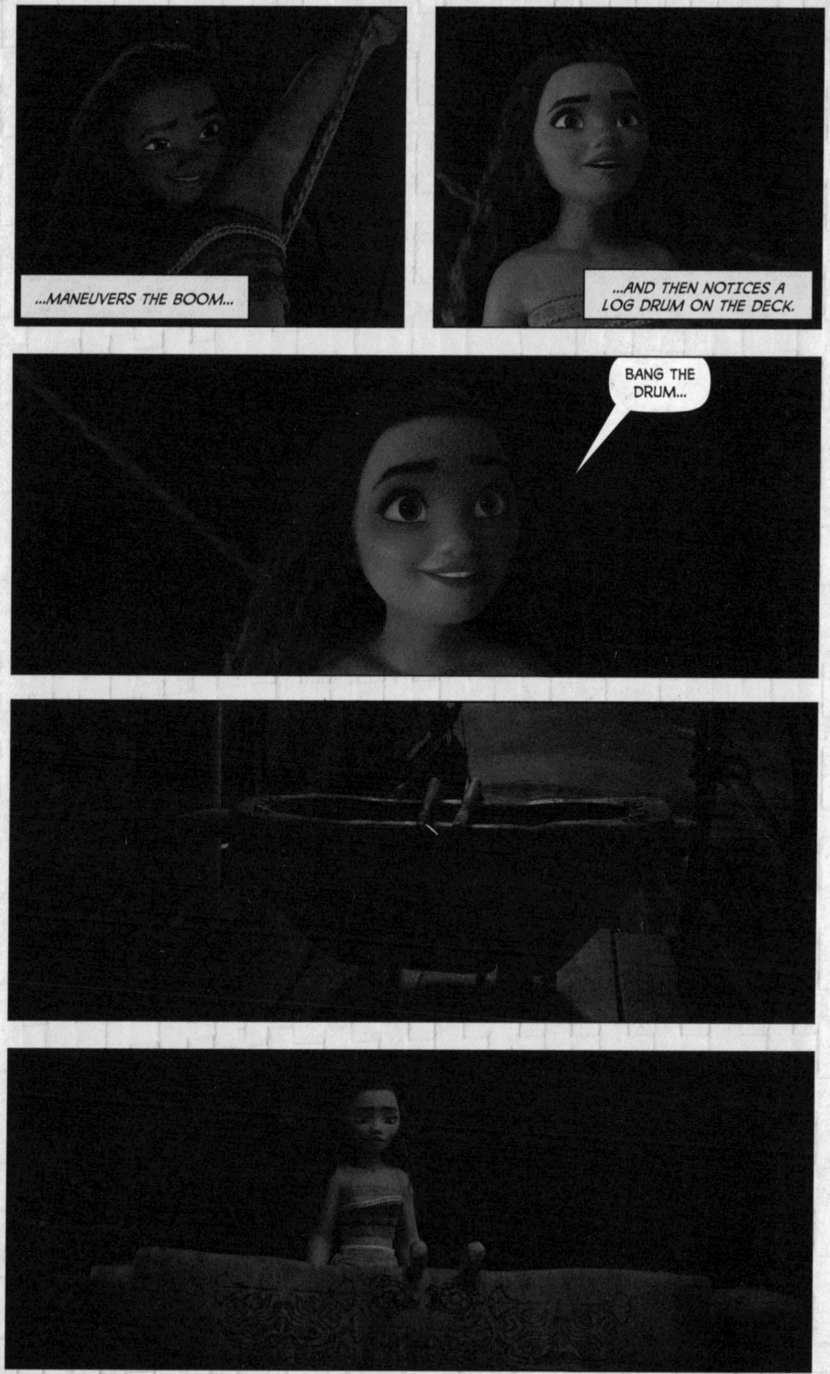
...MANEUVERS THE BOOM...
...AND THEN NOTICES A LOG DRUM ON THE DECK.
BANG THE DRUM...

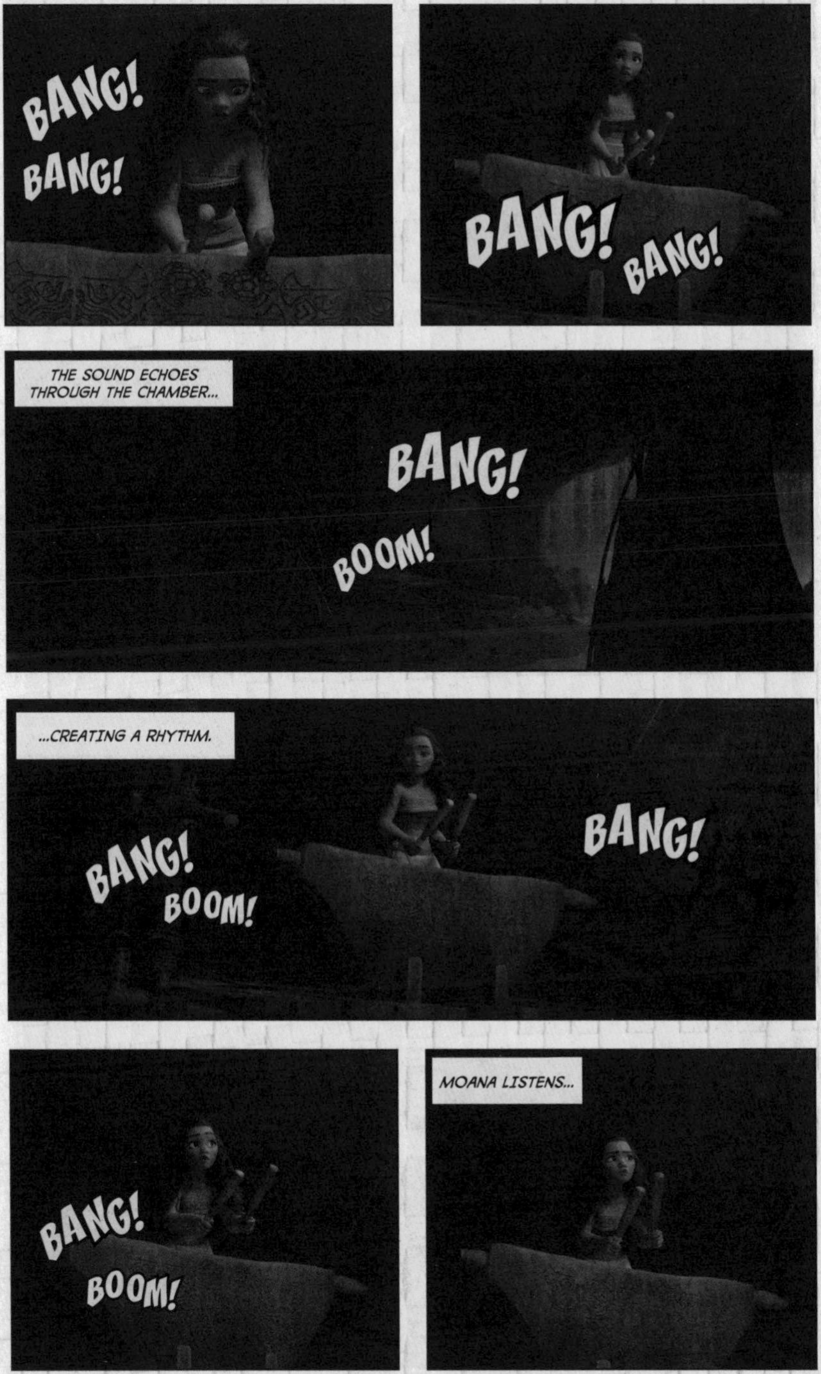
BANG!
BANG!
BANG!
BANG!
THE SOUND ECHOES THROUGH THE CHAMBER...
BANG!
BOOM!
...CREATING A RHYTHM.
BANG!
BOOM!
BANG!
BANG!
BOOM!
MOANA LISTENS...

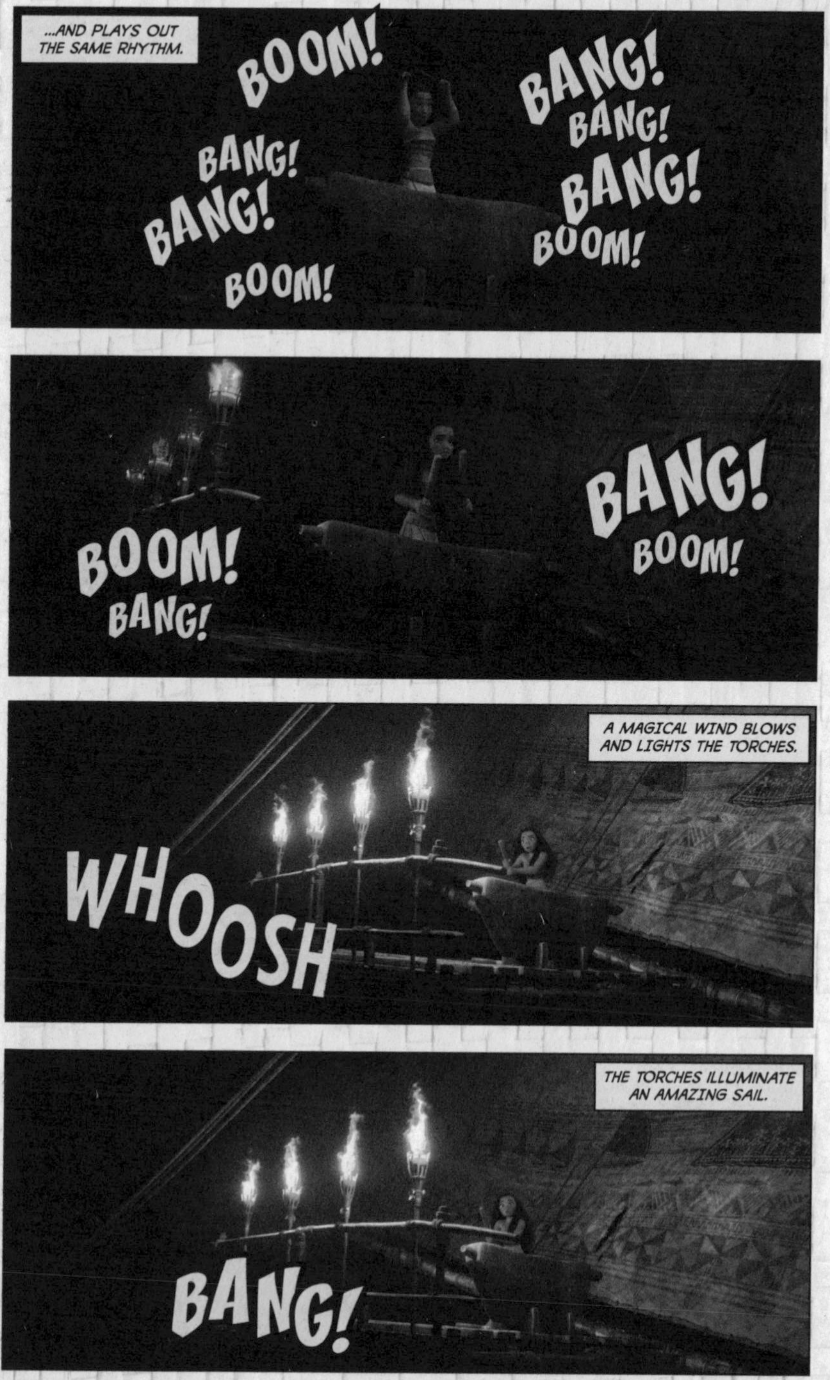

...AND PLAYS OUT THE SAME RHYTHM.
BOOM!
BANG!
BANG!
BOOM!
BANG!
BANG!
BANG!
BOOM!
BOOM!
BANG!
BANG!
BOOM!
A MAGICAL WIND BLOWS AND LIGHTS THE TORCHES.
WHOOSH
THE TORCHES ILLUMINATE AN AMAZING SAIL.
BANG!

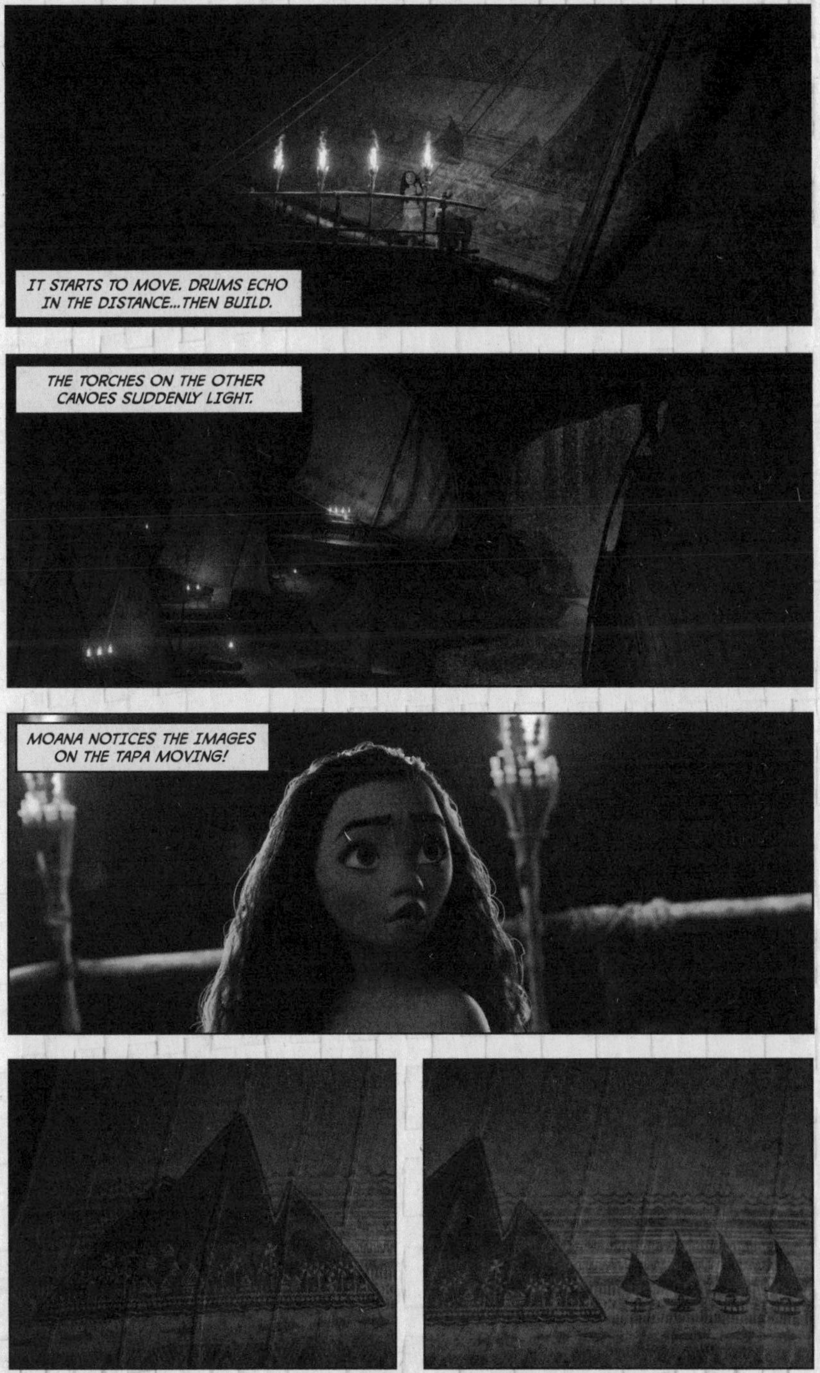
IT STARTS TO MOVE. DRUMS ECHO IN THE DISTANCE...THEN BUILD.
THE TORCHES ON THE OTHER CANOES SUDDENLY LIGHT.
MOANA NOTICES THE IMAGES ON THE TAPA MOVING!

THE TAPA SHOWS THE ANCIENT WAYFINDERS... *VOYAGING* ON THE OPEN OCEAN!

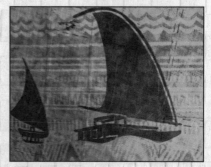

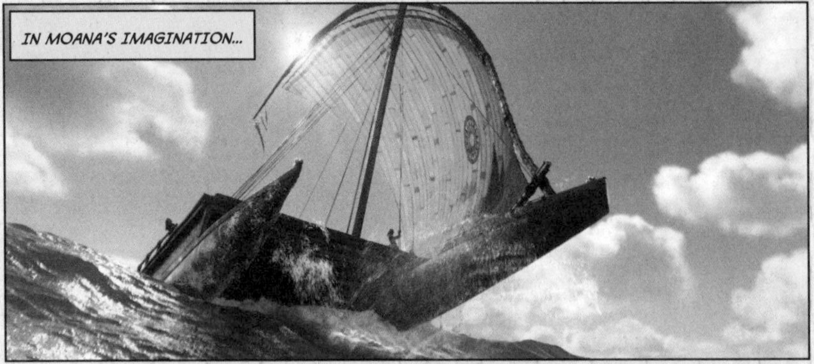
IN MOANA'S IMAGINATION...

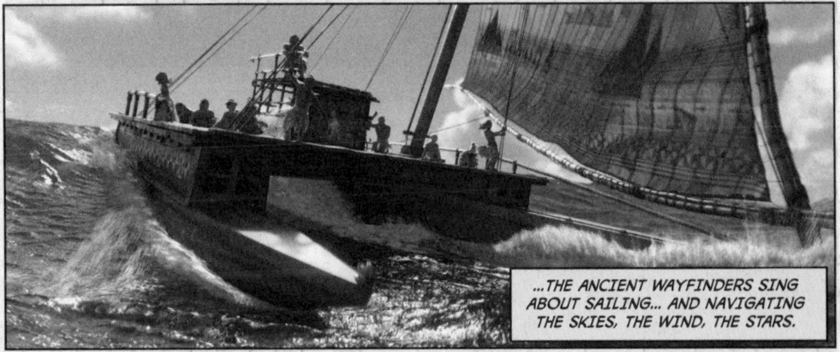
...THE ANCIENT WAYFINDERS SING ABOUT SAILING... AND NAVIGATING THE SKIES, THE WIND, THE STARS.

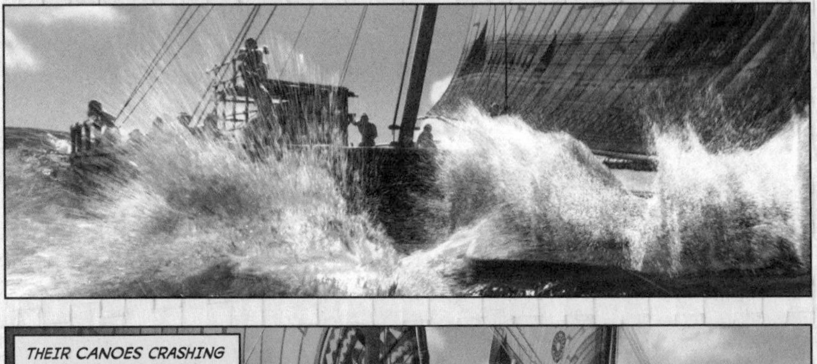

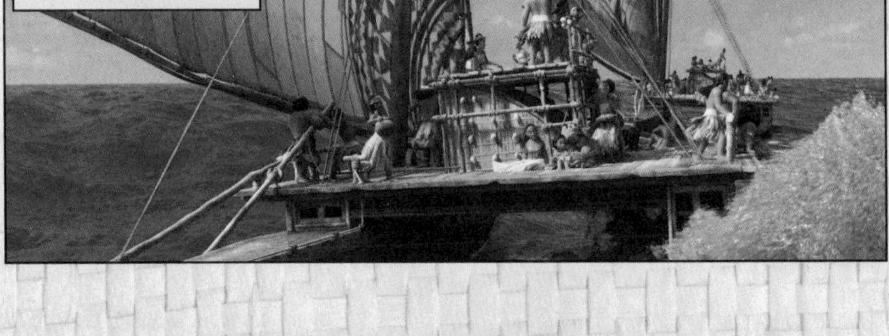
THEIR CANOES CRASHING THROUGH THE WAVES...

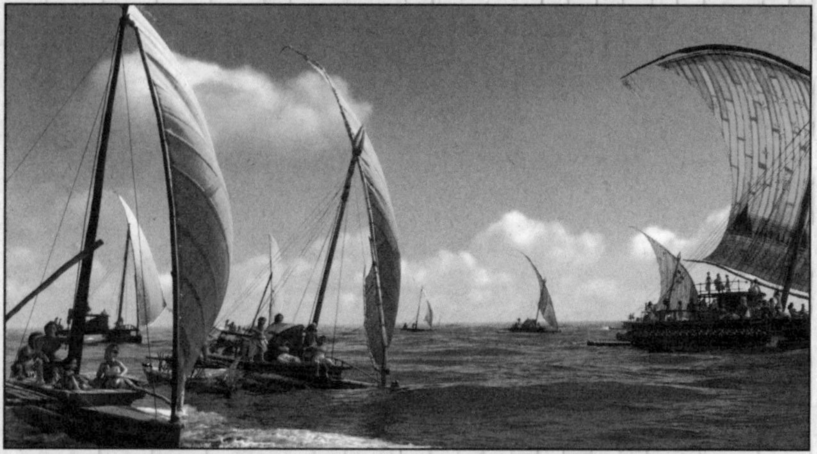

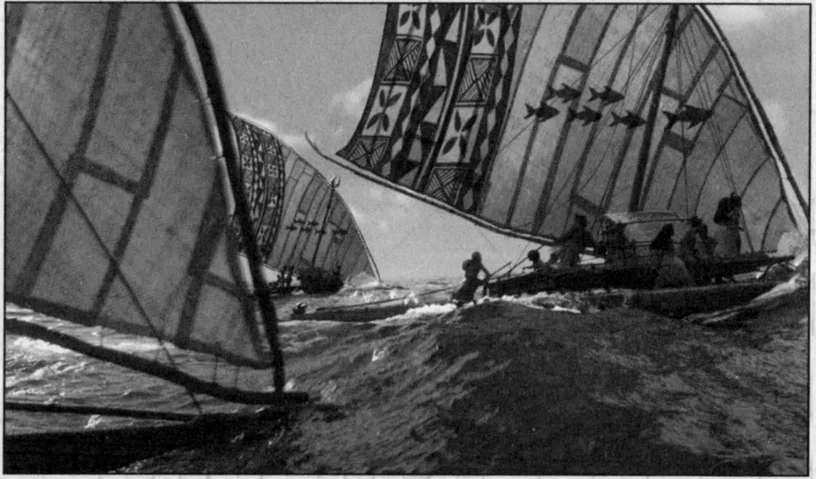

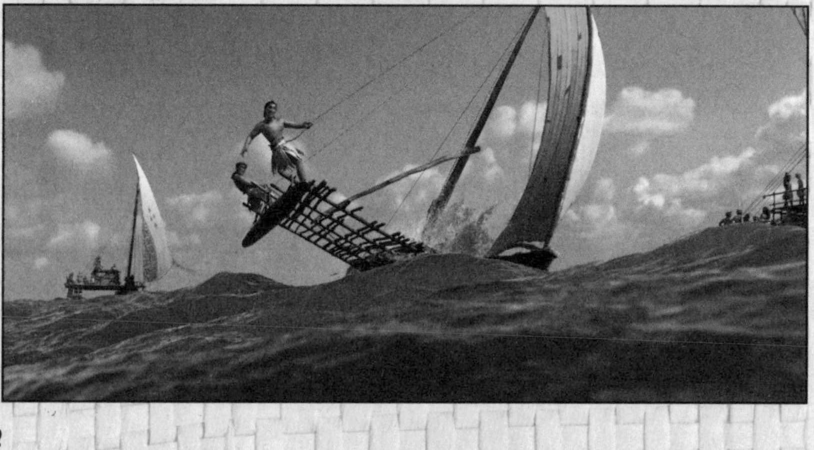

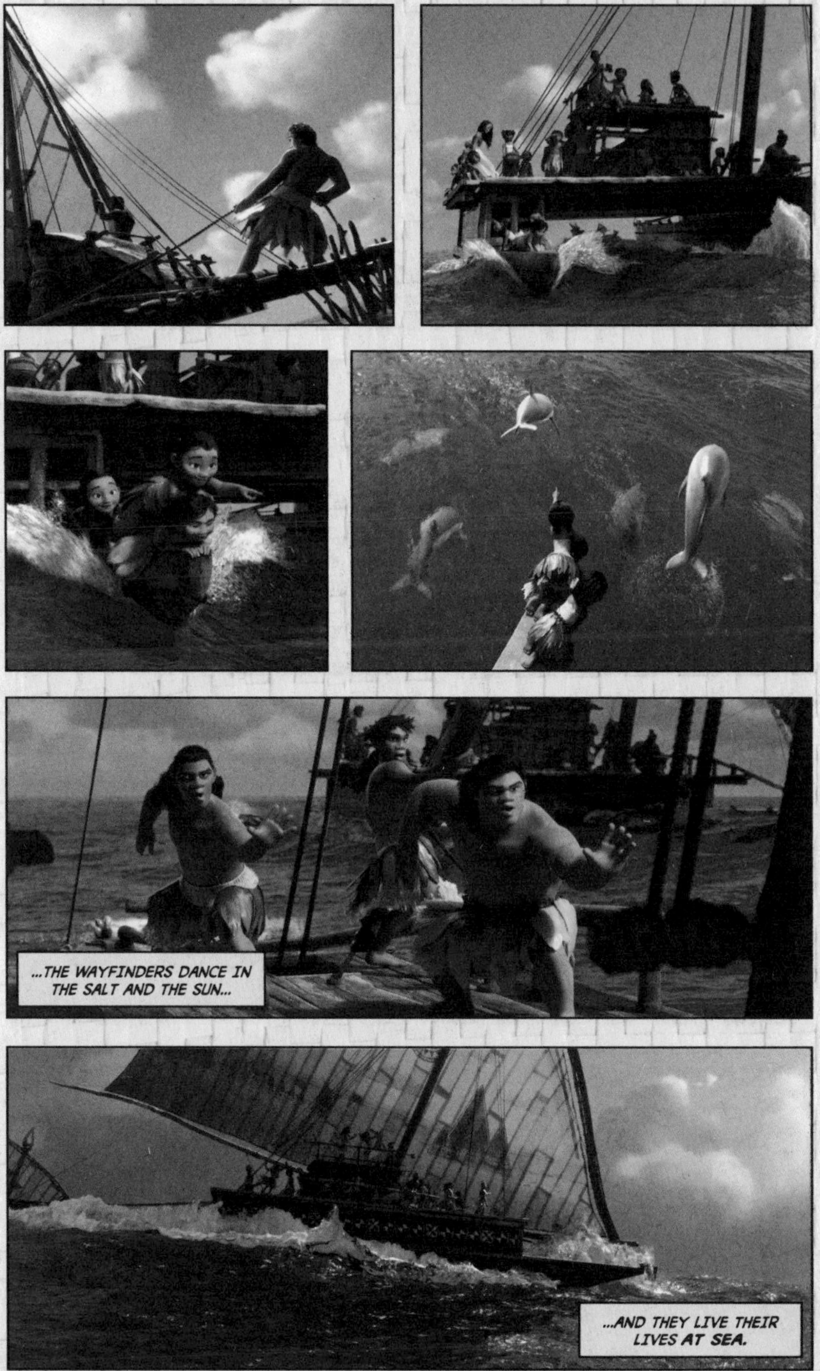
...THE WAYFINDERS DANCE IN THE SALT AND THE SUN...
...AND THEY LIVE THEIR LIVES AT SEA.

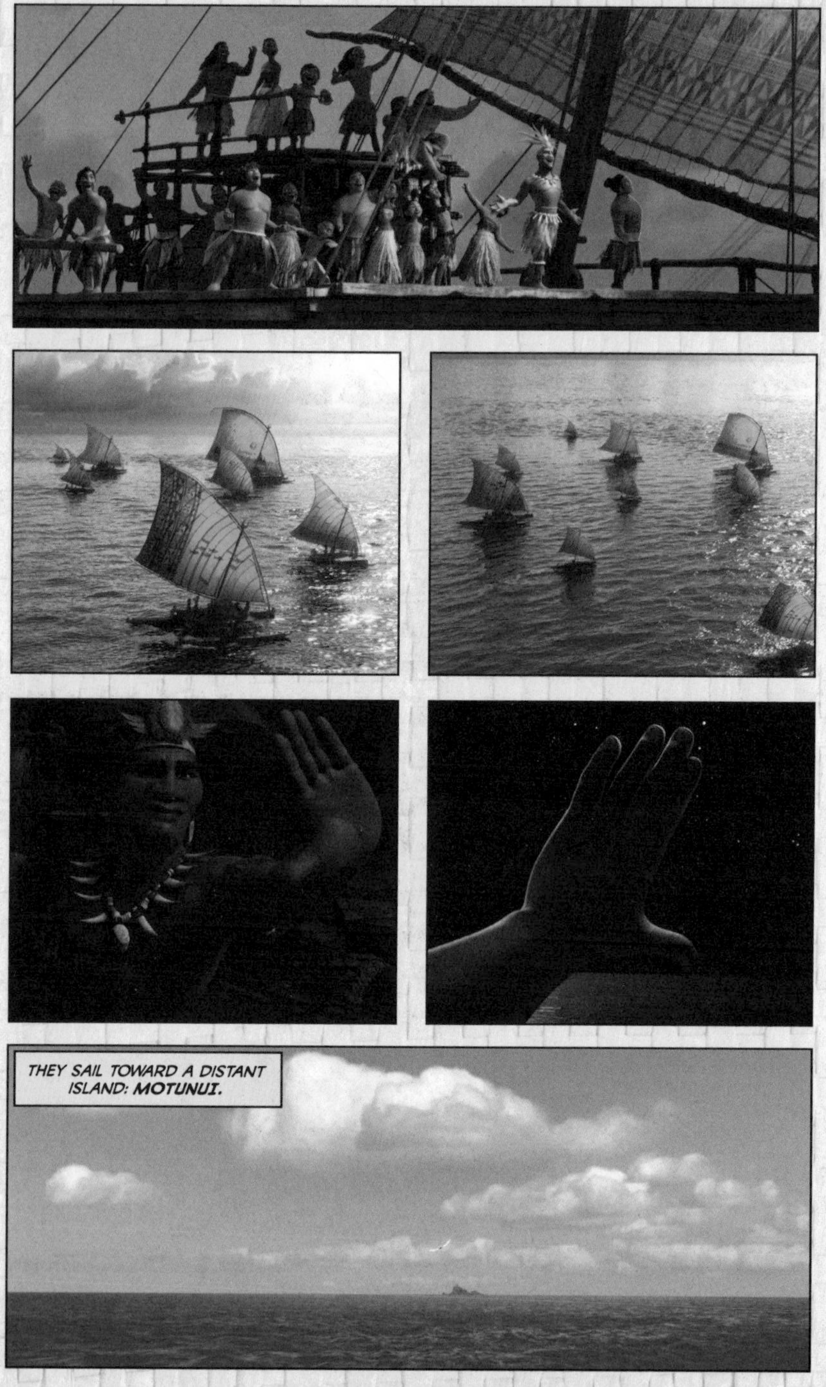
THEY SAIL TOWARD A DISTANT ISLAND: MOTUNUI.

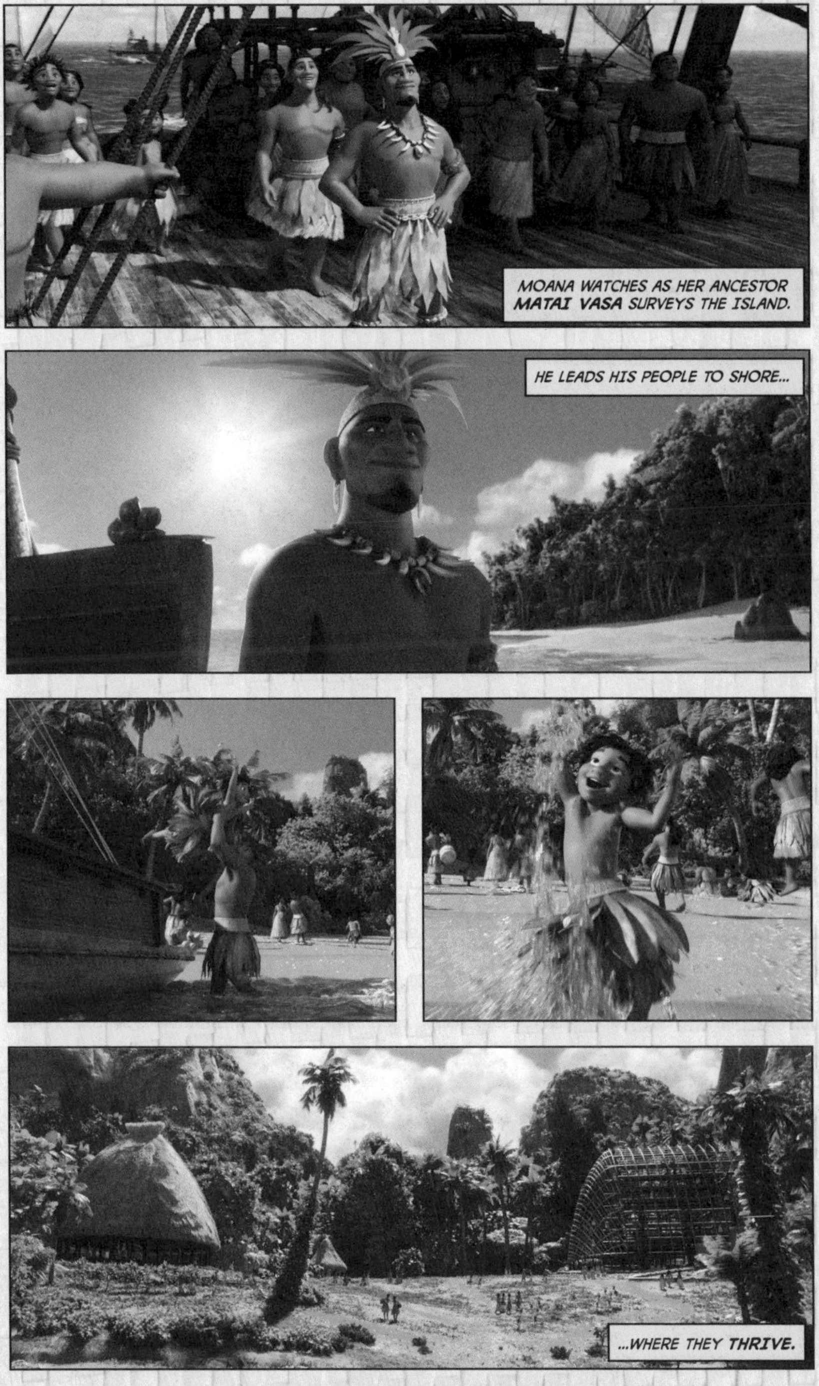
MOANA WATCHES AS HER ANCESTOR MATAI VASA SURVEYS THE ISLAND.
HE LEADS HIS PEOPLE TO SHORE...
...WHERE THEY THRIVE.

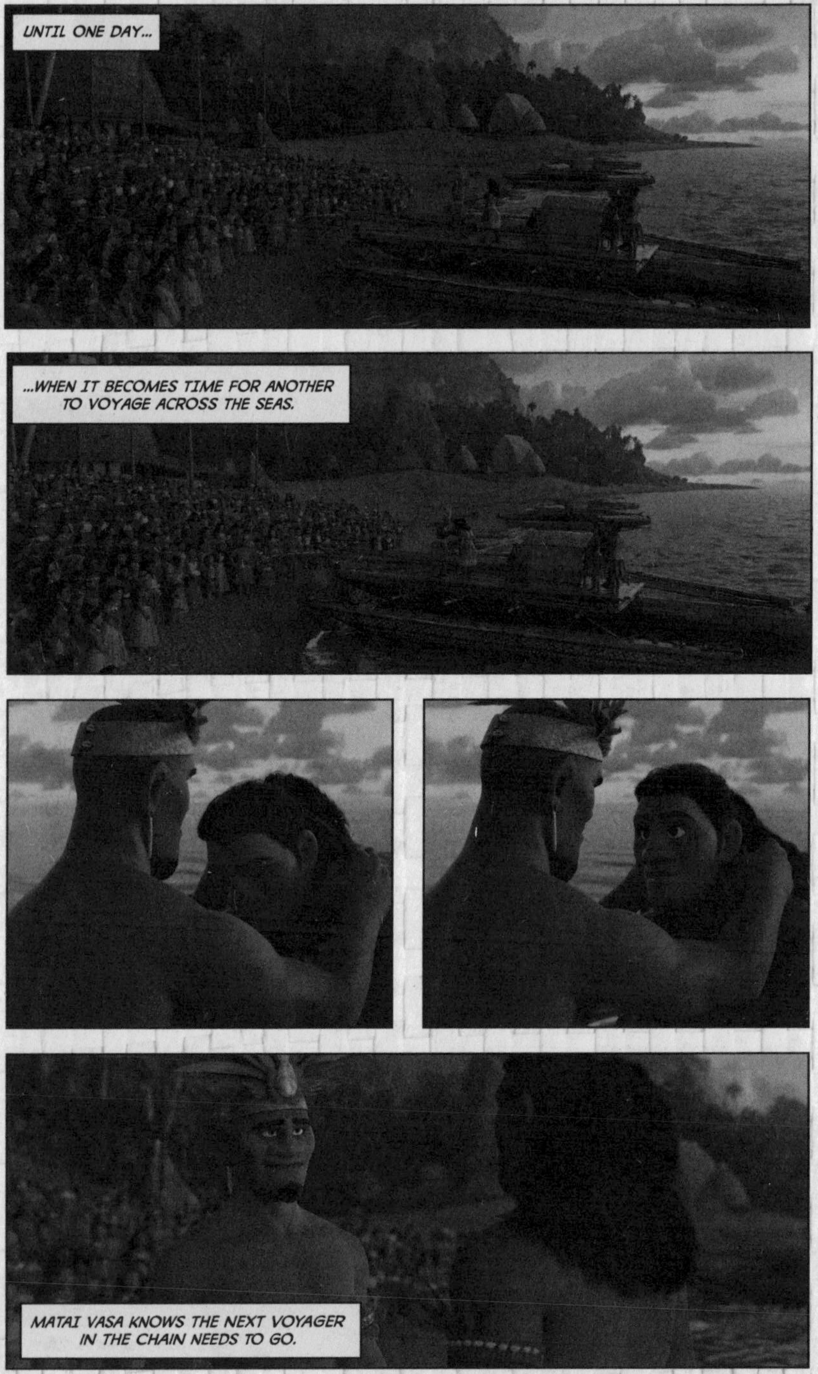
UNTIL ONE DAY...
...WHEN IT BECOMES TIME FOR ANOTHER TO VOYAGE ACROSS THE SEAS.
MATAI VASA KNOWS THE NEXT VOYAGER IN THE CHAIN NEEDS TO GO.

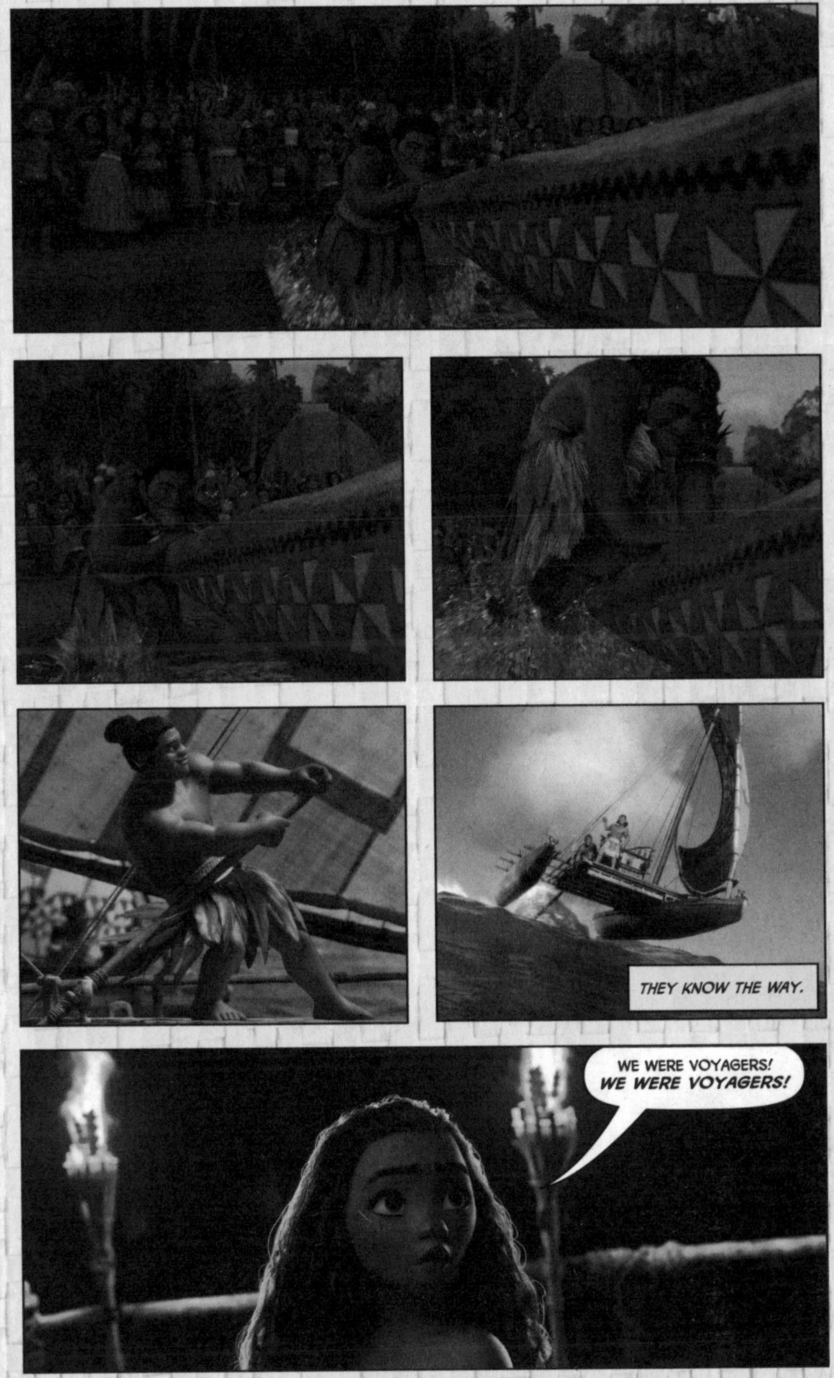
THEY KNOW THE WAY.
WE WERE VOYAGERS!
WE WERE VOYAGERS!

POWERFUL RHYTHMS

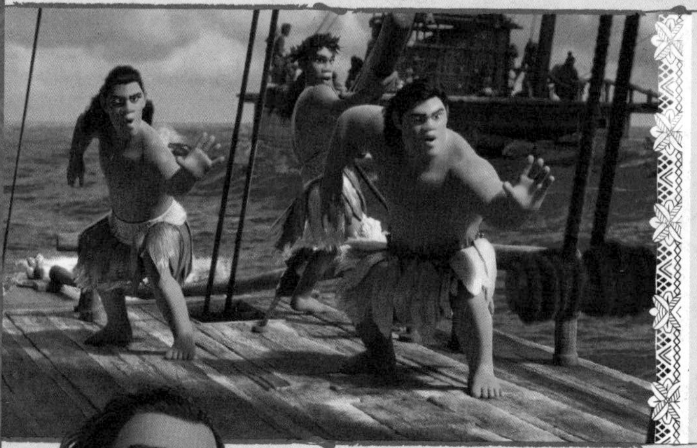

Rhythm is an important part of life in the Pacific Islands. In Tahitian celebrations, known as **HEIVA**, drum rhythm is used to guide the dancers and to announce the different parts of the ceremony. Some of the drums need to be played with sticks, while others are banged on with the hands.

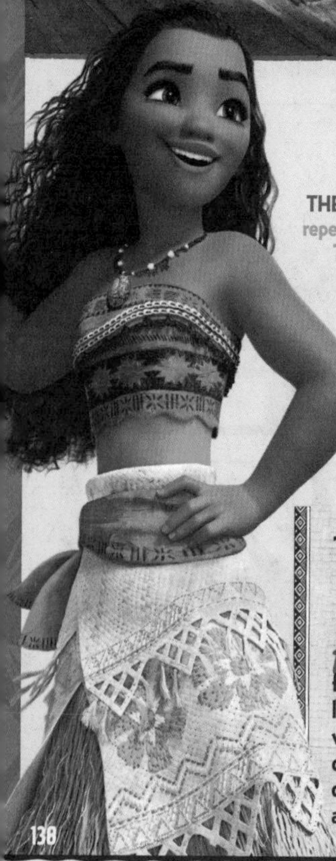

Do You Know?

When Moana enters the **CAVERN OF THE WAYFINDERS**, she bangs on a drum, repeating the rhythm she hears in the echo. Torches light, and she has visions of her **ANCESTORS** sailing on large canoes. Her people were **VOYAGERS**!

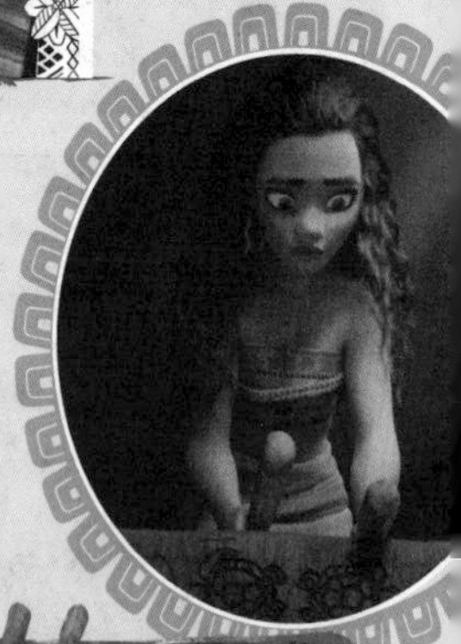

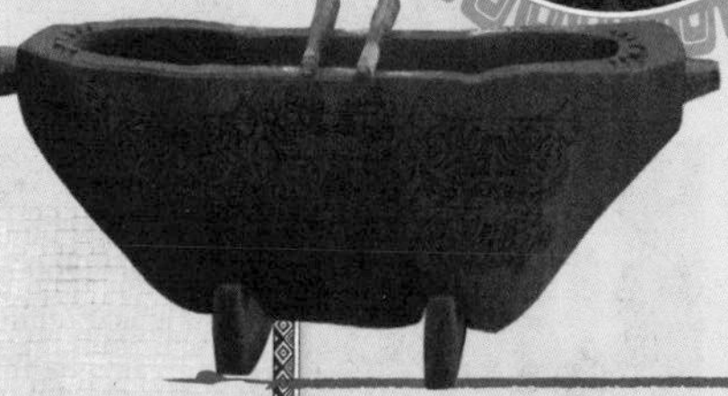

TO'ERE

A typical Tahitian **LOG DRUM** is called **TO'ERE** and is constructed from a hollowed-out hard wood log. The to'ere is played by beating various rhythm sets with a couple of cone-shaped **STICKS**. To'ere come in different sizes; the larger they are the deeper the sound they make.

CRAFT

Build YOUR LOG DRUM

FOLLOW the instructions to create your special **DRUM**, then use it like the people of Motunui to bang your own **RHYTHM** and accompany your exciting songs!

ASK A GROWN-UP FOR HELP!

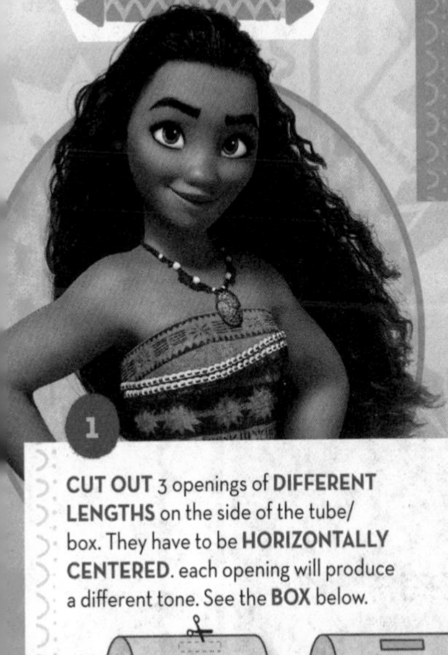

You'll need:

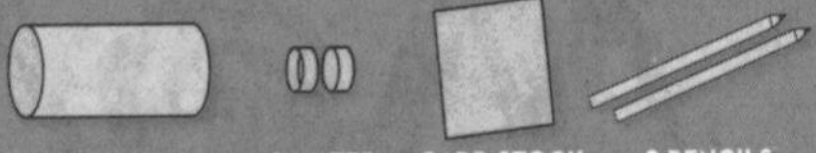

1 EMPTY TUBE OF CHIPS (OR A LONG NARROW BOX) · 2 WATER-BOTTLE LIDS · CARD STOCK · 2 PENCILS

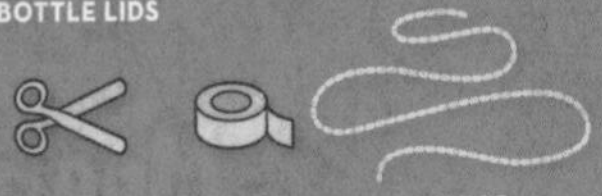

ROUND-TIP SCISSORS · TAPE AND GLUE · A PIECE OF STRING

1

CUT OUT 3 openings of **DIFFERENT LENGTHS** on the side of the tube/ box. They have to be **HORIZONTALLY CENTERED**. each opening will produce a different tone. See the **BOX** below.

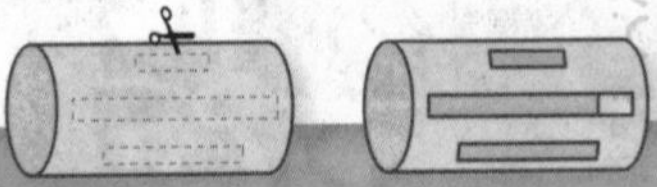

2

If you chose a tube, **DRAW** a circle on the card stock, using the bottom of the tube as a guide. Then, **CUT IT** out and tape it to the tube to **CLOSE** its upper side.

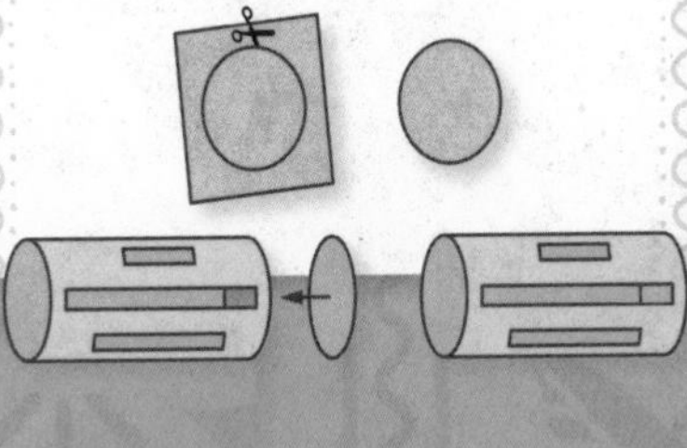

3

ASK A GROWN-UP to make a **HOLE** on the side of each water-bottle lid.

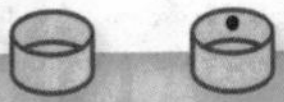

4

GLUE the water-bottle lids to the **TOP** and to the **BOTTOM** of the tube.

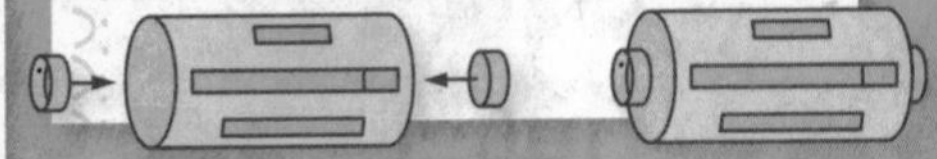

5

Now **TIE** the string to the lids by inserting its ends into the holes and then **SECURING** them with two knots. This will be your strap. **USE** the pencils to **BANG** your rhythm on the drum!

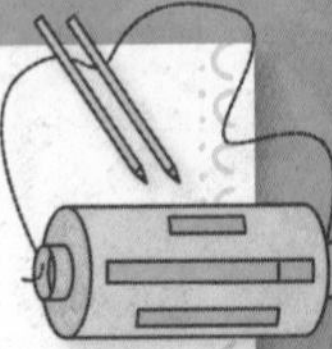

How to play:

HIT the side of each cutout and you log drum will make different **TONES**!

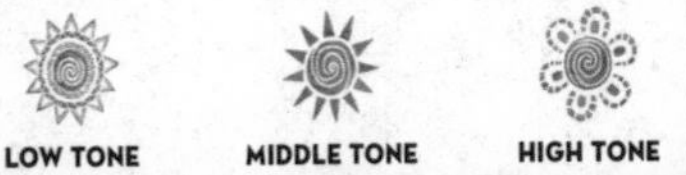

LOW TONE · MIDDLE TONE · HIGH TONE

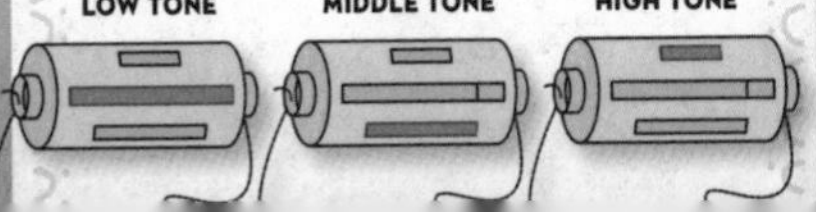

Disney

MOANA

Moana's Decision

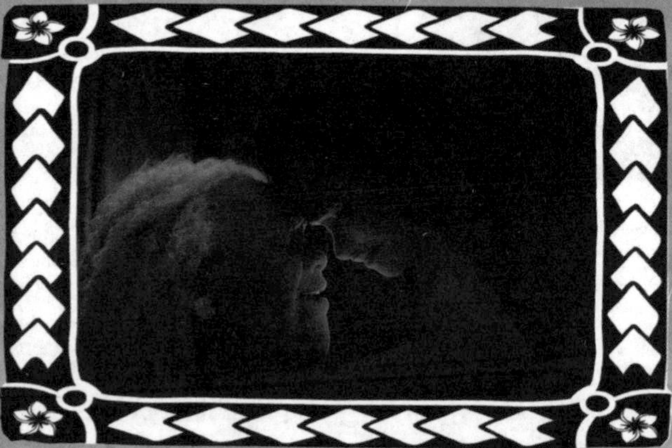

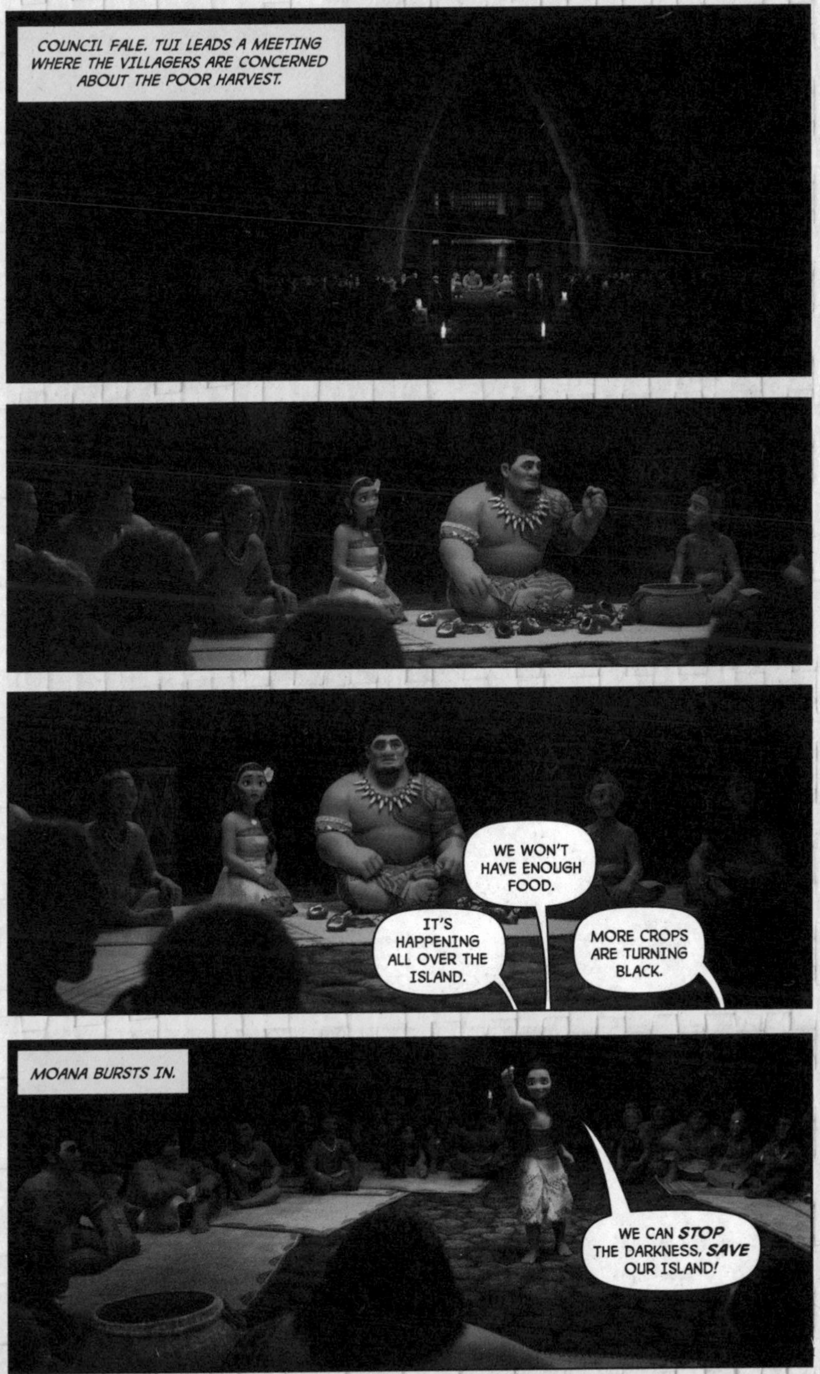
COUNCIL FALE. TUI LEADS A MEETING WHERE THE VILLAGERS ARE CONCERNED ABOUT THE POOR HARVEST.
WE WON'T HAVE ENOUGH FOOD.
IT'S HAPPENING ALL OVER THE ISLAND.
MORE CROPS ARE TURNING BLACK.
MOANA BURSTS IN.
WE CAN *STOP* THE DARKNESS, *SAVE* OUR ISLAND!

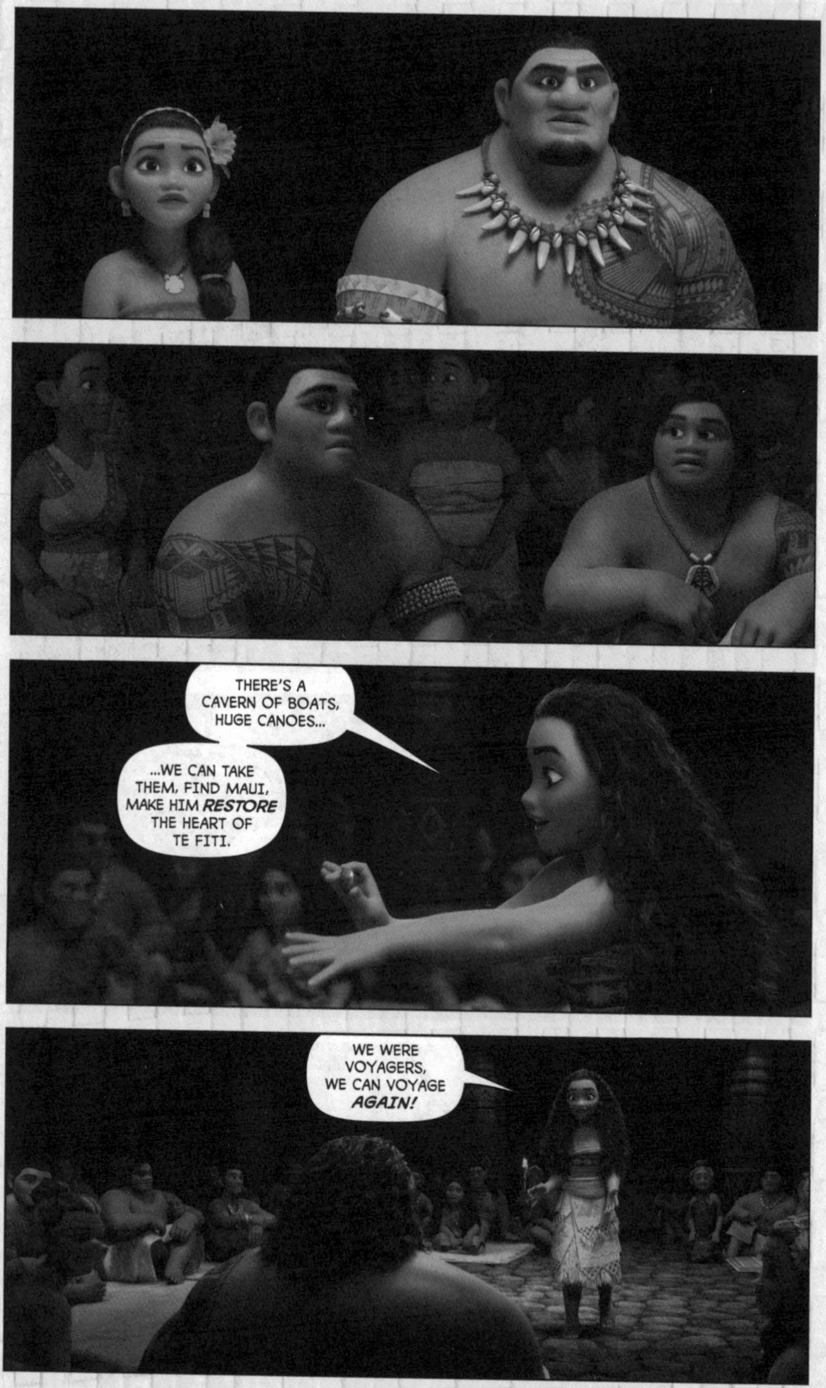
THERE'S A CAVERN OF BOATS, HUGE CANOES...
...WE CAN TAKE THEM, FIND MAUI, MAKE HIM RESTORE THE HEART OF TE FITI.
WE WERE VOYAGERS, WE CAN VOYAGE AGAIN!

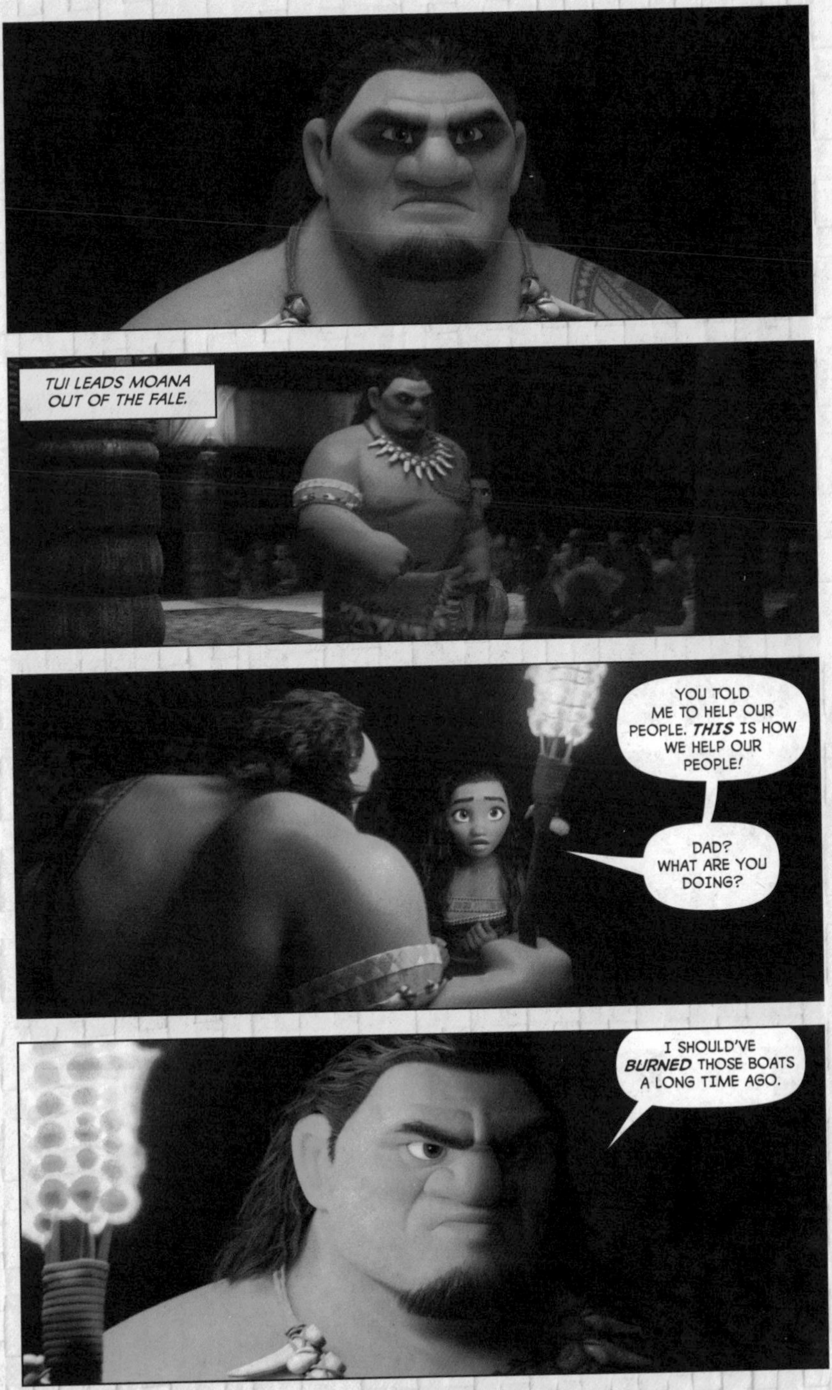
TUI LEADS MOANA OUT OF THE FALE.
YOU TOLD ME TO HELP OUR PEOPLE. THIS IS HOW WE HELP OUR PEOPLE!
DAD? WHAT ARE YOU DOING?
I SHOULD'VE BURNED THOSE BOATS A LONG TIME AGO.

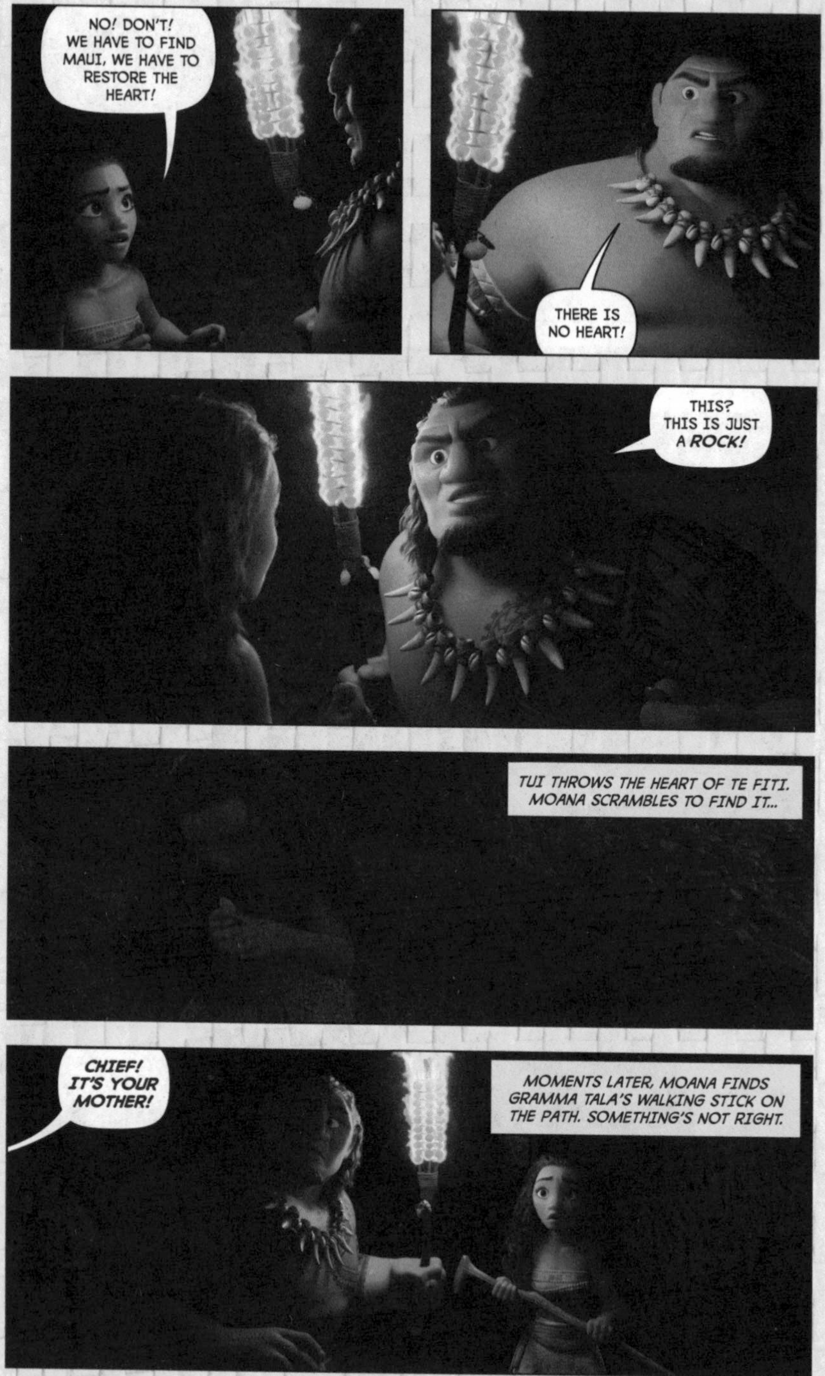
NO! DON'T! WE HAVE TO FIND MAUI, WE HAVE TO RESTORE THE HEART!
THERE IS NO HEART!
THIS? THIS IS JUST A *ROCK!*
TUI THROWS THE HEART OF TE FITI. MOANA SCRAMBLES TO FIND IT...
CHIEF! IT'S YOUR MOTHER!
MOMENTS LATER, MOANA FINDS GRAMMA TALA'S WALKING STICK ON THE PATH. SOMETHING'S NOT RIGHT.

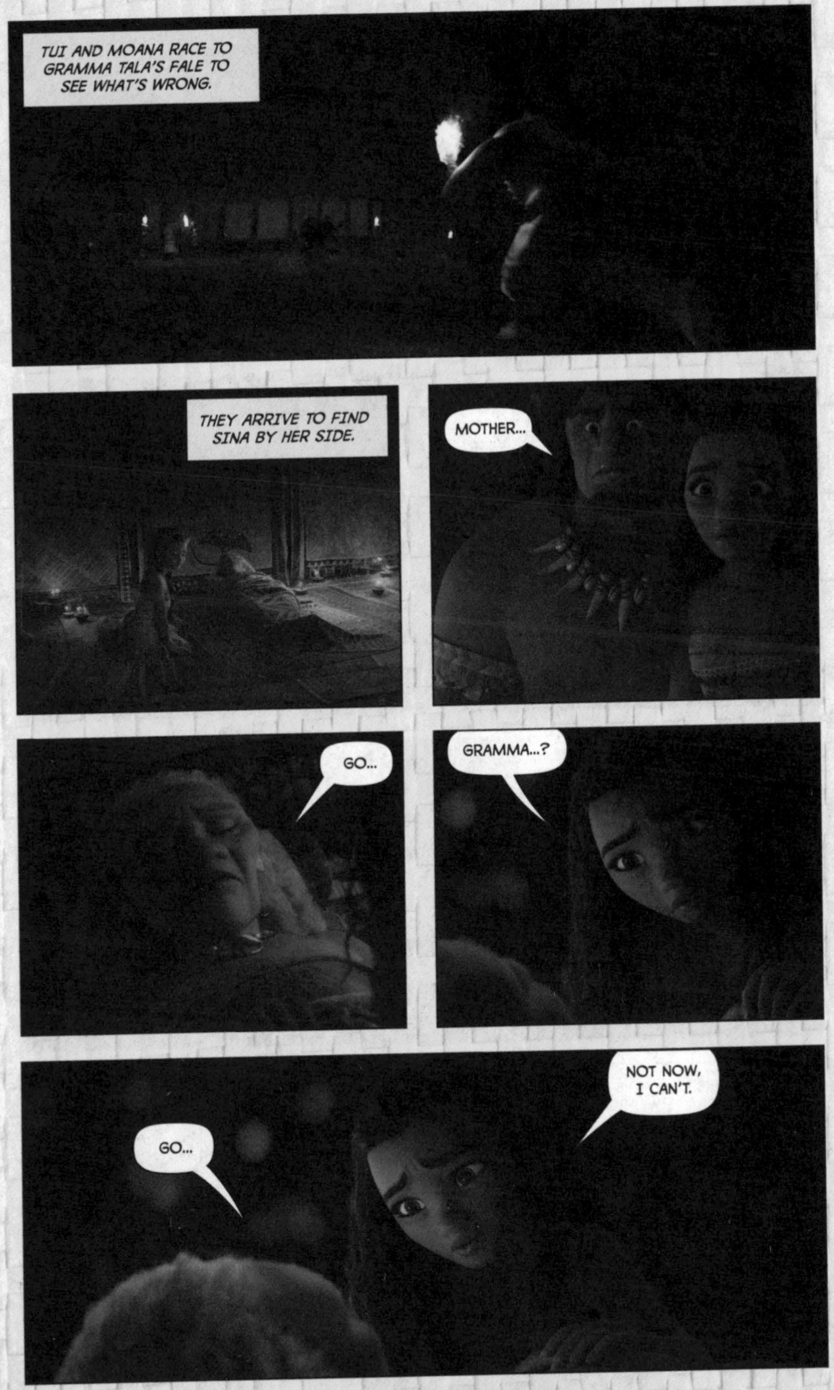
TUI AND MOANA RACE TO GRAMMA TALA'S FALE TO SEE WHAT'S WRONG.
THEY ARRIVE TO FIND SINA BY HER SIDE.
MOTHER...
GO...
GRAMMA...?
GO...
NOT NOW, I CAN'T.

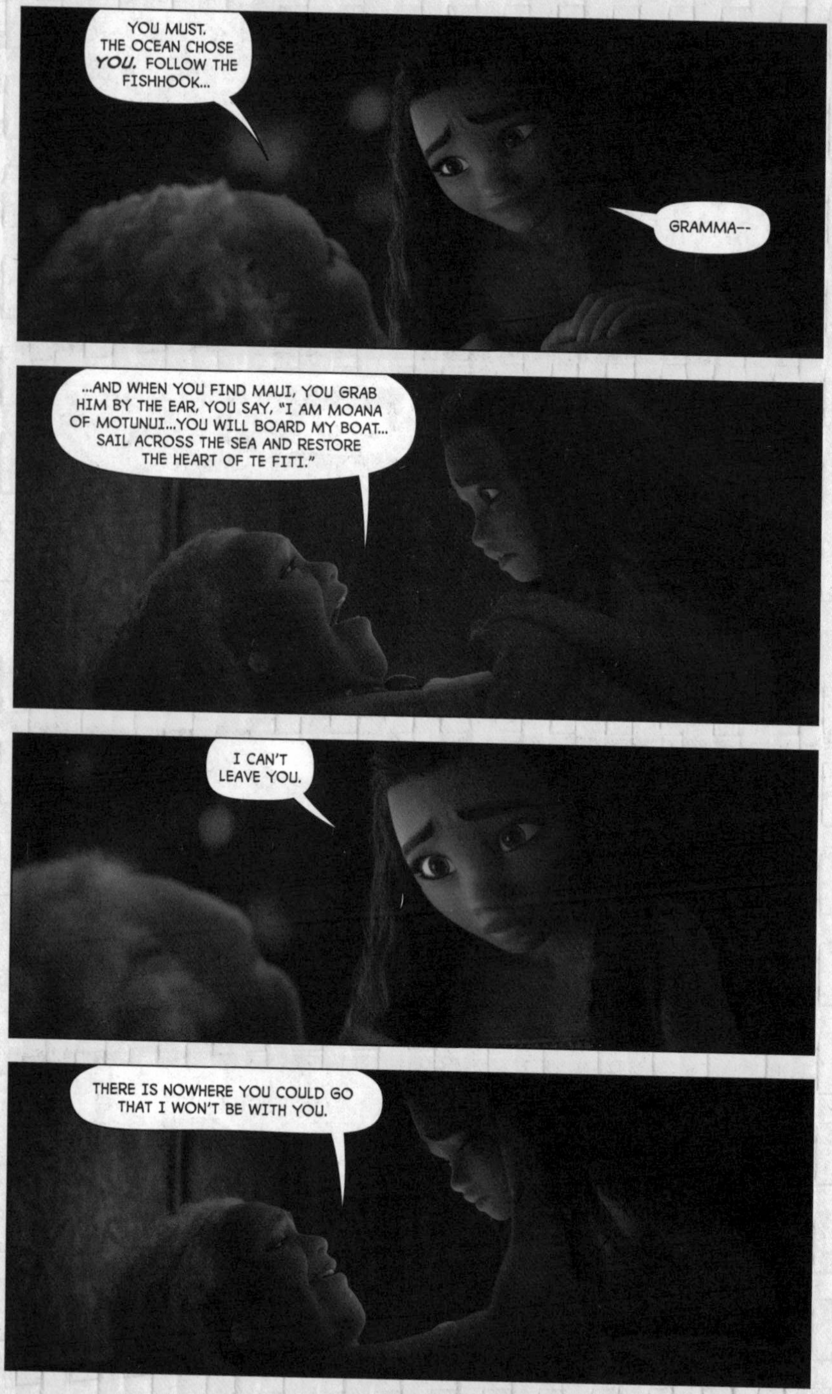
YOU MUST. THE OCEAN CHOSE *YOU.* FOLLOW THE FISHHOOK...
GRAMMA--
...AND WHEN YOU FIND MAUI, YOU GRAB HIM BY THE EAR, YOU SAY, "I AM MOANA OF MOTUNUI...YOU WILL BOARD MY BOAT... SAIL ACROSS THE SEA AND RESTORE THE HEART OF TE FITI."
I CAN'T LEAVE YOU.
THERE IS NOWHERE YOU COULD GO THAT I WON'T BE WITH YOU.

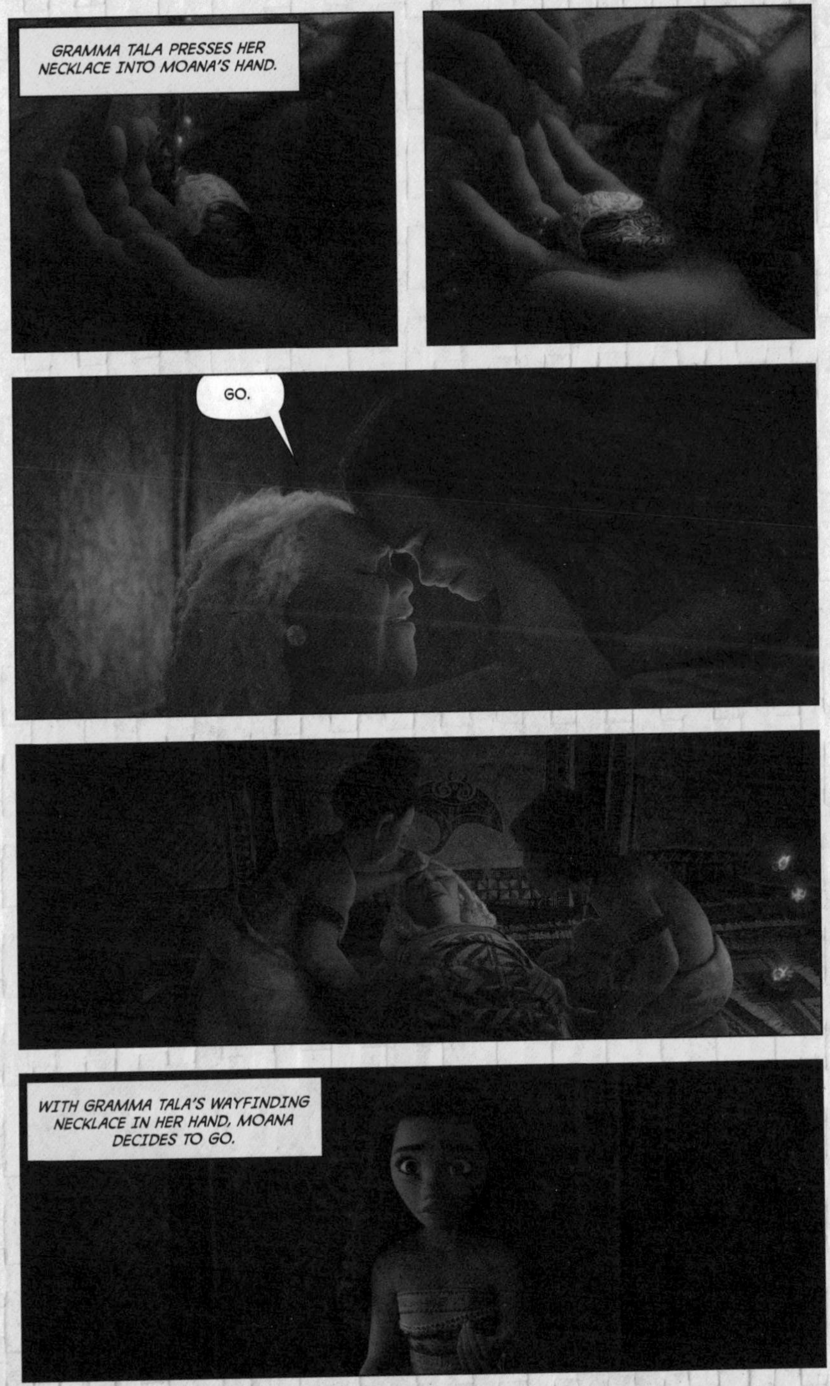
GRAMMA TALA PRESSES HER NECKLACE INTO MOANA'S HAND.
GO.
WITH GRAMMA TALA'S WAYFINDING NECKLACE IN HER HAND, MOANA DECIDES TO GO.

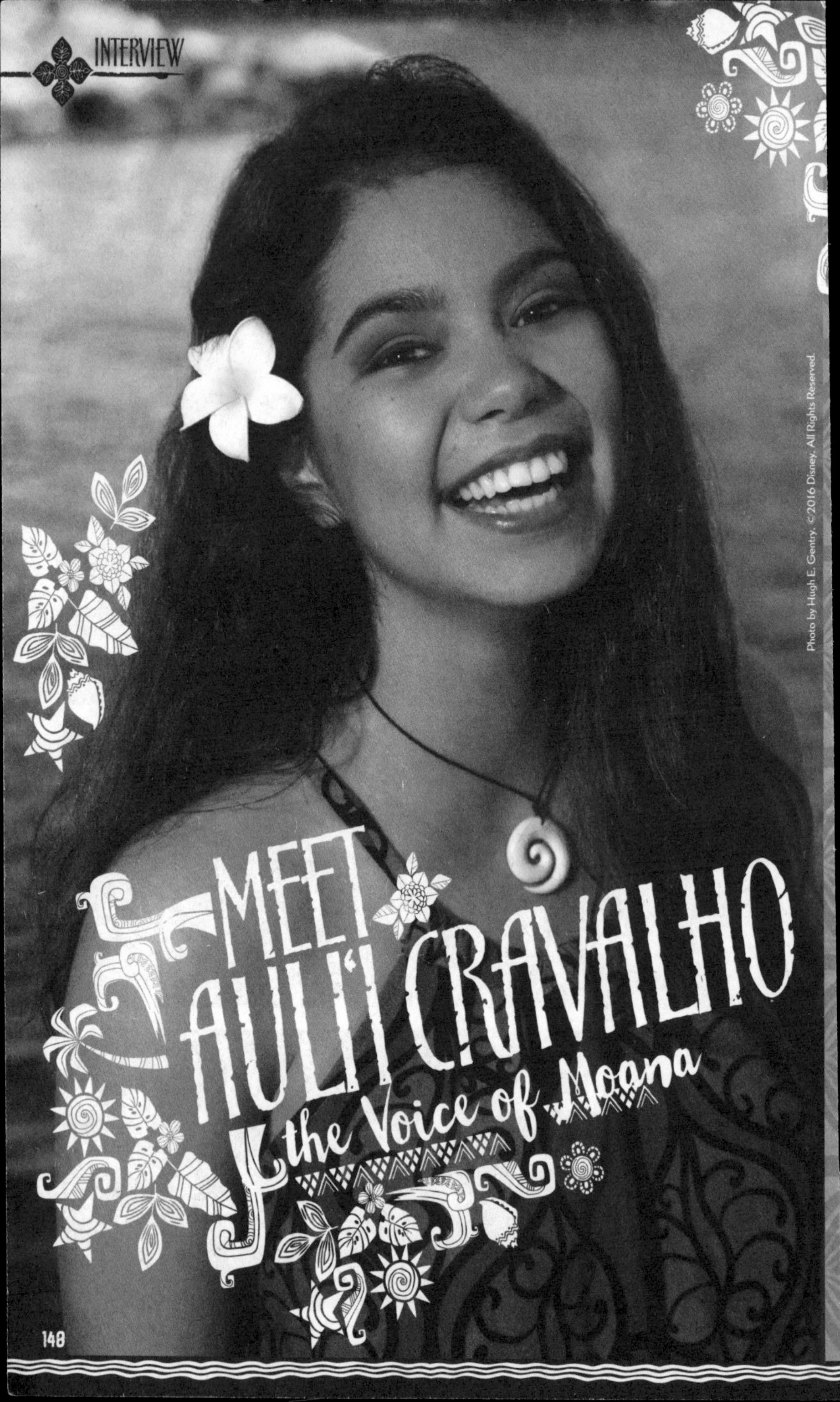

MEET AULI'I CRAVALHO
the Voice of Moana

Connected to her people, her land, and the ocean, 15-year-old Auli'i Cravalho really understands how to play the part of Moana. Find out more about her!

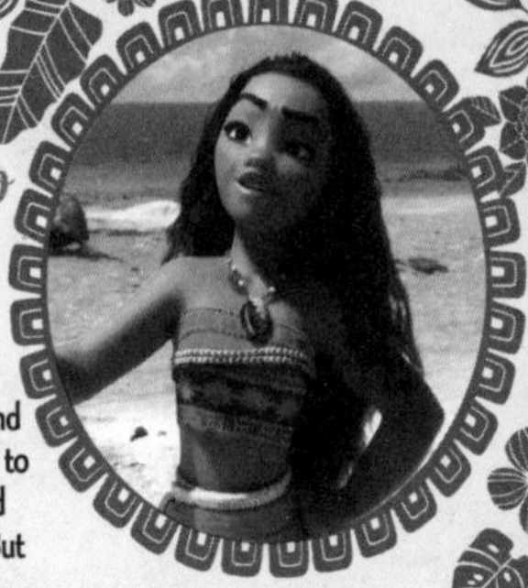

Q: How did you feel when you found out there would be a new Polynesian Disney character?
A: I was so excited when I heard there was going to be a new character. It was such a big buzz on my campus because I go to Kamehameha Schools, which is a school for students with Native Hawaiian ancestry.

> I HAVE BEEN SINGING EVER SINCE I WAS BORN! I WAS A SCREAMER, AND I DEVELOPED AMAZING LUNGS.

Q: How did you get cast in the film?
A: I actually didn't try out. In a totally unrelated audition, my friends and I sang in acapella for a non-profit organization. The same woman who was casting that was also casting for Disney. When she saw my audition, she contacted my mom.

Q: Who are your mentors and what have they taught you?
A: My mom. Mothers teach you everything. She taught me how to do my chores, which I still mess up on. She teaches me to be brave when I feel like I have nothing more to give, and to persevere when I feel like I've given my all. And she teaches me to always remember where I'm from and my roots; and no matter where I go, whether it's to a new city or a new school, to remember to be kind. We are one people. We are all human, and no one is better than another person.

Q: What do you hope people learn from the story of Moana?
A: I hope people learn more about our culture, and I hope they are motivated to learn about navigation and the stars and the ocean. But I also hope they become more rooted.

Q: Have any crazy or exciting things happened while you've been recording?
A: I was very surprised when I had to repeat the lines over and over and over again; that's something that I wasn't expecting. The process of recording is really fun and I love it!

Q: What do you do in your free time?
A: I don't have cable TV, so I read a lot. I LOVE to read. I sing, I have voice lessons. And I love to hang out with my friends.

Q: Other than Moana, who is your favorite Disney Character?
A: It would be between Mulan and Merida. With Merida, she understands that she has to make her own future and become her own person. Mulan, she's just awesome! She's a very empowered character.

Q: If you could use Maui's hook, what animal would you change into?
A: I would change into a house cat, not a lion, just a house cat. Specifically my house cat because I treat mine very well and give them a lot of snacks.

A Bond with the ocean

"I definitely connect to my culture," says Auli'i. "I dance hula, I paddle, I'm a water baby... I swim, I play water polo. Just like Moana connects to the water, so do I. I love the ocean!"

Q: How long have you been singing?
A: I have been singing ever since I was born! I was a screamer, and I developed amazing lungs. I sing in my church choir, and my family has always been very musical.

Q: What advice can you share with young girls who have a dream?
A: If you want to do something, you need to put in the work. When I was little, I wanted to play tag with the boys, but they were really fast. So every day after school I ran laps around my back yard to get faster. And I became the first girl to play tag on the playground in my elementary school!

ABOUT AULI'I

FAMILY AND TRADITIONS

Moana has a really strong bond with her family and traditions. We asked Auli'i how she relates to that. "I have a really big family. Whenever we'd get together we'd kanikapila, which is an impromptu music jam session, and it would be a really great time. And because I'm an only child, being able to see all of my cousins is what made me feel like I had a family. Because when it's just me, myself and I, home with my two cats, it's just a little lonely."

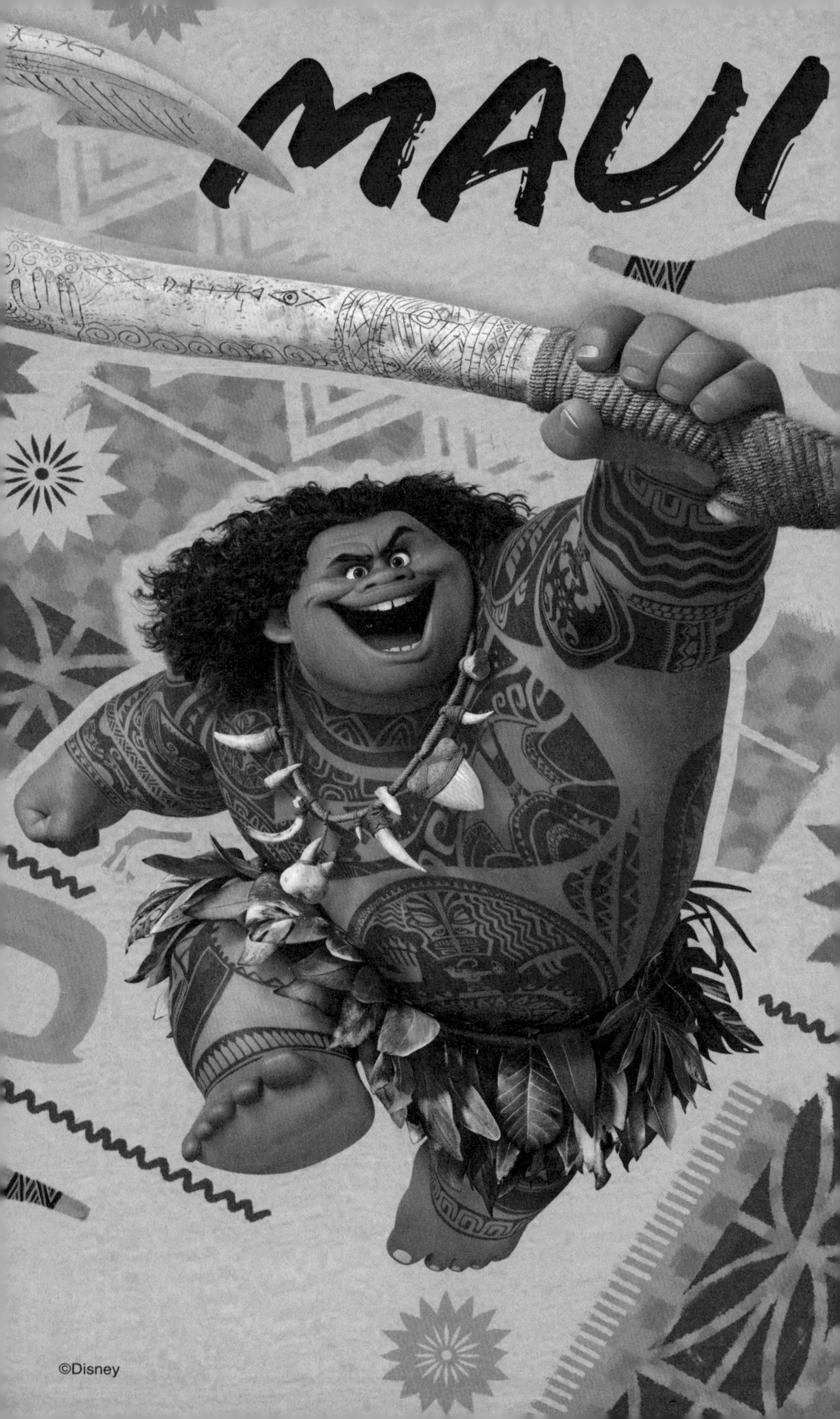
MAUI

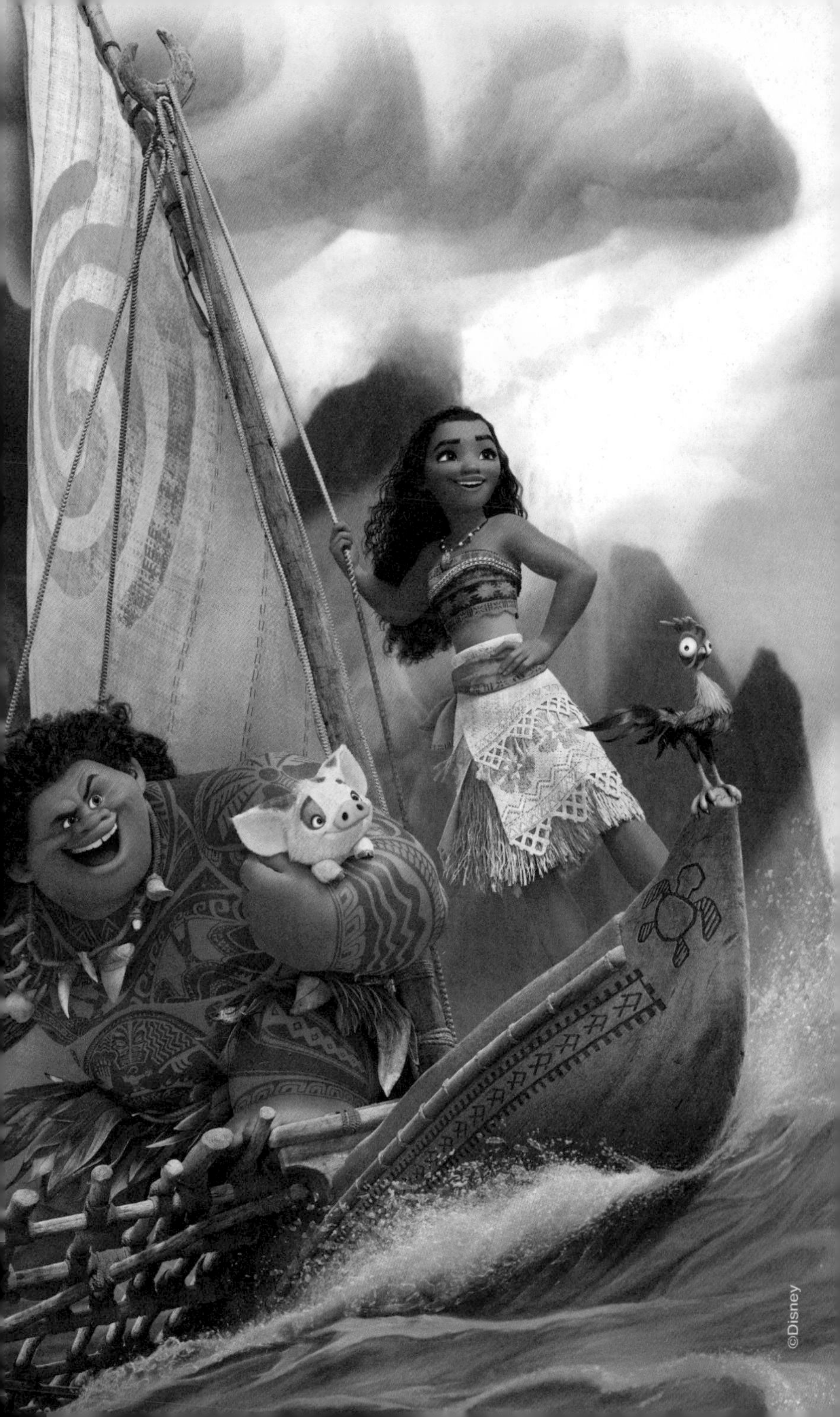

Disney Moana

Moana Meets Maui

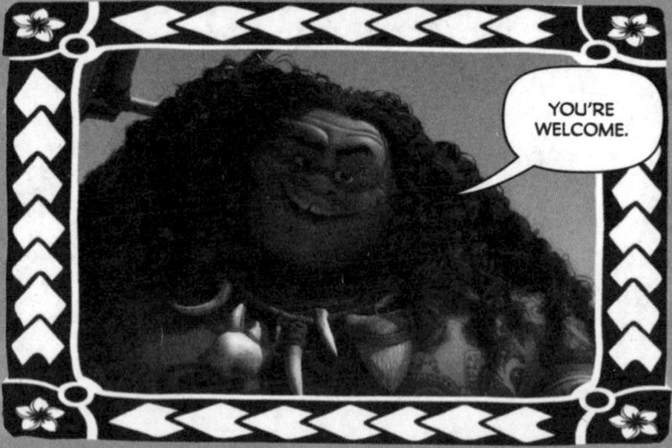
YOU'RE WELCOME.

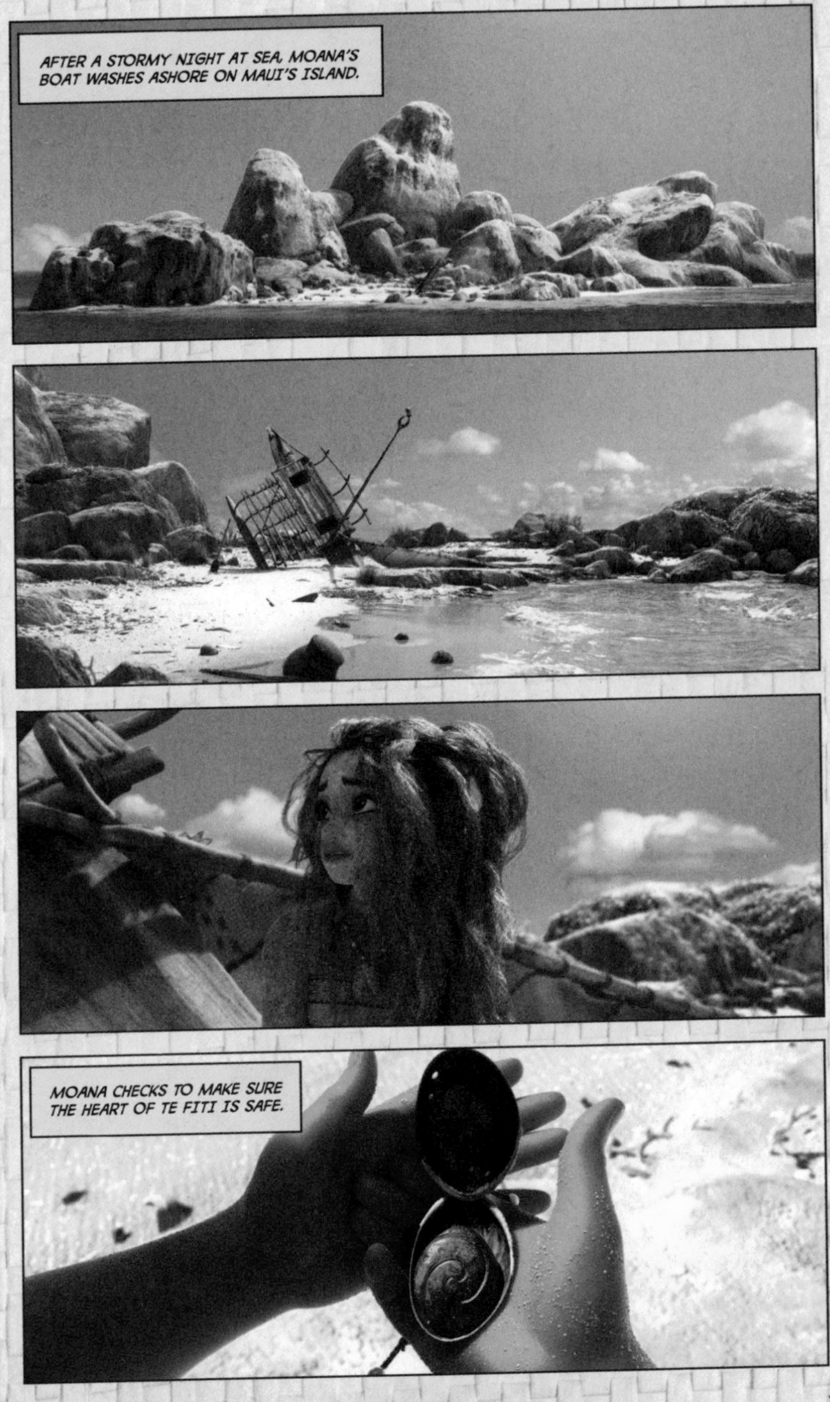
AFTER A STORMY NIGHT AT SEA, MOANA'S BOAT WASHES ASHORE ON MAUI'S ISLAND.
MOANA CHECKS TO MAKE SURE THE HEART OF TE FITI IS SAFE.

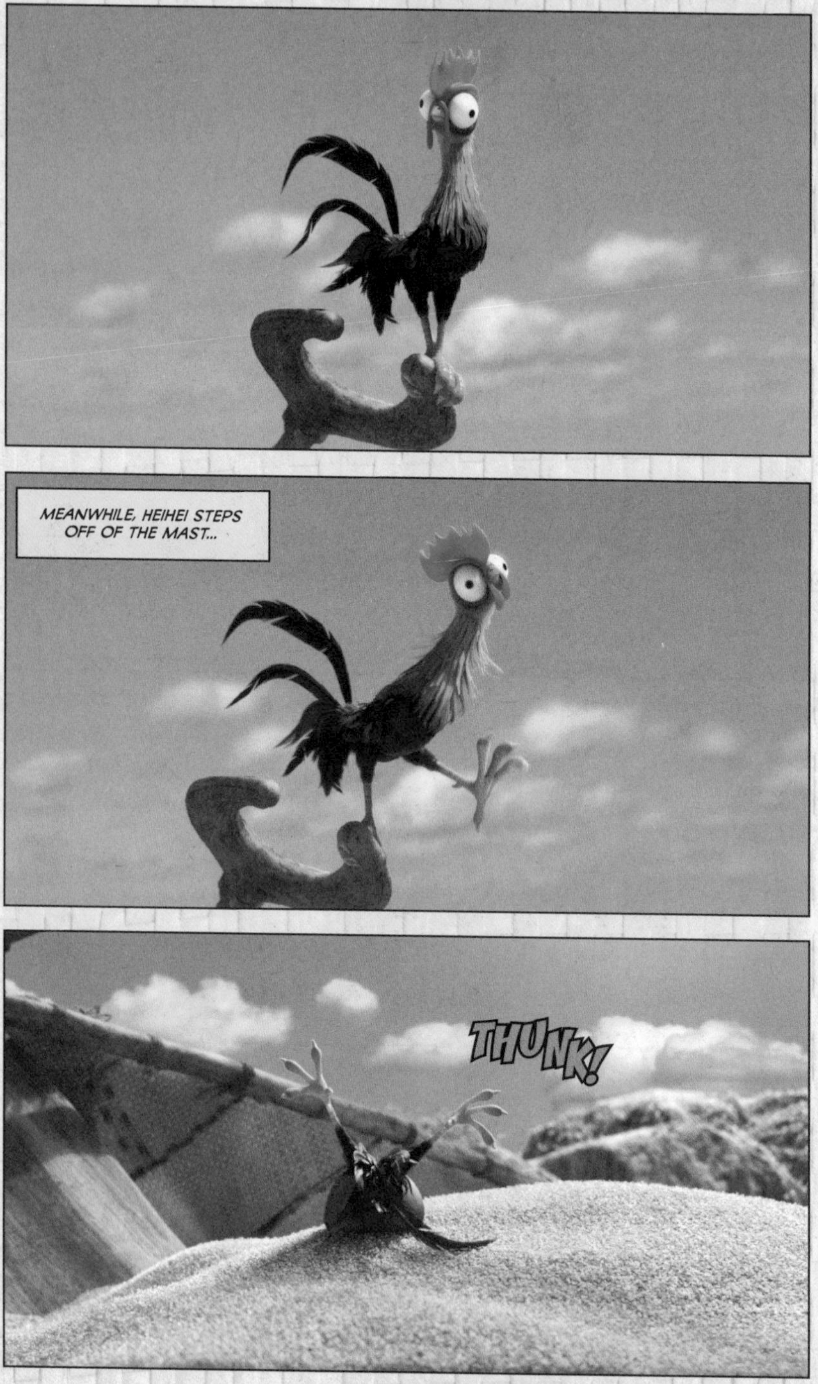
MEANWHILE, HEIHEI STEPS OFF OF THE MAST...
THUNK!

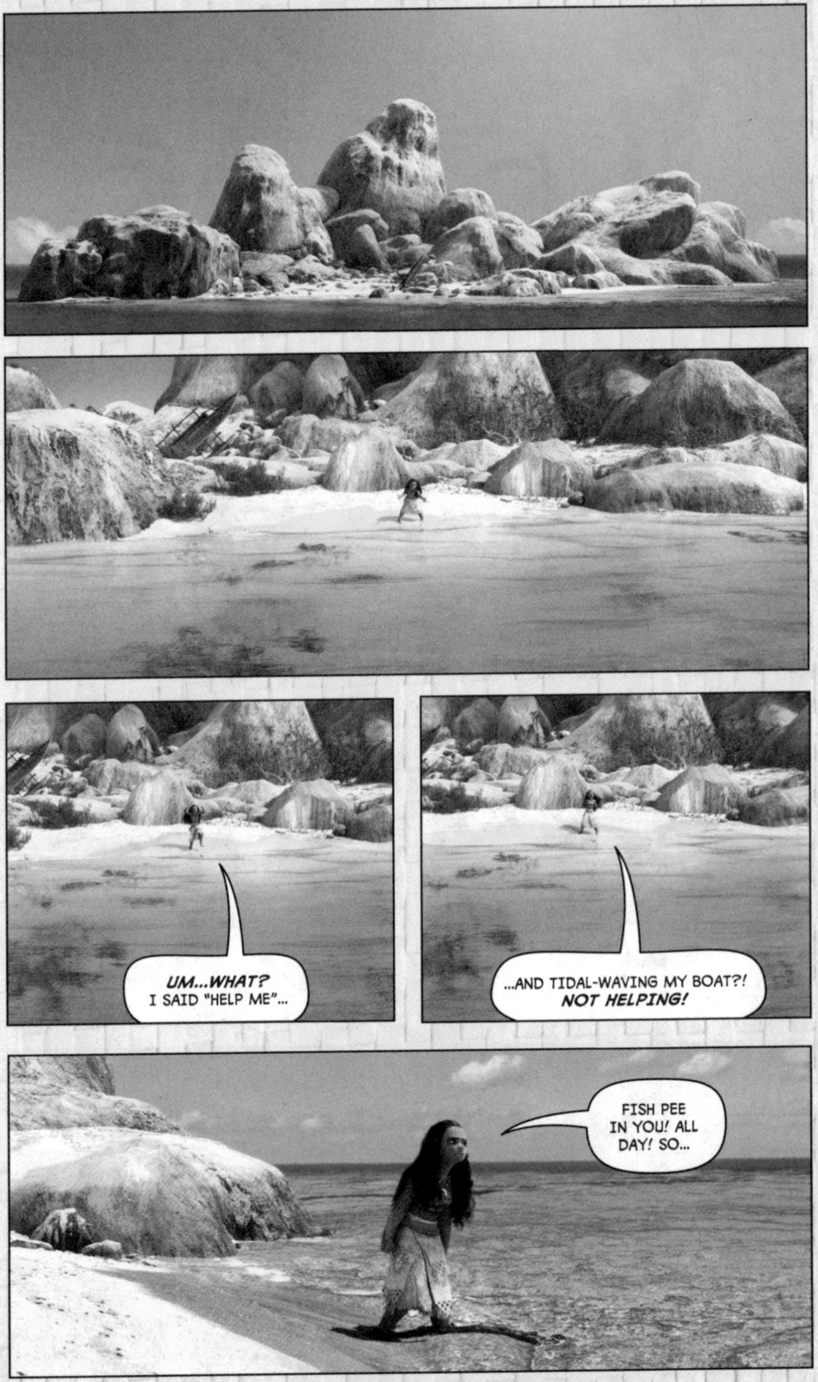
UM...WHAT?
I SAID "HELP ME"...
...AND TIDAL-WAVING MY BOAT?!
NOT HELPING!
FISH PEE IN YOU! ALL DAY! SO...

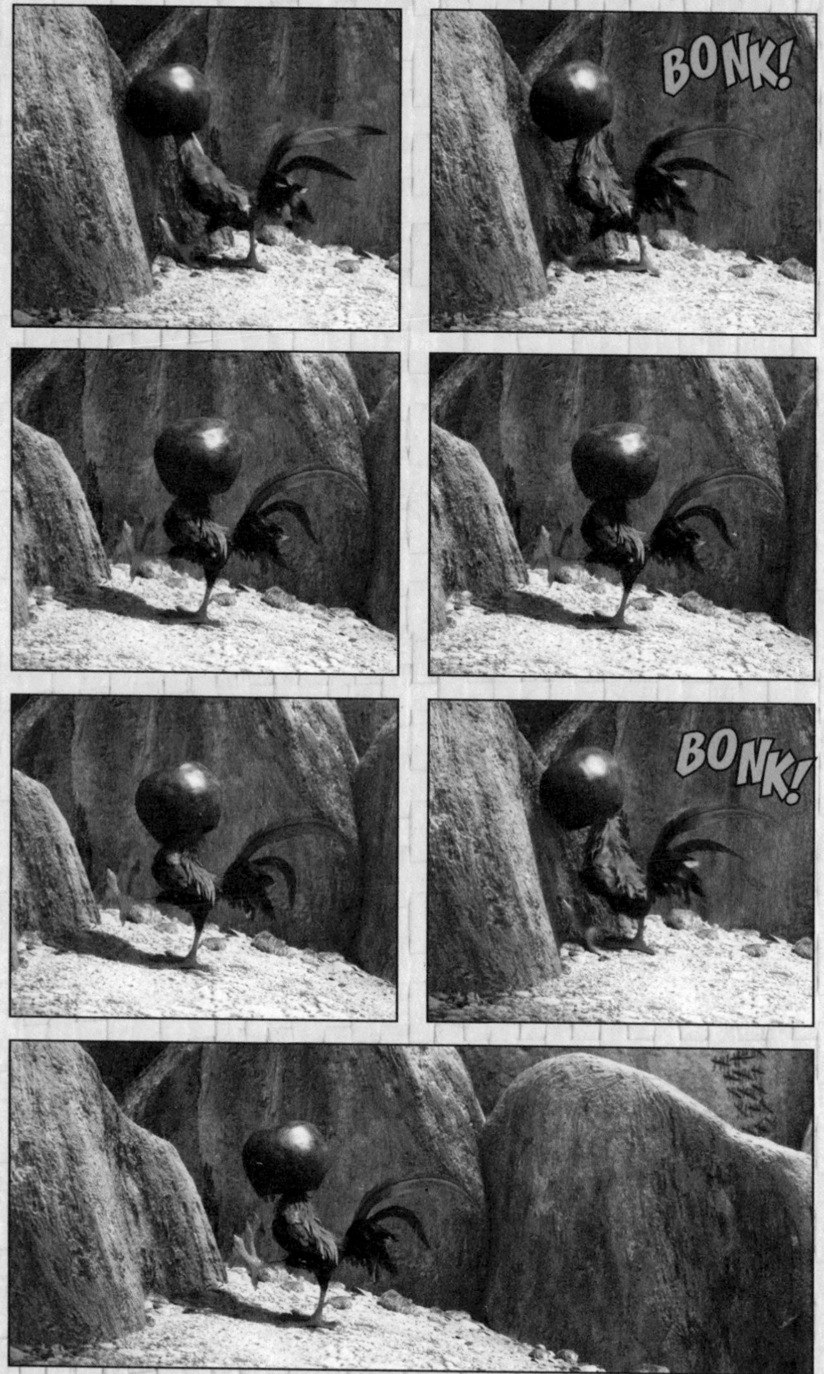
BONK!
BONK!

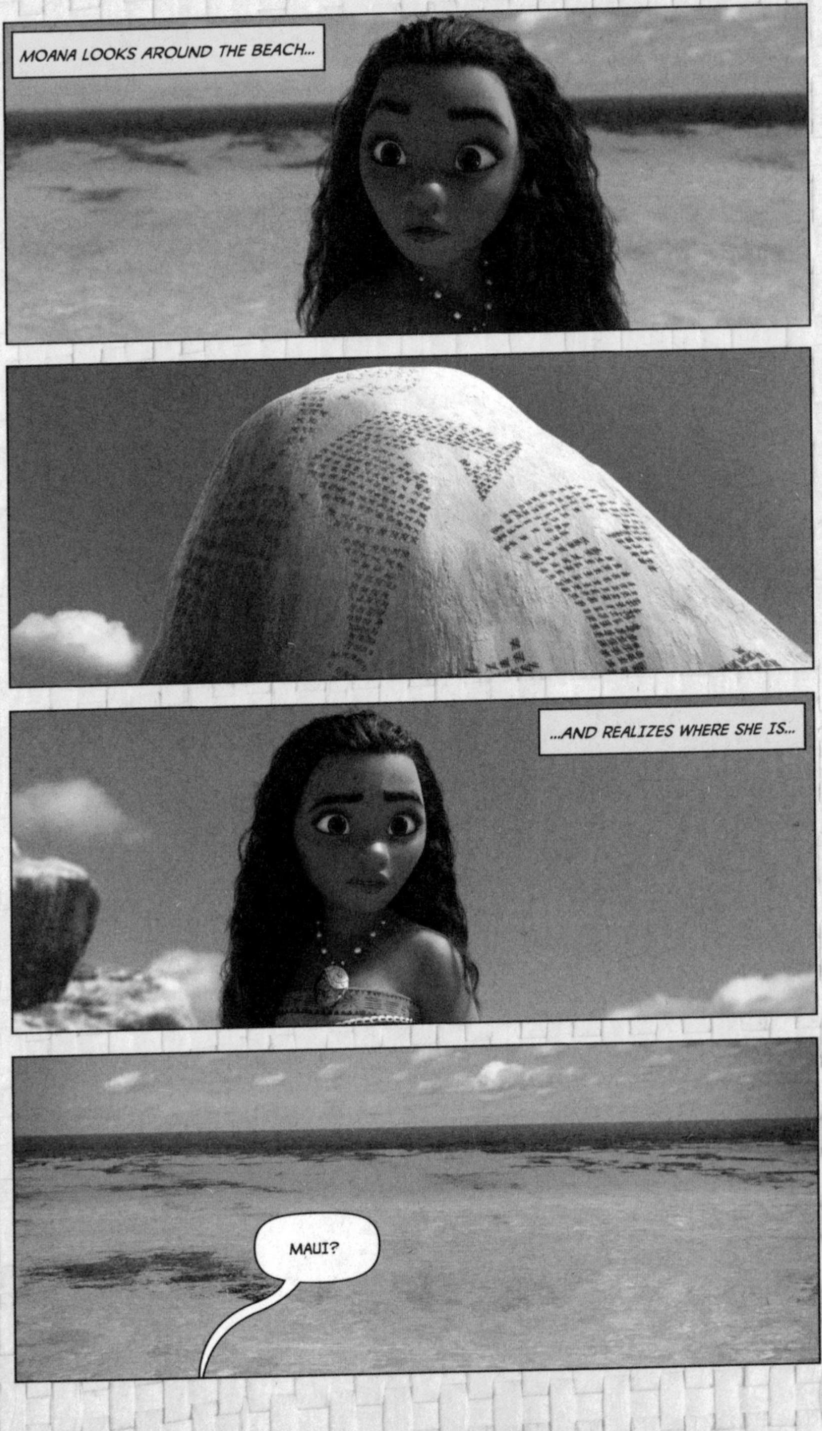
MOANA LOOKS AROUND THE BEACH...
...AND REALIZES WHERE SHE IS...
MAUI?

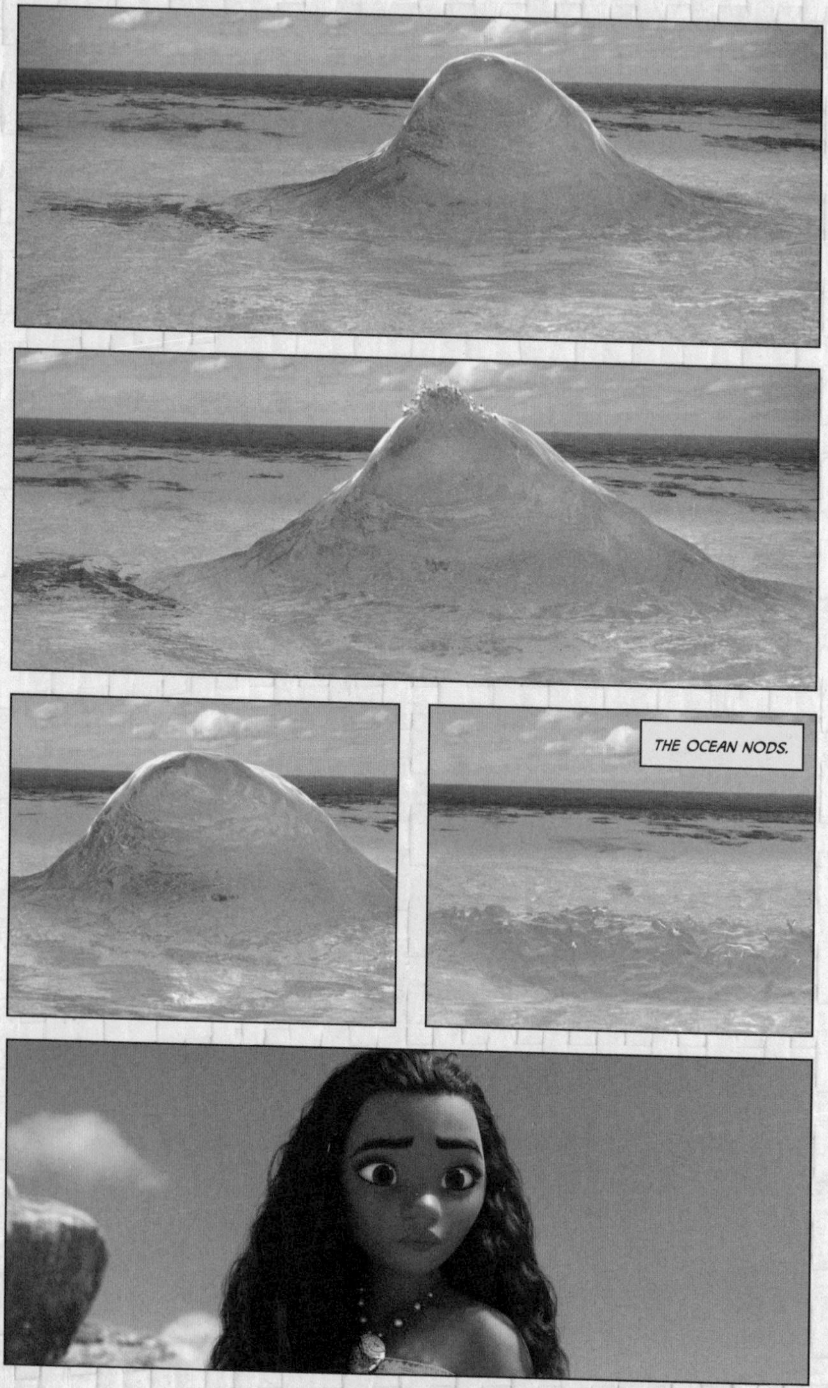
THE OCEAN NODS.

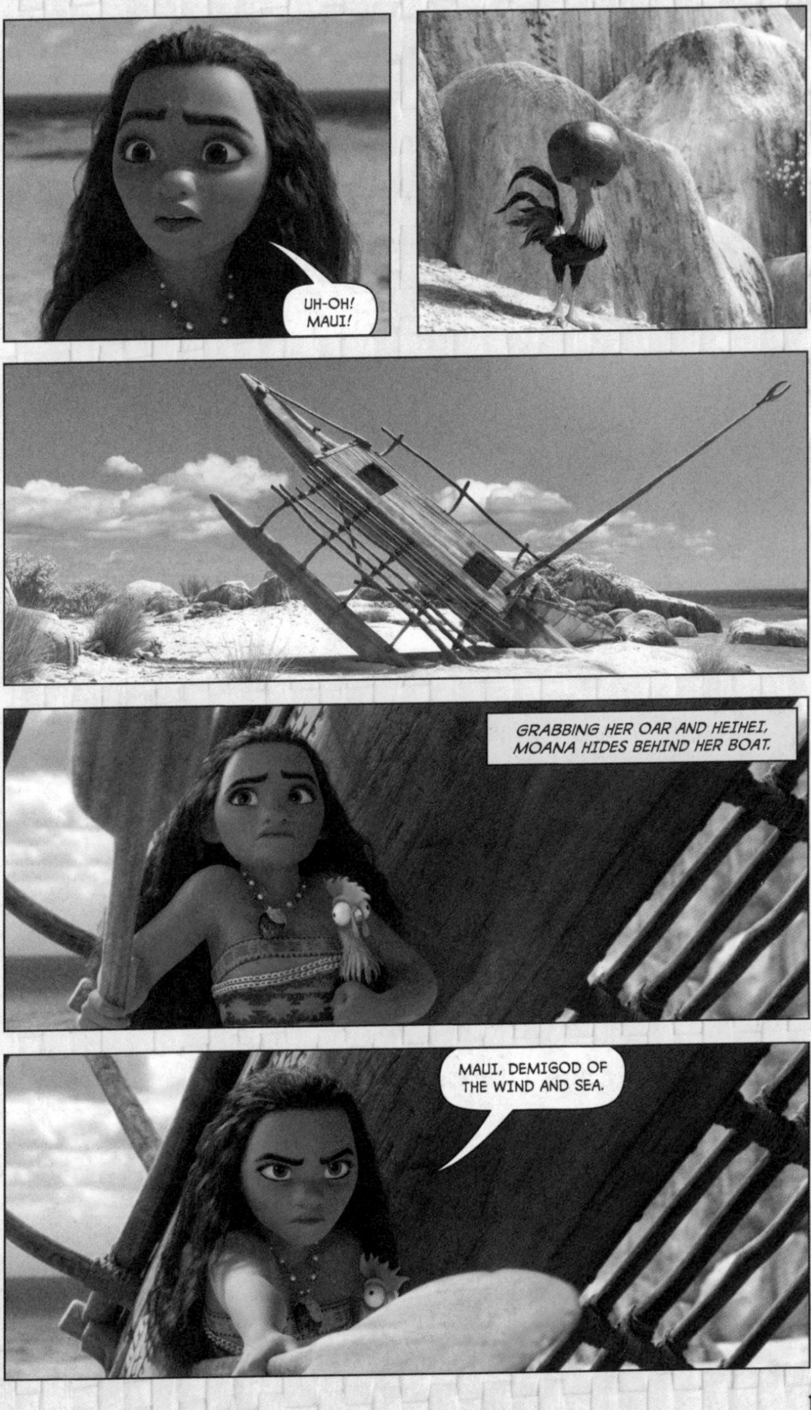
UH-OH! MAUI!
GRABBING HER OAR AND HEIHEI, MOANA HIDES BEHIND HER BOAT.
MAUI, DEMIGOD OF THE WIND AND SEA.

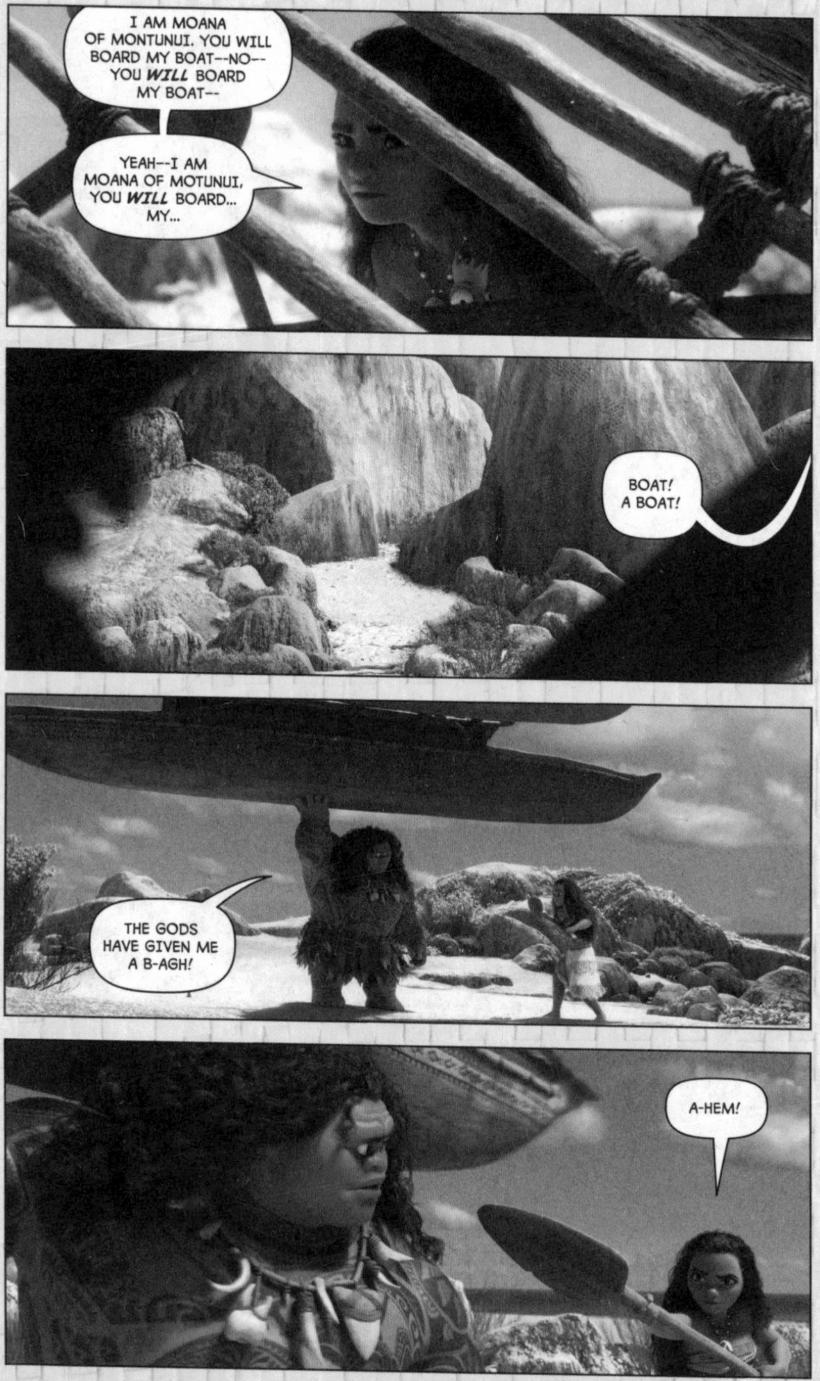
I AM MOANA OF MONTUNUI. YOU WILL BOARD MY BOAT--NO-- YOU *WILL* BOARD MY BOAT--
YEAH--I AM MOANA OF MOTUNUI, YOU *WILL* BOARD... MY...
BOAT! A BOAT!
THE GODS HAVE GIVEN ME A B-AGH!
A-HEM!

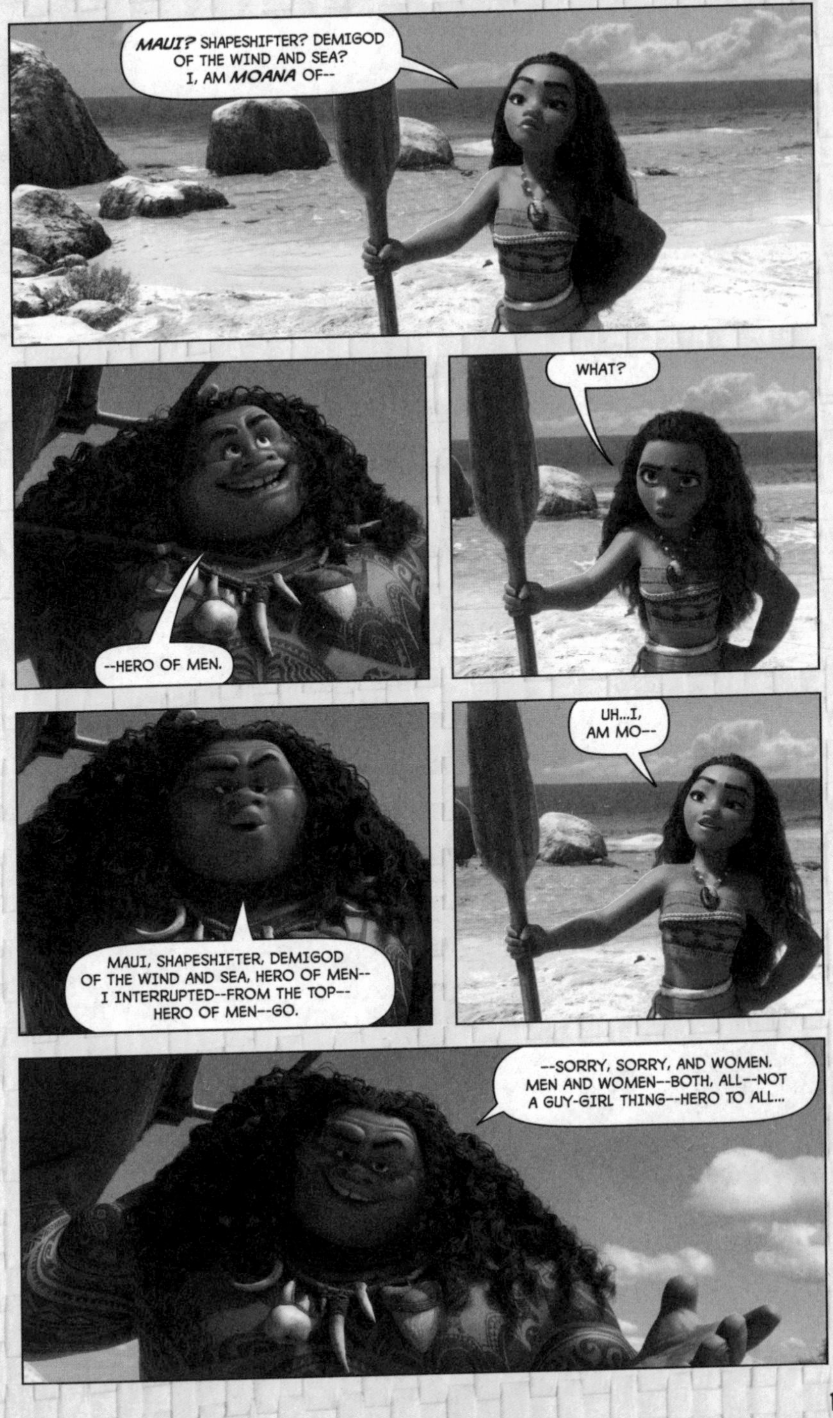
MAUI? SHAPESHIFTER? DEMIGOD OF THE WIND AND SEA? I, AM MOANA OF--
--HERO OF MEN.
WHAT?
MAUI, SHAPESHIFTER, DEMIGOD OF THE WIND AND SEA, HERO OF MEN-- I INTERRUPTED--FROM THE TOP-- HERO OF MEN--GO.
UH...I, AM MO--
--SORRY, SORRY, AND WOMEN. MEN AND WOMEN--BOTH, ALL--NOT A GUY-GIRL THING--HERO TO ALL...

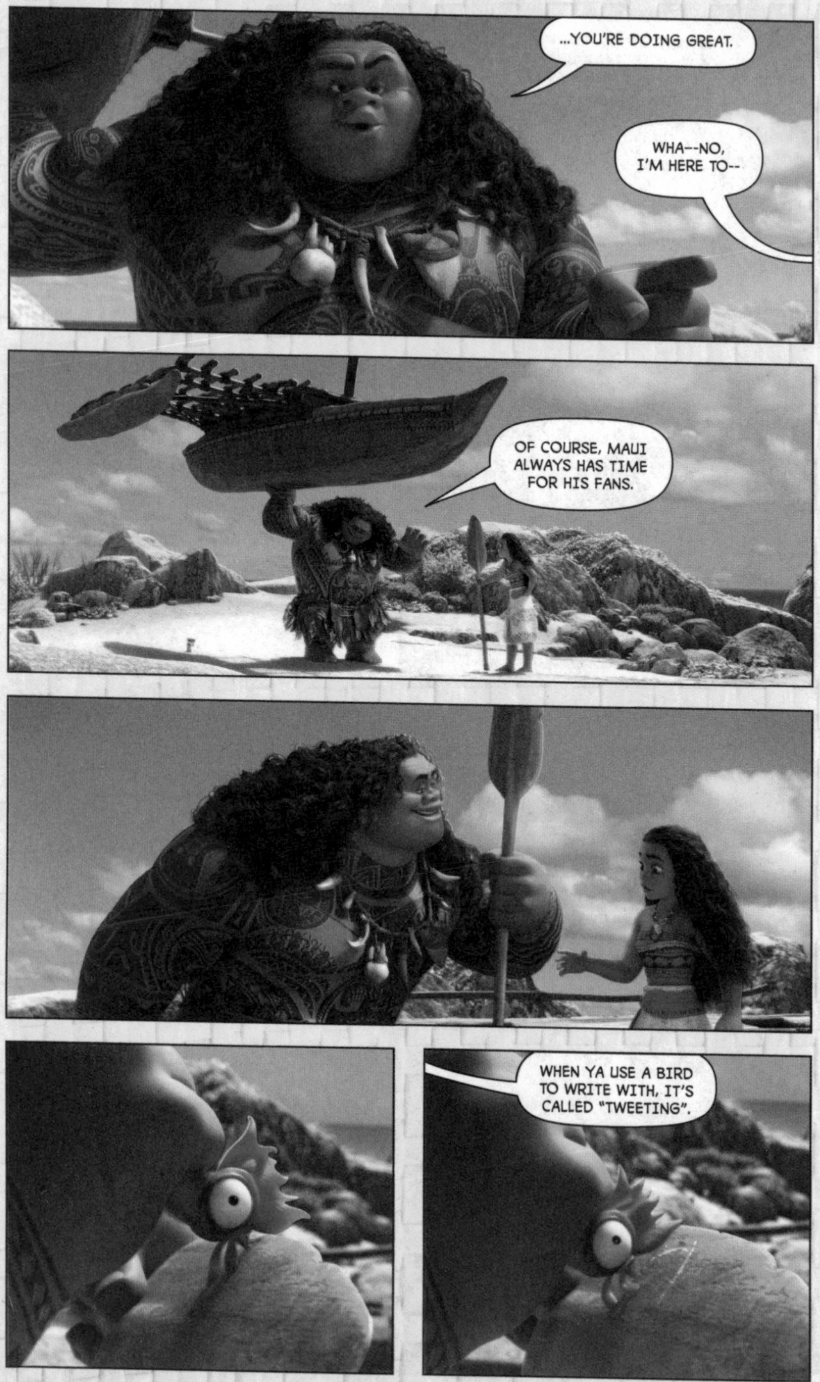
...YOU'RE DOING GREAT.
WHA--NO, I'M HERE TO--
OF COURSE, MAUI ALWAYS HAS TIME FOR HIS FANS.
WHEN YA USE A BIRD TO WRITE WITH, IT'S CALLED "TWEETING".

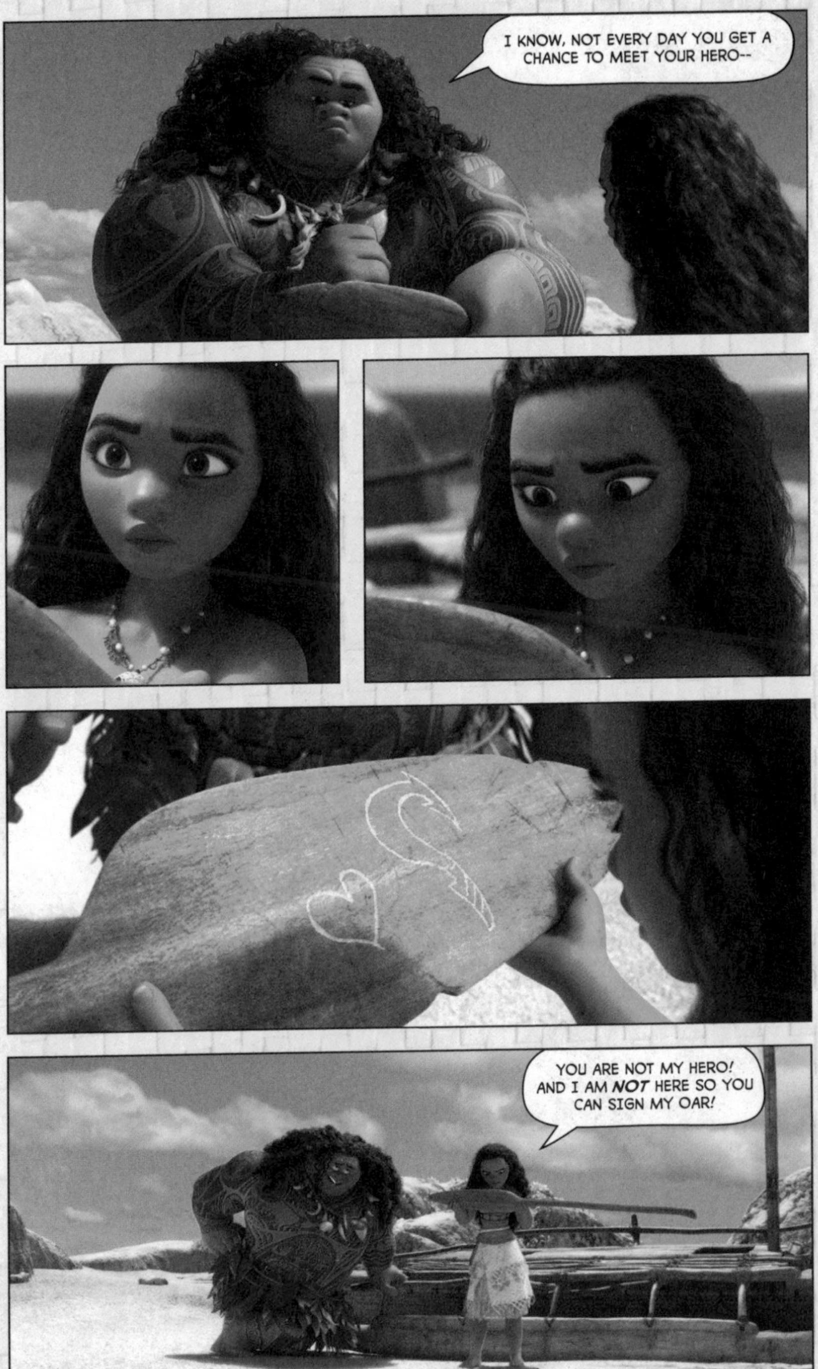
I KNOW, NOT EVERY DAY YOU GET A CHANCE TO MEET YOUR HERO--
YOU ARE NOT MY HERO! AND I AM ***NOT*** HERE SO YOU CAN SIGN MY OAR!

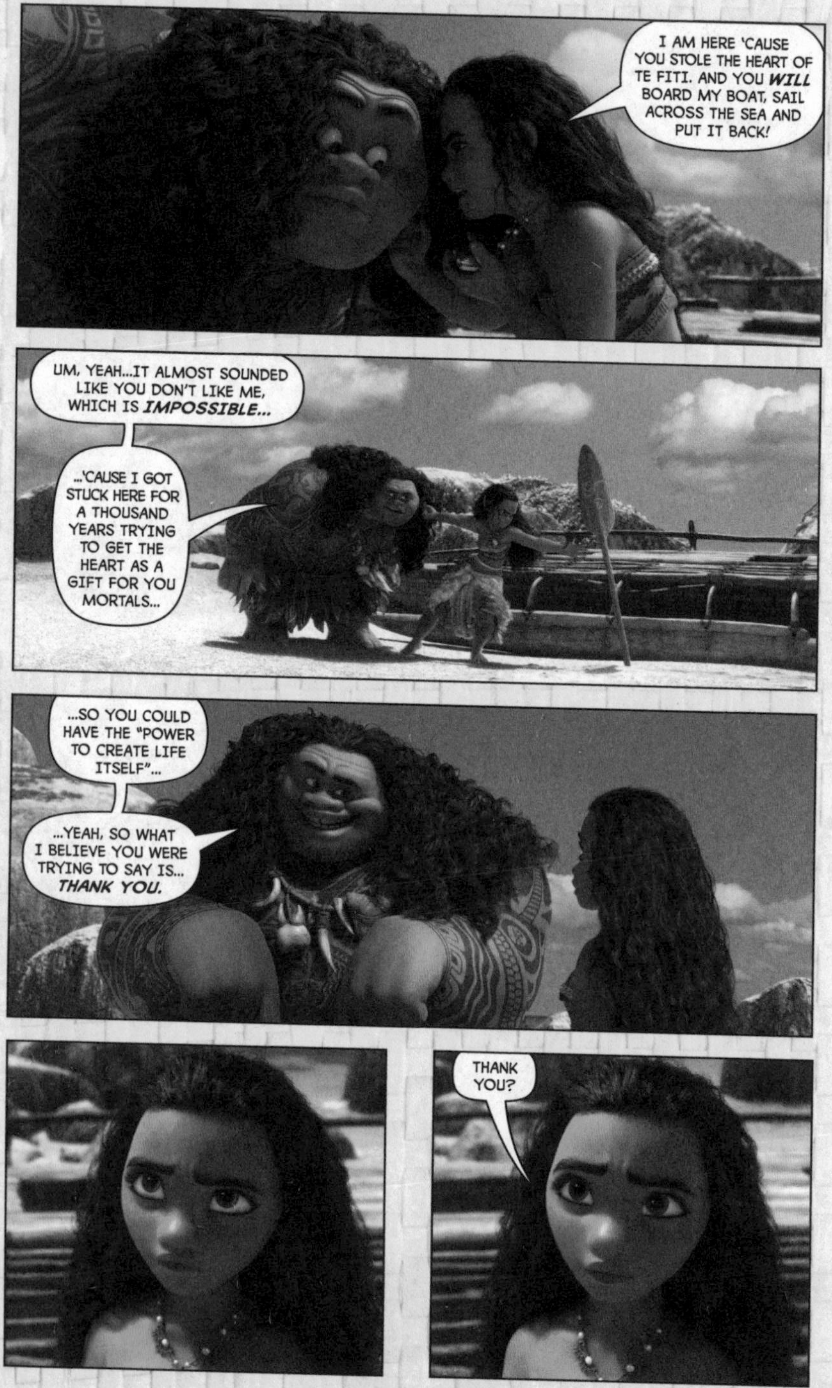

I AM HERE 'CAUSE YOU STOLE THE HEART OF TE FITI. AND YOU *WILL* BOARD MY BOAT, SAIL ACROSS THE SEA AND PUT IT BACK!
UM, YEAH...IT ALMOST SOUNDED LIKE YOU DON'T LIKE ME, WHICH IS *IMPOSSIBLE...*
...'CAUSE I GOT STUCK HERE FOR A THOUSAND YEARS TRYING TO GET THE HEART AS A GIFT FOR YOU MORTALS...
...SO YOU COULD HAVE THE "POWER TO CREATE LIFE ITSELF"...
...YEAH, SO WHAT I BELIEVE YOU WERE TRYING TO SAY IS... *THANK YOU.*
THANK YOU?

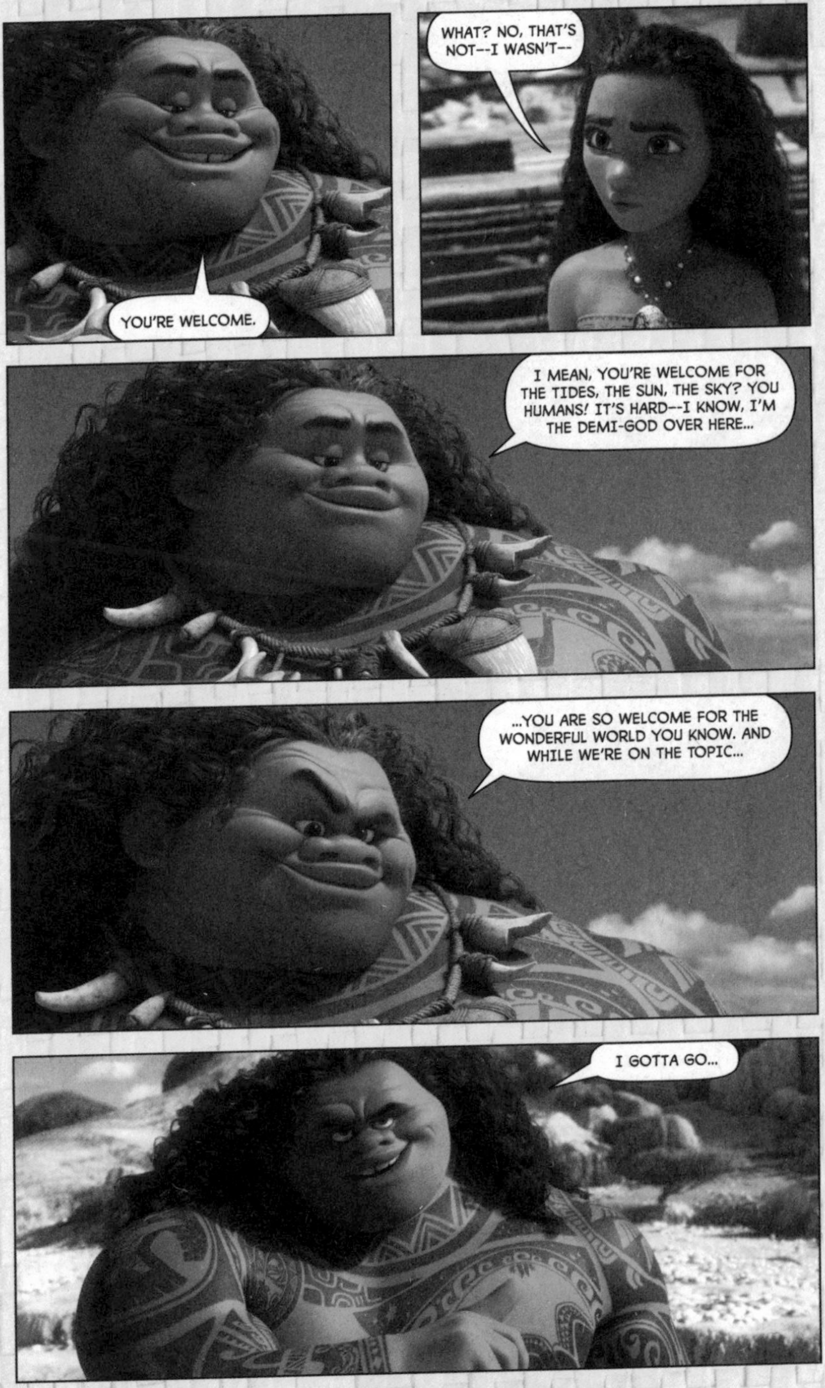
YOU'RE WELCOME.
WHAT? NO, THAT'S NOT--I WASN'T--
I MEAN, YOU'RE WELCOME FOR THE TIDES, THE SUN, THE SKY? YOU HUMANS! IT'S HARD--I KNOW, I'M THE DEMI-GOD OVER HERE...
...YOU ARE SO WELCOME FOR THE WONDERFUL WORLD YOU KNOW. AND WHILE WE'RE ON THE TOPIC...
I GOTTA GO...

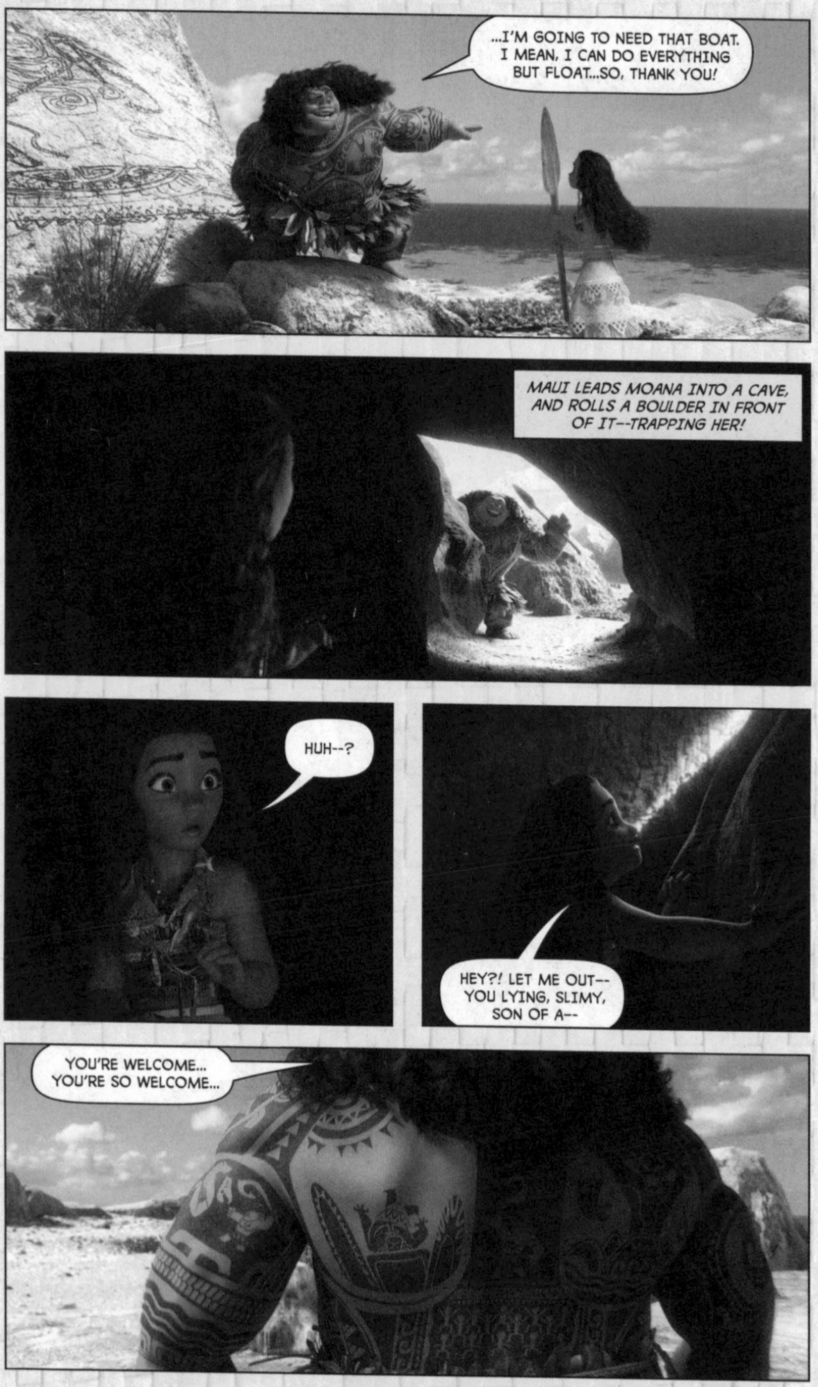
...I'M GOING TO NEED THAT BOAT. I MEAN, I CAN DO EVERYTHING BUT FLOAT...SO, THANK YOU!
MAUI LEADS MOANA INTO A CAVE, AND ROLLS A BOULDER IN FRONT OF IT--TRAPPING HER!
HUH--?
HEY?! LET ME OUT-- YOU LYING, SLIMY, SON OF A--
YOU'RE WELCOME... YOU'RE SO WELCOME...

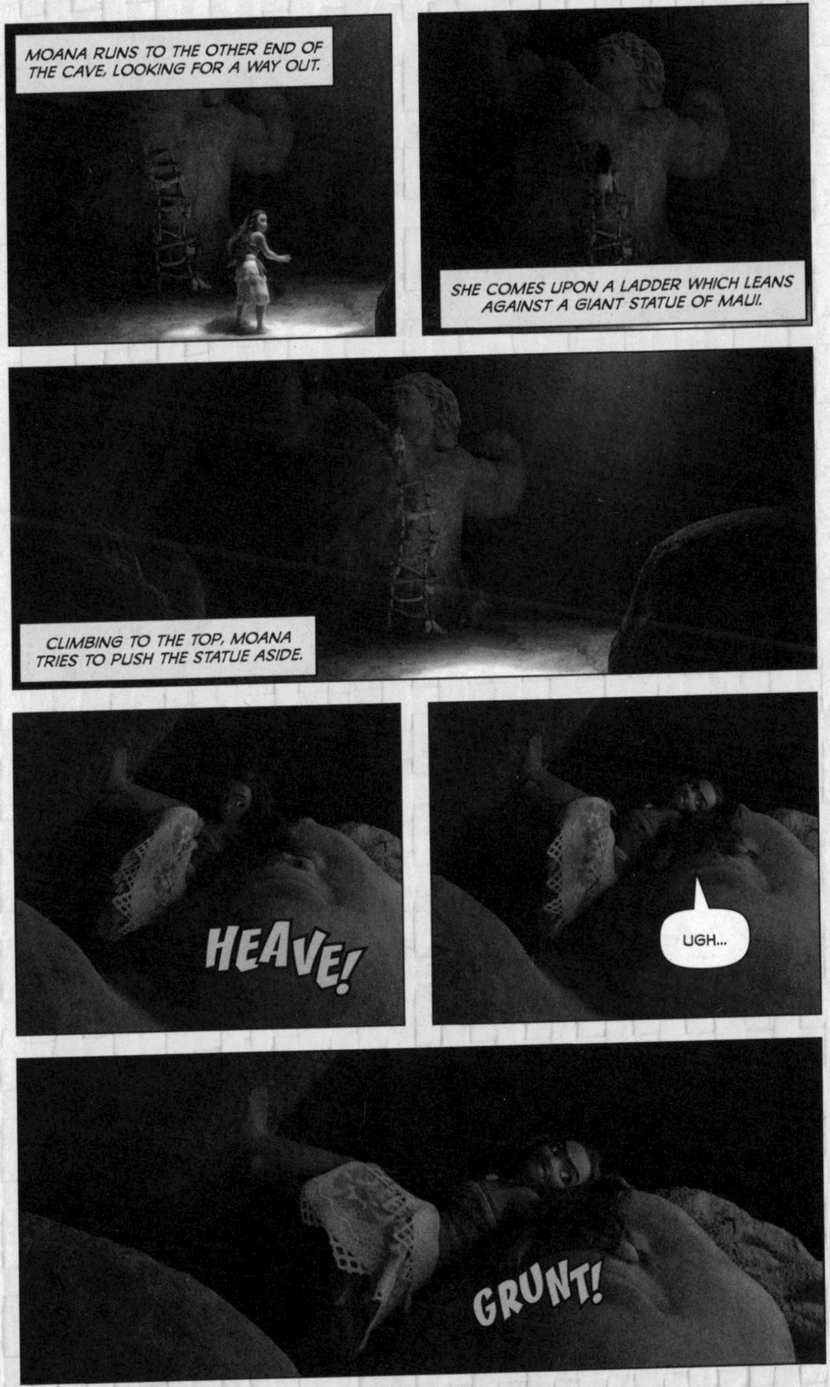
MOANA RUNS TO THE OTHER END OF THE CAVE, LOOKING FOR A WAY OUT.
SHE COMES UPON A LADDER WHICH LEANS AGAINST A GIANT STATUE OF MAUI.
CLIMBING TO THE TOP, MOANA TRIES TO PUSH THE STATUE ASIDE.
HEAVE!
UGH...
GRUNT!

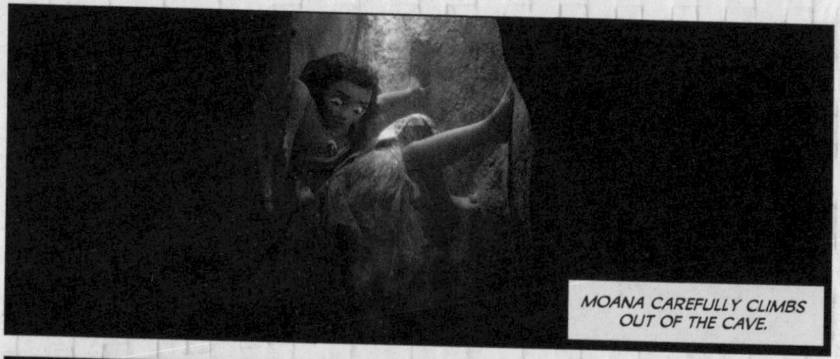
MOANA CAREFULLY CLIMBS OUT OF THE CAVE.

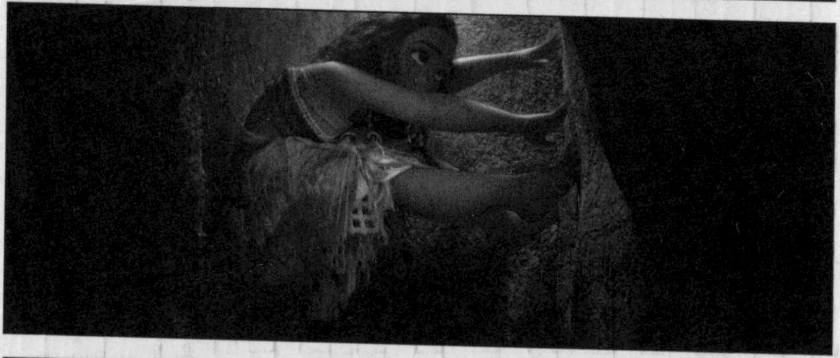

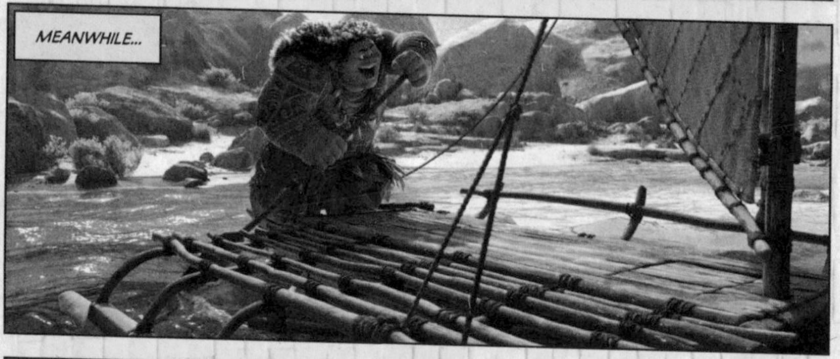
MEANWHILE...

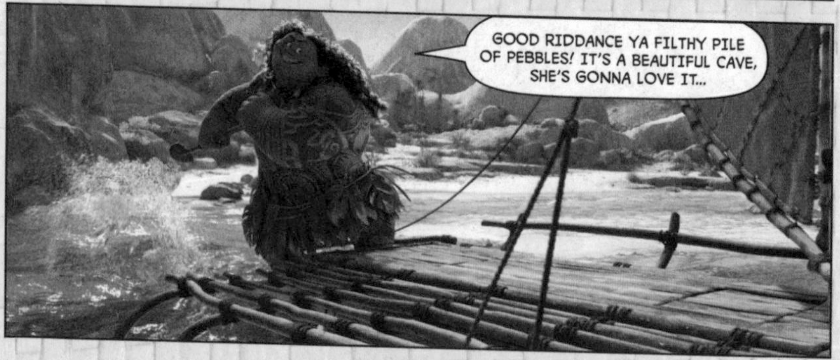
GOOD RIDDANCE YA FILTHY PILE OF PEBBLES! IT'S A BEAUTIFUL CAVE, SHE'S GONNA LOVE IT...

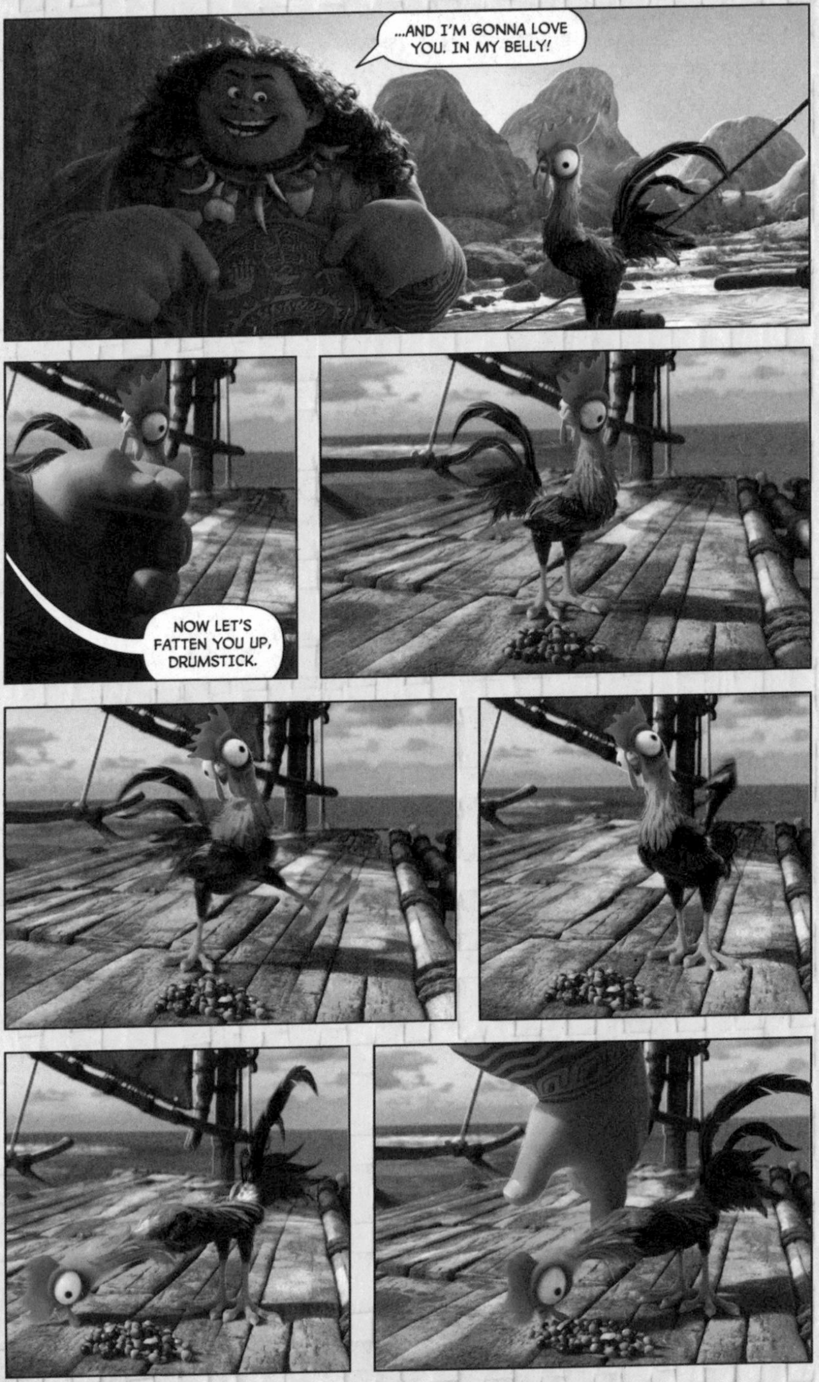
...AND I'M GONNA LOVE YOU. IN MY BELLY!
NOW LET'S FATTEN YOU UP, DRUMSTICK.

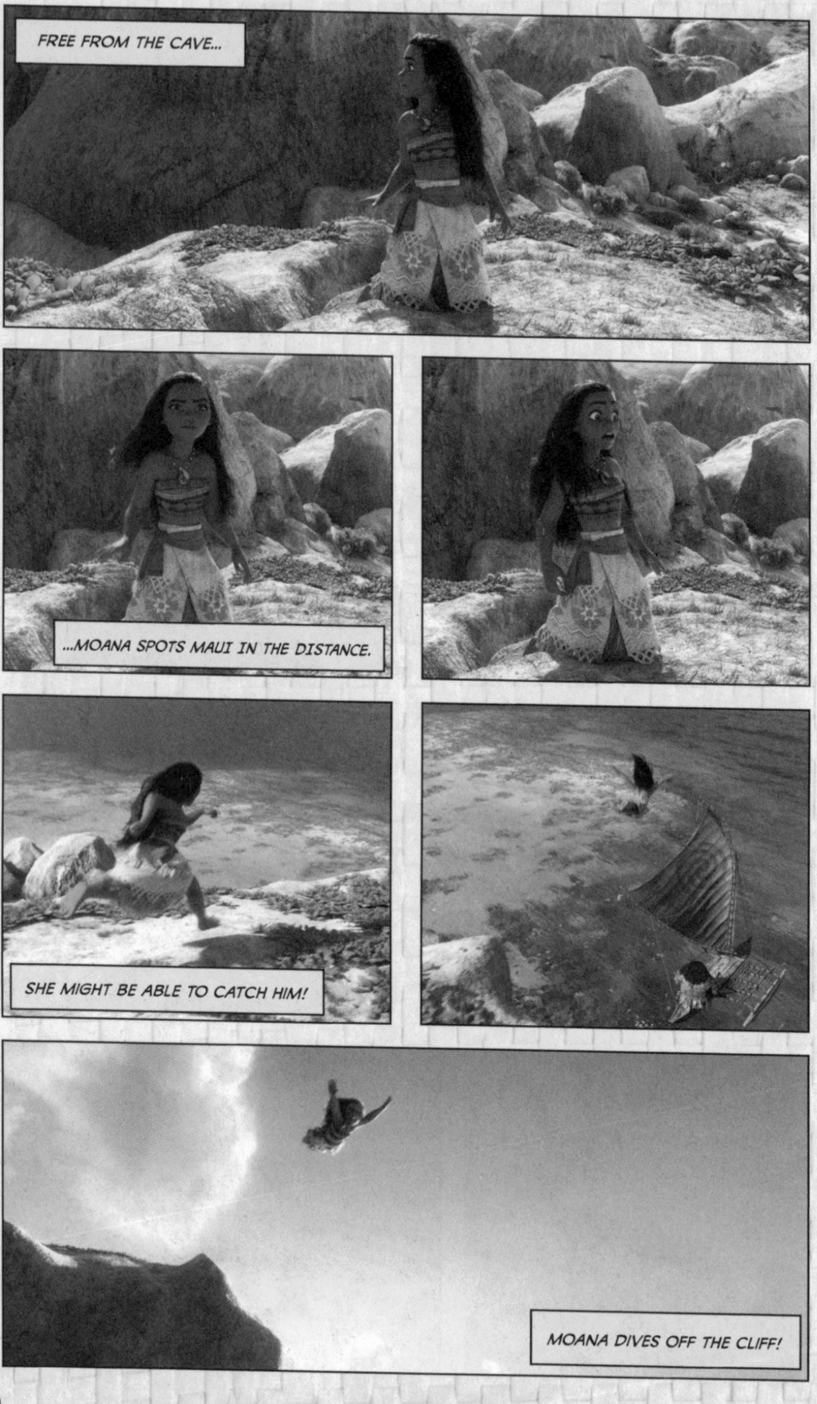
FREE FROM THE CAVE...
...MOANA SPOTS MAUI IN THE DISTANCE.
SHE MIGHT BE ABLE TO CATCH HIM!
MOANA DIVES OFF THE CLIFF!

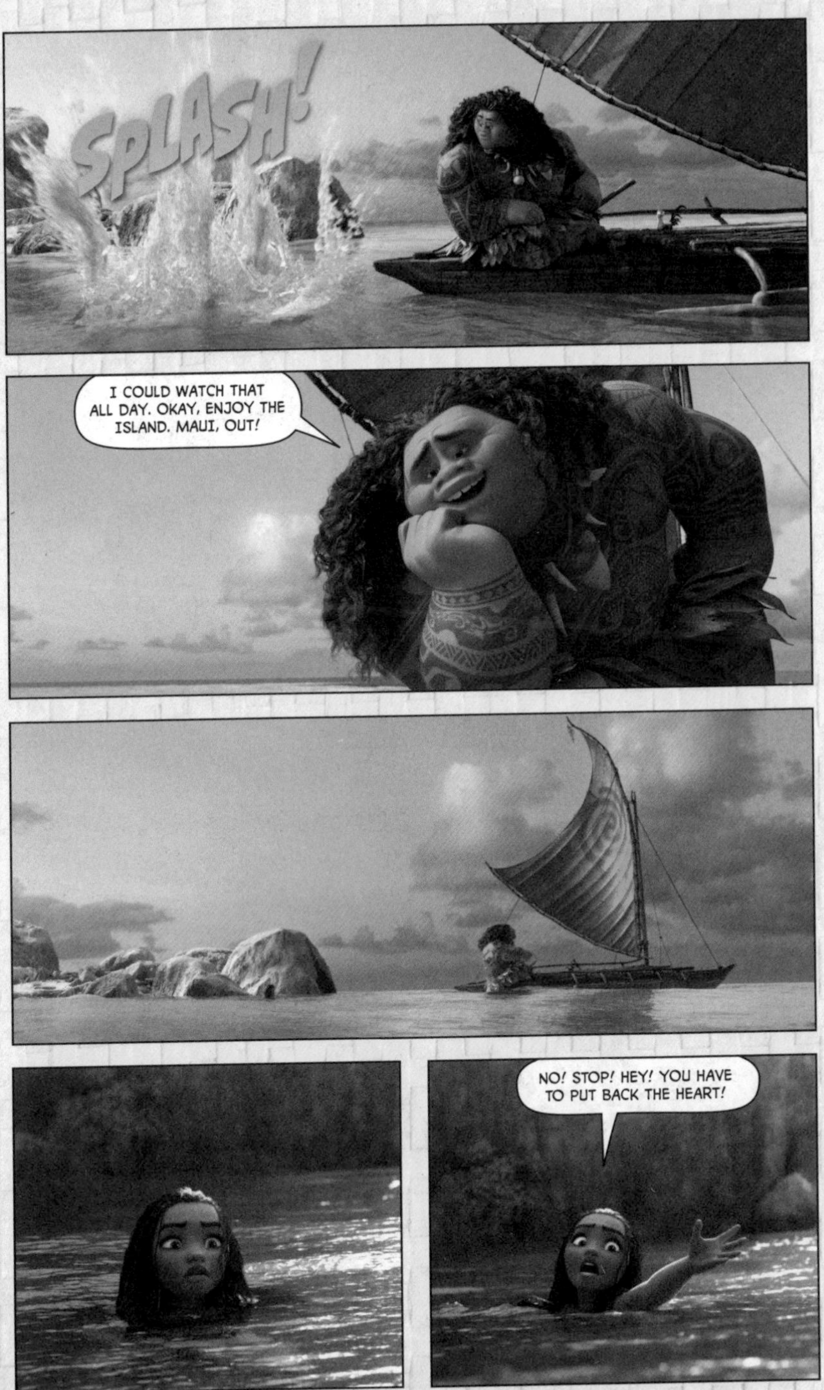
SPLASH!
I COULD WATCH THAT ALL DAY. OKAY, ENJOY THE ISLAND. MAUI, OUT!
NO! STOP! HEY! YOU HAVE TO PUT BACK THE HEART!

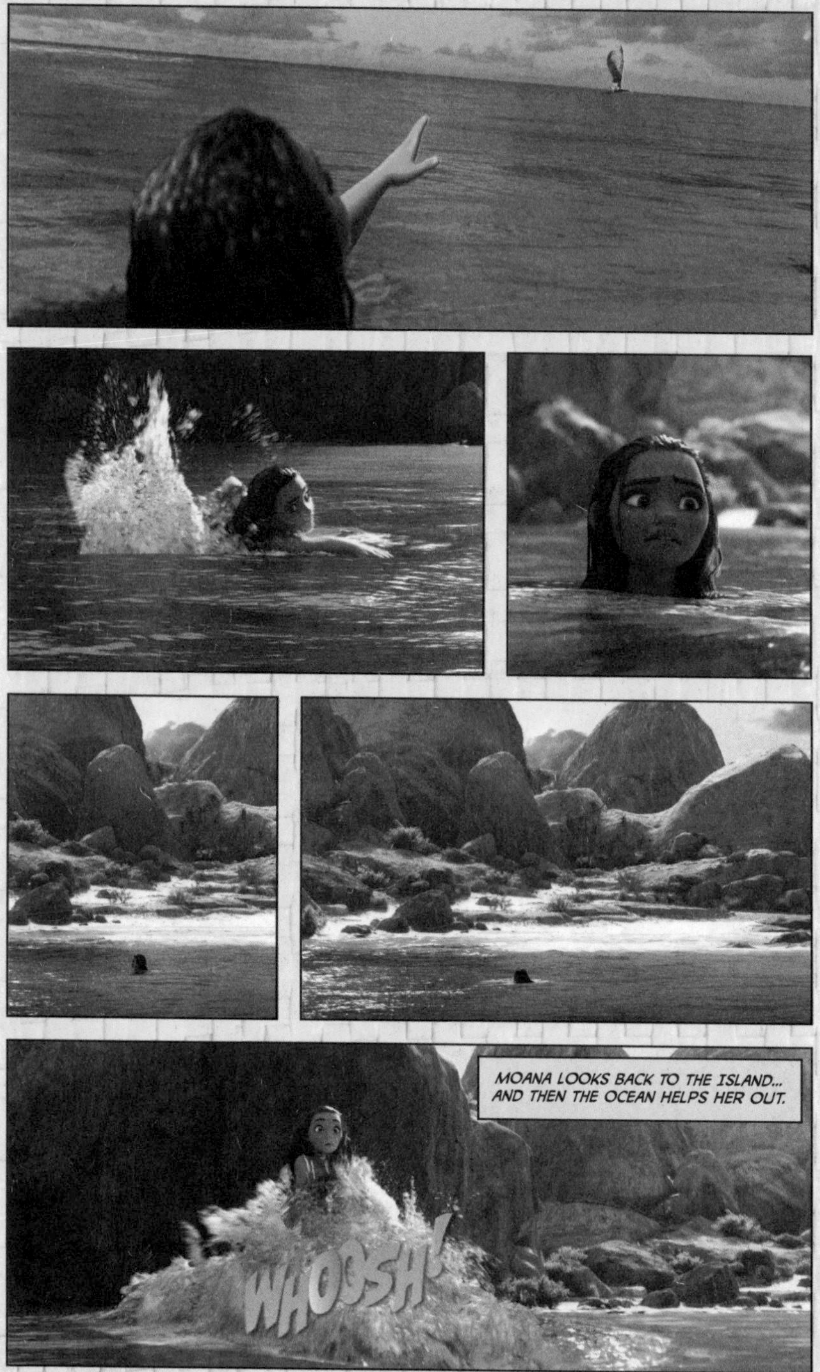
MOANA LOOKS BACK TO THE ISLAND...
AND THEN THE OCEAN HELPS HER OUT.
WHOOSH!

MOANA IS PULLED THROUGH THE WATER AT AN INCREDIBLE SPEED...

...IN PURSUIT OF MAUI.

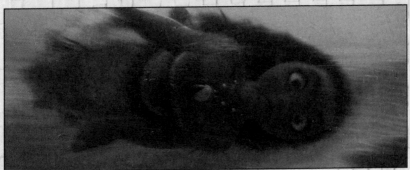

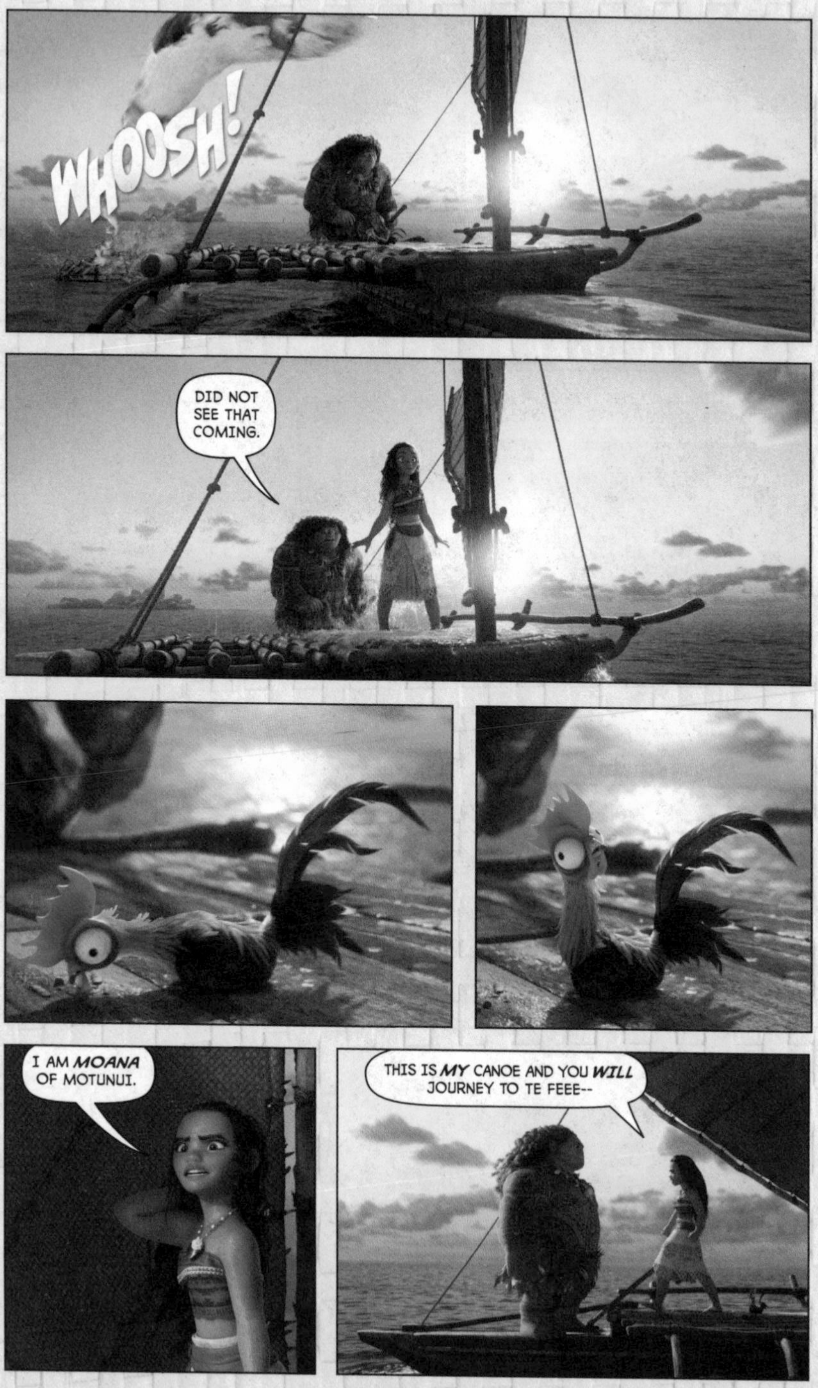
WHOOSH!
DID NOT SEE THAT COMING.
I AM *MOANA* OF MOTUNUI.
THIS IS *MY* CANOE AND YOU *WILL* JOURNEY TO TE FEEE--

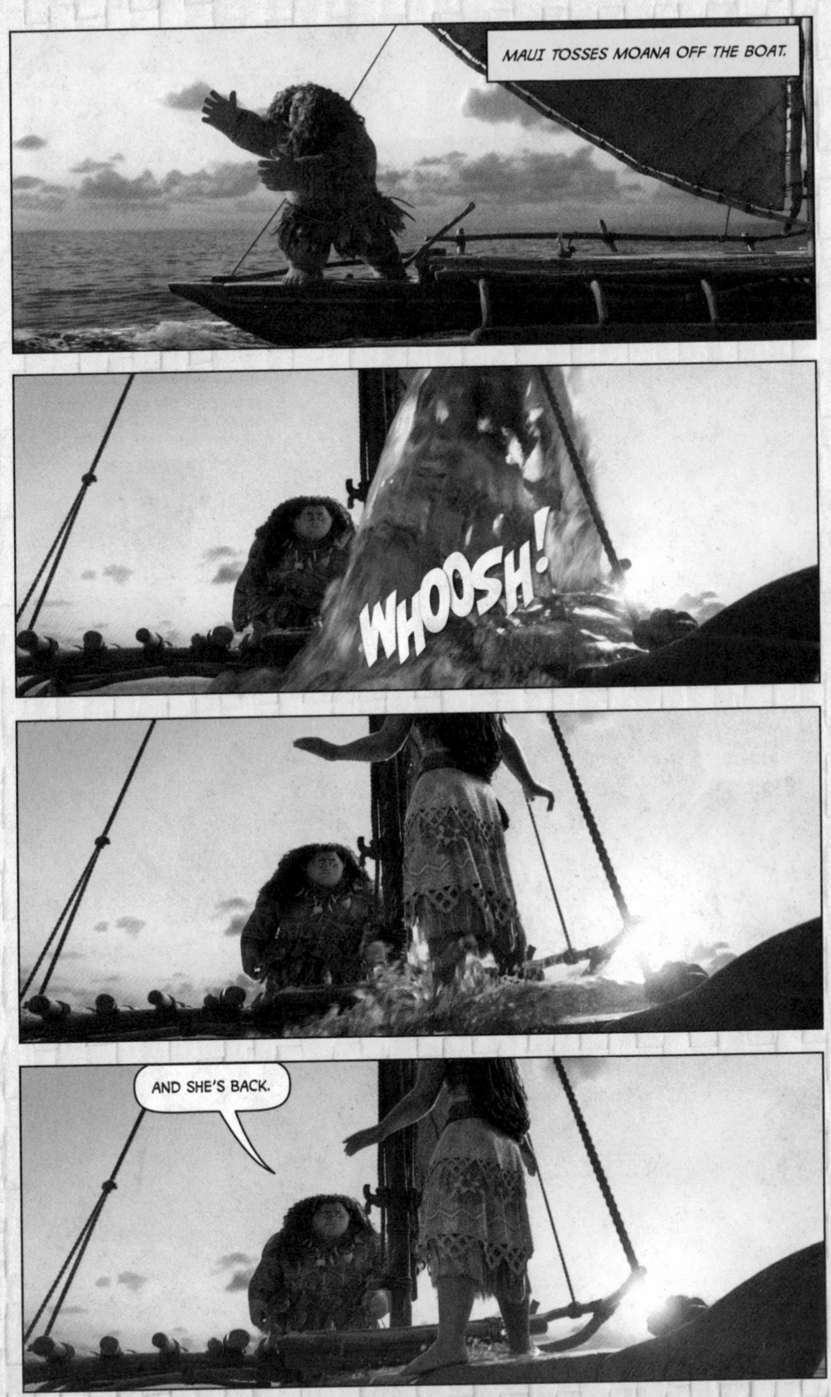
MAUI TOSSES MOANA OFF THE BOAT.
WHOOSH!
AND SHE'S BACK.

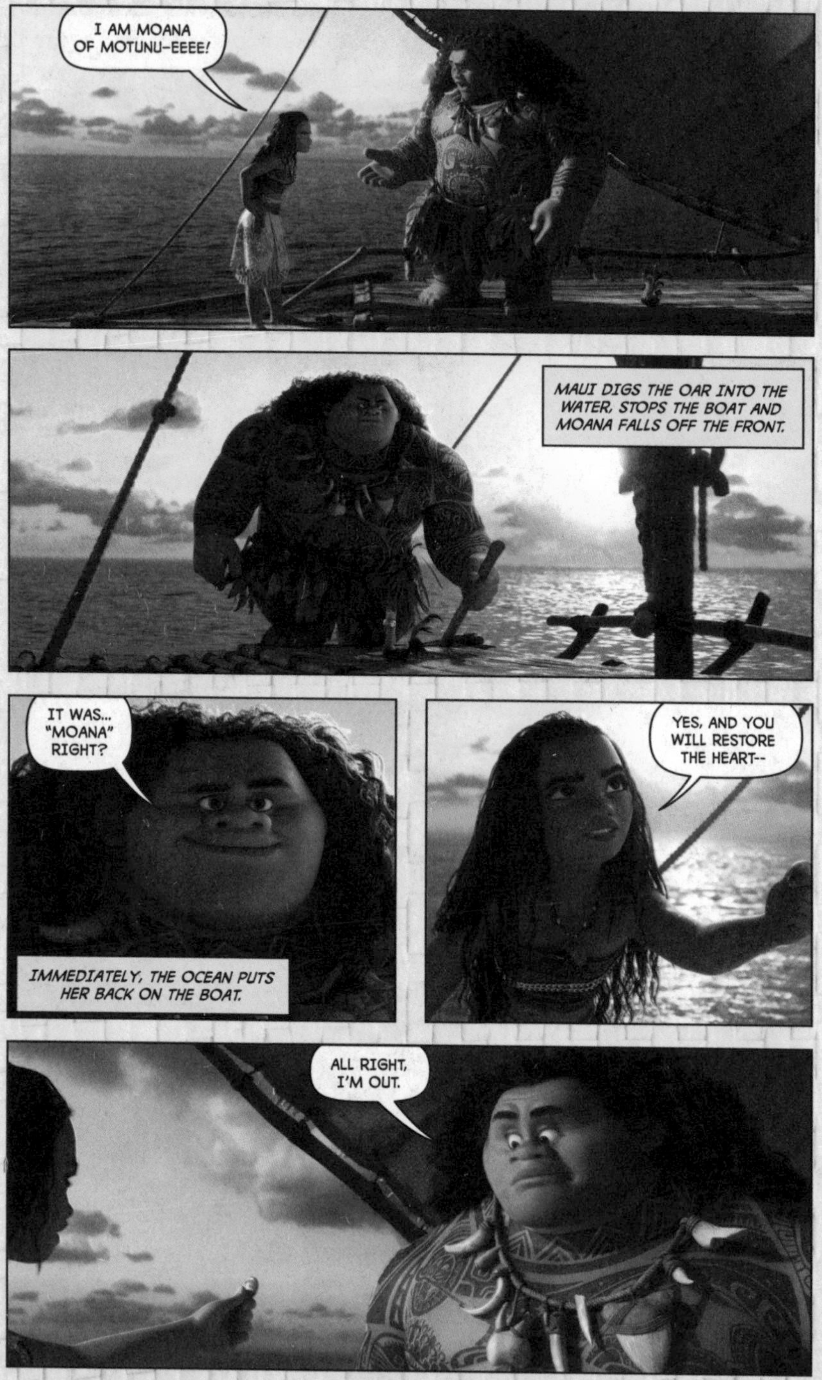
I AM MOANA
OF MOTUNU-EEEE!
MAUI DIGS THE OAR INTO THE WATER, STOPS THE BOAT AND MOANA FALLS OFF THE FRONT.
IMMEDIATELY, THE OCEAN PUTS HER BACK ON THE BOAT.
IT WAS... "MOANA" RIGHT?
YES, AND YOU WILL RESTORE THE HEART--
ALL RIGHT, I'M OUT.

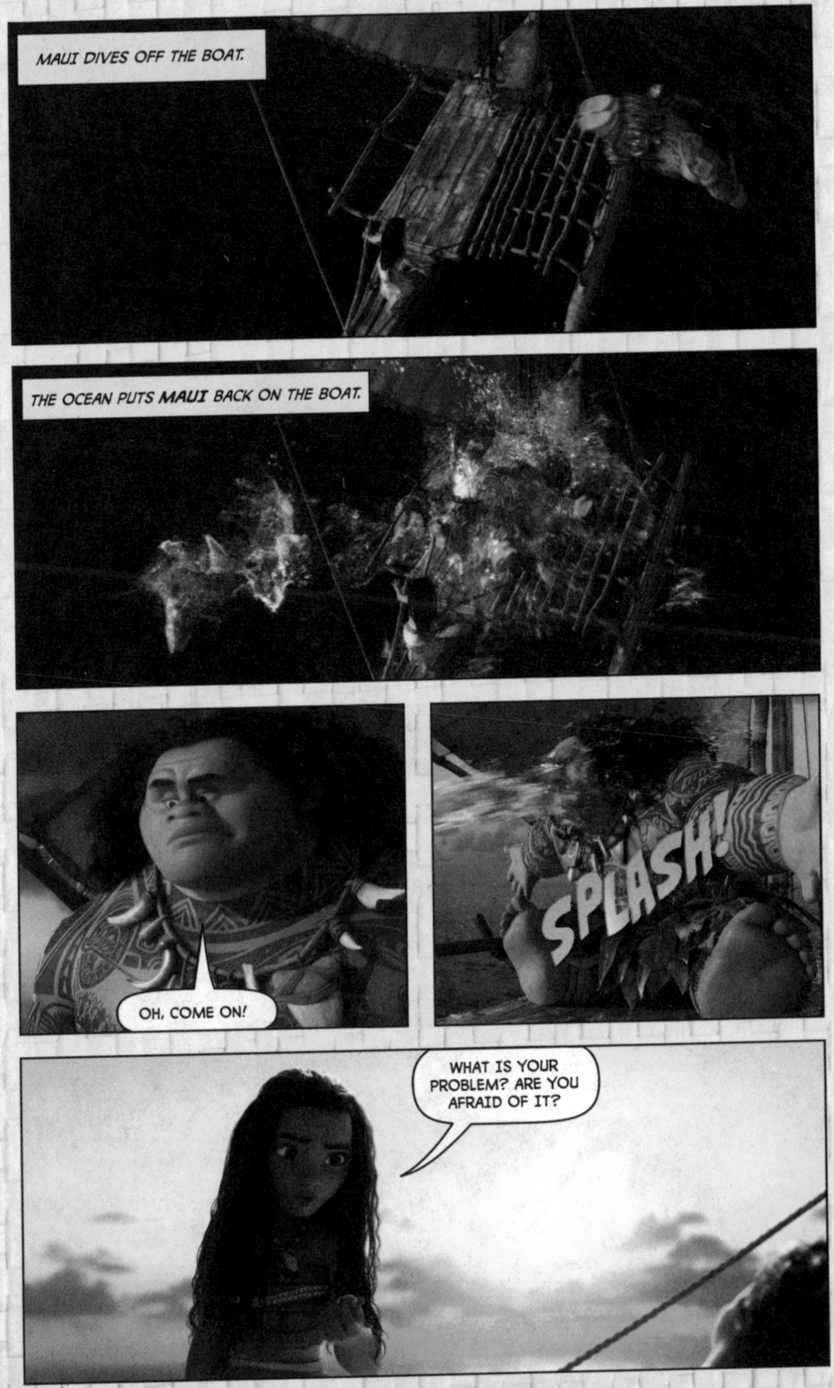
MAUI DIVES OFF THE BOAT.
THE OCEAN PUTS MAUI BACK ON THE BOAT.
OH, COME ON!
SPLASH!
WHAT IS YOUR PROBLEM? ARE YOU AFRAID OF IT?

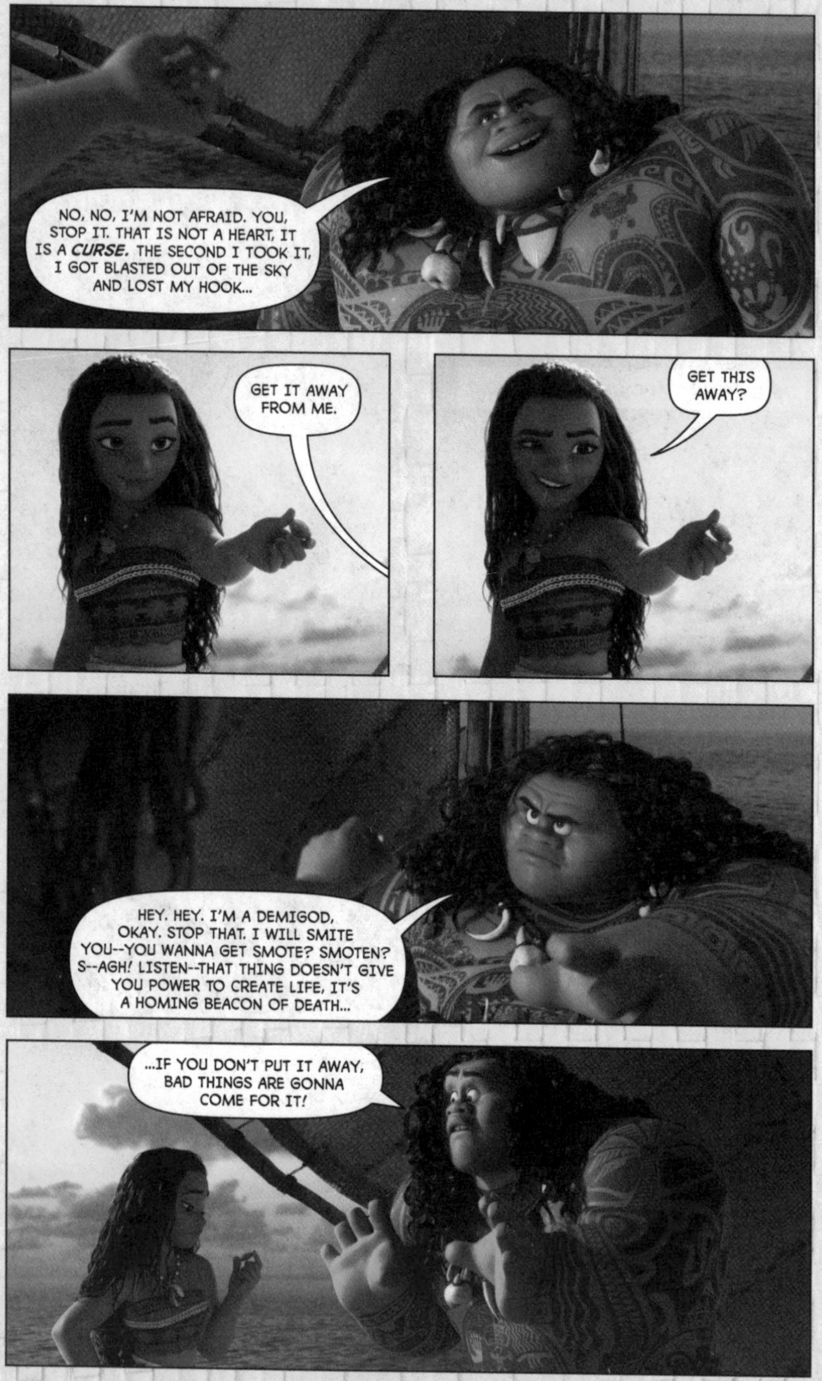
NO, NO, I'M NOT AFRAID. YOU, STOP IT. THAT IS NOT A HEART, IT IS A *CURSE.* THE SECOND I TOOK IT, I GOT BLASTED OUT OF THE SKY AND LOST MY HOOK...
GET IT AWAY FROM ME.
GET THIS AWAY?
HEY. HEY. I'M A DEMIGOD, OKAY. STOP THAT. I WILL SMITE YOU--YOU WANNA GET SMOTE? SMOTEN? S--AGH! LISTEN--THAT THING DOESN'T GIVE YOU POWER TO CREATE LIFE, IT'S A HOMING BEACON OF DEATH...
...IF YOU DON'T PUT IT AWAY, BAD THINGS ARE GONNA COME FOR IT!

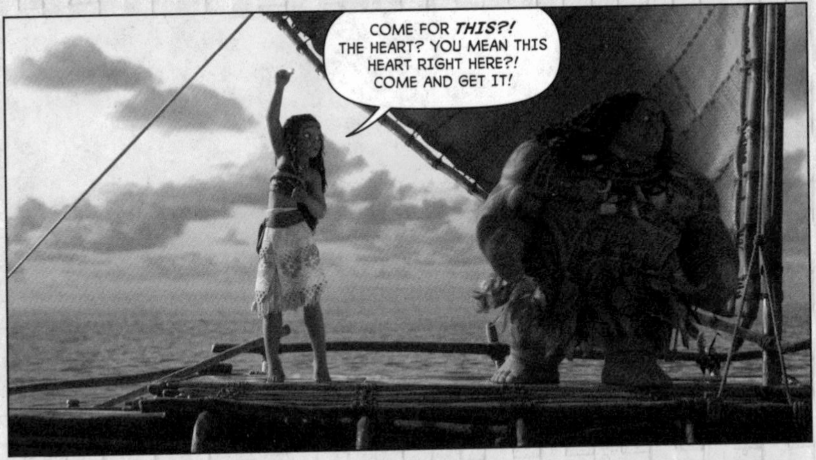
COME FOR *THIS?!* THE HEART? YOU MEAN THIS HEART RIGHT HERE?! COME AND GET IT!

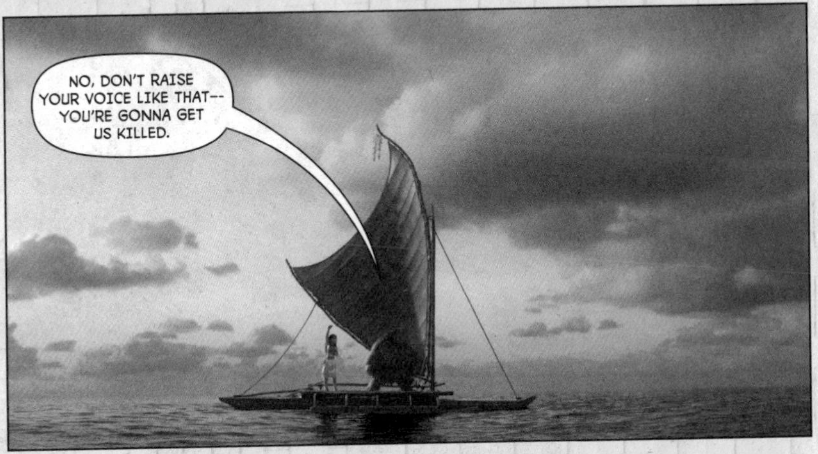
NO, DON'T RAISE YOUR VOICE LIKE THAT-- YOU'RE GONNA GET US KILLED.

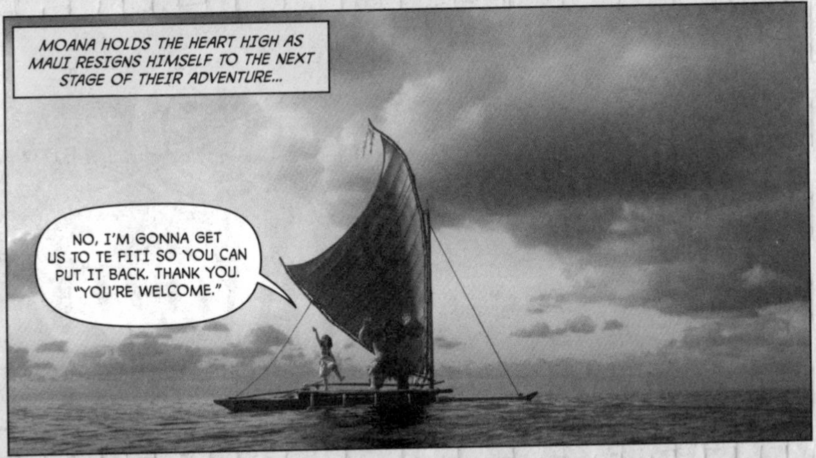
MOANA HOLDS THE HEART HIGH AS MAUI RESIGNS HIMSELF TO THE NEXT STAGE OF THEIR ADVENTURE...
NO, I'M GONNA GET US TO TE FITI SO YOU CAN PUT IT BACK. THANK YOU. "YOU'RE WELCOME."

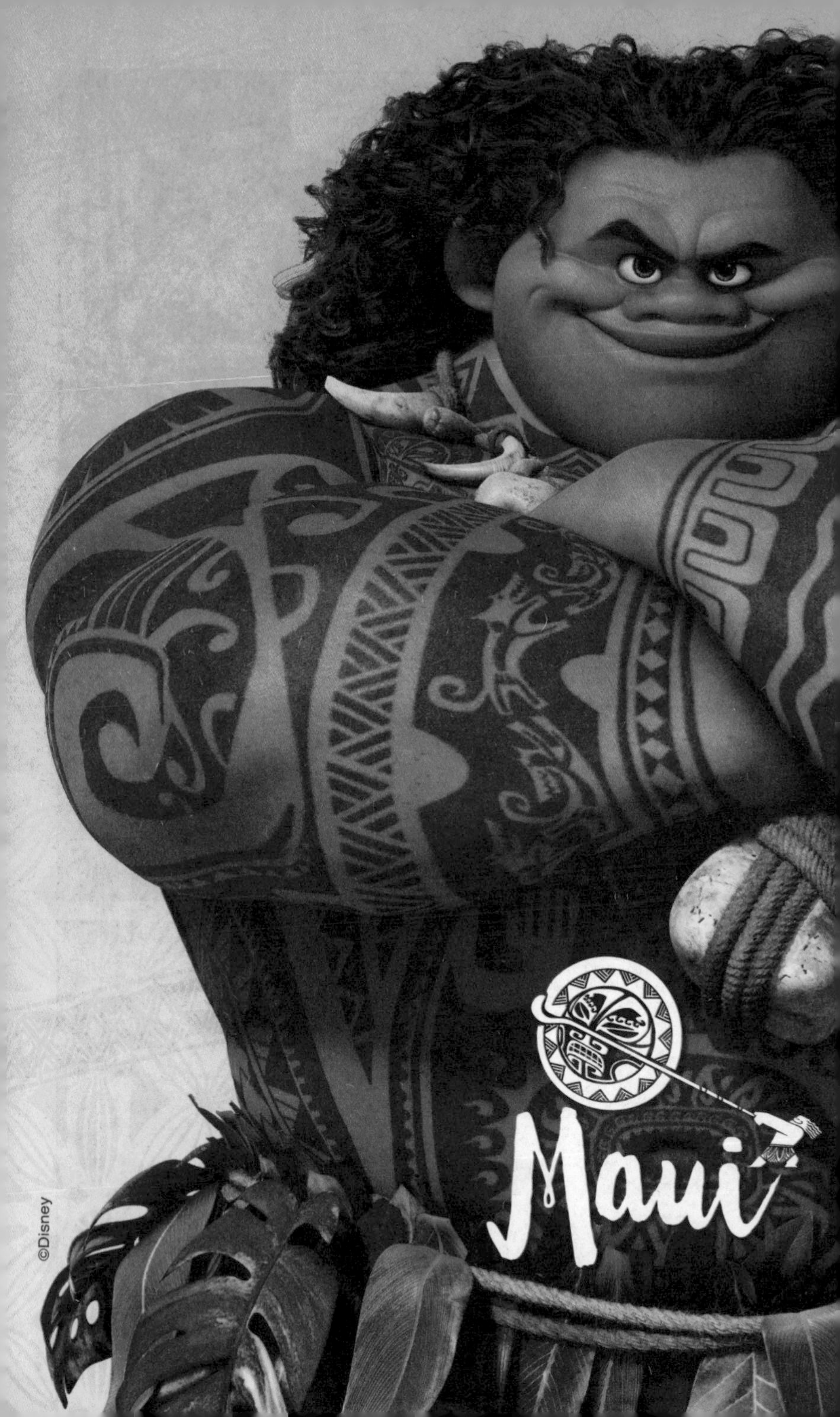
Maui
©Disney

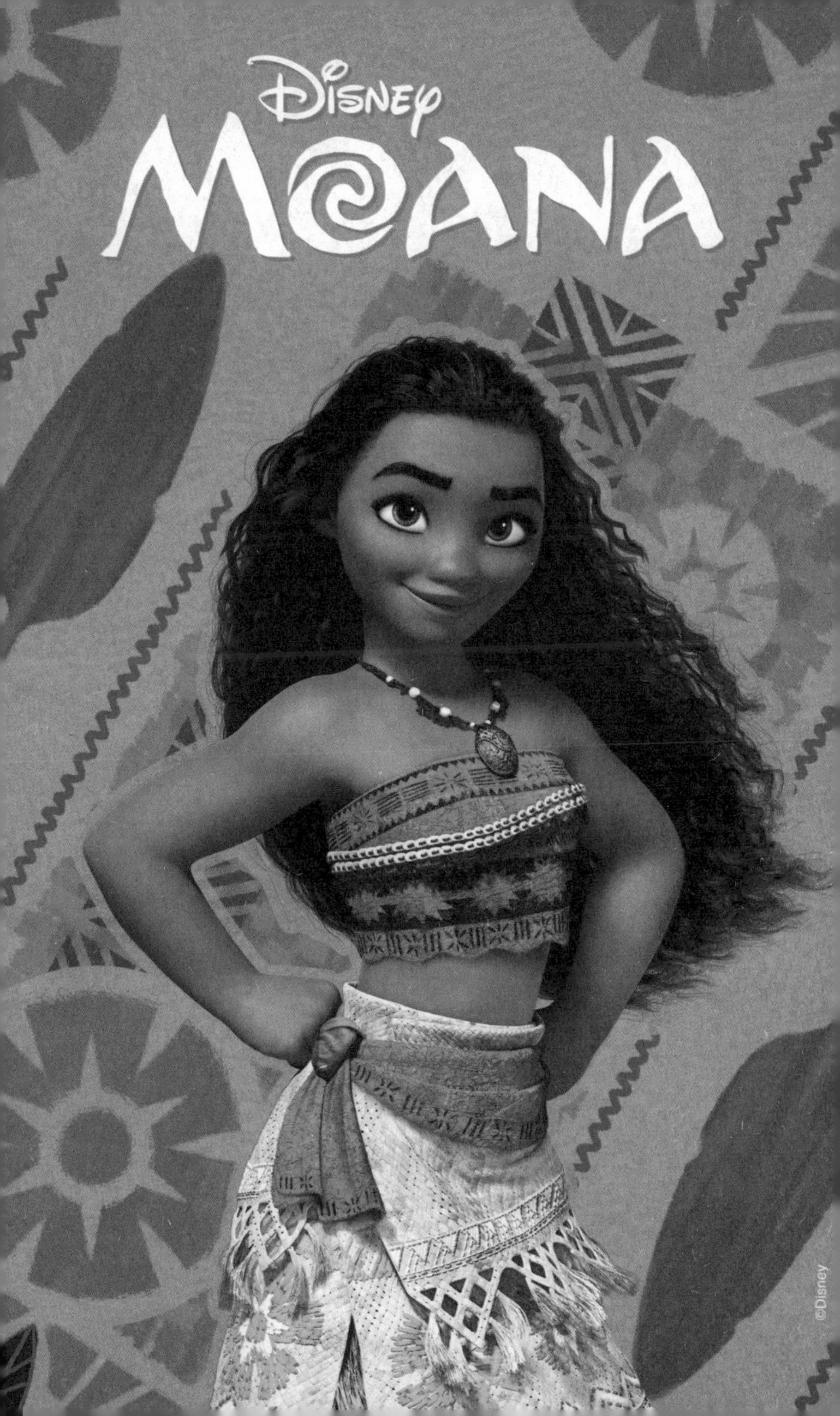
Disney
MOANA
©Disney

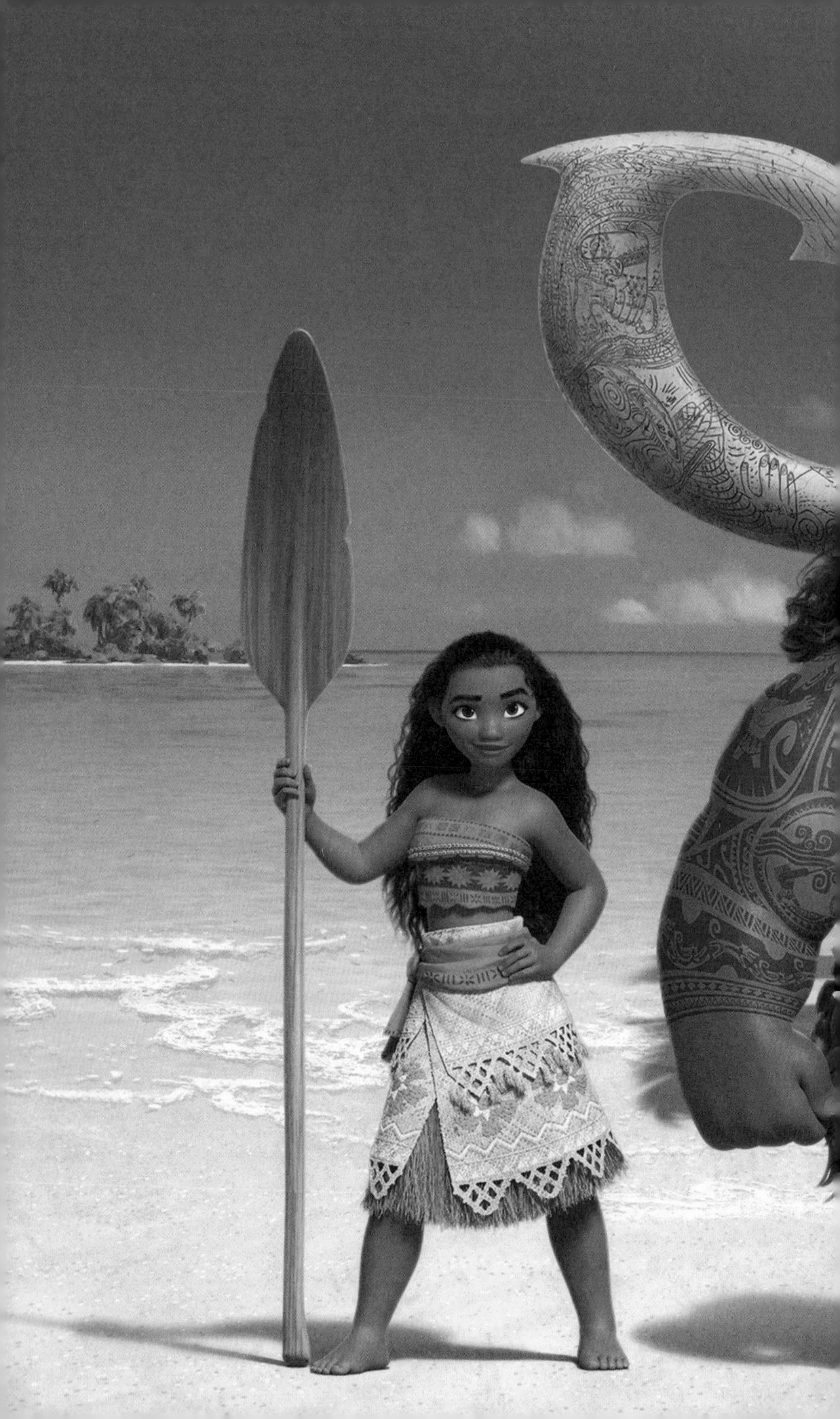

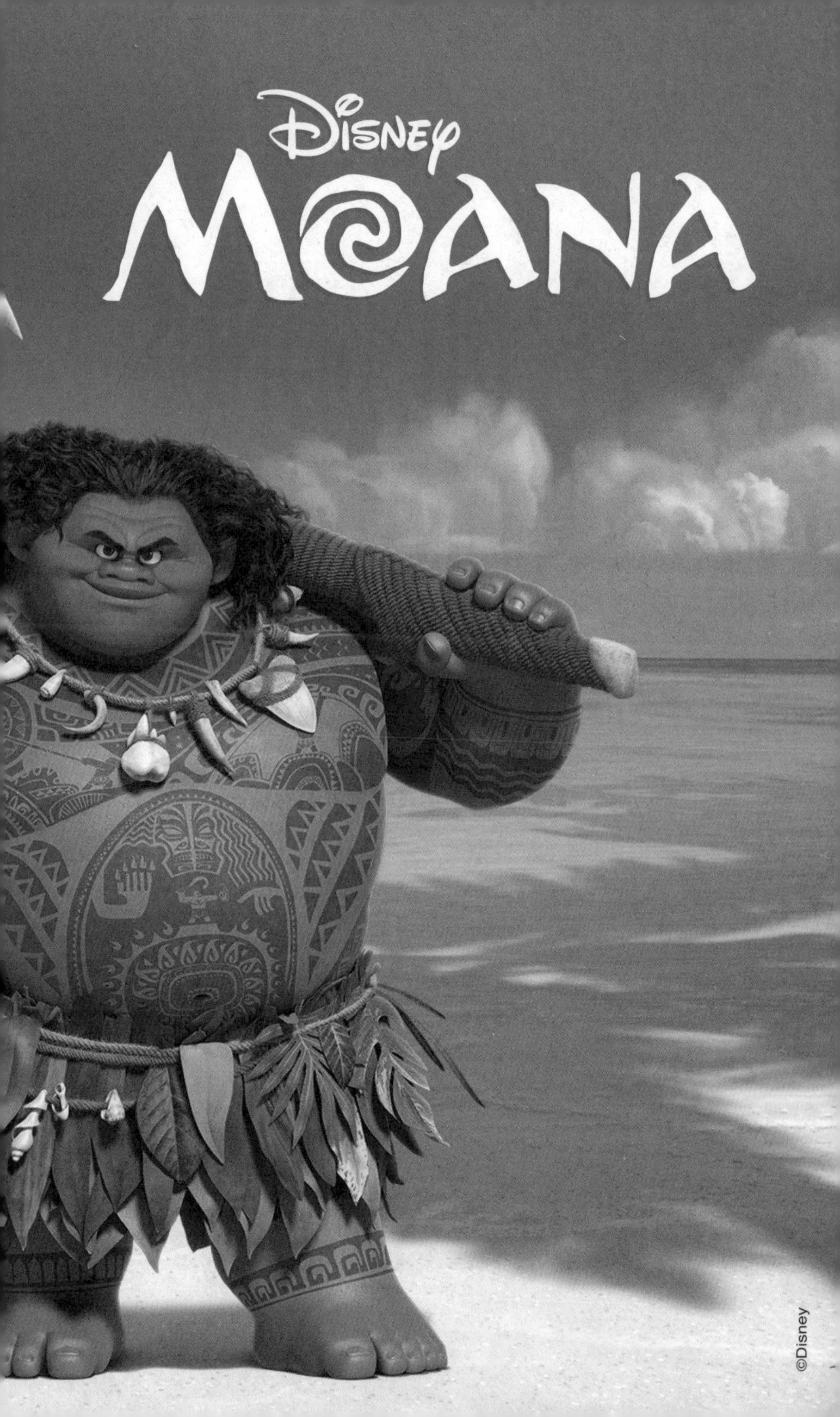
DISNEY
MOANA
©Disney

SPECIAL BONUS CONTENT

The All-New Disney Short Film

Inner Workings

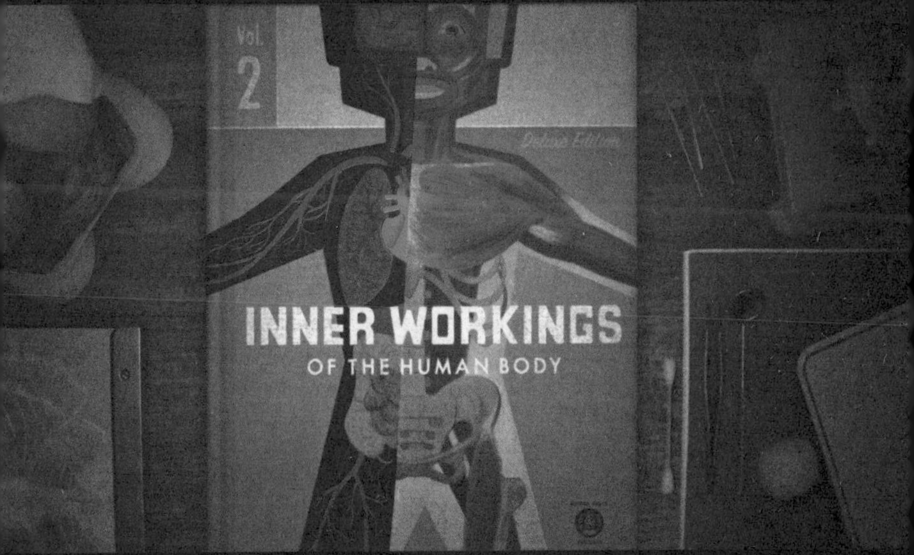

Vol.
2
Deluxe Edition
INNER WORKINGS
OF THE HUMAN BODY

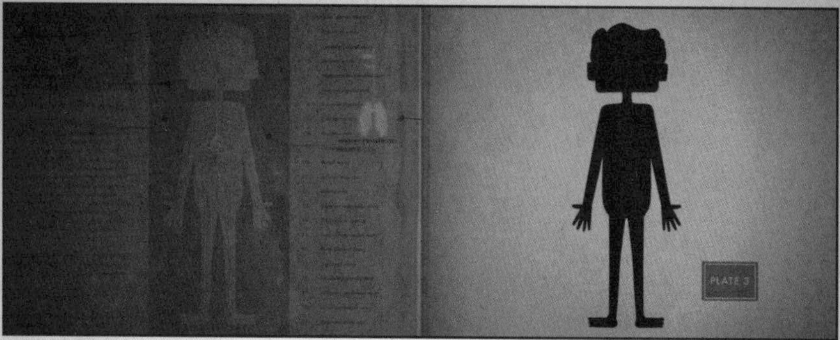
PLATE 3

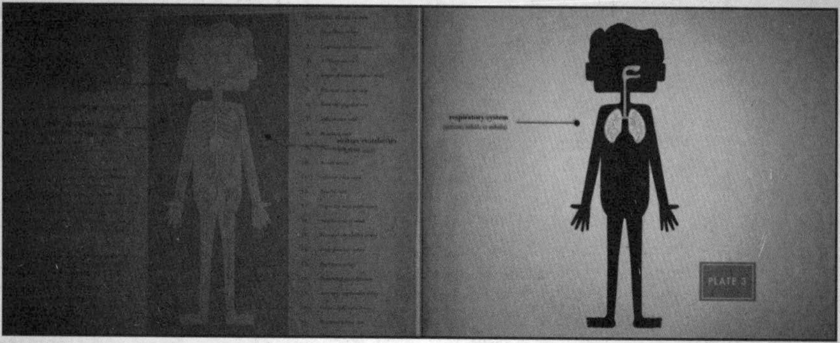
respiratory system
PLATE 3

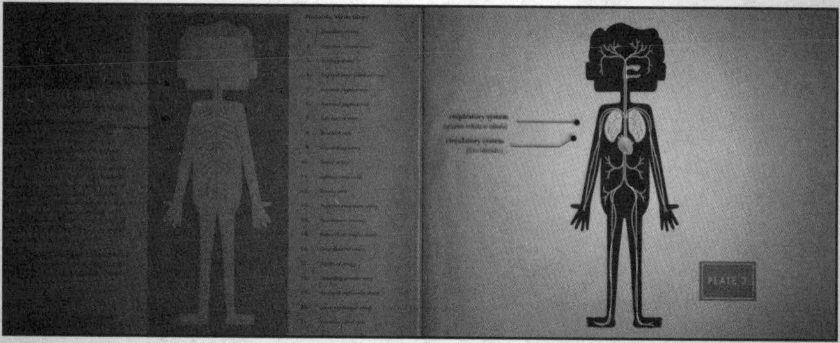
respiratory system
circulatory system
PLATE 3

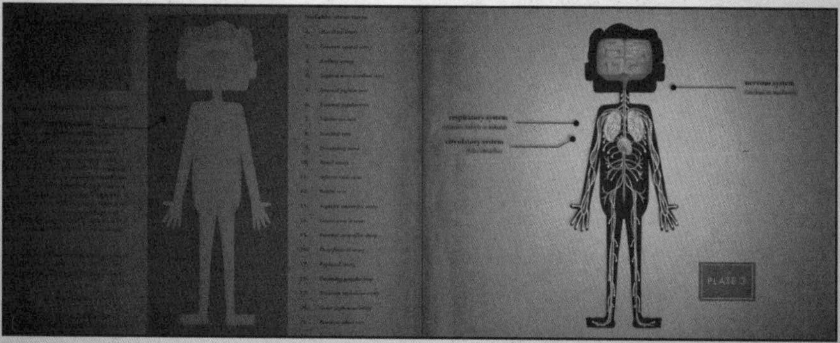
nervous system
respiratory system
circulatory system
PLATE 3

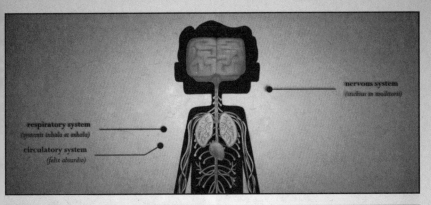

nervous system
(stickius in auditorii)

respiratory system
(systema inhala et exhala)

circulatory system
(felix absurdio)

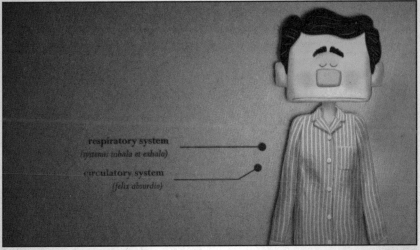

respiratory system
(systema inhala et exhala)

circulatory system
(felix absurdio)

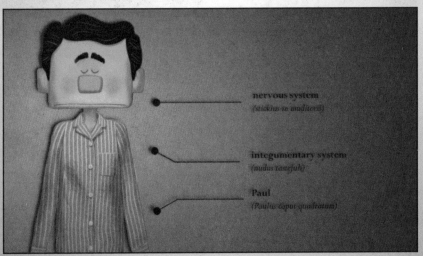

nervous system
(stickius in auditorii)

integumentary system
(nudus tasteful)

Paul
(Paulus caput quadratum)

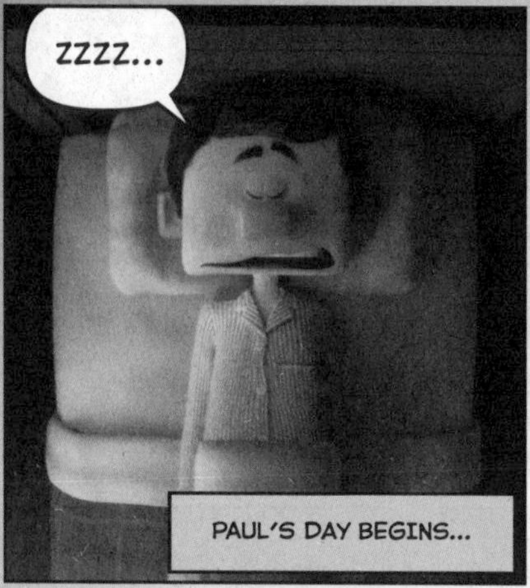
ZZZZ...
PAUL'S DAY BEGINS...

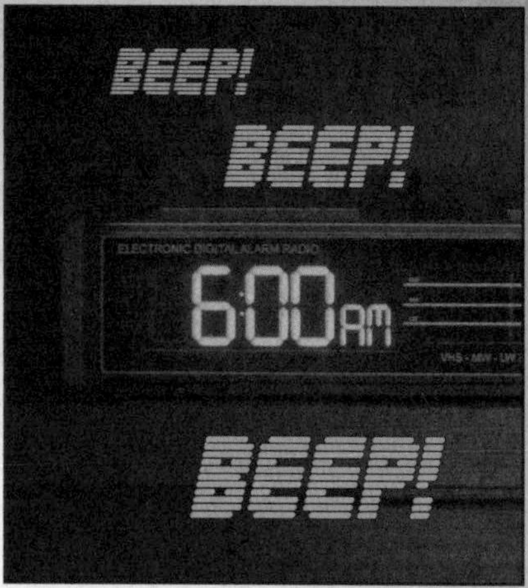
BEEP!
BEEP!
6:00AM
BEEP!

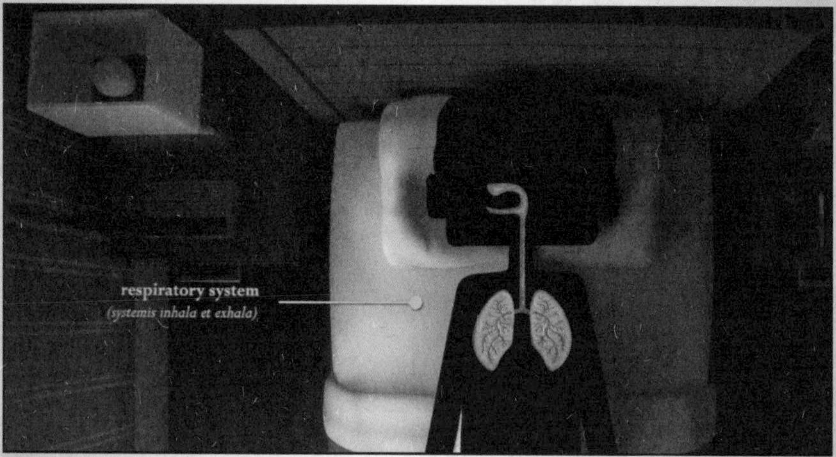
respiratory system
(systemis inhala et exhala)

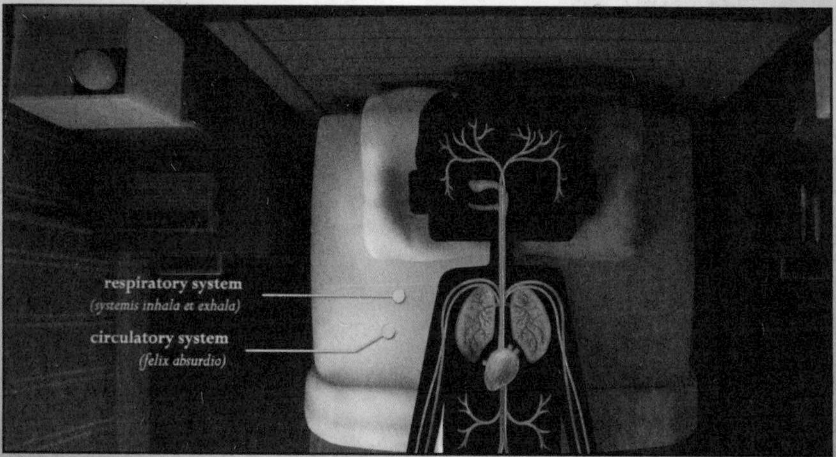
respiratory system
(systemis inhala et exhala)
circulatory system
(felix absurdio)

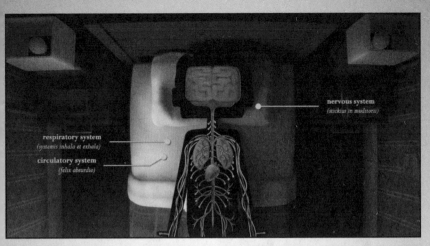

nervous system
(stickius in muditorii)

respiratory system
(systemis inhala et exhala)

circulatory system
(felix absurdio)

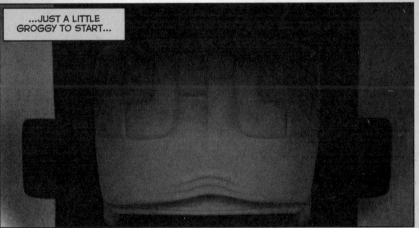

...JUST A LITTLE GROGGY TO START...

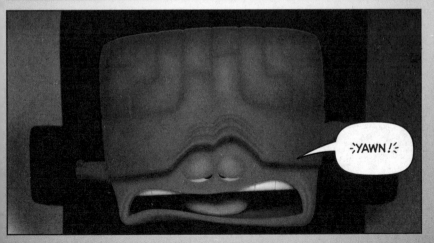

≳YAWN!≲

ZAP!
BEEP!
SLAM!
...A DEEP BREATH IN HELPS...

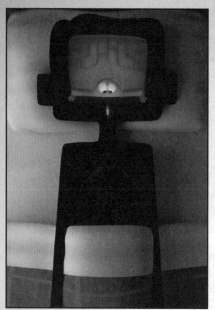

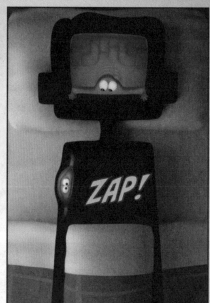

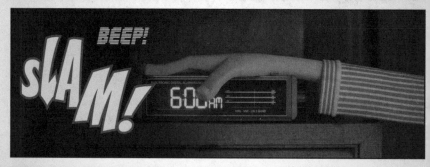

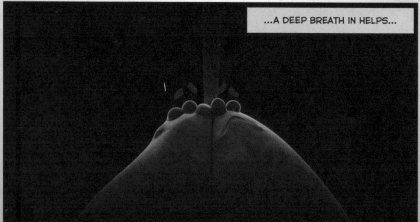

INHALE
EXHALE
INHALE
EXHALE
YAWN!
...STILL. IT'S HARD TO GET GOING.

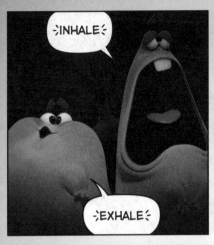

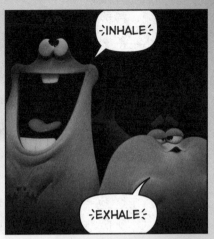

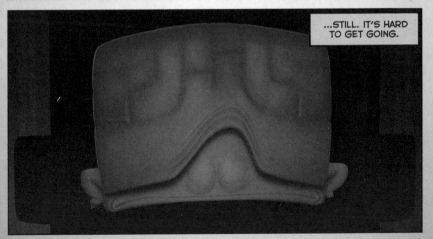

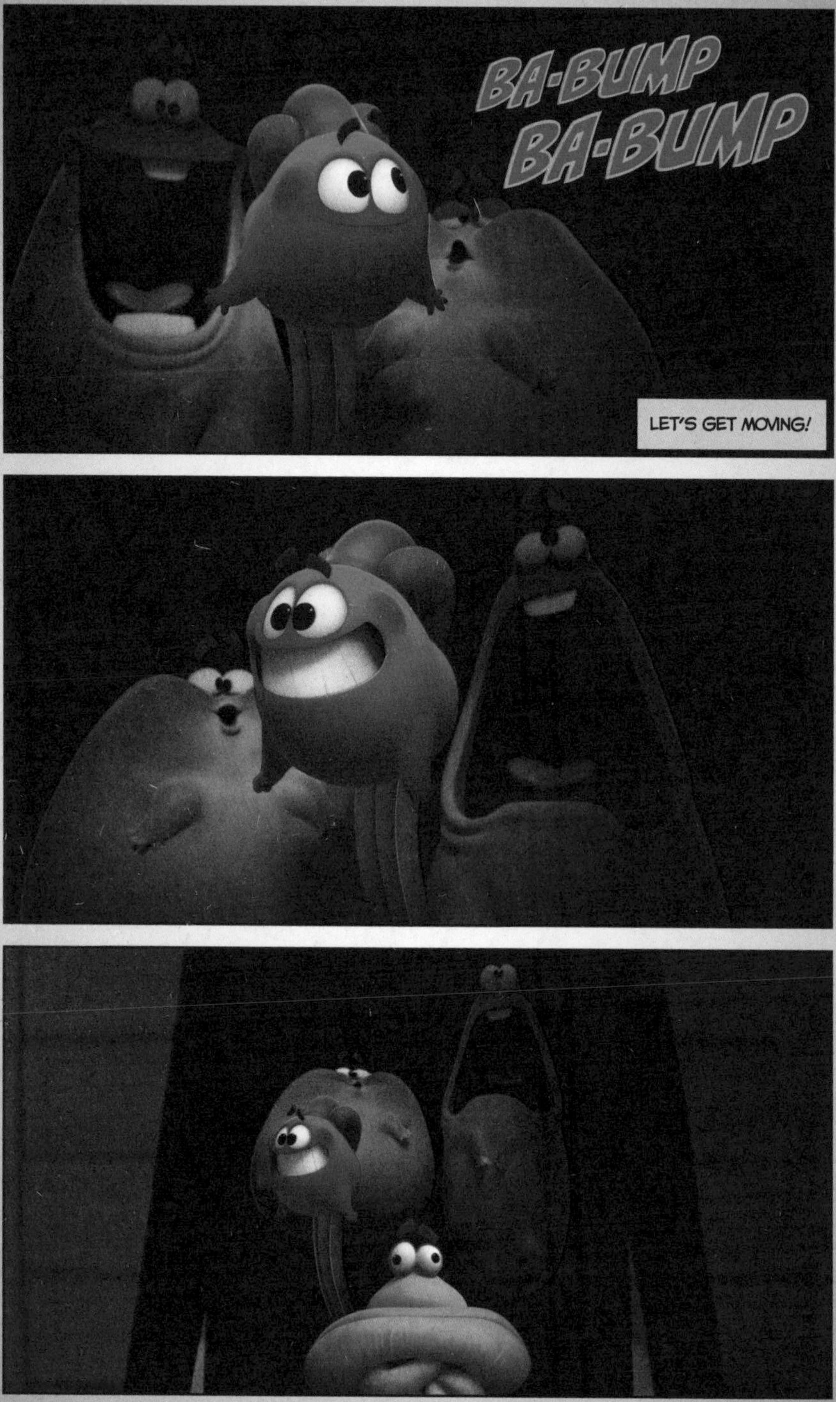
BA-BUMP
BA-BUMP
LET'S GET MOVING!

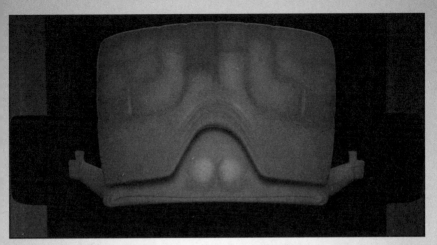

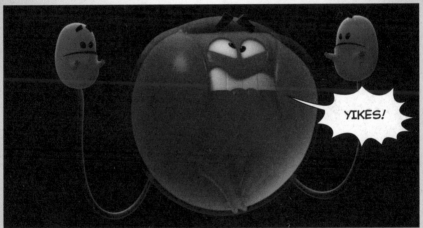

YIKES!

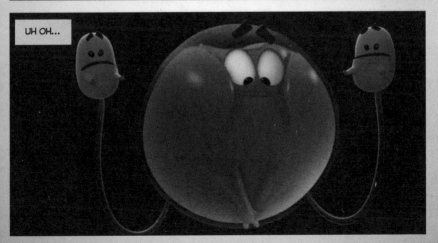

UH OH...

193

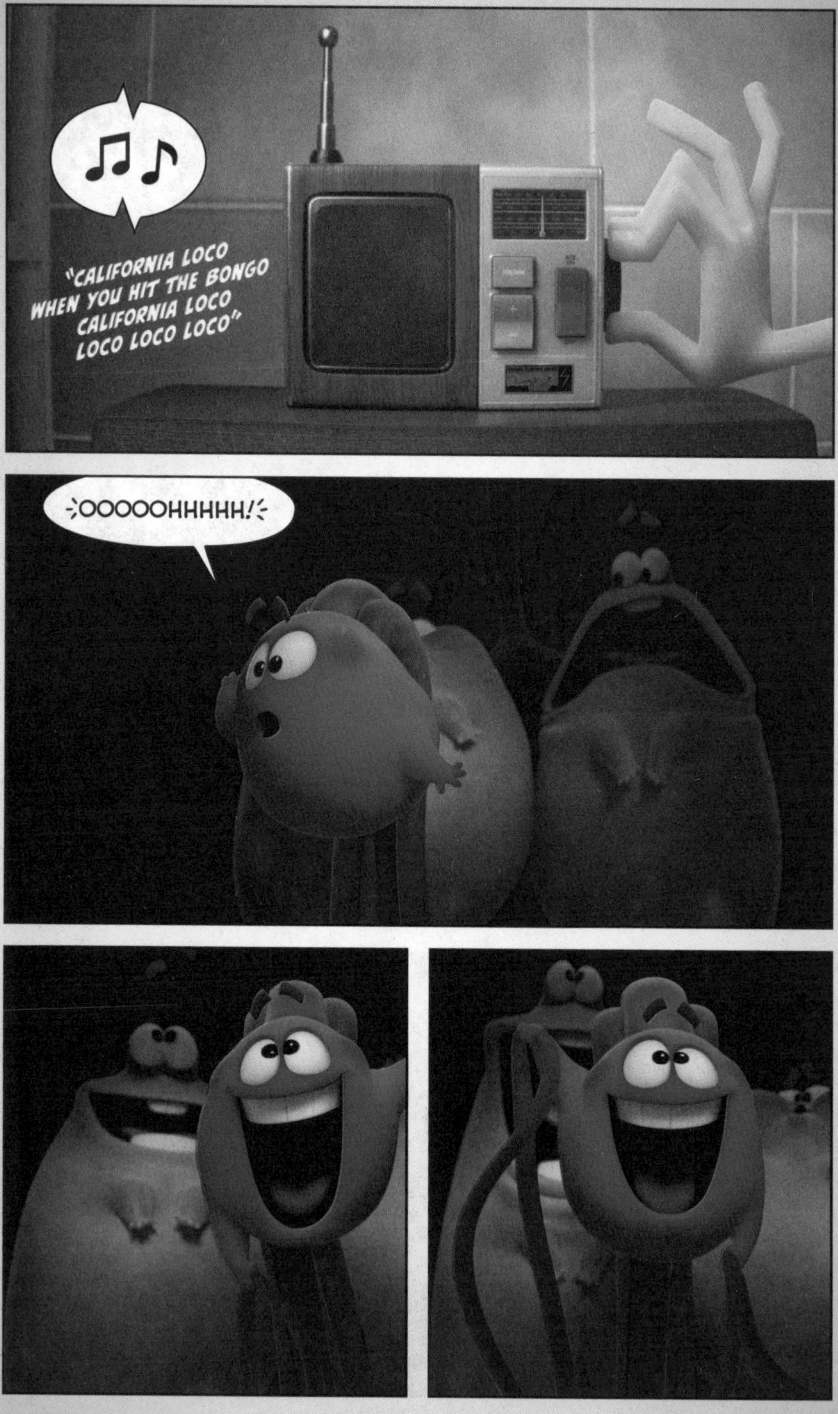
♫♪
"CALIFORNIA LOCO
WHEN YOU HIT THE BONGO
CALIFORNIA LOCO
LOCO LOCO LOCO"
OOOOOHHHHH!

SOAP

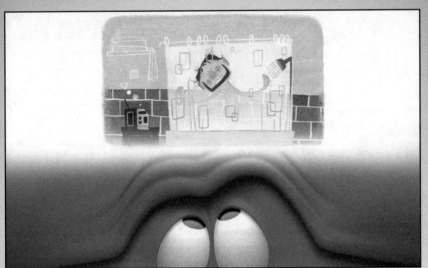

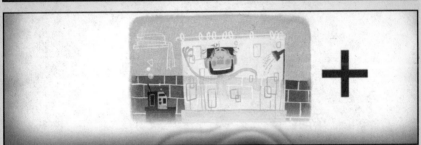

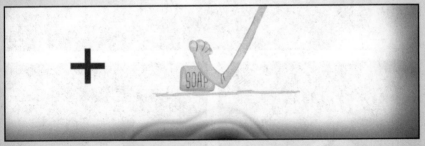

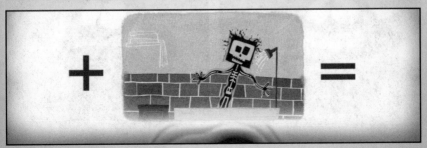

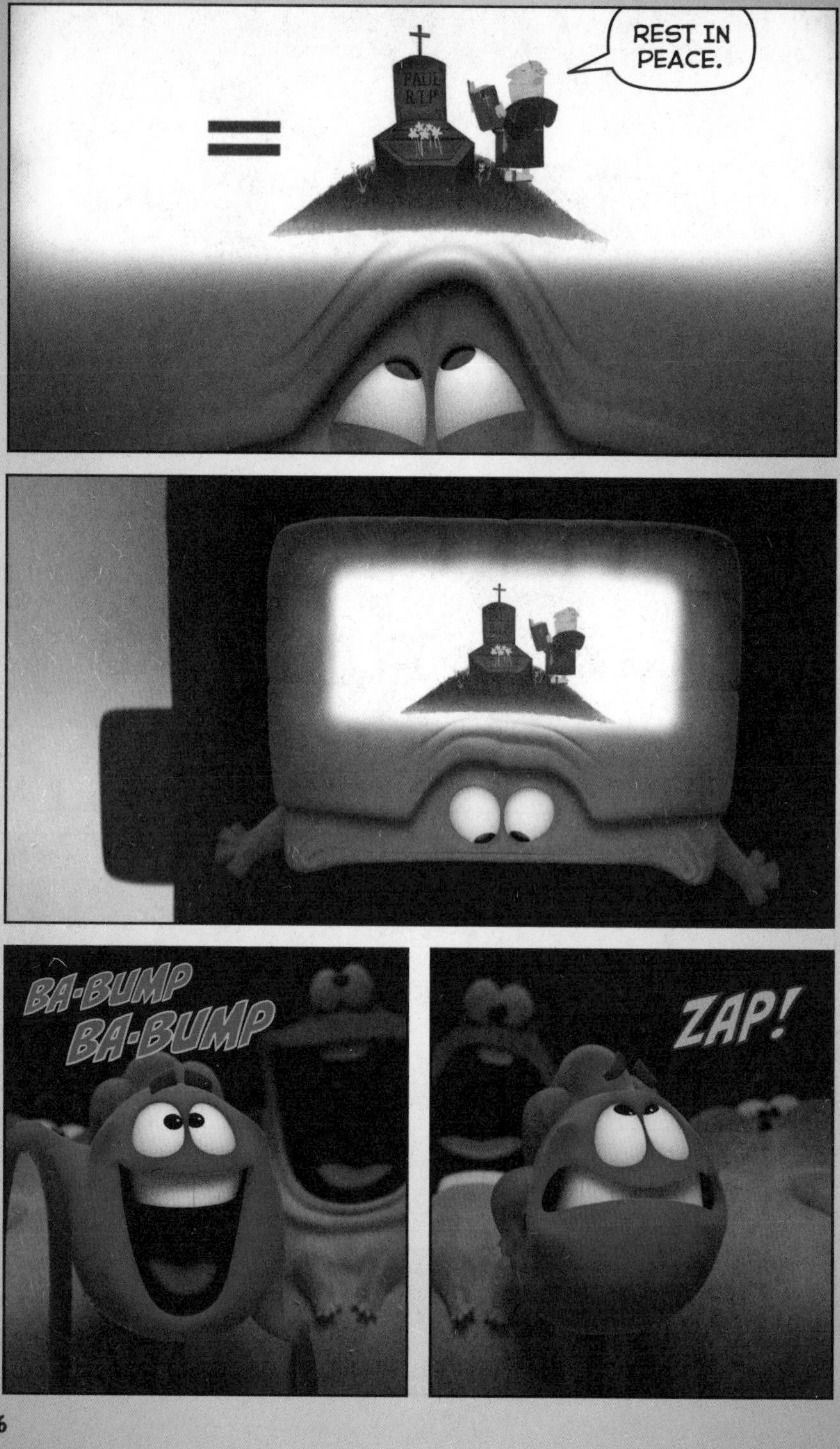
REST IN PEACE.
BA-BUMP
BA-BUMP
ZAP!

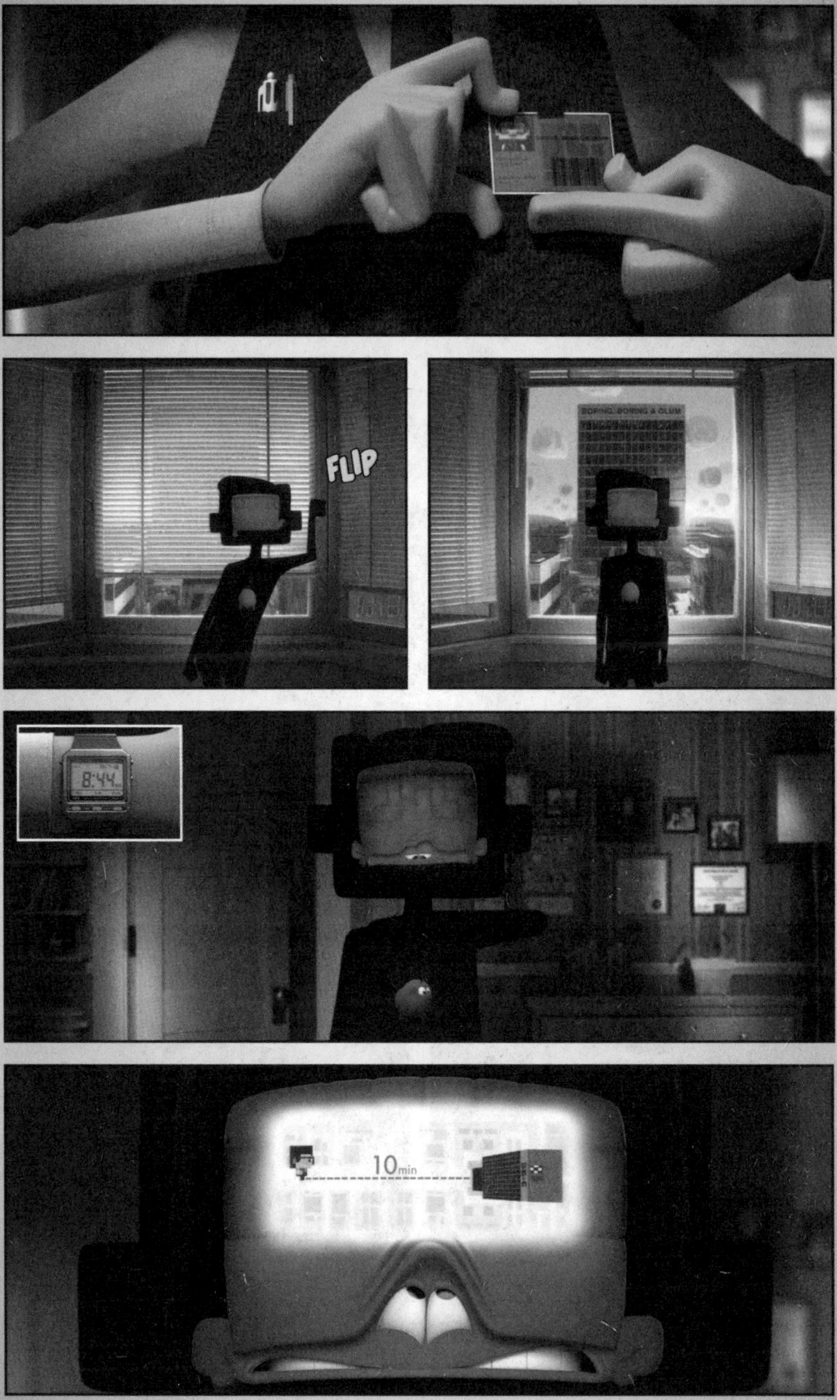
FLIP
BORING, BORING & GLUM
8:44
10min

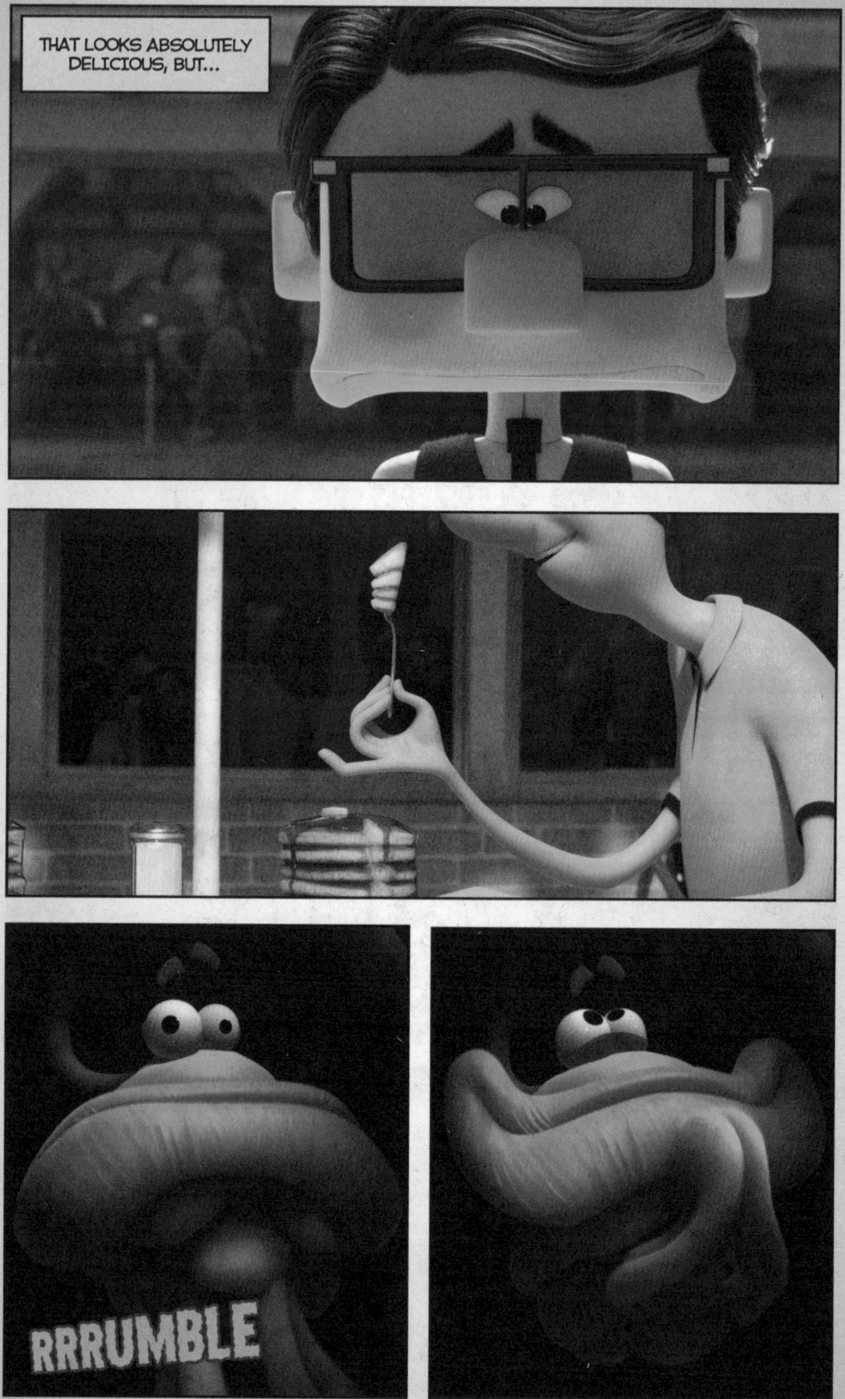
THAT LOOKS ABSOLUTELY DELICIOUS, BUT...
RRRUMBLE

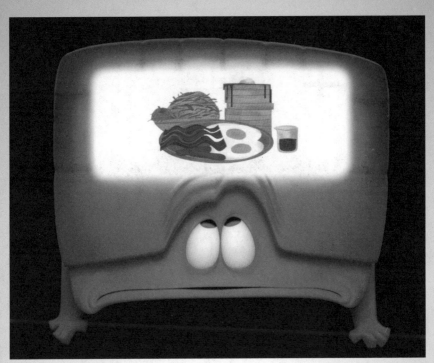

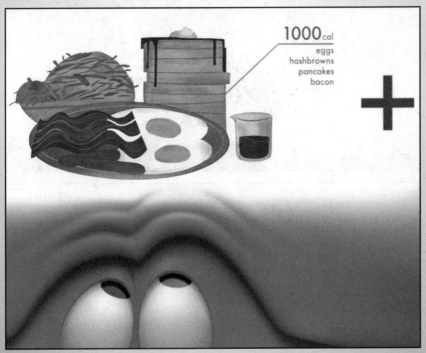

1000cal
eggs
hashbrowns
pancakes
bacon

125lbs
325lbs
325lbs
REST IN PEACE.

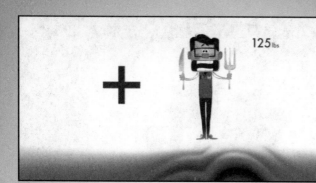

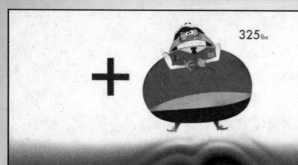

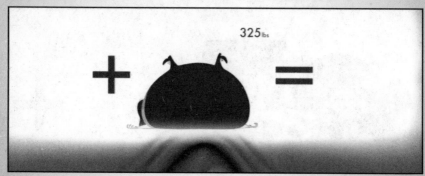

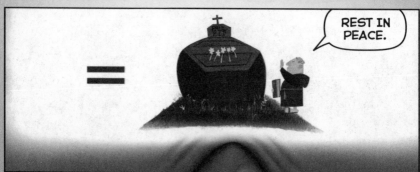

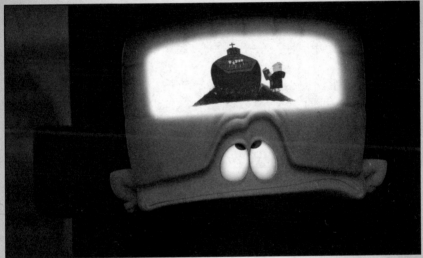

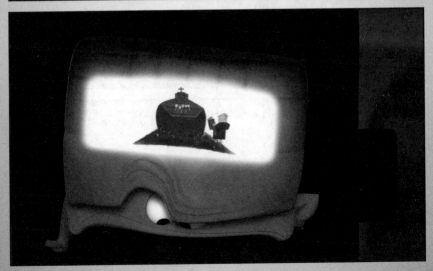

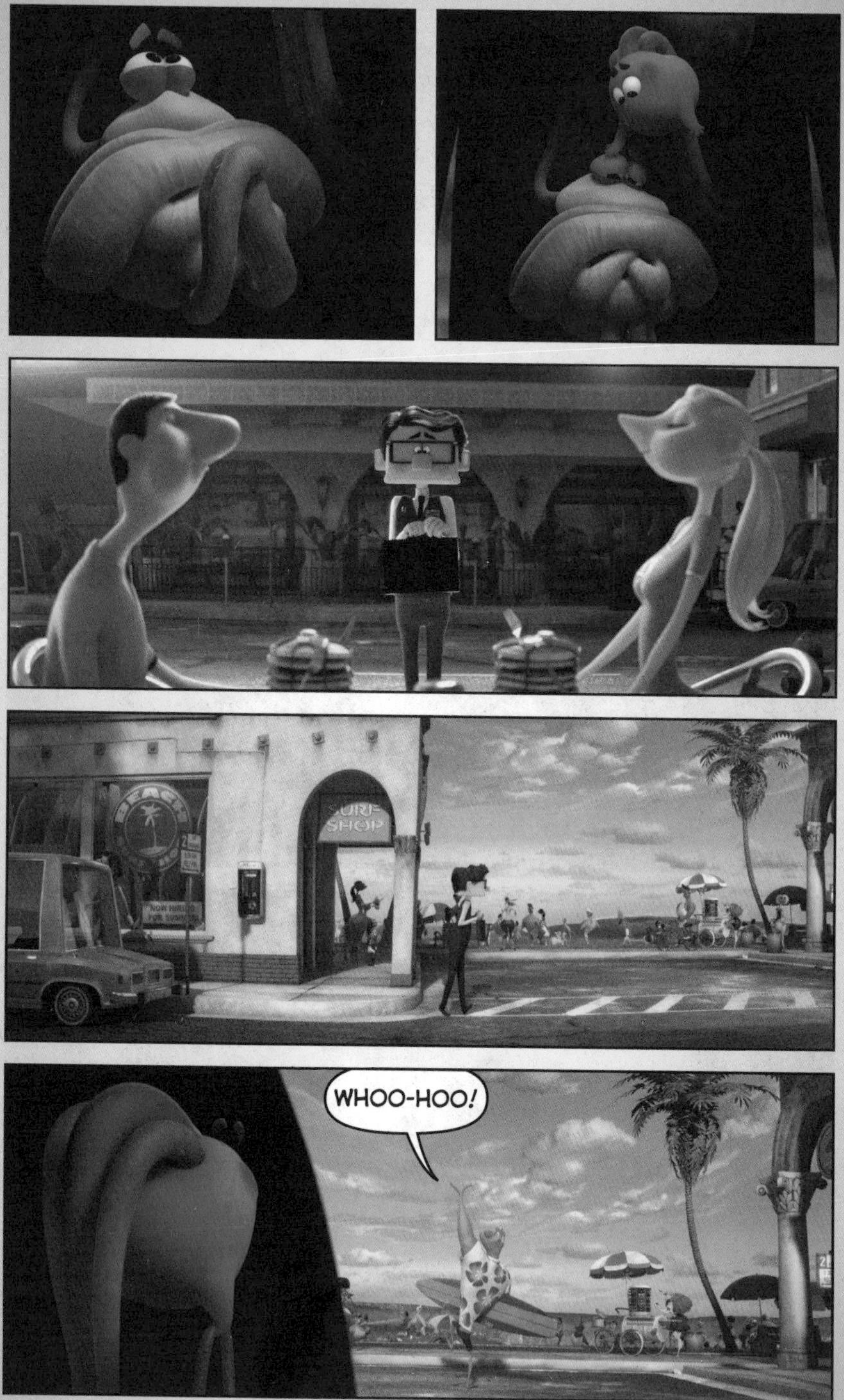
SURF SHOP
WHOO-HOO!

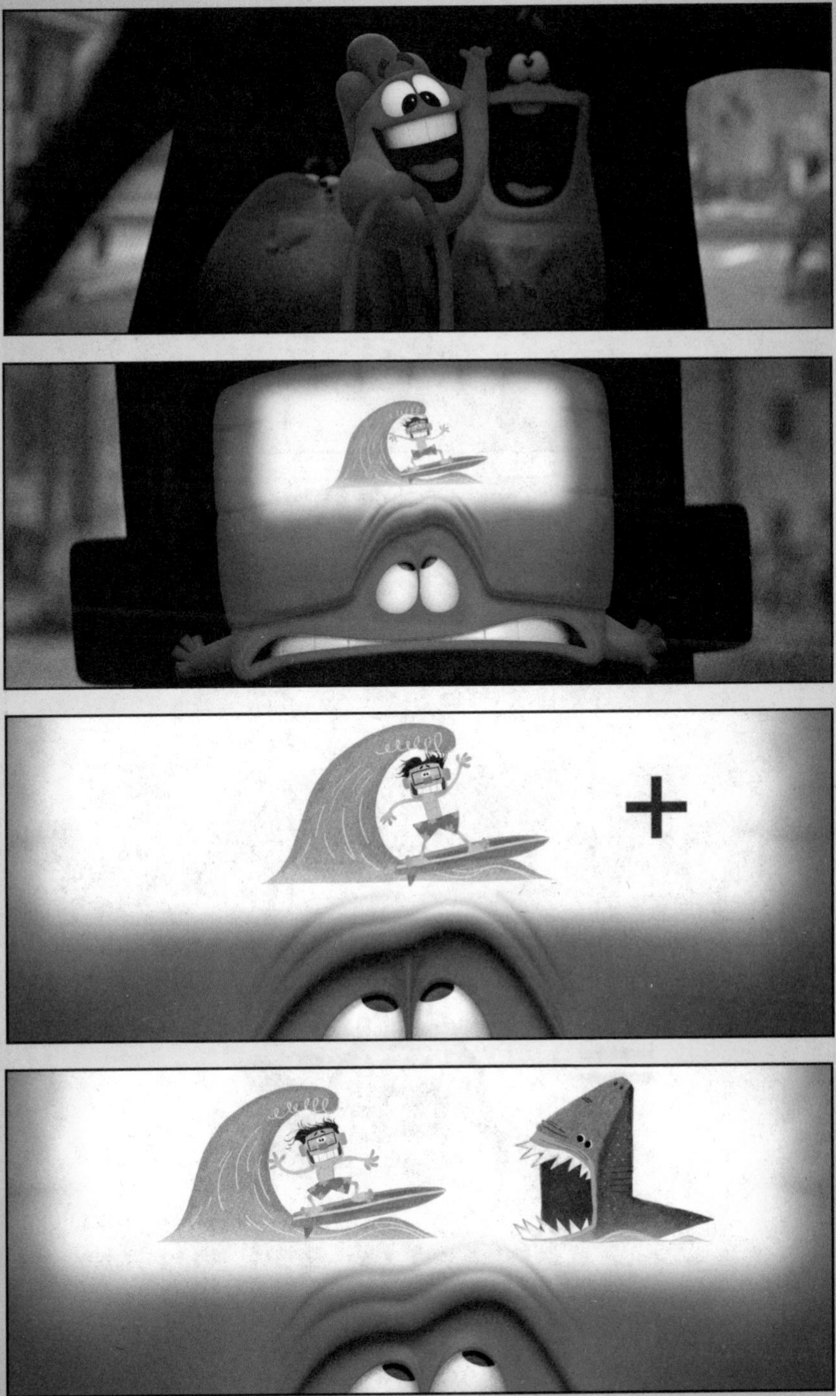

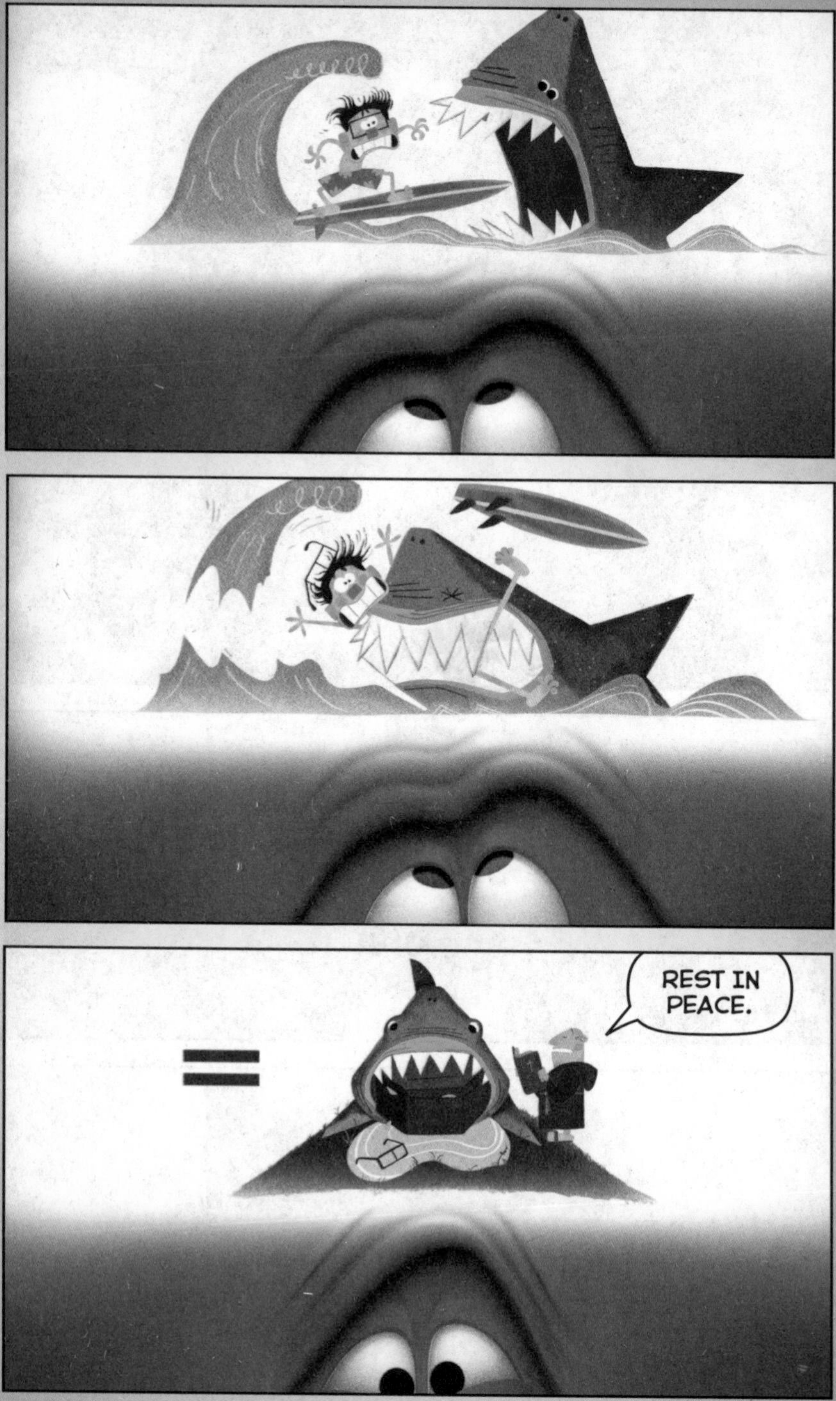
REST IN PEACE.

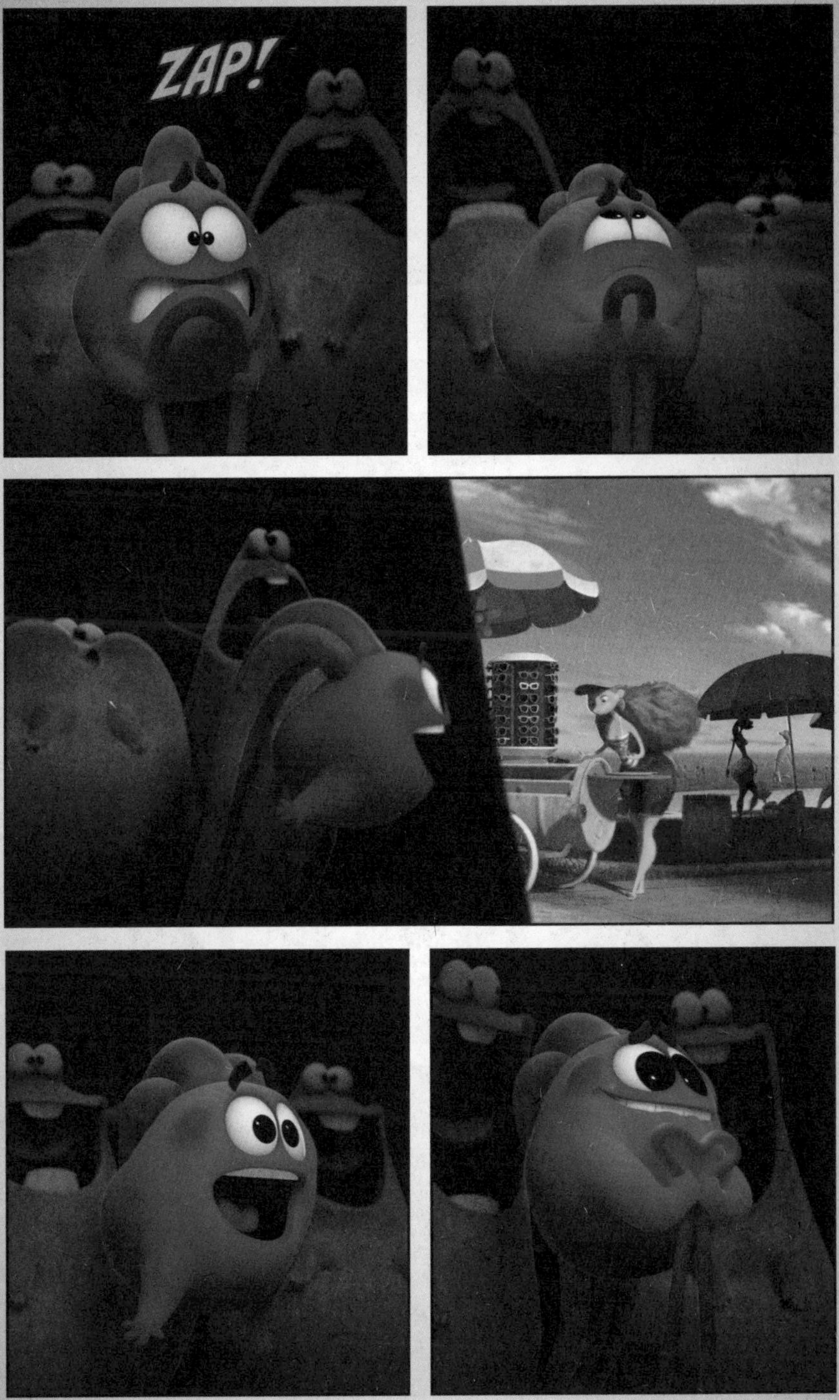
ZAP!

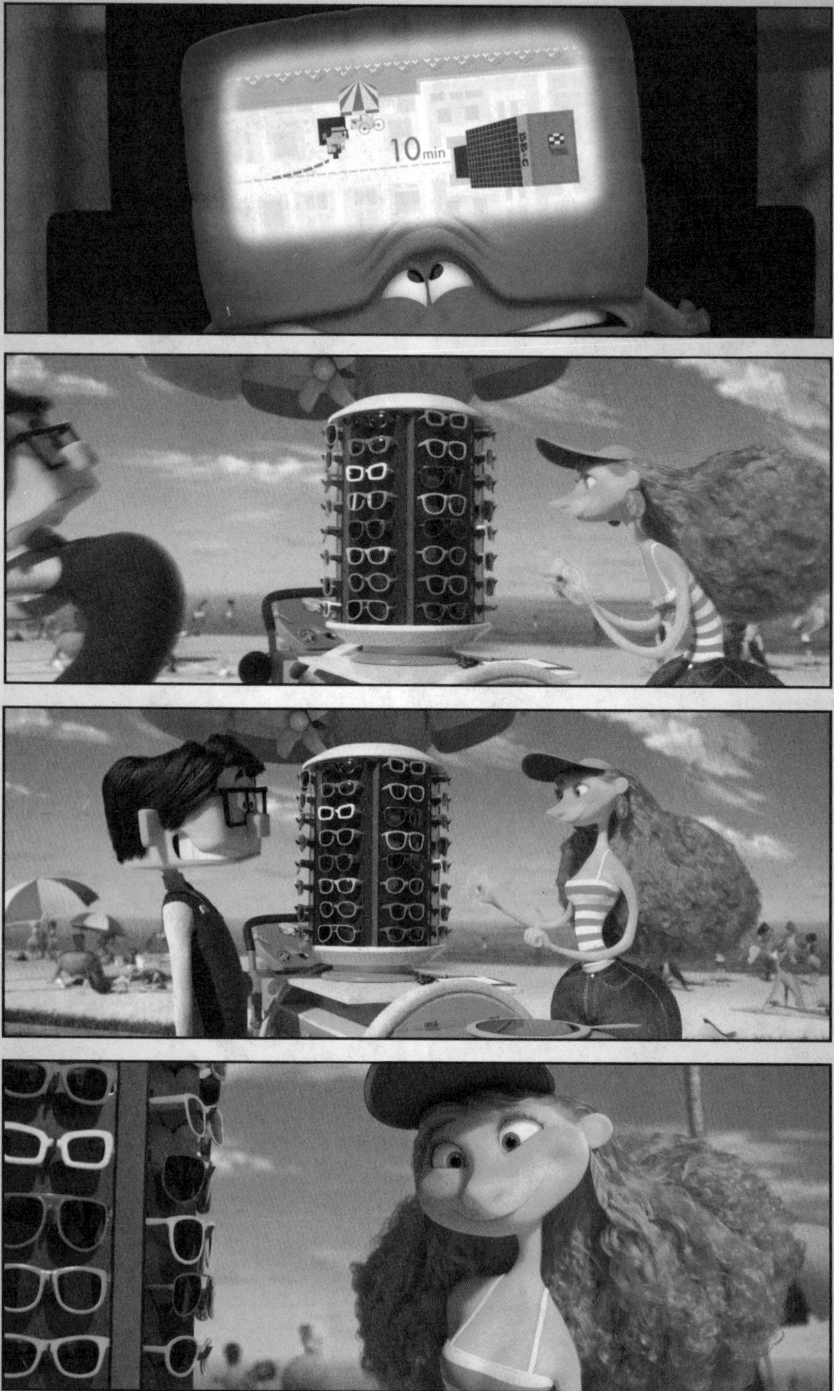
10min

UV

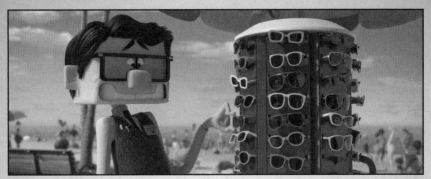

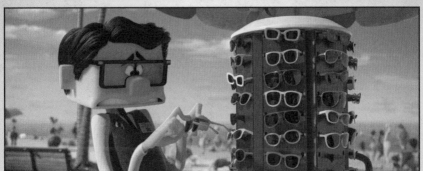

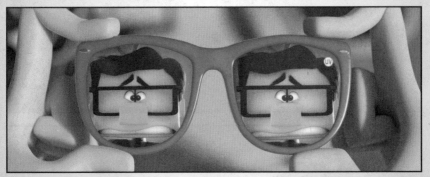

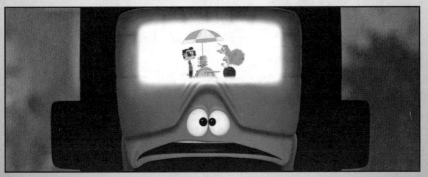

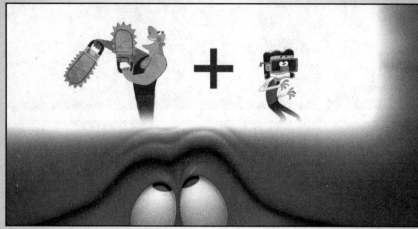

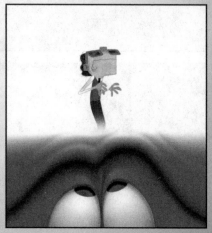

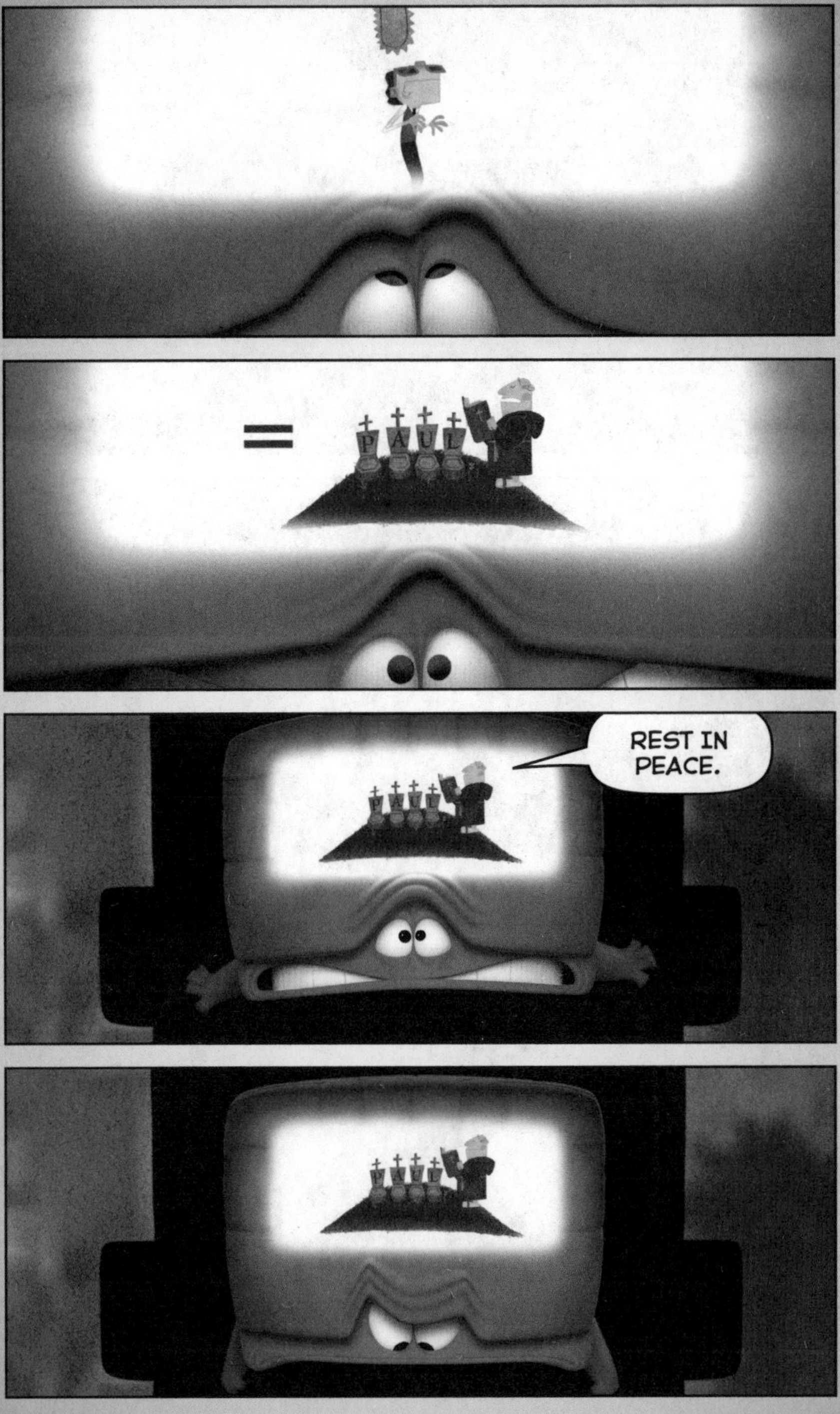
P A U L
REST IN PEACE.

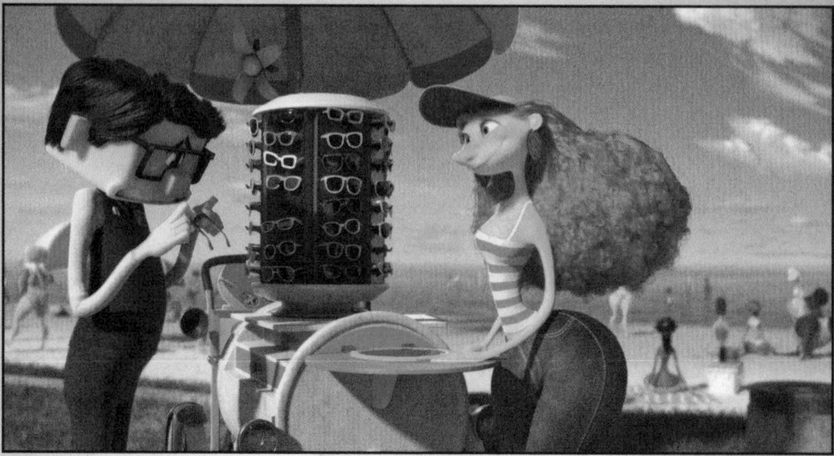

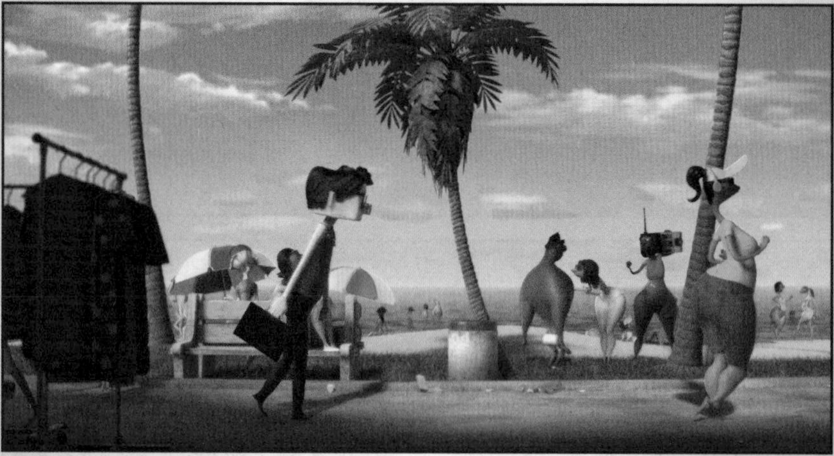

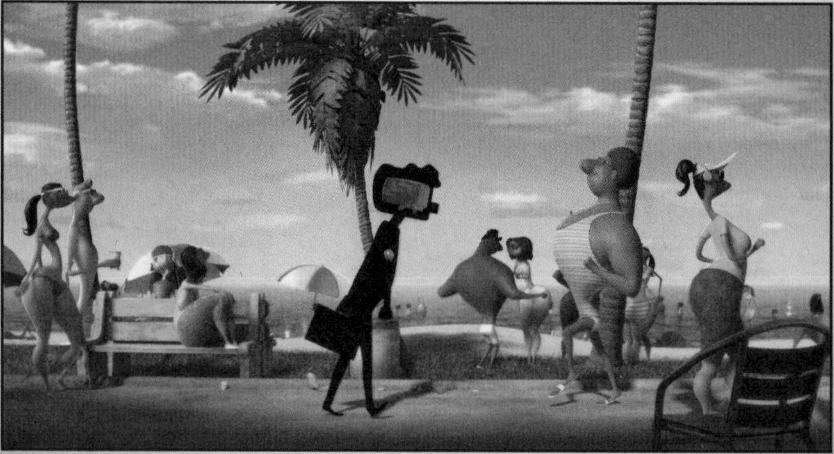

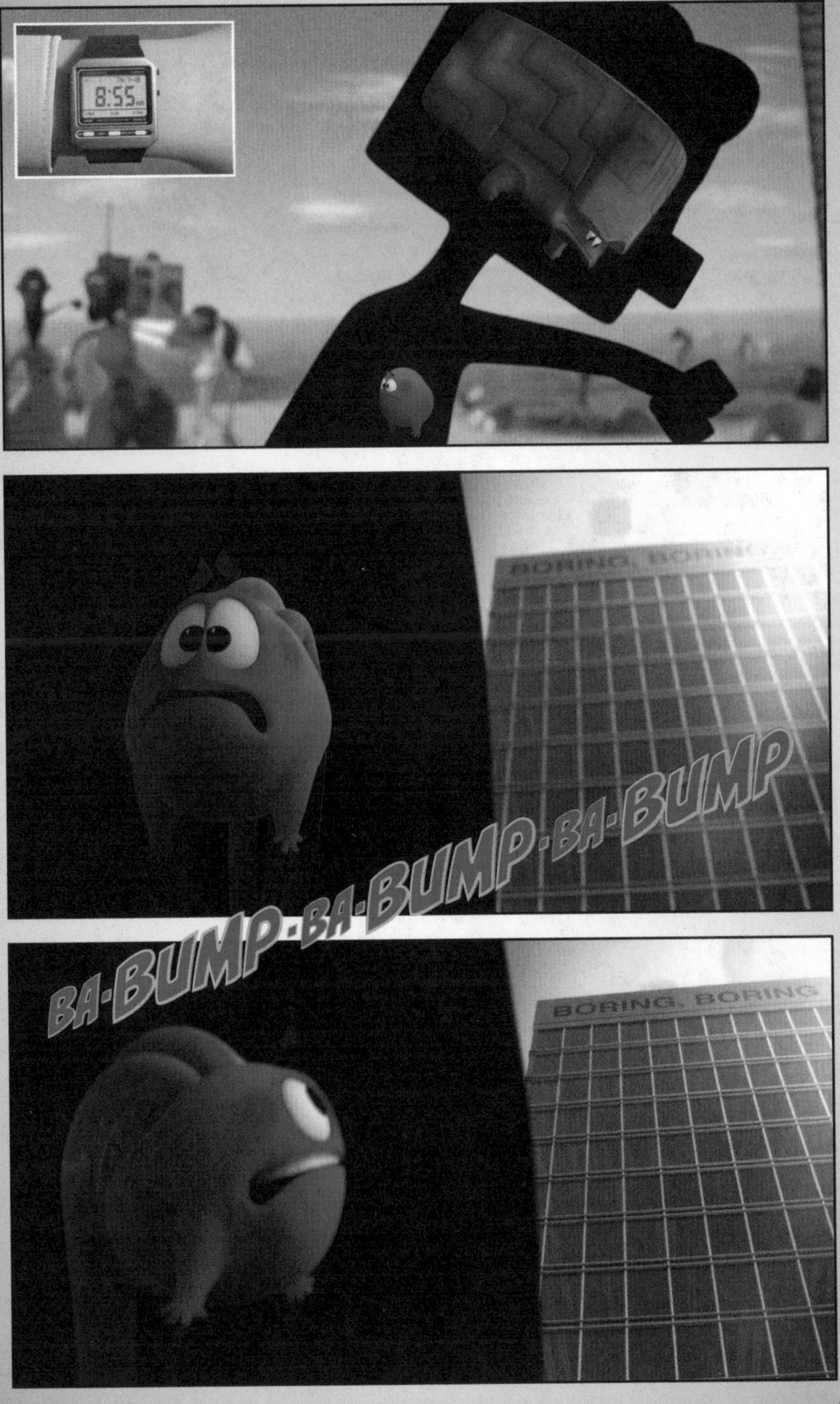
8:55
BA-BUMP-BA-BUMP-BA-BUMP
BORING, BORING

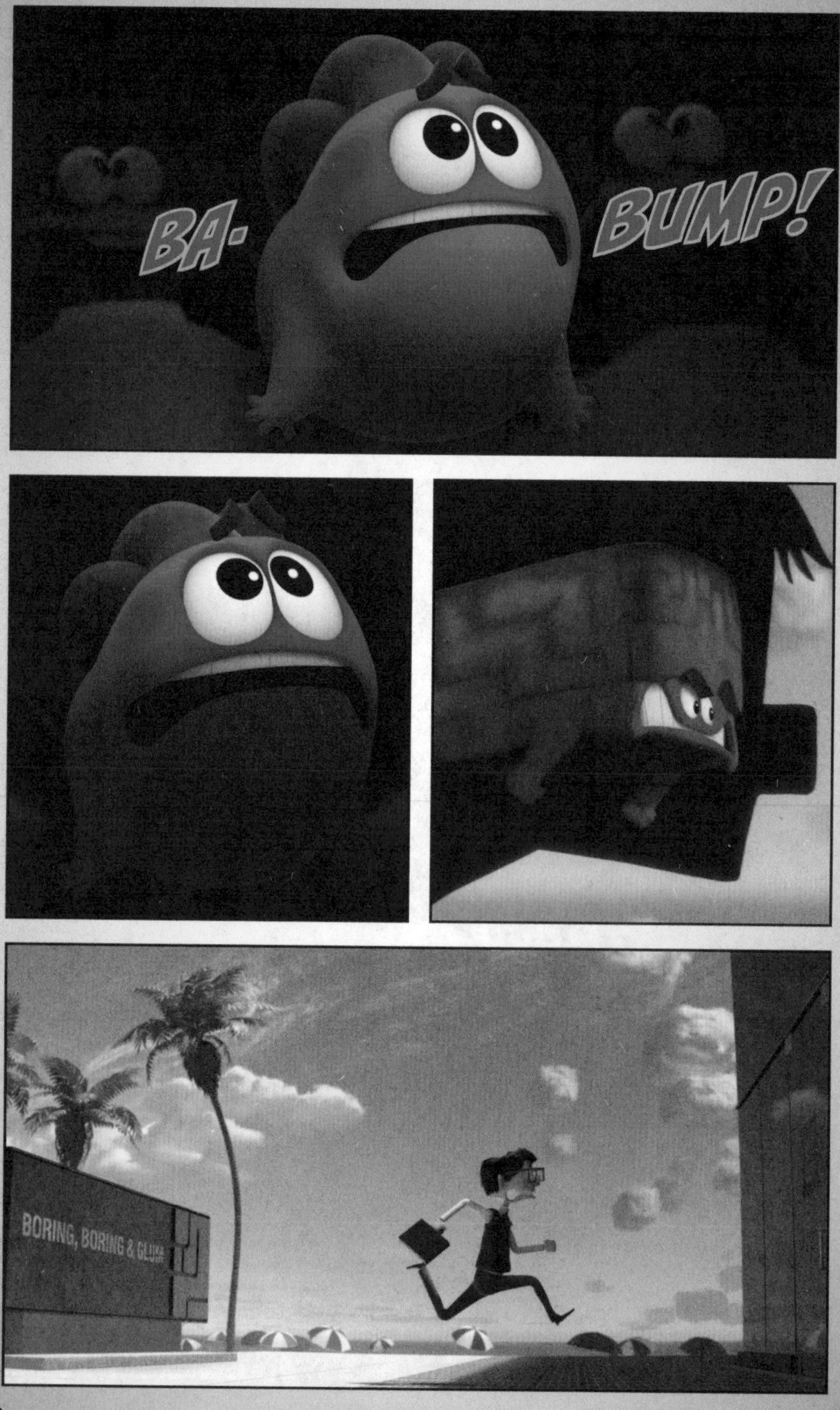

BA-
BUMP!
BORING, BORING & GLUM

BB&G
BB&G
WHEEZE!

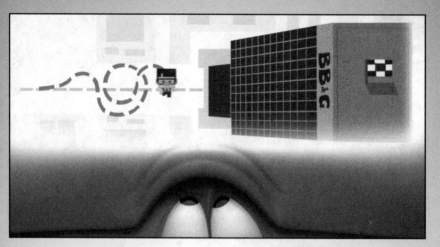

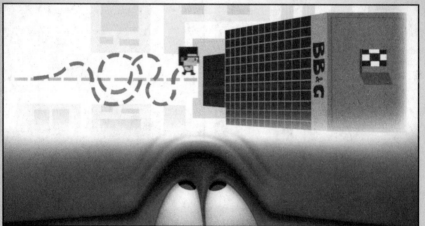

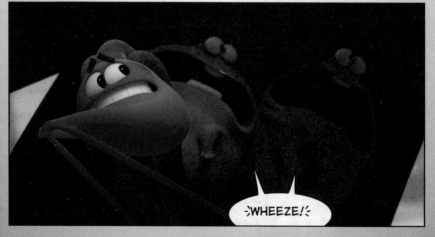

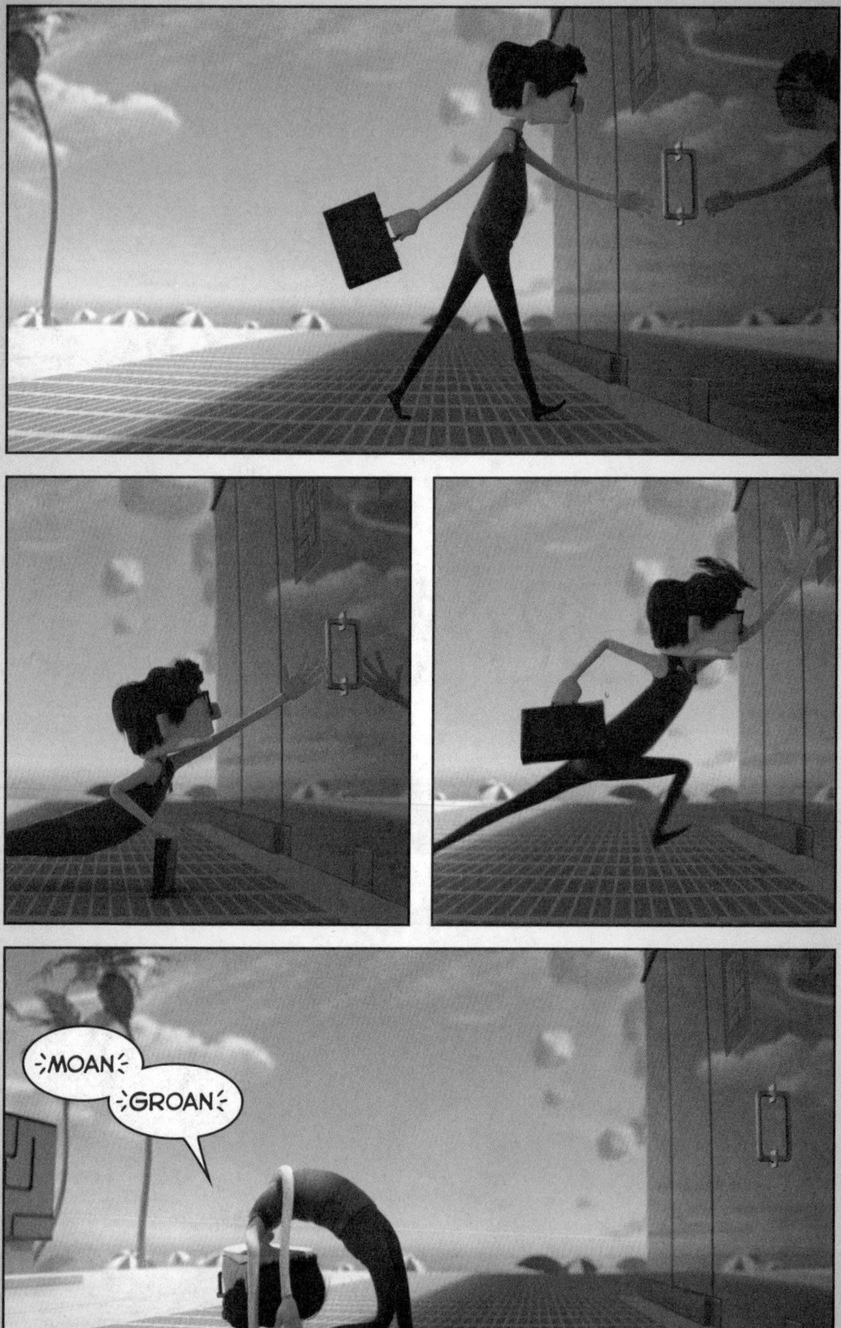
MOAN
GROAN

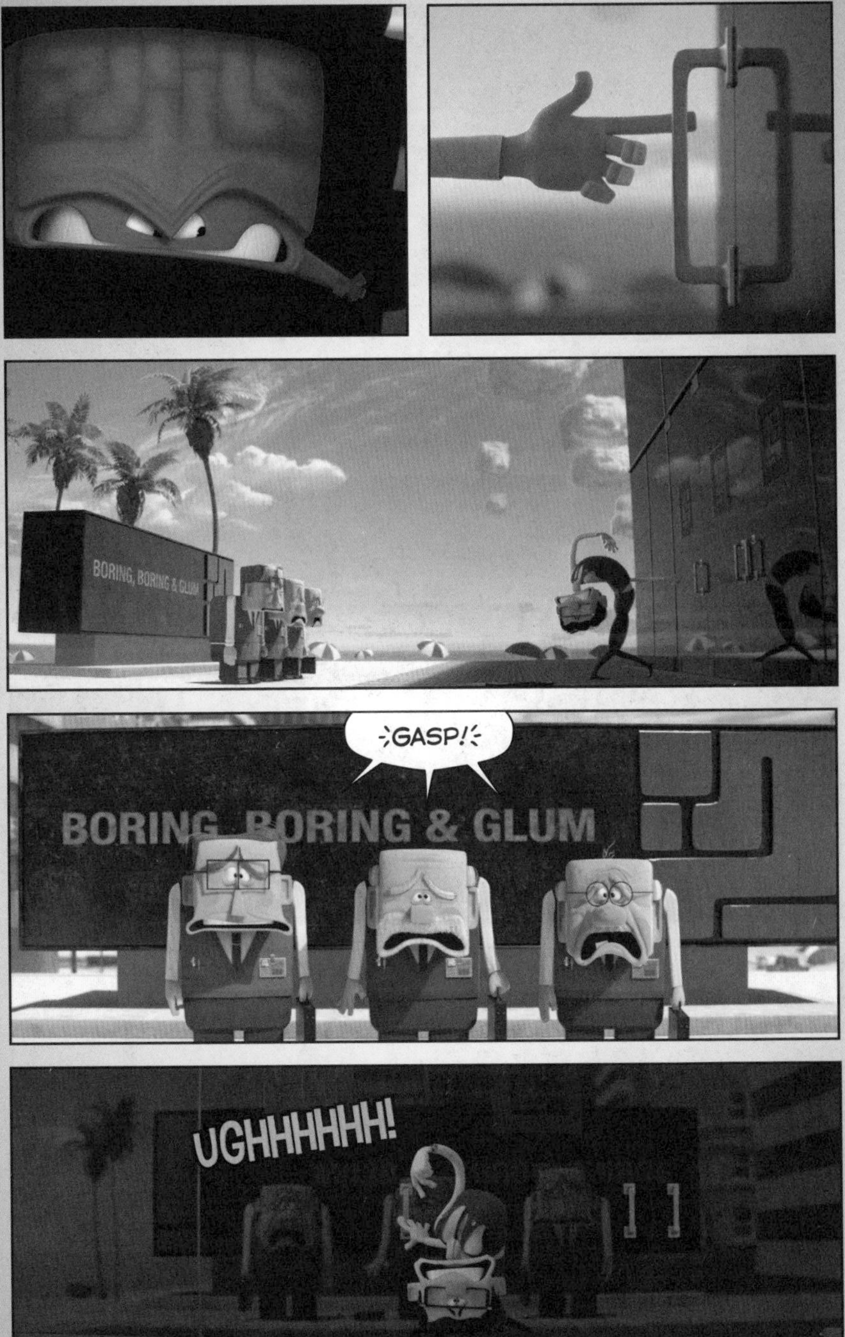
BORING, BORING & GLUM
GASP!
BORING, BORING & GLUM
UGHHHHHH!

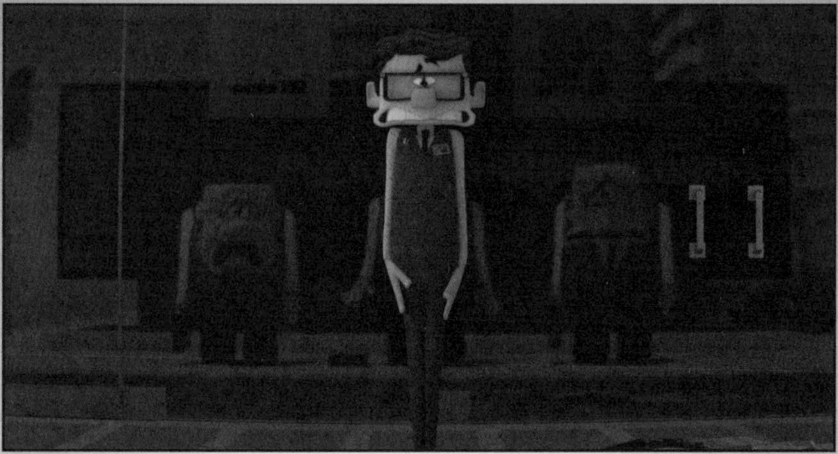

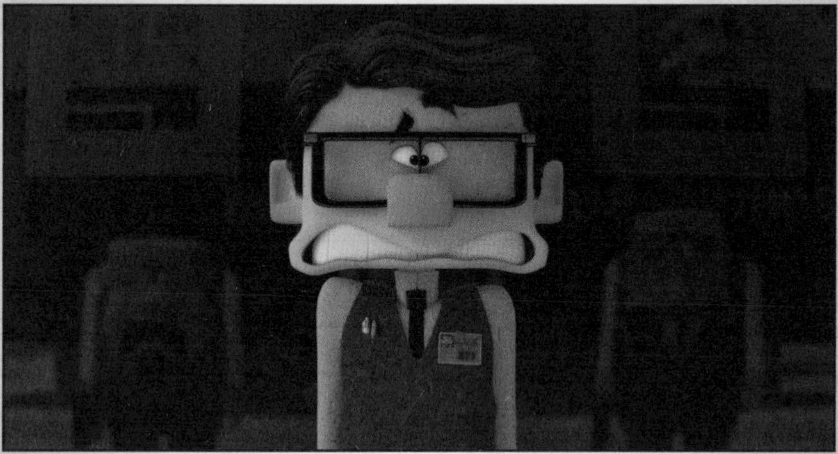

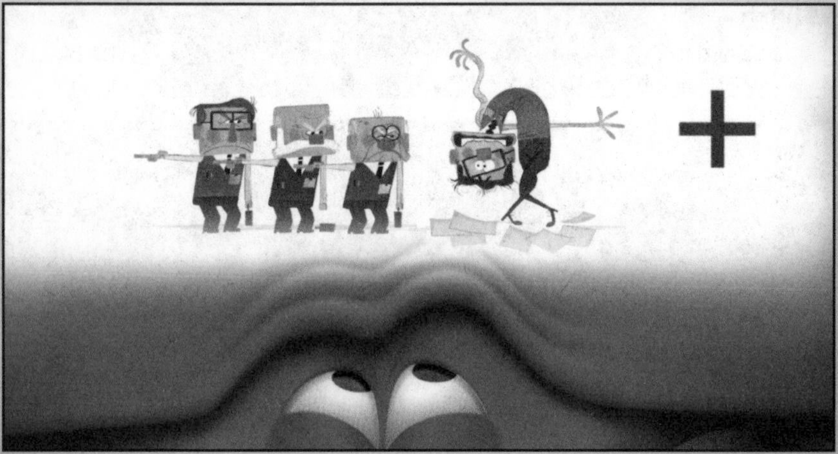

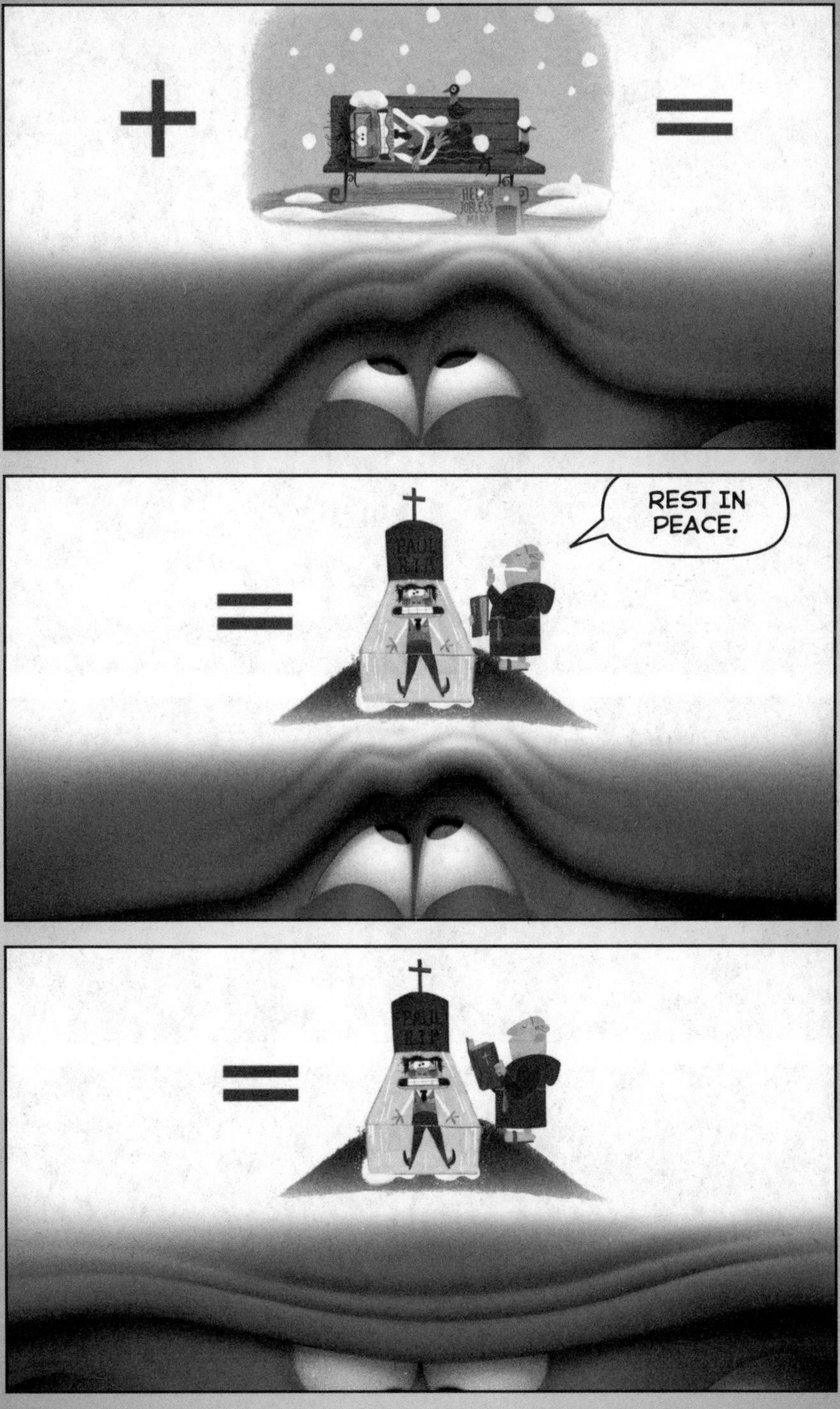
REST IN PEACE.

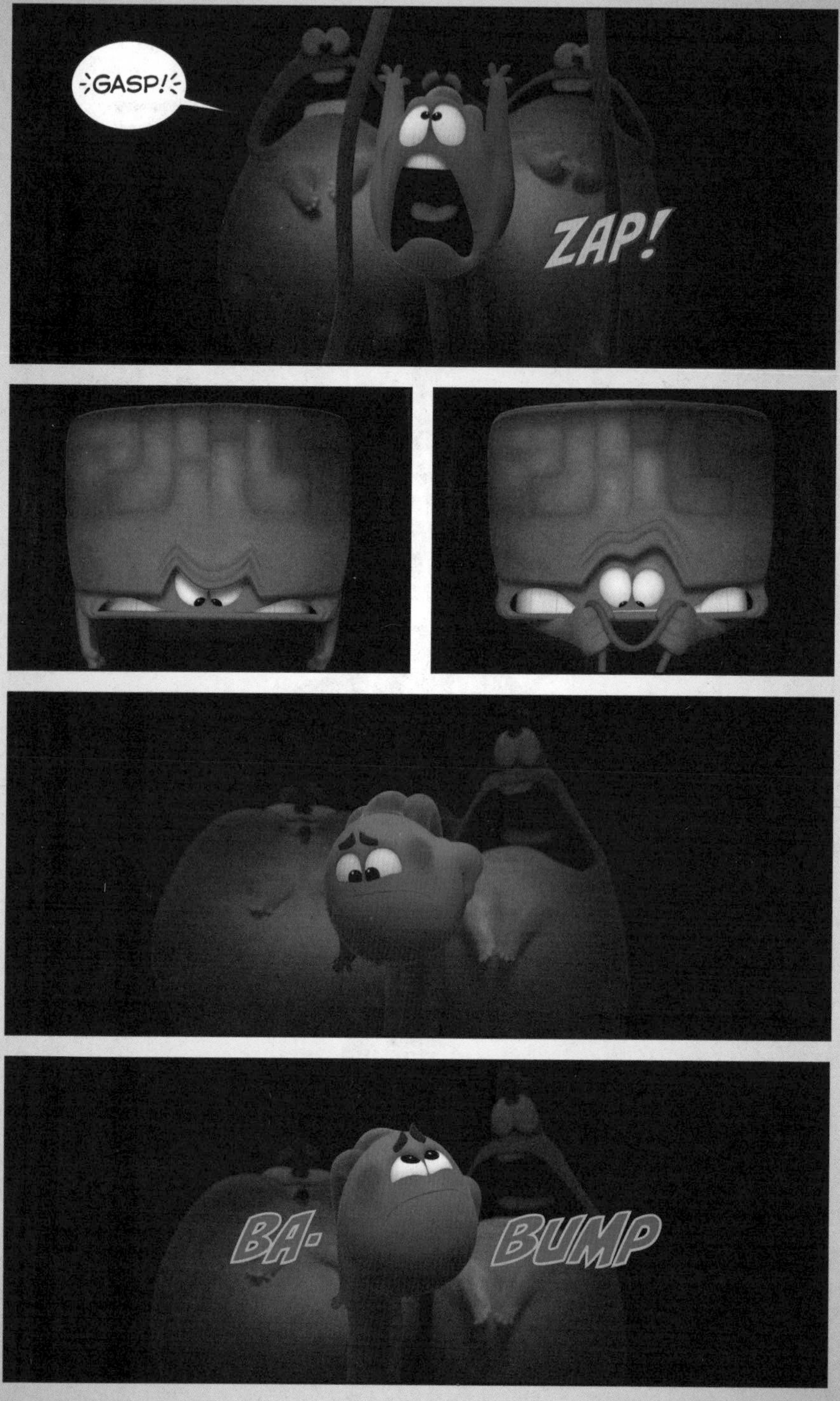
GASP!
ZAP!
BA-
BUMP

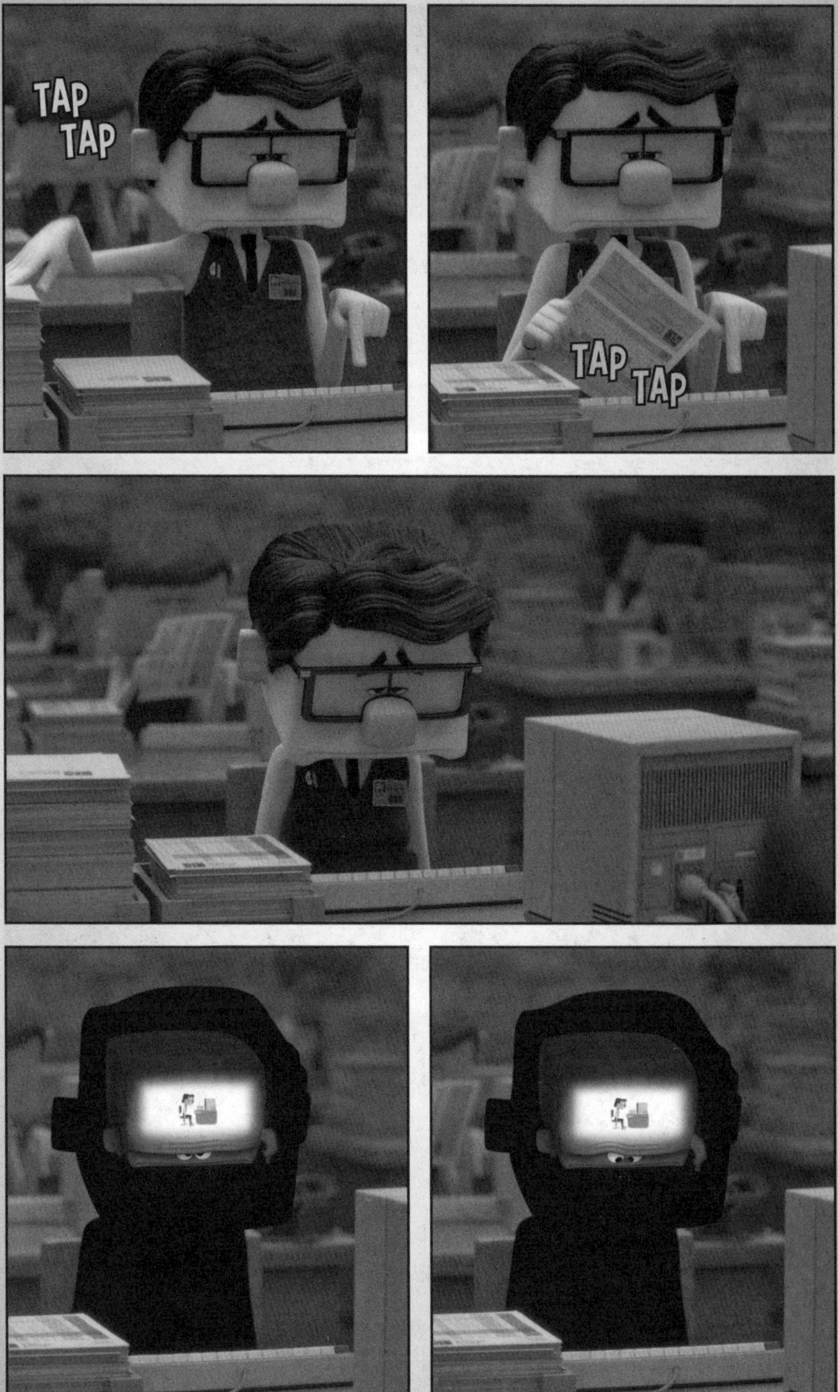
TAP
TAP
TAP
TAP

BETTER KEEP TYPING.

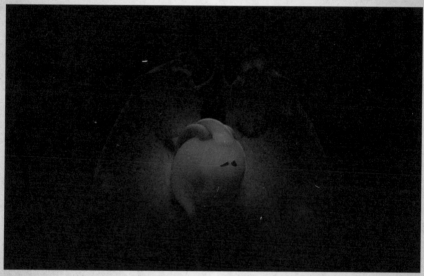

TAP

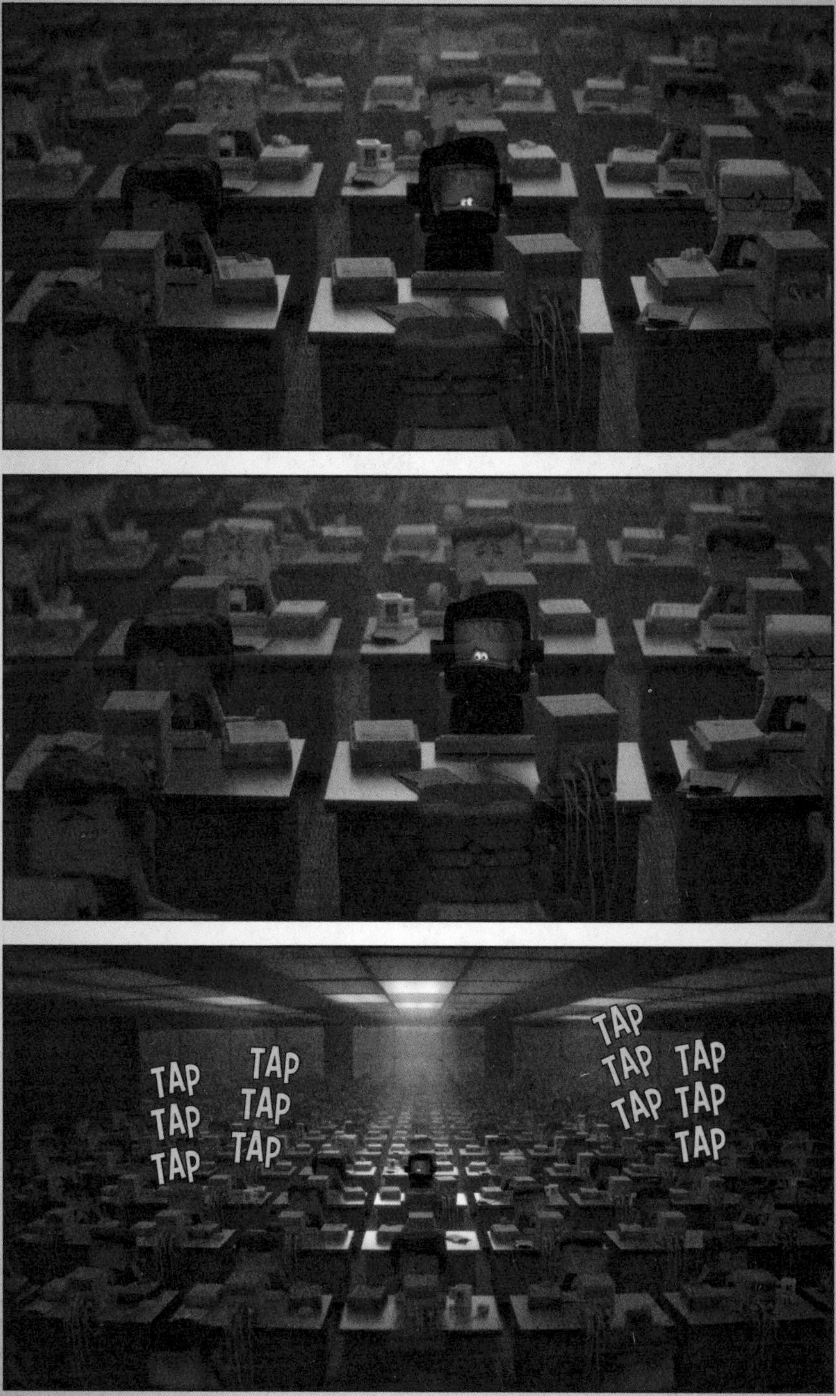
TAP
TAP
TAP
TAP
TAP
TAP
TAP
TAP
TAP
TAP
TAP
TAP

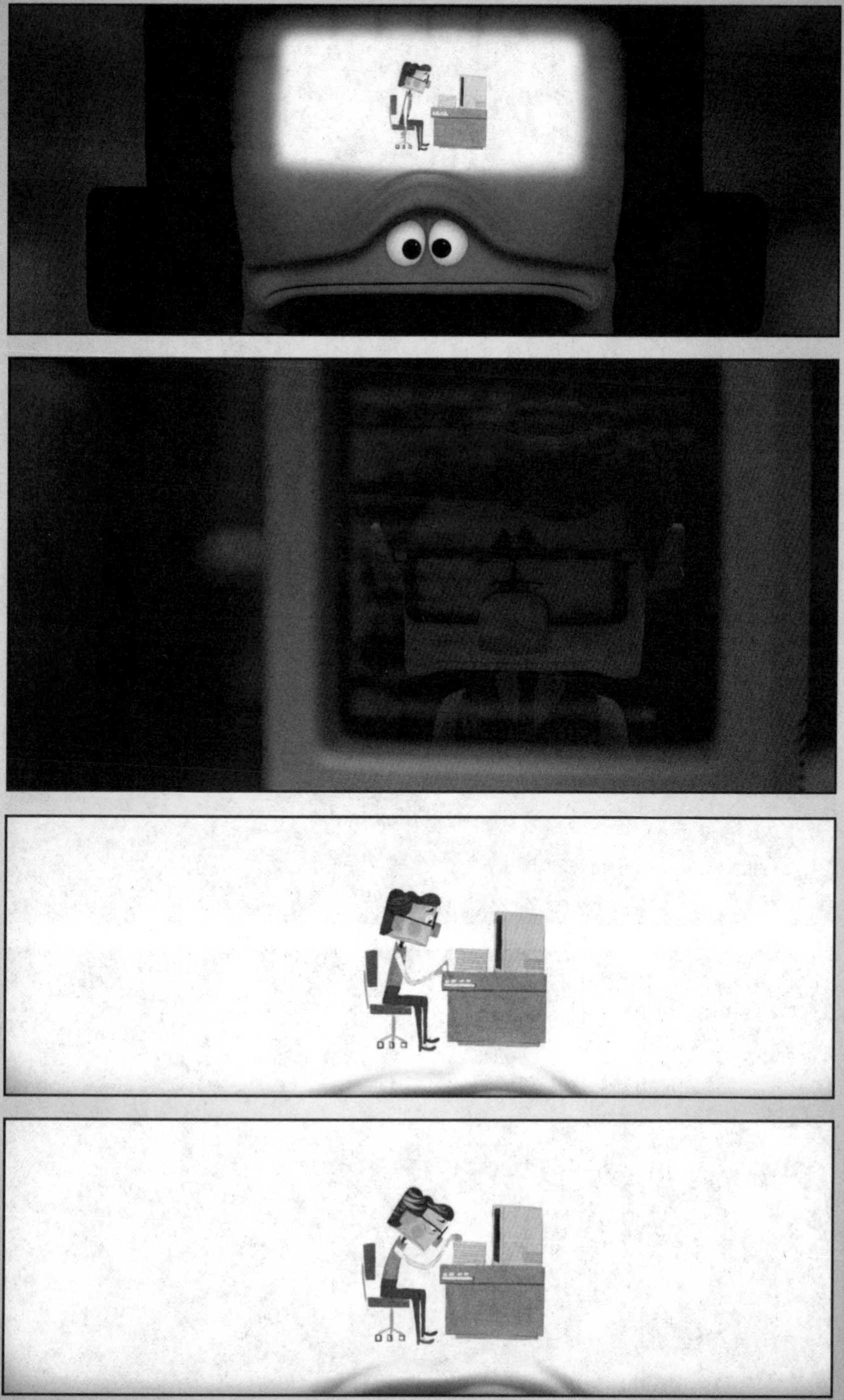

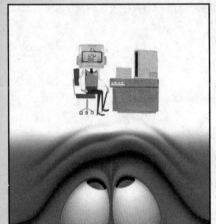

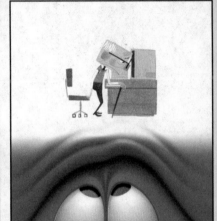

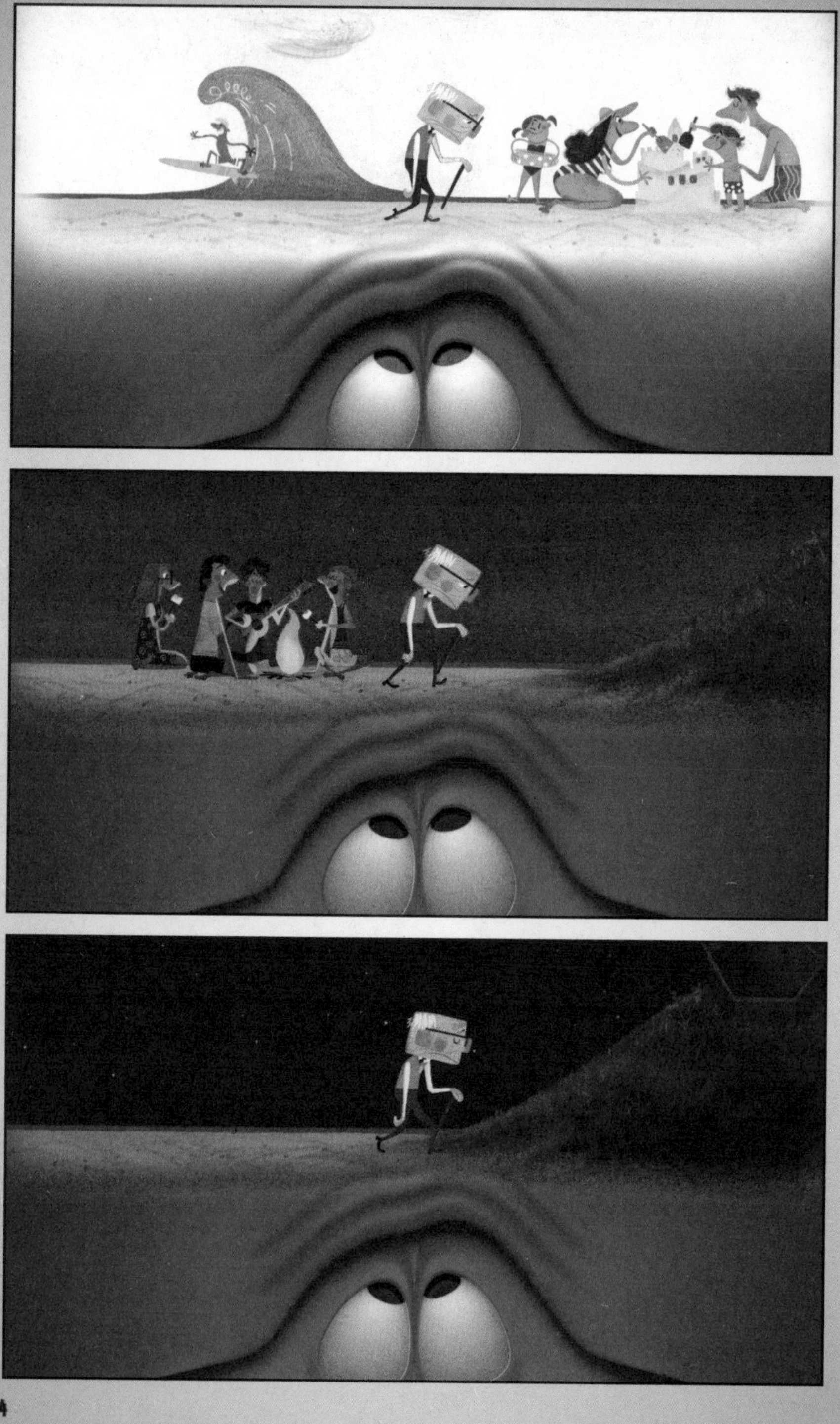

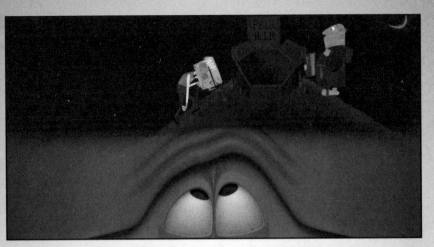
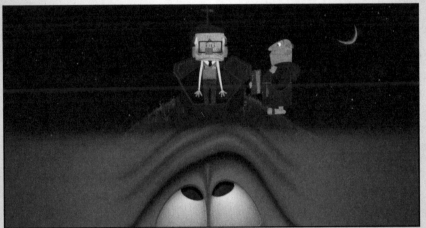

225

12:00 PM: LUNCHTIME
TAP TAP
CHEW
TAP
TAP
CHEW

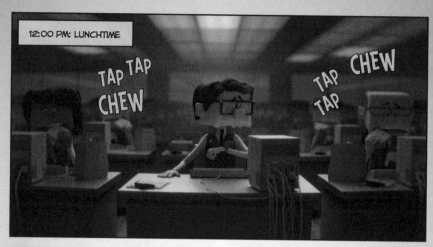

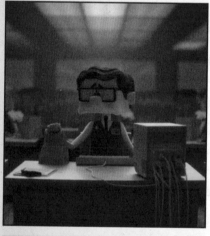

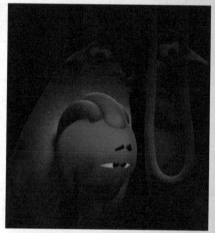

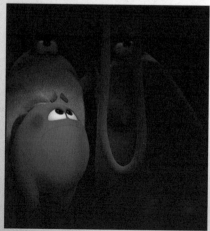

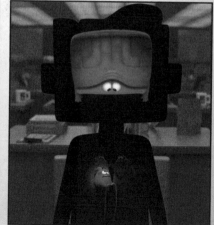

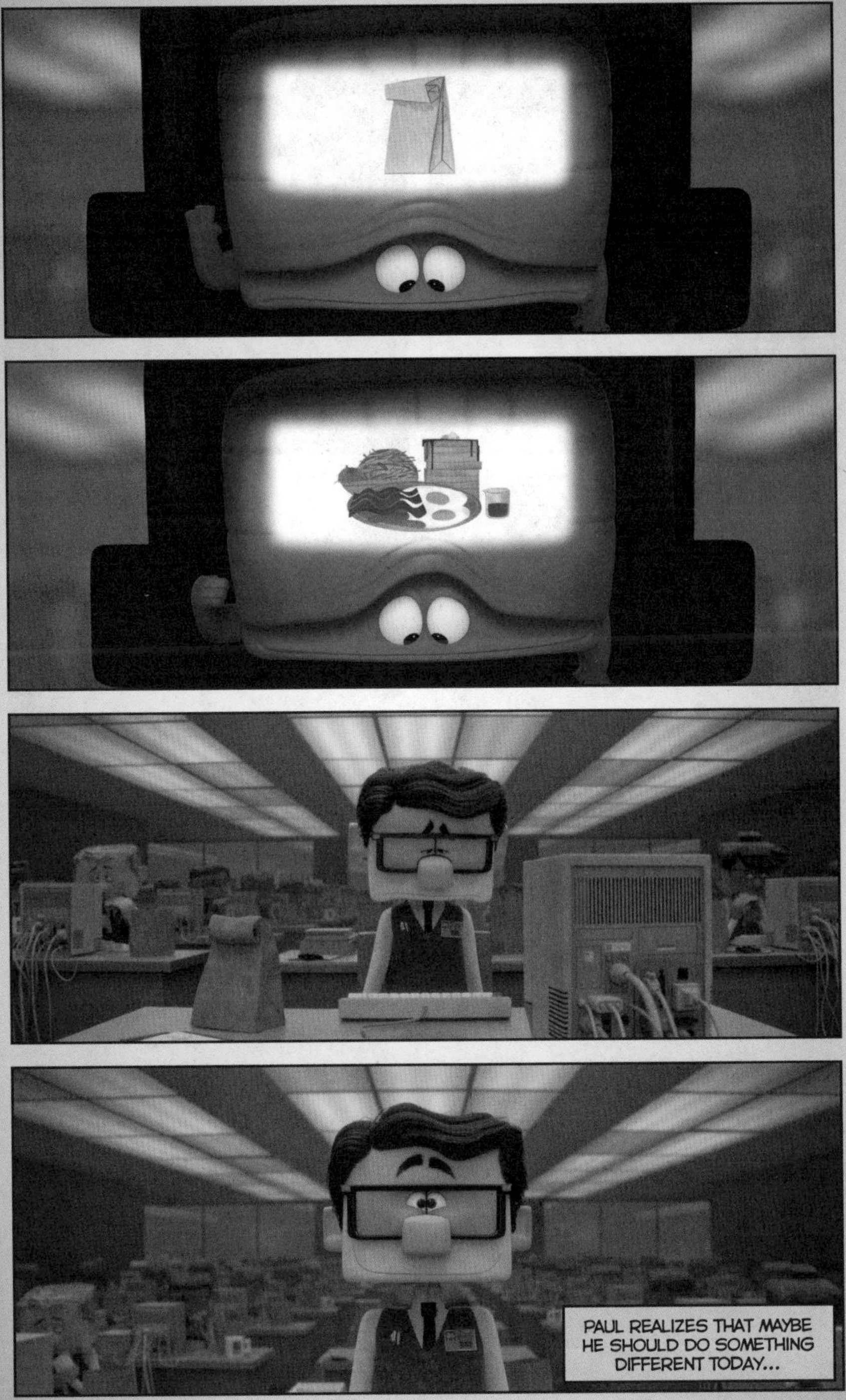
PAUL REALIZES THAT MAYBE
HE SHOULD DO SOMETHING
DIFFERENT TODAY...

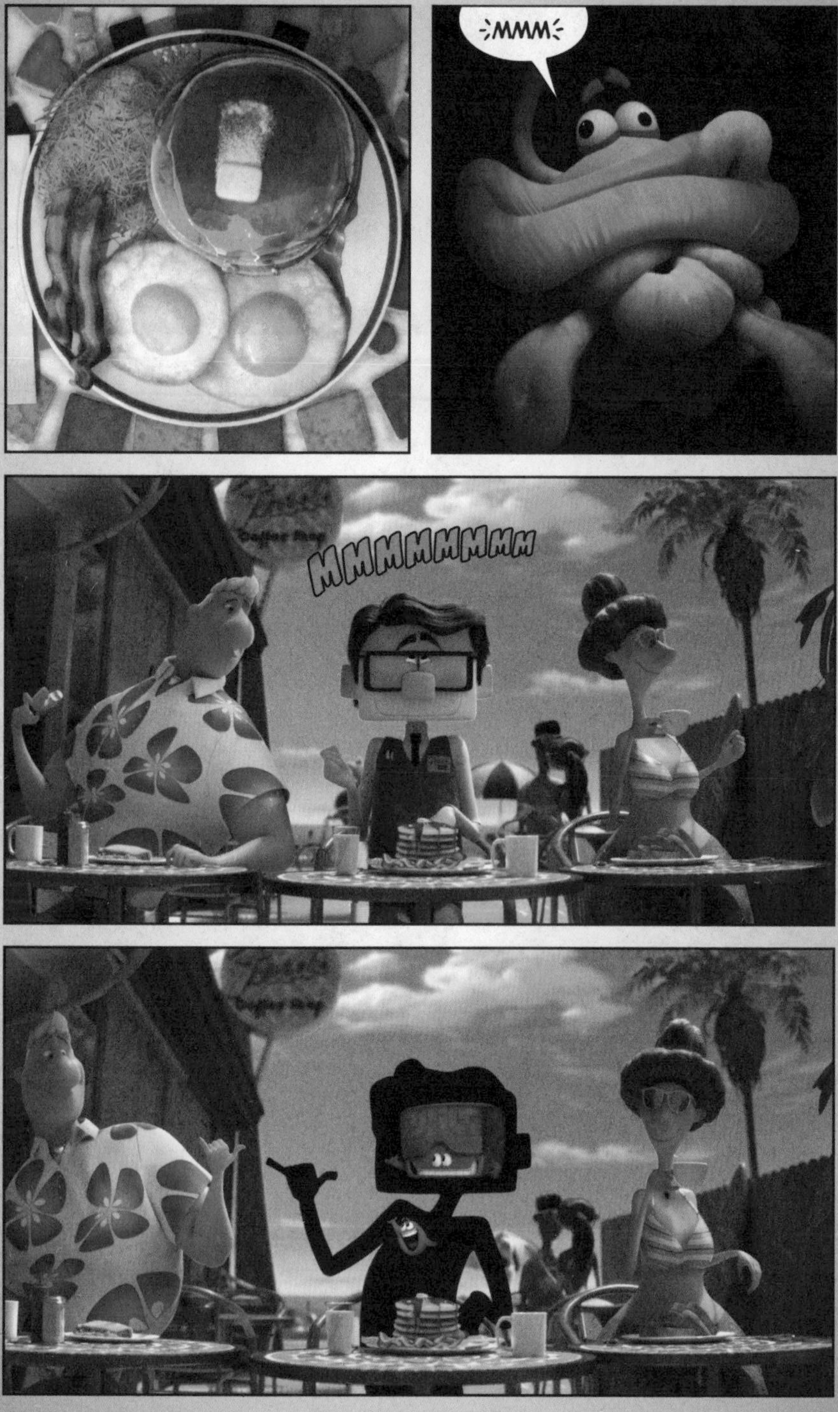
MMM
MMMMMMMM

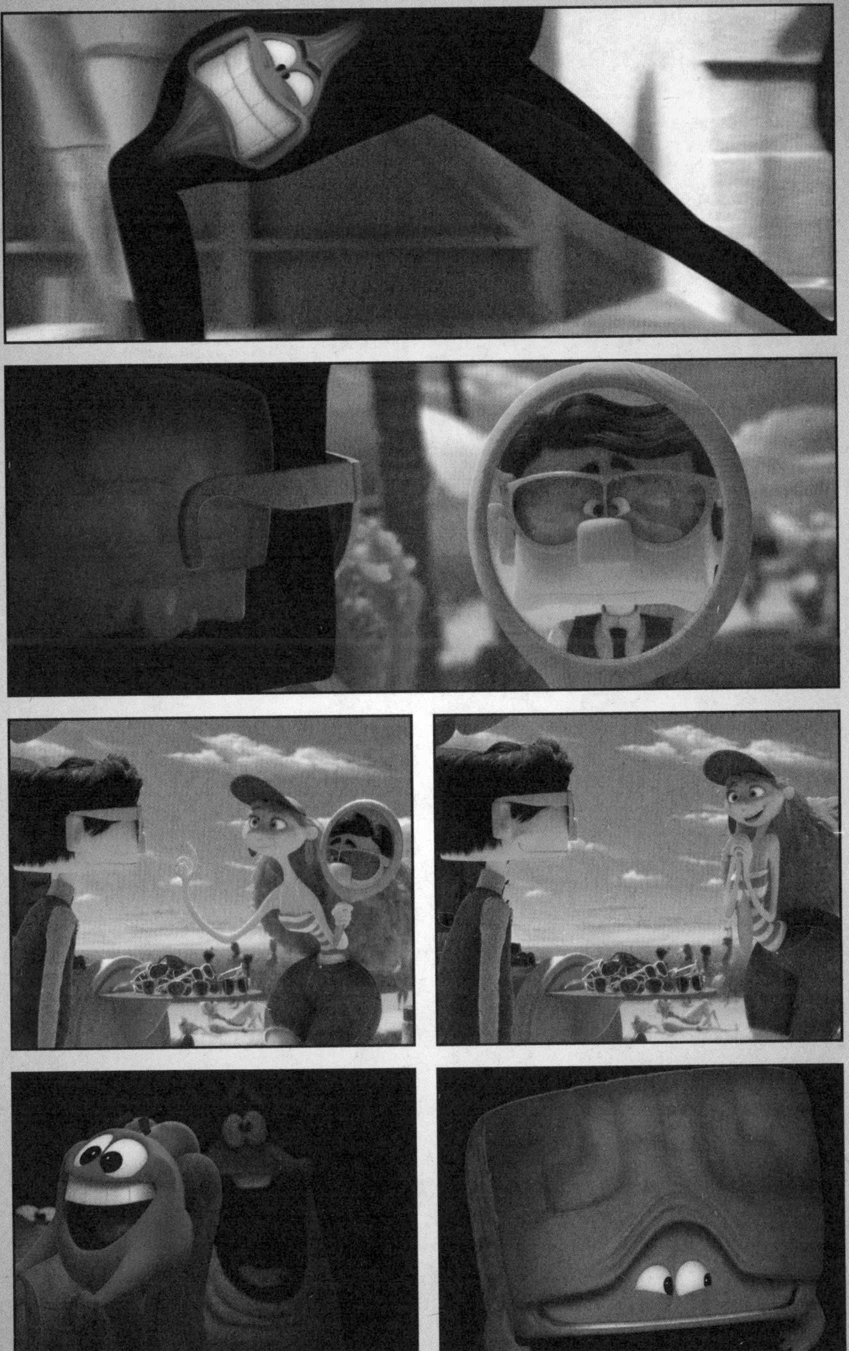

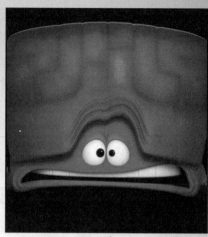
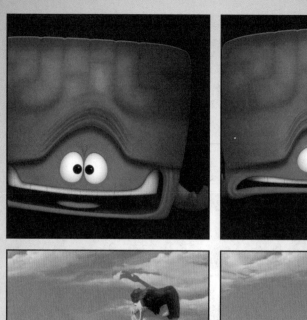

WHOOSH!

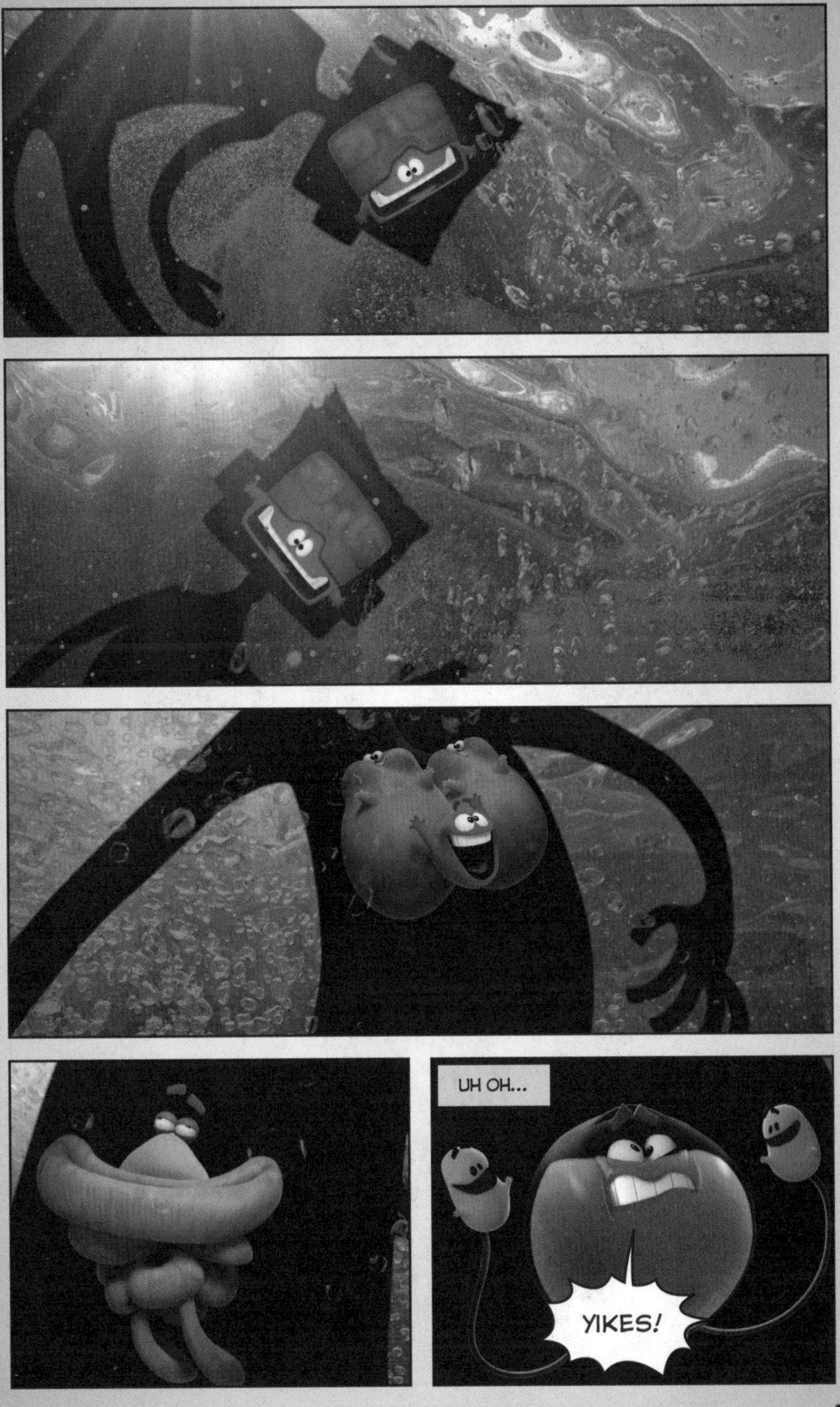
UH OH...
YIKES!

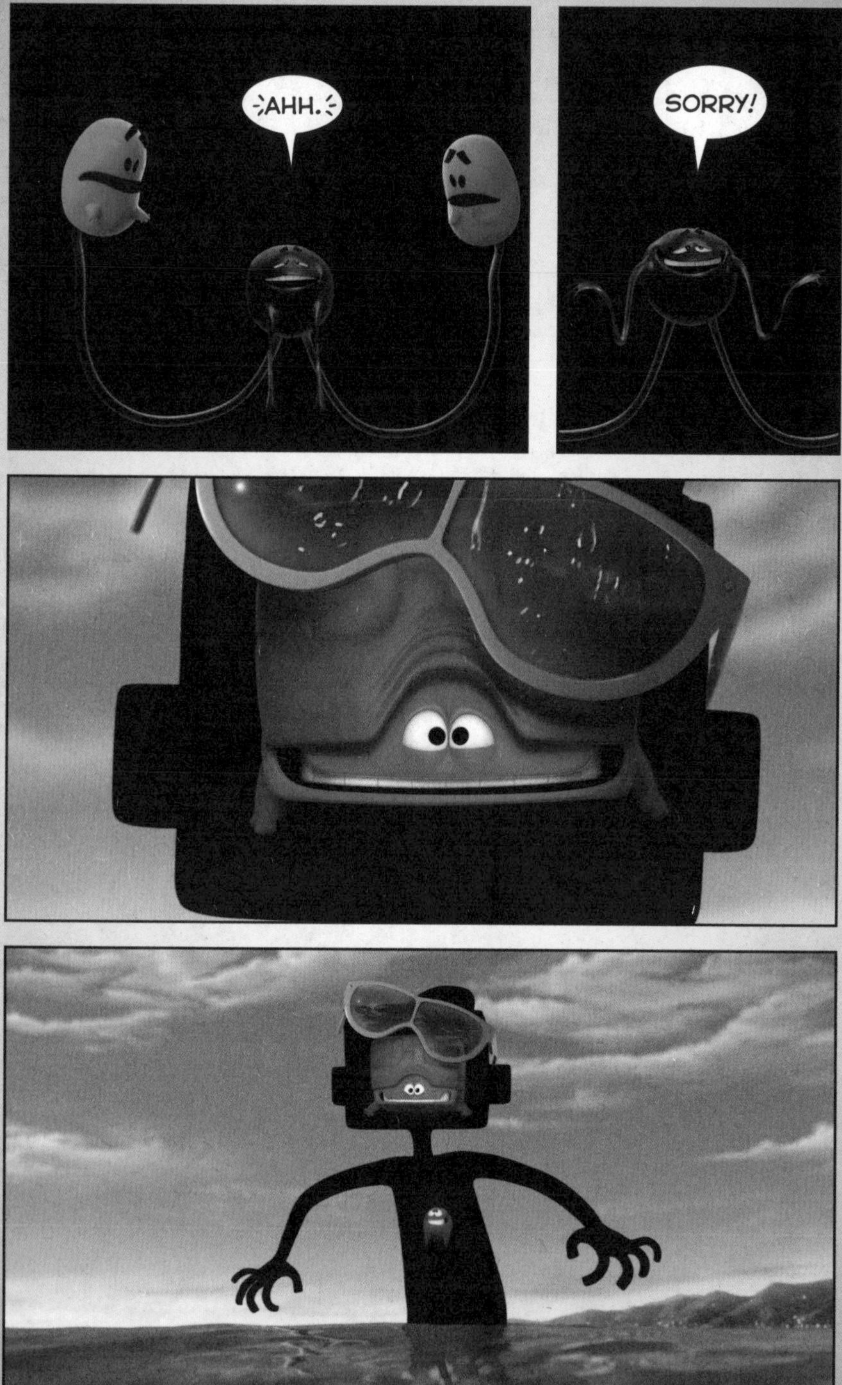
AHH.
SORRY!

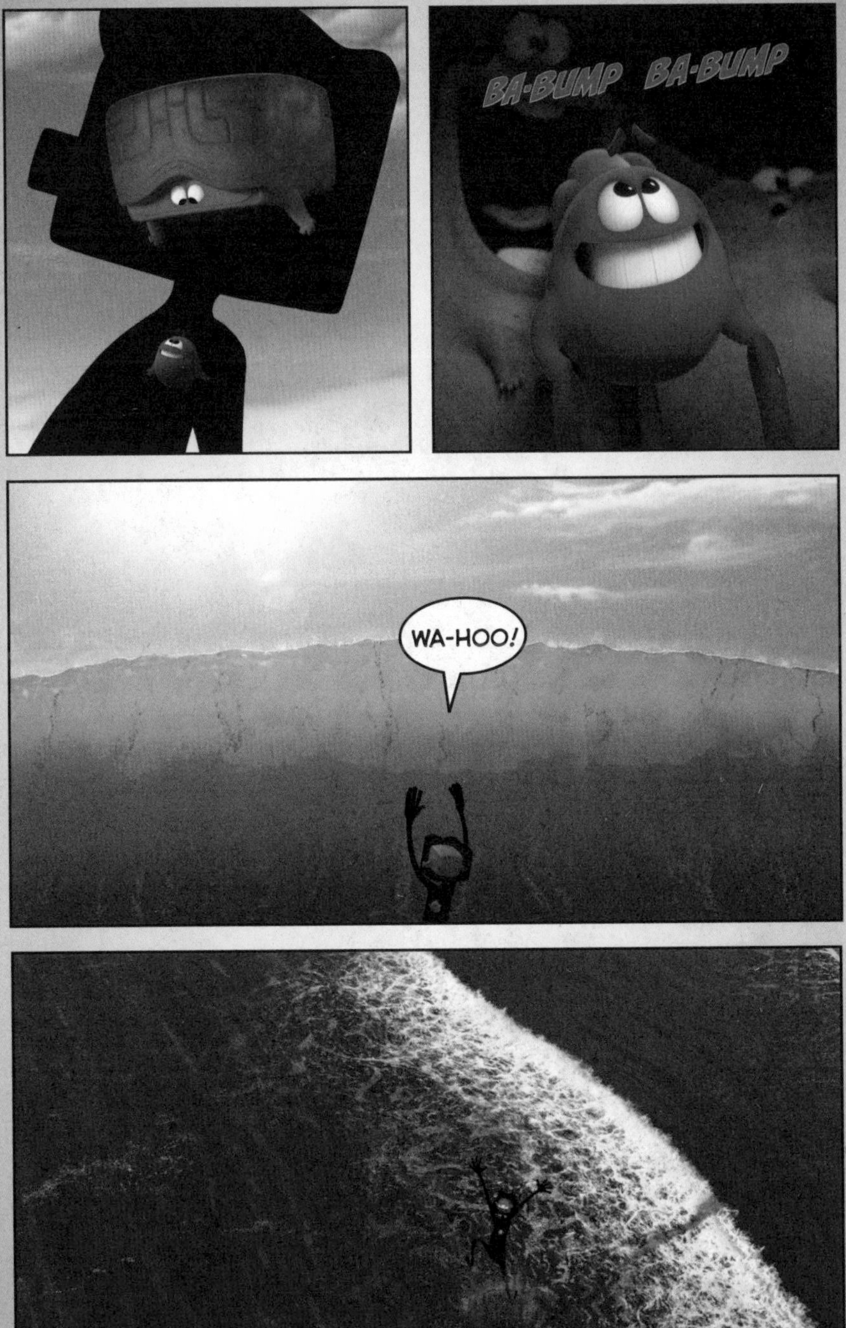
BA-BUMP BA-BUMP
WA-HOO!

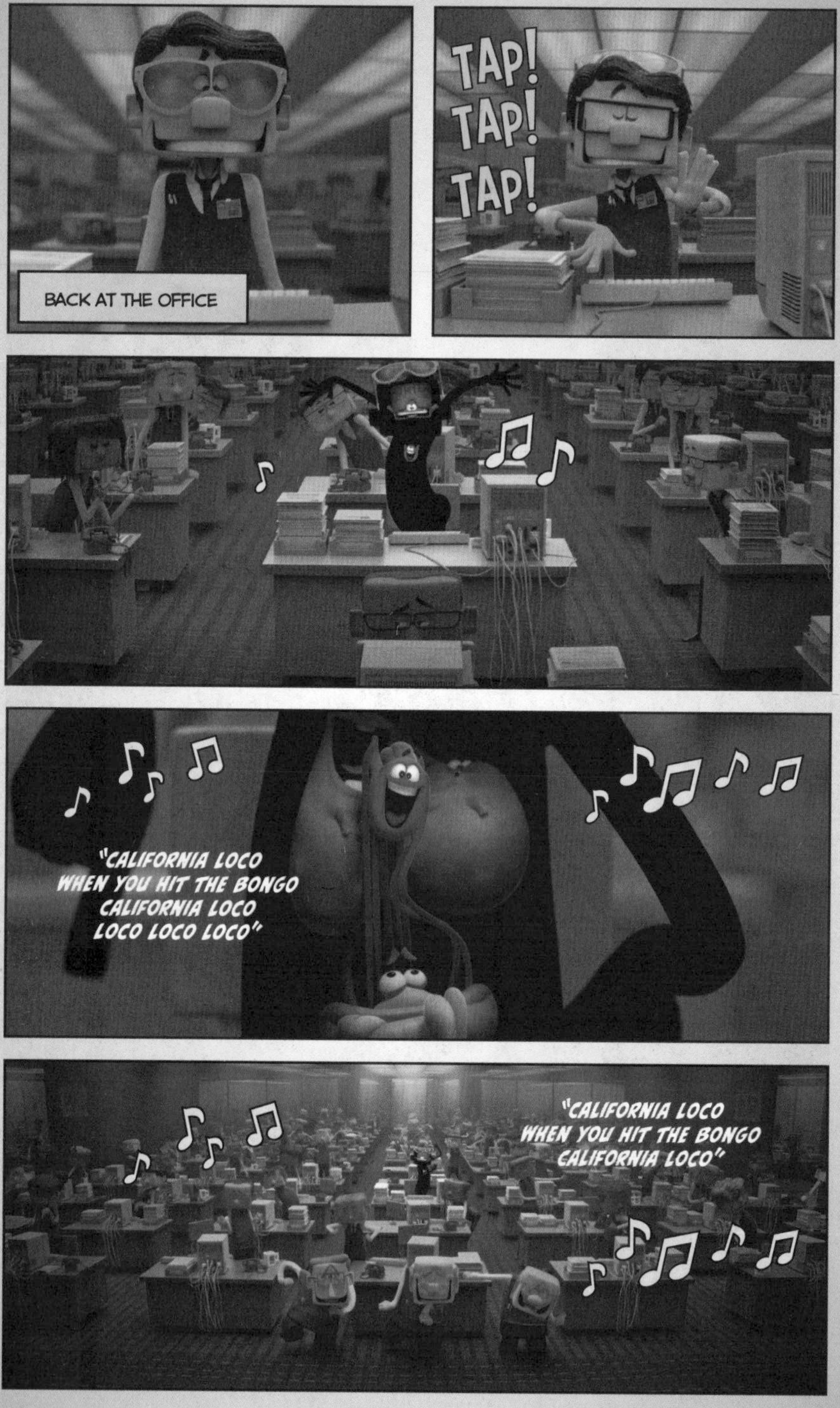
BACK AT THE OFFICE
TAP! TAP! TAP!
"CALIFORNIA LOCO
WHEN YOU HIT THE BONGO
CALIFORNIA LOCO
LOCO LOCO LOCO"
"CALIFORNIA LOCO
WHEN YOU HIT THE BONGO
CALIFORNIA LOCO"

INNER WORKINGS

Director: Leo Matsuda
Producer: Sean Lurie

DIRECTED BY
John Musker & Ron Clements

CO-DIRECTED BY
Chris Williams & Don Hall

PRODUCED BY
Osnat Shurer p.g.a.

EXECUTIVE PRODUCER
John Lasseter

SCREENPLAY BY
Jared Bush

STORY BY
Ron Clements & John Musker
Chris Williams & Don Hall
Pamela Ribon
Aaron Kandell & Jordan Kandell

MOANA: THE GRAPHIC NOVEL

MANUSCRIPT ADAPTATION
Alessandro Ferrari

LAYOUT
Alberto Zanon, Giada Perissinotto

PENCIL/INKING
Veronica Di Lorenzo, Luca Bertelè

COLOR
Backgrounds: Massimo Rocca, PierLuigi Casolino, Pasquale Desiato,
Maria Claudia Di Genova, Characters: Dario Calabria

COVER LAYOUT
Alberto Zanon

PENCIL/INKING
Luca Bertelè

COLOR
Grzegorz Krysinsky

GRAFICH DESIGN & EDITORIAL
Red·Spot Srl - Milan, Italy
Chris Dickey (Lettering)

PRE-PRESS
Red·Spot Srl - Milan, Italy; Litomilano S.r.l.

SPECIAL THANKS TO
Osnat Shurer, Andy Harkness, Ian Gooding, Bill Schwab, Mayka Mei,
Blair Bradley, Ryan Gilleland, Alison Giordano, Monica Vasquez

DISNEY PUBLISHING WORLDWIDE GLOBAL
MAGAZINES, COMICS AND PARTWORKS

PUBLISHER
Lynn Waggoner

EDITORIAL DIRECTOR
Bianca Coletti

EDITORIAL TEAM
Guido Frazzini (Director, Comics), Stefano Ambrosio (Executive Editor, New IP),
Carlotta Quattrocolo (Executive Editor, Franchise), Camilla Vedove
(Senior Manager, Editorial Development), Behnoosh Khalili (Senior Editor),
Julie Dorris (Senior Editor—Project Lead)

DESIGN
Enrico Soave (Senior Designer)

ART
Ken Shue (VP, Global Art), Roberto Santillo (Creative Director), Marco
Ghiglione (Creative Manager), Stefano Attardi (Computer Art Designer),
Manny Mederos (Art and Design Manager)

PORTFOLIO MANAGEMENT
Olivia Ciancarelli (Director)

BUSINESS & MARKETING
Mariantonietta Galla (Marketing Manager), Virpi Korhonen
(Editorial Manager),
Kristen Ginter (Operations)

CONTRIBUTORS
Deborah Barnes, Cecilia Cristoforetti

PROJECT DESIGN
Red Spot, Italy

TEXTS
Tea Orsi, Red Spot, Tea Orsi (comics)

ENGLISH TEXTS
Tea Orsi

PHOTO CREDITS
© Disney; © Shutterstock.com
(pages: 64, 102, 110, 138); H2O

"INNER WORKINGS"
DPD Single-Audio
D002498615

CREDITS
Music by Ludwig Göransson
Featured Vocal Performance by Este Haim
Produced by Ludwig Göransson
Mixed by Chris Fogel
Published by Wonderland Music Company, Inc. (BMI)
"Este Haim appears courtesy of Columbia Records USA,
Universal Music GmbH and Polydor Records UK"

FOR JOE BOOKS
CEO: Jay Firestone
COO: Jody Colero
President: Steve Osgoode
Associate Publisher: Deanna McFadden
Executive Editor: Amy Weingartner
Creative Manager: Jason Flores-Holz
Production and Editorial Assistant: Steffie Davis
Publishing Assistant: Emma Hambly
Sales and Marketing Assistant: Samantha Carr

CINESTORY ADAPTATION
Sayre Street Books

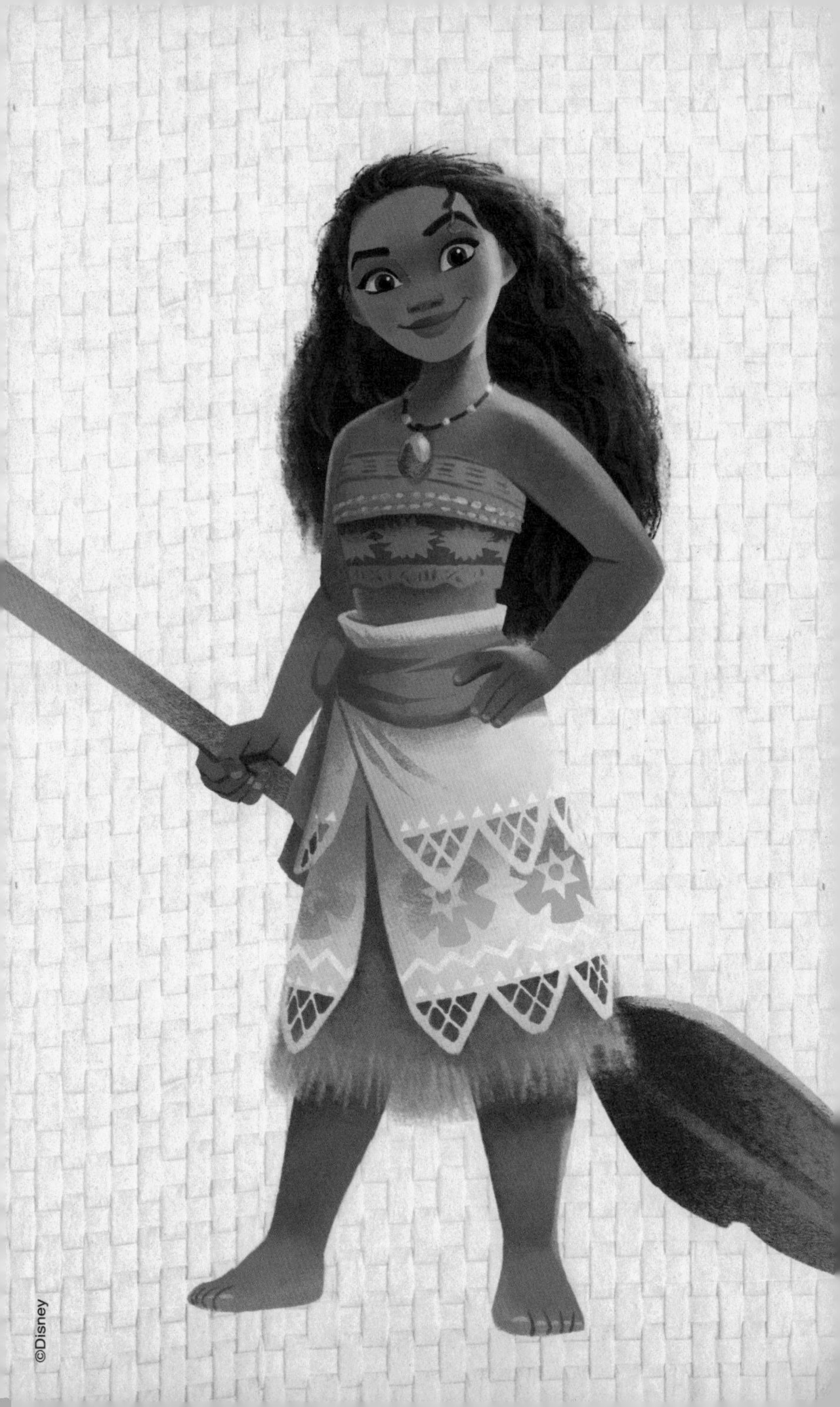